THE

Before turning full-time novelist in 1963, John Gardner spent eight years on the *Stratford Herald* as theatrical journalist and critic, and so built a very close relationship with the Royal Shakespeare Company, even accompanying them on tour to Russia. He is now a top-ranking thriller writer by virtue of novels such as *Golgotha*, his Herbie Kruger trilogy – *The Nostradamus Traitor*, *The Garden of Weapons* and *The Quiet Dogs* – and many, many more. Recently he has assumed the mantle of Ian Fleming and his James Bond novels, *Licence Renewed* and *For Special Services* have appeared on bestseller lists throughout the world. The first volume of his two volume saga, *The Secret Generation*, will be published shortly.

Also by John Gardner in Star

THE LIQUIDATOR
UNDERSTRIKE
AMBER NINE
MADRIGAL
FOUNDER MEMBER
TRAITOR'S EXIT
THE AIRLINE PIRATES
A KILLER FOR A SONG

THE DIRECTOR

John Gardner

A STAR BOOK

published by

the Paperback Division of
W. H. ALLEN & Co. Ltd

A Star Book
Published in 1983
by the Paperback Division of
W. H. Allen & Co. Ltd
A Howard and Wyndham Company
44 Hill Street, London W1X 8LB

First published in Great Britain in
1971 under the title *Every Night's a Bullfight*
This edition first published in Great Britain by
W. H. Allen & Co. Ltd, 1982

Copyright © John Gardner 1971 and 1981

Printed in Great Britain by
Cox & Wyman Ltd, Reading

ISBN 0 352 31230 0

To Peter and Trevor

Who taught me so much about classical theatre, by their work and personal friendship

ACKNOWLEDGMENTS

Grateful acknowledgment is made for quotations as follows: to Longmans, Green and Co. Ltd for *Bull Fever* by Kenneth Tynan; Mr Harold Owen and Chatto & Windus Ltd for *Strange Meeting* by Wilfred Owen; Faber & Faber Ltd for *The Waste Land* by T S Eliot; the Literary Executor of the late Winifred Ashton and Wm Heinemann Ltd for *Will Shakespeare* by Clemence Dane; Penguin Books Ltd for *Shakespeare's History Plays* by E M W Tillyard; Routledge & Kegan Paul Ltd for *After Shakespeare* by Alex Comfort; Methuen & Co. Ltd for *The Ladies* by Rudyard Kipling; Cassell & Co. Ltd for *The History of the English-speaking Peoples* by Winston S Churchill; Mr Rod McKuen for *I Looked at You a Long Time* and *Loving and Losing;* and Mr Irving Berlin for *Heatwave.*

AUTHOR'S NOTE

This book was first published in the 1970s, under a different title, and is a novel very close to my heart. The bulk of my work has been to do with what are now called 'novels of espionage' – *The Director* is different as there is not a spy in sight.

During the late 1950s and early 60s I was lucky enough to work very closely with one of our major classical theatre companies; so it became a natural ambition to write a novel on the subject. Many people have either told me, or written to me, saying this is their favourite theatrical novel – and for that much thanks.

When the rights reverted to me, W.H. Allen asked if they could republish this book under a new title, and I was, naturally, delighted. However, it was essential for changes to be made. As it stood, the original book was firmly set in the late 60s and early 70s. Times have changed and, while the great classics of the theatre – the works of Shakespeare and the like – remain classics because they are ageless, the same could never apply to any work of mine.

So, the book has been updated and, I trust, brought into the 1980s. Like theatre it is for enjoyment and entertainment, in all its forms. I only hope that it tells a story that readers will enjoy.

My special thanks must go to my friend Michael Bailey who has worked so hard to get this book republished, and burned the midnight oil on the mass of up-dating revisions.

John Gardner
Ireland 1981

'. . . "Swordsmen thrust through, and dying in their blood on the arena sand; bulls goring, horses disembowelled, made a meeker vision for the public – a milder condiment for a people's palate – than Vashti, torn by seven devils . . ."

'Now Charlotte Brontë had never seen a bullfight in her life. But I know exactly what she meant; it was a right instinct that made her seek a similitude where she did. *Other plays and other actors evoke for me, the same response; especially Othello, a dramatized bullfight if ever there was one, with its hero the courageously blundering bull, lured to his death by the matador Iago and that maddening handkerchief. Irving was aware of the parallel.*'

Bull Fever: Kenneth Tynan

CHAPTER ONE

Cyprus, goats and monkeys, of course, that's where he should have gone. At least in Cyprus he could have done a little research between lazing. Inevitably he would direct *Othello* one day. *Othello by William Shakespeare. Directed by Douglas Silver. From one hundred and one ideas provided, over the years, by such eminent directors as Tyrone Guthrie, Anthony Richardson, Franco Zefferelli and the Race Relations Act.*

In Cyprus he would have gained just a tiny piece of background knowledge: the feel of the place, its smells; in its villages, the pace of life would not have altered much.

But Douglas Silver was here, in the moist heat and dust of Malta, lying on the bed in this ludicrous pseudo-American hotel perched upon a promontory of rock, shrouded in stifling night, the air conditioning out of action and the jungle beat of the Casanova Trio ripping from the Sand Room, throbbing across the Pool Terrace and in through his balcony window.

The Casanova Trio. Three prancing faggots and a girl vocalist who did not know her B flat from an A Natural.

Silver's mind streamed back as though along an endless road flanked by trees which constantly changed colour, like time lapse photography of the seasons. Loneliness; adolescent anguish; sentiment and the slush of pain which led to revolt. The mind drifting with endless pictures.

It was only yesterday, after lunch, that he realized he had not rested properly for three years. The sophisticated Douglas Silver – *The most promising young director British theatre has seen since Trevor Nunn* they had once written in *The Sunday Times.* Yet here he was, in the middle of the Mediterranean,

11

feeling consciously randy; wanting a woman. Any woman. A man married to a talented, beautiful and international actress.

That's how it goes. Sorry, Jen, he breathed so that she might pick up his thoughts through the static, across the world, among the glittering people.

He sat up on the bed and could see himself, through the open bathroom door, reflected in the mirror. Douglas Silver: twenty-six years old, tall, compact and well proportioned, outwardly composed, with a boyish face, unruly black hair and a manner of diffidence which belied the iron authority he could demonstrate in rehearsal, or the rigid self-discipline he imposed upon himself when directing one of the great dramatic classics.

At Cambridge he had won a first-class honours degree in English and the brilliance of his university productions was blared abroad long before he ever began to consider the theatre as a way of life.

Then Cambridge was over and he was suddenly thrust into the professional world. Provincial repertory companies, work for the Arts Council and then an incredibly lucid production of that director's trap, *Peer Gynt*, in the West End. Success blossomed around him. Recently he had directed one play at Chichester, then a couple for the National, while his *Hamlet* at Stratford last year drew superlative praise from audiences, critics and the profession alike.

He had met Jennifer Frost at a first night party in Chichester. He remembered his surprise on discovering that she was so intelligent. She had two movies showing in London and a third about to be premièred, while the studio publicity still spat out an ignorant and vulgar stream of adjectives which pigeon-holed her into the empty, unobtainable, sex-symbol, bitch-goddess category. The universally adored long dark hair, oval face, brown still eyes and near perfect body fascinated him physically, but it was her mind, leaping with agility, pouring out not screen banalities, but mature, conscious and comprehensive ideas, which captured and captivated him.

12

They had left the party together and gone back to his rooms in the little street near the cathedral. They drank coffee and talked, about drama, the cinema, acting, politics, children, poetry and music, until it was morning when they fell asleep together, not touching, aware only that the use of their bodies together was for some other time.

A month later they were married in the sub-normal norm which trails in the wake of people like Jennifer Frost, retreating immediately into a private shell of exploration.

Now, two years later, Jen had gone back to the grinding, destructive, almost destroyed, over-exposed film world; on location in Mexico with a lead in a *flip*, up to the minute, tricksy little epic titled *Hidalgo*, and it was yesterday, after lunch, that Douglas suddenly became aware that he had time on his hands for the first moment in three years.

It would have been madness to cross the world and join Jen. On location he would have been out of his depth: an abrasive to his wife, her director and the other members of the unit.

In the end he simply walked into the first travel agent he could find in Regent Street and asked if they could fix him up with two weeks in the sun. Somewhere. Anywhere. They suggested Malta. He called his agent, Revill Sutcliffe, and cabled Jen. Finally it had all fused to these moments of sweat, pulsing noise and a wilderness of arid nothingness: the mind bare, the senses dry and no real person to touch.

A knock at the door brought the promise of human contact: a brown-uniformed boy holding a cable and waiting to be tipped.

He expected the cable to be from Jen, so did not quite take in the message as he read: CALL ME MOST URGENTLY. REVILL.

On the telephone yesterday, Revill had said there was nothing urgent. A couple of offers to direct new plays; a haggle over money to do *The Shrew* at Stratford during the following season, but nothing that would not wait until his return.

There was a four-hour delay on calls to London. Four

hours in which to turn imagination into the worst nightmares. Jen was ill in Mexico. There had been an accident. His mind filled with the fantasies of hospitals, planes, airports and the dash to his dying wife's side.

Stupidly, Douglas chose to wait in his room, the solitude groping vividly at his mind and the imagination coloured by the half.bottle of whisky ordered from room service.

When the call finally came through, the line was dreadful and Revill had been wakened after only half an hour's sleep.

'It's Douglas. What the hell's happened?'

Static and the far off voices of operators or lovers somewhere among the electronic network.

'Douglas, what're you ringing for at this time of night?'

'Your cable said it was urgent.'

'It could have waited until morning.'

'Well, what's urgent? What is it?'

'We've had an offer, that's all. I think you might be interested enough to come back and discuss it.'

'What sort of an offer?'

'Director of the Shireston Festival Company.'

'The Shireston?'

'You want to talk with them?'

'It's got to be a quick decision?'

'They want to move. They want to see you now.'

There was a fractional hesitation.

'I'll take the first flight I can get. Call you from Heathrow or Gatwick or wherever.'

He rang through to reception. There was a flight out, via Rome, at eleven next morning and there were seats available. Another cigarette and a long pull at the remaining whisky.

The Shireston. It was not as well organized and certainly not as attractive as Stratford. It had none of the kudos of the National, nor the display facilities of Chichester, but the potential had never been properly exploited. It was a place where one could gather together and build a company, and it was unique. Though they had failed at Shireston, two of its previous directors had become powerfully big names; and, if he had heard correctly, there was money available. It could be a challenge with great possibilities.

Director of the Shireston Festival Company. He repeated it aloud. Elation. The alcohol, combined with the news, began to make Douglas feel the creative need even more sharply. Thinking clearly now, he knew very well how it took him, even though he tried to con himself for most of the time.

'When you're directing,' Jen would say, 'you might as well leave me with a box of king-size candles. Then, when the play's on you're never off me.'

That was why he had never been unfaithful. The time had always been so full even though, however much he tried to disguise it, Douglas Silver's talent and brilliance operated through sexual motivation. The whole drive was directed towards the project, and when that was through the creative urge became more basic.

It was basic now as he thought of Jen: the live texture of her skin and the special smell of her: the particular scent of her sweat when he took her, the gutteral choke she gave at orgasm; the wild look as she prepared for him, or the soft, still, deep quiet as she rested, asleep or pacified.

The Casanova Trio had been silenced by the onslaught of night. Yet the need in him remained. He put on his sandals and padded out of the room. In the main lobby there was nobody except the desk clerk who gave him a mistrustful look.

The Sand Room was silent and uninviting so he went out on to the Pool Terrace, telling himself the urge would pass in the night air. The kidney-shaped pool shone, empty and placid, a whitish-green in the diffused underwater lighting. On the other side of the terrace there was a low wall from which you could look down on to the rocks and the regularly changing surf.

He walked round the pool towards the wall and sat down, squatting sideways on to stare out at the dark water, watching its white foam trimming spluttering in, his mind detaching itself from the present.

Jen came swiftly to the surface. A moment from an afternoon they had spent at Blenheim Palace: a bright cold day in

February and they had walked briskly round the grounds. Later, standing on the bridge, the winter sun reflected in the water: a long spear of light seemed to be pointing at them, embracing, leaning across the parapet. That night they had stayed at The Bear in Woodstock and never slept because of their mutual hunger. He could see the room clearly: the ornate bedhead; coffee going cold on a tray; Peggy Lee's recorded voice filtering an oldie – *Don't Smoke in Bed* – from the radio.

'It's a corny line, but have you got a light?'

The voice had a controlled, husky quality. Douglas turned, startled at its sudden intrusion.

She was a tall coloured girl, dressed to emphasize her slimness in flared slacks and a skinny turtleneck, one hand raised holding an unlit cigarette.

Douglas felt for his lighter. 'You want to be careful doing that. You never know who you'll meet out here in the wee small hours.'

The flame spurted and kindled the tobacco. The girl took a long drag and blew the smoke away with a quick movement of her mouth, as though disgusted by it. 'I know who you are. I saw you at dinner tonight. Then I couldn't sleep and spotted you from my balcony, shameless hussy that I am. How are you, Mr Silver?'

Douglas creased his forehead in an effort to recall her.

'Don't worry.' She laughed. 'I don't suppose you remember me for a moment. I auditioned for you once. . . .'

'In Birmingham.' He almost shouted as memory picked up the clues. He could see her. The empty theatre, her willowy figure in a belted topcoat; green, he thought. It had been a cold morning and there was some trouble with the heating system. He also heard her voice from the stage. How could he have forgotten? The mental note had been made and under-lined. 'Birmingham,' he said again, softly.

'Very good. I'm flattered.'

'Quick Silver.' He grinned.

'I'll bet you can't remember my name.'

The surf crashed once below them. He spread his hands

16

wide. 'Miracles take a little longer.'

She offered a palm. There was a grace of movement. The gesture of an actress. 'Carol. Carol Evans.'

'Now I remember.'

'Liar.'

'I'm sorry.' A pause as he blew out a thin stream of smoke. 'About Birmingham. I mean about the job.'

'As you say, miracles take a little longer.'

'No. You were very good. Very good. It was a matter of casting problems. A little interference.'

'Uh-huh.' She came and sat down beside him on the wall. 'So what're you doing now?'

'I'm on holiday.' She laughed, an infectious, melodic noise, tossing her hair back in a way which had the stamp of habit about it.

'Before that?'

'I had a couple of lines in a movie at Borehamwood. Real hard work. Paid for the holiday.'

'Good lines?'

'Integrated stuff like – Would you prefer the white meat or the dark, sir?'

Douglas chuckled.

'So what's the famous Douglas Silver doing here all alone without his beautiful movie queen wife?' There was no mockery.

He bit his lip. 'Being lonely. Full of self-pity and getting the hell out of here at eleven in the morning.'

'Oh.' A small shock, then with a smile. 'I thought I might have someone to talk with while I improved my tan.'

'You here alone then?'

'No. With a friend. A girl friend, but she got lucky with a nice boy from Hampstead and I get the feeling that I'm intruding. About your wife . . .? Everything's . . .?'

'Everything's fine. Okay. She's making a movie.' He took a deep breath and found himself letting out a sigh. 'Yes, in Mexico she's making a movie.'

'And you?'

'There's work around the corner.'

Her cigarette glowed in the half-light as she nodded.

'If there's ever anything in it for a lanky spade dolly, remember me, Douglas Silver.'

Another pause: counterpoint from the sea eternally slapping away at the rocks. Douglas felt very much alert, his senses tingling, straining like radar antennae. He put out his hand. Carol took it into hers, lightly, rubbing palms together.

They sat there, holding hands and talking: mainly about his productions that she had seen; personalities; mutual friends, the people who, naturally enough, criss-crossed their lives.

After a while Douglas said, 'You want to come back to my ghetto?'

He felt she was looking at him, hard.

'You *that* lonely?' Low and surprised.

'I didn't mean it like that.'

'How else can you mean it, Douglas Silver? A man is alone, his wife far away across the wide ocean and he invites a girl back to his room? He invites her back to screw her. What other way is there?'

There was a shout from somewhere deep in the hotel. A shout of something. A drunken waiter, perhaps, letting off steam now that all the guests were safely tucked away for the night.

Carol got to her feet. 'Okay. Let's be adult. You're a nice guy and you need it. So do I, but it's not for favours. I don't want you beating your brains out when it gets to your next production and you're trying to figure out how you can fit in a black bitch as the Snow Queen.'

She stretched out her arm, took his hand again, firmly this time, and they headed back into the hotel.

In the lobby the desk clerk threw another of his random suspicious looks, shrugging his shoulders once their backs were turned to him.

They kissed by the door in his darkened room. An experimental touching of the lips, no give in either of them. Then, as they undressed, they allowed each other's fingertips to

18

touch and it was as though energy had begun to flow between them. Douglas moved his hand down her rib cage as she bared her small breasts.

She was not just slim, but thin: he could feel the bones, and, while each of her breasts was firm and large enough for him to cup and completely cover with his hand, she had no real waist.

In the end he helped her, sliding the tiny bikini she wore down over her flat buttocks and thighs, lifting his bare foot, placing it against the garment's crotch, pushing down.

She opened her mouth to kiss him, and, this time, there was no experimenting. Her open lips closed on his with a new ferocity.

Douglas woke quickly but without the sudden start which often accompanies a fast return to consciousness. They were edged stomach to stomach and he was in her.

Carol breathed steadily, her face composed, happy. No nightmares haunting there.

Gently he raised his arm to look at his watch. Nine o'clock. His aircraft left at eleven.

He kissed her on the lips and felt his erection strengthen inside her. Jen's face swam over the pillow and Carol opened her eyes.

'It's nine o'clock, he whispered.

She smiled at him, moving her own stomach in response to his steady strokes.

It was the nightingale, and not the lark,
That pierc'd the fearful hollow of thine ear.'

She laughed, but the two lines struck a new fire in him. Delving into his mind he felt for the speech: Romeo's lines –

'Night's candles are burnt out, and jocund day
Stands tiptoe on the misty mountain tops.
I must be gone and live, or stay and die.'

There was no falter, no pause in the movement of her body, as she continued, taking up Juliet's reply, almost whispering the words, her fingers playing round his ear and her lips only an inch from his.

19

'Yon light is not day-light, I know it, I:
Therefore stay yet, thou need'st not be gone.'

Their breath gave out as they arched in mutual pleasure.

During the long winding down, Douglas remained haunted by the way in which this dark girl had come to him suddenly and spoken Juliet's lines with such passion. Common sense nagged at him that his feelings were fraught with emotion; yet, somewhere at the heart of all this and the guilt, fear, obsessions of the mind, an audacious idea had germinated.

'When will you be back in London?' He tried to make it sound casual as he dressed.

'I said no favours.' She was gathering her clothes together on the bed.

'I wasn't thinking about favours.'

'Then you should think of your beautiful wife, Douglas. I don't suppose you'll believe me but I don't sleep around. Just think of it as a mixed doubles that worked because the moon was in the right quarter. What's a screw between friends anyway?'

'I may need to see you back home.'

'Need?'

'Yes, need, workwise – and I'm offering nothing.'

She gave him her private address and her agent's number, dressed and came out to Luqa airport with him.

They said good-bye in the hot crowded entrance hall amidst a gabble of languages. Douglas went straight through to the departure lounge without even glancing back. The creative energy was already being directed into a new channel.

He did not see Carol's eyes or the look of fear on her coffee-coloured face.

CHAPTER TWO

Until 1926 the market town of Shireston had little to offer in the way of tourist attractions. It lay, a community of about four thousand souls, among farming country some twenty miles from the coast, and a good ten from the main South-ampton-London road. Among its eighteen public houses it sported but one hotel, the Blue Boar, and its only real claim to fame was Shireston House: an ugly and rambling mock-gothic and massive building set in one of the largest and most beautiful gardens in Hampshire.

Then, in the August of 1926, Richard Longwell, fifth earl of Shireston, grandson to the third earl who was responsible for the building of Shireston House, died suddenly and without an heir.

If the unexpected death of their relatively young squire jolted the local inhabitants, his will was to shake them even more.

The entire estate, together with a not inconsiderable for-tune, was to be administered by a group of six trustees, the whole to be known as the Shireston Festival Trust.

During his lifetime, Richard, earl of Shireston, had been well known on the fringes of the theatrical world, and slightly better known among academics, particularly for his studies in Elizabethan drama. His will now drew up, in detail, plans that he had intended to implement during his lifetime.

A theatre was to be built in the grounds of Shireston House, *At the bottom of the long lawn where the rose garden and orchard now stand*. A festival director was to be appointed every three years (though there was a provision for the direc-tor to remain in office for a period not exceeding nine years).

21

A professional theatre company was to be engaged by 31st December each year and would perform, from April to September, *the great plays of the classic English theatre, particularly the plays of the Elizabethan dramatists; prices of admission to the Festival theatre being kept low in order that men, women and children from the poorer classes can see great dramatic works in performance, as is their heritage.*

The scheme appealed most strongly to the first appointed trustees, as no less than half of the Trust members were successful men of the theatre. At once they saw an opportunity to display their talents in ideal surroundings while, at the same time, giving more work to an already overcrowded profession.

The inhabitants of Shireston were more sceptical. Who, they said, would travel all the way down to their little town and pay good money to see dusty old plays which they could just as easily view comfortably in London?

They were also dubious at the thought of having actors and actresses living in their midst, even though the will gave instructions that members of the company were to be comfortably lodged in Shireston House itself.

However, in April 1927, the architect's plans were agreed and work began on the conversion of the house into offices, and flats for the actors, while the foundations of the theatre itself took shape over the now mutilated rose garden and orchard.

Work was suspended for a while towards the end of the year owing to the arrival of a long lost distant cousin who steamed into Southampton from Australia, contested the will, and several months later, steamed out again, having lost his case and gained a formidable flea in his ear.

By the end of 1927 the theatre was completed; a large white rectangular building with a capacity for an audience of over a thousand and, unaccountably, a design which showed a marked Spanish influence. Paradoxically this blended with the phoney extravagance of the house itself. Anyone with vision could clearly see that the quiet, lovely garden, lying between house and theatre, would be an ideal place in which to spend a summer evening: picnicking on the lawn before being suspended, moved, slapped against reality, jerked to tears or tickled to laughter in the theatre.

The first season, in 1928, opened many eyes. By the use of judicious advertising, people flocked to the cool lawns of Shireston and were not disappointed. A modern dress *Taming of the Shrew* slightly worried the purists, but any wrongs there were put right by a spectacular *Troilus and Cressida*, an hilarious and magical *Midsummer Night's Dream*, and a haunting *As You Like It* with sets designed to reflect the local woods and fields surrounding Shireston.

All summer, Orlando and Rosalind negotiated the barbed thicket of wit leading to love in a Forest of Arden that could easily have been the coppice visible from the lawns of Shireston House.

For the first few years of its life the Shireston Festival flourished. It also attracted noted actors and actresses whose skills seemed to be more clearly defined, more sharply in focus, amid the calm of Shireston.

Then on 3rd September, 1939, the blow of World War Two fell and Shireston's first flush of success died.

During the war, the house was used as one of the many Combined Services headquarters, the theatre acting as a most adequate briefing hall. Both Montgomery and Eisenhower spent much time there before D-Day, and so a small and not insignificant patch of history was added.

It was not until the early fifties that the festival got back into a reasonable stride, but that success was short lived. Money was available, if not always forthcoming from the trustees, but the right actors and directors seemed to be elsewhere.

The decline was rapid. The other major companies – Stratford, the National, Chichester – began to make the headlines of the sixties. Slowly Shireston became almost a joke. Living on a memory, always on the brink of recovery, yet dogged as a second-rate repertory company, sometimes playing to houses less than a quarter full.

This was the situation when the trustees reached out to

clutch at Douglas Silver. He was a bright talent whose personal magnetism might provide both the dynamic means to respark interest and bring Shireston back once more under the artistic microscope.

They had made no bones about the situation on their first meeting with Douglas. They were prepared to offer him the appointment of festival director only if he came up with the answers which appealed to them.

Now, a month after that first exploratory interview, with the ghost of summer outside, Douglas sat at the foot of the oak table which ran almost the length of the trustees' board room, a pretentiously panelled chamber that had once been the Longwell family nursery.

The trustees themselves were a formidable body. The chairman, Sir Basil Daley, was a kingpin of industry, as were Rupert Crown and William Dempsey; the latter being a heavyweight in the world of big business accountancy.

George Tupnall, a small, sad and precise looking man, was a local solicitor and son of one of the original six trustees; while only one member could claim to have ever played an active role in the theatre, Sir Lewis Roland, now a faded and fumbling caricature of the famous comedy actor he once had been.

The sixth trustee, old Sheridan Whitney, was on his death-bed, as, in fact, he had rejoiced in being for the past three years.

They mumbled together at the far end of the table like a Dickensian workhouse board. Revill Sutcliffe, who had travelled down with Douglas, more to protect his ten per cent than anything else, began to shuffle uncomfortably.

Douglas kept his eyes fixed on the oil painting of Richard Longwell, which, inevitably, hung behind the chairman's seat. The afternoon sun slanted in through the leaded windows as neatly as if it had been arranged by a cunning lighting expert. The smell reminded Douglas of that Elizabethan scent they had used in the Long Gallery Alan Tagg designed for the Shakespeare Exhibition at Stratford in 1964. He had a vivid picture of that room. There had been a girl then, before

24

Jen, and they had driven down from London to see the exhibition and do some of the plays. He had been very impressed with that room hung with great portraits: Robert Dudley, earl of Leicester; Sir Philip Sidney; and Elizabeth herself, a golden queen, one hand resting on a globe, the shattering of the Armada in panels above.

He could not remember the girl's name which probably meant something dire and psychological because he could see her clearly: how they had stood together in the Long Gallery and looked out of the windows at the mock-up of Elizabethan London which seemed so real. He could feel her hand and, pressing back into the memory bank, recalled that he had her three times that night. Yet the vivid thing was the phoney gallery. It was probably something to do with being a director. One spent time making people believe that the unreal is real: a weaver of fantasies trapped by his own lack of stable memory.

The portrait stared back at him and Douglas wondered what kind of man Richard Longwell must have been. One thing was certain, he would not have approved of what Douglas was about to propose. Neither, he suspected, would these five most conservative gentlemen whom he now faced. He did not have to look at them, there had been ample chance for observation during the first interview. The reason for Shireston's descent, he suspected, lay right here among the trustees, too tied to rigid convention to risk a brave artistic gamble. Indeed, from the few inquiries he had been able to make in the City, it seemed that Basil Daley had more than once tried to find some legal method of closing the festival in order to channel the still large amounts of stocks, interest and capital into schemes which smacked of safe and large returns.

There was a shuffling and consultation of watches at the end of the table. There was a particular exactness about these men which Douglas found irritating. To him it suggested that under the business worldliness there was a pettiness, a quibble in their minds.

Sir Basil Daley, thin as the proverbial wraith, punctilious as God, coughed and gave Douglas a wintery smile.

'Mr Silver, it is three o'clock, time for us to start.'

Douglas could not resist taking a long deliberate look at his watch.

'Exactly one month ago we asked you to prepare a report for us,' Daley continued. 'A summary of your plans for this festival and its company. We are now gathered to hear this summary, upon which we will base our final decision regarding the appointment as director of the Shireston Festival to your good self.'

Douglas nodded. A far from pretty speech, but it was an accurate reflection of the type of people he had to convince.

'I feel that I should tell you,' Douglas began, 'that I have taken certain steps, in complete confidence, to assist me in formulating the ideas I'm about to put before you.'

The faces did not change.

'I've talked about the nucleus of my own ideas with Sir Laurence, Peter Hall and Trevor Nunn, all of whom have had great experience in this kind of venture. But, while they have given me the benefit of their advice, I cannot claim that all, or indeed any, of them are in sympathy with my proposals.'

As a light joke it was a frost. The five men still did not change their positions. Sir Basil seemed to be doodling.

'My first proposals are, I think, obvious. It goes without saying that they're going to cost money. Primarily you're going to need a totally new and first-class publicity machine.'

It was the glaring thing that had struck Douglas on examining the Shireston Festival executives. Publicity had been handled, not from the house, but from the local Information Centre, a grubby converted shop attached to the *Shireston Gazette*, a three men and a girl type weekly newspaper.

'Preferably I would want one top-rate man, an assistant of his own choice, a couple of secretaries and good office space up here where I can keep an eye on them. PRs and their minions are servants to an organization like this and eyes have to be kept on them otherwise they think they're running the show. Most of you already know that, notwithstanding, a

26

good PR set-up costs money.' He paused for breath, realizing that he was playing the whole scene to Sir Basil. As if to rectify this he shifted his chair slightly.

'A good publicity machine cannot operate in a vacuum. What we need is a clean sweep. A solid carefully chosen company. Actors who are not just box-office names but capable, reliable and efficient players around whom I'd hope to build a semi-permanent company: much as Peter Hall did in his early days at Stratford. An ensemble. A company that would work and go on working together in order to develop a style, a trademark within the profession. A group of actors who would, in turn, draw other actors to them, sharing skills and abilities. Yet the company must also be flexible enough to take in the unique talents of the theatre, the cinema, show-business even.'

He was leading up to the big moment. The one studded with mines and traps. Overplay it and there would be no chance. Underplay, and perhaps the roof would fall in.

'Given that I have my publicity machine and at least the beginnings of such a company, I am now faced with using them to the best possible total effect. One cannot hope to create style and ensemble acting in one short season.' He glanced up at the Longwell portrait. The eyes now seemed to mirror distaste. He looked away quickly. 'But we can create a talking point. We can open the doors of that theatre out there and let in a great rush of air followed by a purging flame. I make no apology for being theatrical in my choice of language. That's my business. Theatre. In particular the kind of theatre that I believe ought to be on display in this place. The Theatre of Re-examination.' Again he paused briefly, histrionically, slapping the table with the flat of his hand as he had rehearsed it a dozen times on the previous evening. Douglas was not a man to leave things to chance.

'Gentlemen, I want to inflame you with this idea. I would like you to feel for it as much as I do.' On his feet now, leaning forward, Douglas had the whole attention of the trustees.

'During my first season I would like to throw this company in at the deep end and make a public re-examination of four

27

great Shakespearian plays. Take them apart, if you like, in the light of current, international and social problems. There's nothing new in this, I know; but if Shakespeare is the genius master playwright, then a novel, off-beat interpretation can be of dynamic assistance: to the theatre as a whole and to this theatre in particular.'

'We don't want gimmicks. Tell him we don't want gimmicks.' Old Lewis Roland looked towards him with trembling lips.

'What are the plays, Mr Silver?'

Before Douglas had time to answer Rupert Crown's question, the chairman, Basil Daley himself, cut in –

'You see, Mr Silver, this is all very interesting but we've already talked to directors who have made similar passionate pleas. The problem is that their manifestos, on examination, have always boiled down to personal whims aimed at increasing their own stature. We would not like to see that happen in your case. I will grant that this theatre needs a strong company and an efficient publicity machine. But how will that machine be used? Who will really benefit? Yourself?'

Douglas dropped back into his chair, willing the look of anger from his face. He swallowed hard, taking a deep, controlling breath before speaking.

'Inevitably any radical change here is going to reflect to some extent on personalities. But what you must see is that, while myself and the many actors who will be concerned, may benefit, so will the festival. On the other hand, my bad judgment, or an actor's failure, can damage the festival as a whole.'

Daley nodded. 'And how would you build this first season? The productions?'

'*Othello*, *The Merchant of Venice*, *Romeo and Juliet* and *Richard III*.' He tried to sound matter-of-fact.

'Favourites all. Can't monkey with them.' Lewis Roland smiled.

It was time for the first bombshell. 'At the core of the season,' Douglas began, 'I want *Romeo and Juliet*. The

28

Capulets will be played by coloured actors and the Montagues by white.'

'The Capulets coloured? Coloured Capulets?' It was the first time that the precise Tupnall had spoken.

Douglas nodded. 'Black Capulets.'

'In fair Verona?' Tupnall was gay, Douglas would put money on it. The mocking rise in his voice. A man who gratified himself and nibbled in the twilight areas of art, picking up a few facts, a little knowledge and the right phrases, listening to semi-academic chat from gay actors.

'They were there. There were black people in Verona.' Douglas spread his hands as though to pacify the five men whose facial expressions now ranged from incredulity to amusement. 'Just think of the play for a moment. I realize there's nothing in the text to assist a racial slant to the play; but there's nothing to hinder it either.'

'I would have thought,' Daley leaned back with steepled fingers, an elder statesman humouring a young back bencher. 'I would have thought that there's enough about racial prejudice in *Othello*, and of minority groups in *The Merchant*, without building it into *Romeo and Juliet*.'

'*Othello* does not entirely stand or fall on the colour question,' Douglas countered quickly.

'*Even now an old black ram is tupping your white ewe.*' It was the kind of quote that would have readily stuck in Tupnall's mind.

Douglas waved it away with a flick of his right hand. 'In the final analysis, as people are fond of saying, it doesn't matter a fart whether Othello is black, puce, or vermilion – excuse the Elizabethan language. The play makes many points, colour is one tiny facet. As for *The Merchant*, go and examine that more thoroughly and you'll find it's not just about anti-Semitism. These are all subjects that call for new production slants. But just think. A black Juliet. Think of the tragedy of the play and put it into the spectrum of the colour issue. All right, it may not be a revolutionary idea, but, my God, it'll be a talking point.'

Surprisingly, he saw that Daley was nodding agreement.

'You'll have a problem with casting.' It was a statement from the chairman, as though Douglas had already won his case.

'Yes, a small problem. I know the actress who could do Juliet. I would want a black actor or personality of some standing to play Othello. . . .'

'Mr Poitier, I presume.' The scoffing Mr Tupnall again.

'I've checked,' said Douglas coolly. 'He's not available. I would like to get Joe Thomas.' The second bombshell.

'But he's a nightclub entertainer.' From Crown.

'One of the best. He's acted as well. Has a lot of movies and one Oscar to his credit.'

'And is a very difficult and costly gentleman.' Daley's smile was less wintery but in some ways more dangerous. 'Would you be able to get him? And if you did . . . could you . . .?' He hesitated, picking his words with care, 'Would you be able to control him?'

Sir Basil Daley was not altogether the square that Douglas had thought. Joe Thomas was the epitome of the American Negro club entertainer who had made it right to the top with limitless talent and ruthless morals. Now a multi-millionaire, Thomas could command huge fees for short appearances, small fortunes for television spectaculars. His ego was unbelievable, his energy unflagging, while the world's press made it plain that his flashpoint was exceptionally low.

Vivid stories gushed in the wake of Joe Thomas. In the past six years he had got through as many wives as a normal man gets through motor cars; his sexual excesses were whispered about through every capital he visited; there were the usual, eagerly reported, brawls; the occasional, and unpredictable, outbursts in favour of black militants; the fact of his heavy drinking; the rumours of drug abuse which were not unnaturally exaggerated to include the popular fantasy that he was mainlining it on the hard stuff: a tale that could be discredited by simply watching him work, or checking on his exhausting schedule.

Among the private information that Douglas had gleaned about Joe Thomas was the fact that he had no firm commitments for the following year. Also his doctors had advised a complete change of environment. For a period he had to be unobtrusively removed from the bright lights and the remorseless nightclub scene.

Douglas smiled back at the chairman. He had no idea whether he could handle Joe Thomas or not, but, at this moment, confidence was essential.

'I said that I would *like* Joe Thomas. Not just because he's a very big name, but I think it's the kind of off-beat casting that just might come off. In the middle of all that talent there's a rich vein that's still waiting to be tapped.

'I've only met him once, but, yes, if I could get him I think I could control him. You see, for him it would be a huge gamble. He'd need help and I think he'd know that. I think I could gain his trust. Tap the vein.'

'Cost?'

'Astronomical,' Crown answered.

'Not necessarily.' Douglas had them going now and he was not giving up. 'There is a way to Joe Thomas. Straight through his ego and into his guts. That's the way I would go. Present a big enough challenge and you might bypass the salary problem.'

Even Tupnall showed interest, though he seemed to be switching the conversation away from *Othello*. 'You said you already had an actress in mind for Juliet?'

'Yes. Unknown. But she'll do it easily. A girl called Carol Evans. She's very good.'

The snake in the brain; the taste of tobacco and whisky and brandy; the smell of melon on her body.

'And your Romeo?' Tupnall was asking.

'I'm not certain yet. Unknown. I've got to find him.'

'What about Desdemona?' Bland.

The catch question? Douglas allowed the pause to build until Tupnall, over-anxious, tried to slide the knife home. 'No chance of your wife playing it?'

'Would you want that?' Douglas tried to sound surprised. They all knew that she was the obvious choice in the circumstances.

'Was it in your mind?'

31

'Not until you put it there.'

'I think we would like it,' interrupted Daley.

'Then I imagine it would be possible.'

'Good. Shylock?'

'Straight casting. A Jewish actor. A comedian. Maurice Kapstein.'

'Plays the lead in that television thing?'

Douglas gave an abrupt nod. '*The Game Game*. Yes.'

'I wouldn't have called it "straight casting".'

Daley once more proving that he was no fool.

'And Richard?'

'Not easy. Larry still lingers constantly in the public mind because of the movie getting so many playings on television. Ian Holm topped the lot at Stratford in '64. Not easy at all. I want a genuine power politics motivation: a live dictator. And there's something else. I want an actor capable of playing Richard as a bisexual. I had thought of Conrad Catellier.'

He saw Tupnall's eyebrows rise a fraction.

Dempsey smiled. 'You'll have The Fellowship of the Boar around your neck.'

'Everyone has The Fellowship around their necks when you do *Richard III*. They're nice people. They just don't happen to believe the political propaganda Shakespeare was spreading around about Richard Crookback.' He suddenly realized that Dempsey's smile was not friendly.

'Catellier will be high, he'll cost a great deal,' said Dempsey. 'I think the whole thing is too high. The budget on the company alone is going to be a strain.' He had been playing with a pencil throughout the meeting. Douglas could now see, across the table, that he had been scribbling lines of figures.

'Bill.' Daley held up a restraining hand. 'Might I suggest that we discuss this in private?' He turned back to Douglas. 'We do realize, as businessmen, that you have to spend a bit to make a bit.' His smile had become tinged with warmth. 'If we accept your plans in principle, and then, perhaps, supply you with what we think to be a realistic budget, you could let us know if you think it possible to come anywhere near fulfilling your intentions.'

It was more than Douglas had hoped for.

'God,' breathed Revill in the car outside. 'You're a bloody maniac. Joe Thomas as Othello. Do you know about Thomas?'

'I know.' Douglas grinned.

'And Kapstein. The problems you're going to have with Kapstein.' He held up a hand. 'A great actor. Okay. But you've got to keep a company happy. Kapstein, the lovable old Jewish gent. He'll insist on at least six seventeen-year-olds who'll play. And how are you going to keep him out of your wife's dressing-room? She's the first he'll make for. The full exposure bit. Are you really going to throw in with that lot?'

'I'm going to throw myself in.'

'And that raging old queen Catellier,' muttered Revill.

'Listen, Revill.' Douglas put his hand on the driving wheel. 'I can compound the most spectacular and mind-blowing Shakespearean season this country's ever seen. They'll remember it for decades.'

Revill Sutcliffe put his Rover into gear and drew away from the house. 'Maurice Kapstein already. And impossible Joe Thomas. Mad. You're bloody crazy, and another thing, who's Carol Evans?'

'A great Juliet.' Douglas was looking at the burning white of the theatre's façade rising among the trees across the velvet lawn.

CHAPTER THREE

He was quite a tall man, around six two; but well proportioned, slim-hipped, standing in the centre of the spotlight, one arm raised high, the other clutching the microphone, the head bent and sweat dropping to the floor.

Energy exuded from him: a kind of dazzling static which flowed out in warmth, caught the audience by the throat, and made each of them a part of this electric figure: white pants and shirt contrasting obviously with the striking black face, cropped hair and strangely sensitive hands.

For ninety minutes Douglas Silver had been engrossed in Joe Thomas's performance. The songs; the chat from the stool in the middle of the floor; the sentiment; the impersonations and dancing. This was a unique entertainer. *A fluid ball of black fire*, the quick quip ad men called him.

The more Douglas watched, the more his mind became encased in the idea of harnessing this talent and energy to one production: one performance.

It seemed impossible that he could be sitting here in the lounge of the Thunderbird Hotel on The Strip at Las Vegas, with the crap games, roulette, and the constant churn of fruit machines going on only a few yards away.

Basil Daley's letter had arrived ten days ago, a lifetime, only three days after the interview with the trustees. On reflection, Daley said, the trustees would back Douglas Silver, though it had to be made clear that not all the members were happy about what they called 'the sensationalism which seemed to lie behind Mr Silver's attitude to some of the proposed productions'.

As far as Douglas was concerned it still constituted a minor miracle. Daley himself was a man to have in your pocket, and Daley seemed to react sharply and favourably to the core of Douglas's plans.

With the letter came the budget. Again far more than Douglas had dreamed of. Daley obviously had a healthy arm lock on the rest of the Trust and had talked them into opening up the vaults for one last big throw. They were allotting a staggering £2 million for the first season with a review of the situation in May of the following year. In other words, unless Douglas retrieved about three-quarters of the initial investment of festival funds he would find himself in difficulties for his second season.

Within thirty minutes of receiving the letter, Douglas telephoned his acceptance.

An hour later he set up the first meeting with the stage director and the productions' manager. Both had been at Shireston for two years; both had been on the point of resignation; both were old acquaintances of Douglas. Ronnie Gregor, the stage director, had worked with him in Birmingham; while he had known Art Drays, the productions' manager, when Drays was an ASM at Stratford.

Within half-an-hour, Douglas had persuaded them to forget about resigning.

'I don't wish to be rude, but you'll never do it,' said Ronnie.

'*I'm* not going to. *We* are.' Douglas made it plain from the outset that it would be a team venture.

'It'll be one hell of a job fitting up a company around names like Conrad, Maurice and your wife.' Art was already scratching names and queries on his clip board.

'Not to mention the incredible world of Joe Thomas,' grinned Ronnie.

'We haven't got any of them yet,' countered Douglas.

'And Thomas we're not likely to get, thank God.'

'Be patient and let us see.' Douglas began to set them their first tasks. He would deal with Conrad Catellier, Maurice Kapstein, Carol Evans and Joe Thomas himself. They had

35

two weeks to draw up preliminary casting sheets, check on actors' availability, set up auditions, where necessary, and provide names for second strings for the most important middle billing players.

'Whoever we get in the leads,' Douglas told them, 'and whatever talent comes to light from the small part people and the walk-ons, remember that our middle men, our Brabantios, Cassios, Roderigos, Tybalts, Friar Lawrences, Lorenzos, Gratianos and Jessicas have got to be more than just good. They've got to be very strong and very professional. If we do manage this spectacular lead billing I need men and women around the leads who are absolutely grade one. I'm going all out for an integrated company.'

He realized immediately that Art was going to pick him up on his use of the word 'integrated'.

'How integrated?' asked the productions manager. 'What percentage of coloured actors do we use? All those Capulets are going to be difficult to place in the other plays.'

'No.' Douglas was firm. 'They're not going to be difficult to place. We draw attention to them in *Othello* and *Romeo*, but I'm having no sharp divisions in the other two plays. As far as *The Merchant* and *Richard III* are concerned it's to hell whether people are white or black. In those two plays we really drive it home and make the audiences forget about the colour of men's skins.'

'What percentage?' Art again asked with diffidence shadowing his voice.

'Forty-five per cent coloured. I'd like to make it fifty-fifty, but even I've got to be realistic.'

Ronnie was given the additional job of checking around the repertory companies; sitting night after night in the provincial theatres as Shireston's talent scout: searching for the spark of talent which Douglas might be able to fan and produce a conflagration: a memorable Romeo.

That night, Douglas called his wife. The location work in Mexico was over and she was now back in Los Angeles doing the daily drive to and from the studios, still with four weeks to go before they finished the picture.

On the telephone he held himself back, not daring to tell her everything at once. In the following weeks they would have to find a space, a vacuum into which he could pour his plans and ideas.

She was missing him and edgy about work, but full of joy when he told her of the appointment and naturally inquisitive when he asked her to make no plans for next year.

'We're going to work together, aren't we?' she asked excitedly.

'I hope so, but I've got to talk to you about it first. I may even be seeing you before you think. Oh, and not a word to anyone yet. The whole thing, my appointment, everything's under wraps until I give the okay.'

He had to get close to Thomas, and fast. Practically the rest of the night was spent in tracking down the coloured entertainer's manager. He finally found him in Las Vegas where Joe was playing the Thunderbird with his retinue around him.

Sure, why not? He could come out and talk to Joe any time he wanted. Sure Joe remembered him. Joe never forgot anybody. Yes, he would give the matter his personal attention.

'Call as soon as you arrive, as soon as you get into town, Douglas baby. There's always a welcome here. Okay?'

Douglas could almost hear the man saying, 'Some British kook, a theatre producer with a sick idea trying to sell Joe short. Don't worry, Joe, we'll handle it if he turns up.'

He lunched with Catellier's agent next day and met Maurice Kapstein's agent in the afternoon. Both actors were free, except for Maurice's television commitments next year. There was certainly a chance, but a great deal of negotiating would be needed.

Already he had called Carol's agent and there was absolutely no problem there. In the evening he met Carol for dinner.

She came into the restaurant late, breathless and full of doubts. 'You're having me on, Douglas, I just don't get that lucky, what's the catch?'

'What did your agent tell you?'

'Well, Bernie called and said you wanted to see me. I thought it was just the old. . . . Well, you know . . . Malta. Then he told me that you were going to Shireston and wanted me to play Juliet.'

A waiter circled the table like a lone vulture. She took another deep breath. 'It's a gimmick, isn't it? You really want me for a tiny part – which would be great.' The melodic laugh again. 'Honestly, just to work would be terrific.'

'There's no gimmick unless you make one. Let's order and then I'll talk about it. One thing though . . .' he laid his hand over hers. 'The offer is not payment, for Malta or anything else. I want you down at Shireston as an actress. And that's the one reason I want you down there: whatever else.'

The matter which, more than any other, nagged and worried in the back of Douglas's mind was the question of the new publicity department.

It was now mid-September. Announcements would have to be made before the end of the following month and he wanted the whole deal handled from Shireston. That would set the pattern for the future.

The best theatre public relations people were already at Stratford, or Chichester, or with the National. Outside that circle it meant going to one of the larger PR firms which would not suit the situation.

There was one name, however, that kept reasserting itself: Adrian Rolfe.

Rolfe had backed out of theatre PR work about a year before, in order to join one of the big publicity houses that had been courting him for years. In this instance, the promise of fast promotion and an eventual seat on the board had been the carrots dangled and accepted.

With an impeccable army background, Rolfe had a genius for organization. His contacts were spread amazingly wide, and, having worked in the theatre, and around actors, for fifteen years or so, he knew all the tricks: the sensitive areas; the ways of smooth-tongued diplomacy; the subtle bribes.

He could take a mundane story and place it, with sniper's accuracy, so that it would get maximum coverage. He was also gifted with impeccable good taste when it came to matters of style for the layout of programmes and advertising copy.

A brilliant gem, but with the flaw of a waspish tongue which made him occasional enemies within the profession. One was Douglas, with whom Adrian Rolfe had indulged himself in a stand-up public shouting match, over a minor error in the wording of a press release concerning the famed production of *Peer Gynt*.

Douglas, who had been in the wrong, lost the battle of words. Now he thought hard before attempting to woo Adrian Rolfe into the Shireston fold. Under normal circumstances it would be difficult enough, but, with old wounds still festering, the negotiations would have to include a humiliation which Douglas did not relish.

In the end Douglas became convinced that, if he could possibly be persuaded, Adrian Rolfe was the man for the job. He decided that the festival must come before his own pride and some approach had to be made. Yet, still side-stepping the issue he took Revill Sutcliffe into his confidence, asking the agent to start sounding out the ground. An actual meeting would have to wait, like a hundred other things, until he returned from America.

Slowly things were taking shape. Terms were agreed for Catellier and Kapstein, though Douglas still had to speak to the actors on a personal level.

Ronnie and Art worked steadily and were making a little progress. Each evening, Douglas met Carol. It became a kind of habit. The meeting of two people who could talk on a different level after Douglas had completed a day filled with telephone calls, lists and the interminable problem of dovetailing appointments into an ever-tightening schedule.

Basil Daley had loaned them an office, awaiting repair and decoration, above an Indian Restaurant in Rupert Street on the fringes of Soho.

When the day there was finally through, Douglas would

walk up and meet Carol, usually outside the Swiss Centre gleaming with watches and posters of green slopes, chalet-backed and overhung by mountains.

They would dine and talk. He regularly kissed her good night on her doorstep, like some uncertain teenager; and there was nothing else until the night before he left for Vegas.

For once, Douglas went to pick her up from her flat off the Bayswater Road. At the top of the steps by the front door he pressed the buzzer next to the sliver of cardboard on which her name was written in careful, schoolgirl copper-plate. The intercom speaker crackled into life and her distorted voice asked who it was.

'I'll unlock the door, Douglas. Come straight up. Third floor. My name's on that door as well. I'll leave it open. Wait for me, would you, I'm having a shower.'

Slowly he climbed the stairs and entered the flat. A large bedsitting-room, unspectacular, but clean and comfortable. Doors off to the kitchen and bathroom, from which he could hear the sound of the shower.

He called out, and she replied that she would only be a minute. Her dress was laid out on the bed next to her under-wear.

The naked coffee body, beaded with water under the shower.

He crossed to the bed and allowed his hand to touch her dress lightly, then the bra and pants. He felt hot, an intruder.

'Pretty?' she asked from the bathroom door, shrouded in a towel. 'I'm sorry, love, I've been rushing about all day. I'm terribly late.'

He walked to her and took hold of the towel. For a second she hesitated, pulling away with a half 'No' forming on her lips. Then the damp cloth fell from her and there was the skinny figure again, arching towards him in all its glorious golden brown sleekness.

They made love for three hours, went out for a quick meal and returned to her flat.

Then, before he had time to think, Douglas was on a jet doing the long haul over the pole to San Francisco where he did not have time to call Jen, but did make time to cable Carol, before getting the local jet to Vegas: hot, sticky, a wild maelstrom of mass pleasure at one hell of a price. Gaudy, horrific in its pressures, yet slick as artificial silk in the manner of taking your money and making you feel good about it.

During the afternoon he spoke briefly to Tommy Carr, Thomas's manager, giving away no details and concealing his dislike for the arrogance of the big man, ring-decorated and overdressed, acting as though he was St Peter next to Joe Thomas's God.

Thomas called later and it was obvious that the man did remember their one meeting in London. Somehow they had found themselves next to one another at a movie party, and for two hours they had knocked holes in the world and then put it back together. But that was in London. Here, Thomas was on his own ground and far from being alone, or even remotely lonely.

'See you in my suite after tonight's show, eh, Doug?'

'I'll be there.'

'Okay, baby, I ain't goin' no place tonight.'

And here it was, the end of the show, with Joe Thomas curving the note up to a deep finish.

Joe could feel the sweat dripping from him. Running into his eyes. He needed a drink and cigarette, but he still punched the energy from every pore because that was the way he always played it. Throttle full open, heading straight for that mountain into which, one day, he knew, he would crash. But the mountain was still a long way off.

Half opening his eyes he had to blink the sweat away. He dropped an arm and let the applause, the cheering and stomping of feet, flow into him, embracing him. It was food. Joe's fix, the recharge. This was the payback and the payola for all the bad years, the hoofing and insults, the common indignities he shared with his black brothers.

He allowed his body to sway and his head to roll so that he saw the bowl of faces: smiling, laughing, a tear here and there

41

near the surface, and the hands like a sea of acceptance swelling and bubbling around him.

He made a quick gesture with both hands, shaking his head, as though warding off praise. At last there was silence.

'Thank you, folks. Thank you. All good things must come to an end. I wish I could go on for another two hours.' Applause. Quieten them again. 'No. Really. Thank you. Thank you. I have a limited time here and it's just not possible. I ain't allowed no more time.' Groans. Quieten those quickly and get ready to hightail it out but fast. It's been a long night.

'Quite sincerely, folks, I want to say what a great thrill it's been for me tonight. I mean that. You don't know what a thrill and honour it is for me.' A scatter of applause. 'No, really. You've been the best audience this stay in Vegas. Hope you've enjoyed it. Come back again real soon, I'm here for another four weeks. God bless you and let's live together in peace, huh?'

Jesus H Christ, he thought as the hands started again, every white bastard in this room I can take, and I can screw every and all of their plump little wives just by twitching my finger. Shit to you. Shit to you all.

The boys were at the exit to flank him and hustle him through and into the performers' elevator and up to his suite on the sixth floor.

'You were great tonight, Joe.'

'Really great, you knocked 'em, baby.'

There was another ring of applause as he entered the suite.

About thirty people were there, making little impression on the long wide drawing-room. Tommy Carr was smiling his wide insincere smile. Who else? Two or three folk he had taken to during the first couple of weeks in Vegas, and the 'personal friends': leeches, there to tell him what a great show it had been. Monro, the bartender, stood smiling and white jacketed. The whole place, furniture, junk art, expensive non-decor and all, thought Joe, looked like an airport departure lounge.

'You want a massage, Joe?' From Smiley, one of the boys

on his right.

'Nah. I'll settle for a shower. Bring me a big, and I mean big, Bacardi and coke.'

Smiley nodded to Jones, the other boy. Smiley took his job seriously and rarely moved more than ten feet away from Thomas.

Joe summoned up the energy and began the dancing little walk across the pile to the bedroom. It was a question of running the gauntlet of approbation. The distant smiling faces down in the main room had nothing on this. These geeks wanted to touch you and fawn. It helped, but the same old routine began to pall after a time. Joe was ready for new kicks.

'Joe I've never seen anything like it. You were a sensation.' He was a heavy, pudgy-faced man in a lightweight tartan tux, armed with a blonde. Through the off-focus vision, the desire for a drink and other needs, Joe remembered that the blonde was the reason he had taken a liking to the guy, who was turning to fat and would not see forty-eight again. His young wife was meticulously bored and a good twenty-two.

Tommy Carr reached the bedroom door at about the same time as Joe.

'I got four in tonight, Joe. Over by the bar.'

Joe inclined his head. Four girls and a couple of men chatted with the animation of basking lizards on a hot day.

'You want now, baby?' asked Tommy.

'Not them.' Joe's head snapped round. 'That. If you can prise it away from fat gut.' He indicated the blonde with the man in the tartan tux. Tommy nodded.

'No sweat though.' Joe looked at him, almost a threat in his eyes.

'I understand.'

'Anything else I should know?'

'I'll join you in a minute.' Tommy was away across the room and Joe, Smiley at his elbow, slipped through the door.

The cigarette tasted good. Smiley held it for him while he showered, then helped rub down his boss, sprinkling the friction lotion on the tough, hard body.

Dry and feeling more like himself, sensing the urge to continue, Joe took the drink that had been brought through, rinsing his mouth, throwing back his head and taking great gulps.

'Shit, man.' He shook himself like a dazed boxer. 'That's been a rough couple of days.'

'Mr Carr is waiting.' Smiley seldom smiled, hence his name.

'Send him in and wait outside.' Joe slipped into a towelling robe, crossed the room to the dressing table, looked broodingly at the single tape cassette lying there and nodded. Finally he picked it up, slid it into the machine, part of the built-in equipment of the bedroom, and pressed the key.

His own voice came gliding from the hidden speakers. A backing of muted strings and percussion. The lyric was sad, haunting, yet he would bet it would lay a few ghosts out there in the world of true love and romance. His voice dipped and swerved softly to the words: about a girl who was going away and how he knew that was the best thing that could happen, though he was still fighting it and would wait for ever. All the clichés, all the spiked darts to reach the emotions of the young, the desires of the middle-aged, and the memories of the old. He heard the door close.

'I got Mrs Delroy outside. Man has she got hot pants for you.'

'Good track.' Joe pointed to the tape machine. 'Who's Mrs Delroy?'

'The blonde broad with the gutsy husband. He's drinking himself to death out there with some of the boys. He won't know if his wife's coming or going.'

'She'll be doing both before long.' Joe nodded wisely. 'Still a good track.'

'It's very good. Pete's pleased with that one and seven more, but he wants another four for the album. We go to LA at six o'clock tomorrow morning. You do the session and Pete's promised to get you back here by eight, in time to rest up before the show.'

'Real nice of him. I get a rest. So what else is new?'

'That British director's here.'

'British director?'

'Douglas Silver, the one you got buddies with at some party. Remember? You spoke to him this afternoon.'

'Yea. Yea, I spoke to him. He's class, Tommy. Shakespeare, Ibsen, Chekhov. Legit. Find out what he wants?'

'He wants to see you. Hush-hush.' Tommy grinned his wide grin and put a finger to his lips.

Joe nodded again. 'We'll keep him waiting a while. Send Mrs Delroy in, and I'm not to be disturbed. Not yet anyhow, and not by the husband.'

'Anything you say, Joe.'

'You got it. Anything I say.'

The track on the tape had changed to a bouncy soul number by the time the blonde tapped at the door and entered in answer to Joe's call.

'You come right in, Mrs Delroy, and make yourself comfortable and at home.' He did an Uncle Tom around her, realizing why he had been attracted to her a couple of nights before.

For a blonde the girl gave off flesh radiations, each move almost calculated to condition a man into trying to make her. And she does it all, thought Joe, without even trying. We'll see.

'You like a drink, Mrs Delroy?'

'I've had a drink, Joe. And the name's Janice.'

'Uh-huh.' He stood in the centre of the room in front of the bed as though thinking. 'Janice? You know why I invited you in here?'

She stood up and took two paces towards him.

'Because you have a reputation to keep up. You need stimulating and you don't use whores. You do the picking and you pick only the best.'

He grinned and let the robe slip from his shoulders. 'So here I am, white mama. Take me.'

There was a sharp hiss as she drew in her breath on seeing how magnificently he was endowed. Like a black stallion, gleaming and proud. A jet lance on which to impale herself.

Carefully she reached up behind her neck to the fastening of the little black dress, the inevitable evening uniform of vacationing wives. Her right hand pulled downwards on the zipper and the dress fell to the floor. She was naked underneath. White and unmarked where her bra and bikini pants usually were, a light reddish brown elsewhere, over the areas that had been exposed to the sun.

Joe stood quite still, looking at her with a touch of disgust on his face.

'I'm ready, Joe.' She came towards the bed, but he caught her by one shoulder.

'You want a bit of Joe? You want to be able to go back to Cleveland or St Paul or Buffalo, or wherever else home is, and whisper to the other adulterous wives at the coffee morning that you made Joe Thomas? You had that big black guy who so's wonderful on TV? The star? You had him right here on that great trip to Las Vegas?'

'No, Joe.' She whined, her brow creasing with incomprehension. 'I just want to give you something in return for all you've given. Joe, I've watched you. On television. The first time I saw you live was in New York and I've seen you every night here. While you're on it's like you're doing it to me. To me personally. Give it to me now, Joe.'

He rested both hands on her shoulders. 'It ain't as easy as that, lady. You want a bit of Joe then you've got to pray for it. On your knees. And you've got to eat it, baby. If you want jungle juice you've got to drink at the fountain.' His hands pressed harder on her shoulders.

She opened her eyes wide. For a moment his stomach turned over in a butterfly panic. He thought she was going to run straight out there among the others. It had happened once with a quickie like this and the aftermath had been unpleasant.

'I. . . .' She tried. 'I . . . don't. . . .'

'You don't do that kind of thing? Like hell, darling.'

'No. I do. I do it. See, Joe.'

And she was on her knees. He encouraged her by sliding his hands over her breasts. Like hell she did it. Regularly and eagerly by the way she licked her tongue across him, taking him into her mouth and pulling like a famished baby at the breast. She even clung on as his body jerked in three fast spasms, only letting go and lunging sideways for the bedside table and the box of Kleenex when it was all through.

Joe sighed and sat down on the bed. The blonde was stretched out at his feet, her body going rigid and then relaxing in a quick regular motion.

Joe laughed quietly. 'You get yours as well?'

She nodded violently, her face averted.

'Well, there you are. Another dream come true. Thanks, baby.'

She got to her feet, making heavy weather of it, and started to dress, do her hair and repair the fractured make-up.

'Another thing.' He was already pulling on a fresh shirt as she reached the door.

'Yes?' She desperately tried to regain some of her lost poise. She was confused, knowing that, in spite of the delicious post-orgasmic throb, she had been humiliated, her role as she had planned it had been reversed. In reality what she had wanted from Joe Thomas had been unctuous and gratifying appreciation: a sexual *Te Deum*.

'Just, if you happen to pass by again, Janice honey, wear underwear eh?'

'I thought. . . . It's going out of fashion.'

'Not in my circles, kid. Ladies wear underwear. Maybe it's because when I was small my ma and pa went without food to see my sisters decently dressed. Anyhow, I like the old-fashioned unwrapping game, so remember.'

Her hand clutched at the door handle.

'And let's live in peace and harmony, eh?' Joe laughed and began to snap his fingers to the beat coming from the tape machine.

The crowd had not thinned down at all by the time he left the bedroom. If anything there were more people than before.

Cigarette in one hand and drink in the other, he came out like a boxer spoiling for a fight. The same old greeting and spontaneous murmur of approval gurgled to meet him. Shit, he thought, I might as well have a tape made and play it in here every night. That way I might get rich.

As he moved slowly among them, grinning and acknowledging, Joe let his eyes scan the crowd. He used a carefully devised search pattern that he had perfected through the years. He liked to know who was around, invited or uninvited; who were free loading and, not the least important, who was not around.

Janice and her husband had left. His grin broadened. That was what the Janices of this world needed and deserved. The genuine thing could happen at leisure, later, with one of the four who had offered themselves and had been brought up by Tommy for that purpose.

Now Tommy was at his elbow.

'I've got Douglas Silver over here.'

Joe nodded and allowed himself to be steered over to the young looking man with long black hair, nervously smoking at the bar.

'Hi there, Douglas baby, nice to see you again.'

Douglas was nervous. The whole scene jarred with him. The people were not really of his world: half of them the garishly extrovert side of show-biz, the other half hangers-on. An hour had passed since his arrival and conversation was difficult. He wanted to keep his head clear so three Martinis were enough, and he had just witnessed the beginning of an unpleasant public brawl between a young blonde and her slightly drunk, over-blown, husband. In some ways Douglas was appalled to see the way in which trouble had been averted by having them hustled out of the suite.

When Joe came out the atmosphere was equally nasty, a mixture of adoration and blatant sycophancy: the whole unhealthy and based almost completely on the emotions.

Douglas wondered if he had made a terrible error of judgment. He cooled his thoughts by facing the fact that Joe Thomas was not likely to agree to his proposition anyway.

Douglas stretched out his hand to greet the tall man.

'Hello, Joe. Great show. Really great.'

'Yea, I'm pretty fabulous.' Joe grinned, speaking as though he meant it. 'Well, come on, man, tell me what you been doing? What's your scene?'

Douglas made a quick intro, a précis explanation of the Shireston Festival.

'That sounds healthy.'

'Well it's not Stratford, but it can be pretty big. I wanted to talk to you about it.'

'To me? Is it money? You want a hand-out? Or for me to do a benefit maybe?'

'No, for Christ's sake, Joe, nothing like that.'

'Well, come on, man, give.'

'Can we talk somewhere privately?'

'Ah, shit to that, let's talk here, there's fun here.' He waved away a couple who were bearing down on them. 'Over here.' Leading Douglas to a corner far away from the bar. Smiley was close behind them and, as they sat down on a short beige settee, Joe turned to him. 'See that Mr Silver and I ain't disturbed: right?'

Smiley nodded and took up a post several feet away.

For a moment, Joe was distracted, looking hard at someone across the room. It gave Douglas a chance to make a quick observation of the man now that he was off-stage with the true personality emerging.

Outwardly there were the trappings of wealthy success, hell they were all around anyway, but he admired the intelligence with which Thomas presented himself. A simple glance at him and you saw a big slim man dressed in white shirt and pants. Look closer. The shirt was silk and there was probably some hand stitching in there somewhere. The chunky gold cufflinks could have come from any cheap store, but get right down to it and the work could not have been done by anybody but a master craftsman. There were other things, the broad alligator belt, the rings on his fingers and the calf that shod him, or the intricate design on the medallion hanging from a thin gold chain around his neck.

'Sorry, baby, I got carried away. You want to look at the piece over there. Tits like riot helmets.' Joe was back with

49

him. 'So tell me about this Shireston Festival and the Shakespeare bit. Something I ain't never done, the Shakespeare bit.' He giggled, the giggle turning into a low tempo guffaw. 'Me doing Shakespeare. A gas.'

'Sorry you find it funny, Joe.'

'Huh?' His face assumed a mask.

'I was going to ask if you would play some Shakespeare for me.'

It took a couple of seconds for it to sink in. 'Oh yea. Yea. A great gimmick. Good thinking, buddy. Forget it and let's stay pals. You couldn't afford me anyhow.'

I'm sorry, Joe. Really sorry, because with your talent I think we could have produced something memorable.'

'Come on. I'm an out of proportion ugly black bastard who sings and dances and does the other schtik really well. What did you have in mind for me? That I should play Hamlet?'

'No. Othello.'

The pause was terrifying. For a minute, Douglas thought Thomas was going to hit him. Then –

'You're on the level aren't you? You must be nuts, baby. Me? Othello? Now, Doug, if I was an actor, just if I was, even then, would I make an Othello? Man, I saw Robeson play it. With his voice and stature he only just made it. I saw Sir Laurence as well, mind you I was the only guy in the whole world who didn't like that. Othello needs dignity, height, authority. That one was like a Jamaican drummer, man, and I've got nothing against Jamaican drummers.'

Douglas nodded. There was hope. Joe Thomas was no fool.

'Now just think hard,' Joe continued. 'Get that picture in your mind of me, the pug ugly spade, walking on and squalking *Most potent, grave, and reverend signiors*.' He did it in a Jerry Lewis voice. 'A laugh a line.'

'I've had that picture in my mind for some time and I don't think it would be a laugh a line. You see, Joe, I believe that yours is one of the unique talents. I could be wrong, but I think that you're capable of giving the role everything it needs. You're capable because of your talent, and because of the way you've used it so far. All right, so you're ugly. But who says a guy like you cannot have dignity and authority? You've got it already.' He let it slide home.

Slowly, Joe nodded.

'Christ, Joe, you give out both of those qualities every time you walk out in front of an audience.'

'Ah.' He flapped a hand and made a drinking motion towards Smiley who gave the signal to Munro at the bar. 'Forget it, Doug. Like I said, you couldn't afford me anyhow; and my voice, sure I've done a few movies, but that doesn't equip me for things like this.'

The drinks arrived, Douglas became conscious that the whole background to their conversation had been filled in by Joe's voice, swinging and singing in stereo. One of the speakers was embedded in the wall above them.

'You really mean what you said just now?'

'That you could do it?'

'Yea, that I could do it. Or have you got another angle, Doug, pally?'

Douglas let a smile spread slowly. 'I've got several other angles, Joe. As well as you playing Othello I'm going to do *Romeo and Juliet* with all Juliet's folks as uppity black people.'

He waited for the reaction. It came out with a splutter. 'Hey, man, that's great. You got a place for me in there?'

'If we came to some agreement I might ask you to play Juliet's poppa, old Capulet.'

'I can see it all. Yo come right in heah, Juliet gel, 'way from that white trash or ah'll tan yo' hide.' He gave a little giggle then leaned forward, serious again, putting a hand on Douglas Silver's knee. 'Say it again, you really think I could get away with it, huh?'

Douglas shook his head. 'No, not get away with it. You could do it. We don't know each other very well, Joe, but I should imagine that you're pretty disciplined when it comes to work. This would mean self-discipline like you've never known. It would mean leaning hard on the director. Putting all your trust in me and working twenty hours a day. It would

51

mean being part of a company, not just being Joe Thomas the glitter man, the one on top. It would mean something.'

Joe laughed. 'Who's playing the chick? Desdemona?'

'I hope it'll be Jennifer Frost.'

'Now. There's a nice lady. I could. . . .' Realization crossed his face. 'Oh sure, you're married to Jen Frost, aren't you? Well, that figures.' He nodded, seriously. 'How long does this set of charades go on for?'

'April to September'.

Thomas gave a sour laugh. 'You mean you'd want me to give up everything else: movies, clubs, everything, for six months?'

'More than six months. Rehearsals for *Othello* will have to begin in the first week of January. And let's face it, Joe, if you're going to do the thing at all, you're going to need some expert coaching before you even step into a rehearsal room with actors who've played Shakespeare for most of their working lives. It's a whole new scene. That's why I thought you'd be interested. I felt that the challenge. . . .'

'Yea.' He flapped his hand again. 'I can feel the damn challenge. Right here I feel it.' Pumping his stomach with a balled fist. 'A challenge that's going to take a year out of my professional life and, maybe, leave me chewed up and spat out in little pieces.'

'Or a bigger, wiser and more accomplished person than you've ever been.'

'What you payin'?' Joe grinned, digging the director hard in the ribs.

'Nothing like what you can get anywhere else.'

'Pity. It's attractive. I ain't had a real challenge since I played the Ku Klux Klan Commem in Memphis. You're right though, why the hell shouldn't an ugly swivel hips black man play Othello? Let's see how it grabs the rest of the folks.'

Instinctively, Douglas put out a hand to stop him. Too late, Joe was on his feet, strutting out into the centre of the room, his voice raised against the chat and his own singing, recorded, voice.

'Gather round, folks, I got news. Cool that lousy off-key beautiful black vocalist. C'mon, c'mon.' Beckoning with the fingers of both hands, little waving motions.

The tape went dead and the chatter died. A few couples moved in closer to Joe, others turned to look at him.

'Okay. Now we've got a celebrity here tonight. A director. Ah shit, you say, directors are a dime a dozen. Well I'm not talking about your dime a dozen movie directors. I'm talking about a real director. The living theatre, folks. A guy who directs live actors on the live stage.'

Douglas felt his stomach churn.

You want to know why he's here? You want me to tell you why he's come all the way from England to talk to me? Okay. The man's name is Douglas Silver, a great director and married to another name you'll know, Jennifer Frost.' A little more interest as Jen's name was mentioned. 'And he's come all the way from the green fields of England to ask me . . . Me. . . .' He thumped his chest. '. . . To play . . . Othello.'

Silence. A slight shuffling. Then a chuckle from the far end of the room. The chuckle spread and grew. It seemed to swamp Joe and bore down on Douglas's ears like some terrible electronic noise used for torture. Laughter. Rising to a higher note. Joe still stood in the centre of the room with his arms spread wide. He turned, almost a gesture of supplication, towards Douglas, his face a mask of disbelief. But the laughter continued. Even Smiley had a twisted expression, though he was looking down at his shoes.

'Cool it.' Joe pitched the shout too high and it came out like a shriek. 'What the hell is there to laugh at? The idea of me playing Othello? We'll see.'

Another giggle, this time a nervous reaction from one of the girls.

To Joe the whole world shrank to that giggle of laughter. It became total. Most personal. The faces he trusted. The faces he did not know. Jungle faces. Piss off, black man, get back to Africa. Treating him, Joe Thomas, like an ignorant spook. Shit on you. He turned back to Douglas Silver. He knew now

53

that he could trust the Englishman. He put out a hand and rested it on Douglas's shoulder.

'Okay.' He spoke in a whisper. 'You got yourself a deal. The press needn't know, but I'll come for just my expenses.'

'Your expenses?'

'Mine. You don't think I'd bring along any of this trash. A year away from all this'll do me fine. It'll be like nothing else.' He swivelled to look at the guests. 'And you can all get the hell outa here. Go. Go back to the sewers. I don't want to see any of you again.'

Tommy Carr took a step forward and opened his mouth to speak.

Even in his fury, Joe was careful. 'All of you, except those I have to see legally.' With the motion of a snake's head he spat towards Carr, then again turned to Douglas. 'We can see my lawyers in LA. Tomorrow. They'll fix the deal.'

He stopped to watch the people drifting out. At the end of the procession were the four girls that Tommy had brought up.

'Hold it. Who told you to go?'

The girls clustered together: a redhead, brunette and two blondes. Like sheep. Long young legs, tired faces and eyes which were windows to nothing.

'You.' Joe pointed at the brunette.

'Me?' Disbelief and adoration mixed with fear.

'Nobody else, unless Mr Silver wants one of the rejects.'

Douglas shook his head. He was worried sick by what he had seen. It was going to be difficult enough controlling Joe without freaking out in a merry foursome with him.

'Up to you, baby. Speak now or hold your piece.'

'I'd rather not.'

'Okay. Fly with me in the morning. Tommy'll give you the details. I have to do a recording session but we'll fit in the bit with the lawyers. I'll call them now. Sleep well.' He turned his full attention on to the brunette. 'And remember, baby, I do the funnies.'

Wrapping an arm around her, Joe began to pull the girl, unresisting, towards the bedroom.

CHAPTER FOUR

Ronnie Gregor was impressed. Every night he had been dashing between London and all points to sit in large and small, comfortable and seedy, aged and modern repertory theatres. To Ronnie it seemed that he had been doing this all his life. In fact it was only a matter of ten days.

He followed Douglas's instructions to the letter.

'Don't be influenced by the standard of the productions,' Douglas had told him. 'We're looking for one thing only: a young, unknown actor whom I can mould into a Romeo. To be honest, Ronnie, I don't care a damn if he can't do anything else, or if he never does anything else. I want a great Romeo. So just look at actors. Watch the way they move, the way they stand, their command, their voices. Hell, I don't need to tell you what to look for. I've got a Juliet. You find me a matching Romeo.'

One night after Douglas had left the office, a few days before leaving for Las Vegas, Art asked, 'You ever see this girl, Carol Evans, our Juliet?'

'No.' Ronnie was too busy to worry about people who were already signed up.

'Then let's look at the mug shots.' Art began to leaf through *Spotlight*: the casting directors' *vade mecum*, two massive volumes cataloguing practically every actor and actress in the country.

It was a good photograph of Carol. A three-quarter profile that showed off the bone structure to beautiful effect.

'Nice from the neck up, but can she act?'

'Three movies last year, it says here. I'll bet they were walk-ons. That's the problem with coloured actors in this country, they have a hard time getting experience.'

Art laughed, a touch of bitterness. 'Don't come that, Ronnie. All actors have a hard time getting experience. You concentrate on finding Douglas's Romeo.'

Ronnie concentrated. There was one possibility at the Belgrade Theatre, Coventry; another in Nottingham.

But here he was really impressed.

A contact in the north had said that he would not be wasting his time if he looked in at the Stanthorpe Repertory Theatre's production of *As You Like It*.

So he took the train one Tuesday afternoon, to Manchester, watching the smooth green of the south transform into the harsher beauty, the granite and the hard realism of industry, the toiling bowels of the land.

A bus ride to Stanthorpe, and a quick taxi trip to the grimy Victorian façade of the repertory theatre.

Originally, the building had been a music hall. Gilt and red velvet, the walls saturated with belly laughs, and a stage where the greats of that dead era once walked. Dan Leno, Tom Costello, Vesta Victoria, Marie Lloyd, Ada Reeve. They all passed that way, and, when the Stanthorpe Town Council acquired the old Music Hall, saving it from the Bingo-Hall-Bowling-Alley fate worse than demolition, to become a civic theatre, the first director had enough foresight to unearth a couple of dozen rare old posters from the scenery dock. He then framed and hung them in the shabby foyer, a reminder to all that, above everything else, this was a theatre: a place for people to relax and be entertained in the fullest possible sense.

Strangely enough, in the hard cold climate, Stanthorpe Repertory Theatre flourished. It captured a large audience by intermingling standard favourites, comedies, farces and thrillers, with more *avant garde* work. They even managed to fill the house for a fortnight each year with their annual Shakespearean production.

Within less than an hour after the curtain had risen, Ronnie circled the name Asher Grey in pencil on his programme.

The production itself was a moderate and modest affair. In

spite of its poetic simplicity, *As You Like It* is not a pushover of a play. Its romanticism, magic and comedy are not easily balanced, and the mixture comes out heavy if the director does not follow Shakespeare's blend with accuracy.

There was no doubt, though, that young Asher Grey's Orlando stood head and shoulders above the production and the rest of the company.

Physically he was stocky with broad shoulders; black curly hair and a face which had all the markings of good looks, carved ruggedly from a lump of weathered granite. He could not be more than twenty-three or four, yet the face was already adaptable. A pop face: not smooth, girlish or sensual, but the features of change and endurance. As Orlando, he moved with a grace that accentuated his masculinity. So many actors of his age would have confused the issue and equated grace with an overlay of high camp.

His voice had a soft resonance. Ronnie reckoned that he was only using it at half strength, but there was control, a sense that young Grey understood the words.

The considerable subtlety of his performance was that Asher Grey managed to sustain the strength of character even in the most moonstruck moments of comedy.

He would do, this small blossom of unknown talent. He would do very well. In the interval, Ronnie scribbled a note on the back of his card and took it round to the stage door.

'Mr Grey says if you'll hang on, he'll be down in a minute,' the doorkeeper told him when he went round at the end of the performance.

There was a light drizzle outside, occasionally swept up the street by light gusts of wind. A couple of actors and one of the girls came running out shouting loud 'Good nights' to the doorman.

Ronnie was annoyed. He thought it a somewhat cavalier gesture for Asher Grey to leave him standing there in the cold by the stage door. But when young Grey arrived the actor could not have been more apologetic.

'I'm terribly sorry, but it's bloody murder in there. Eight

57

of us in one dressing-room.' The voice that had so lovingly caressed Shakespeare's poetic prose seemed harsher now.

In his note, Ronnie had asked if Grey would have a drink with him to discuss a business matter. Now he found that the actor planned to invite another guest.

'Do you mind if I bring Julia along? Julia Philips that is.'

Ronnie's mind did some mental gymnastics to remember Julia Philips. He decided that she was the pudgy-faced girl who had played Phebe without any noticeable talent or ability.

'Well. . . .'

'Julia and I. . . . We sort of live together,' Asher sounded almost coy.

'I think it would be better if we were alone.' Ronnie felt for the right words, he was not one of nature's diplomats.

Asher Grey nodded, a fleeting look of relief on his face. 'Okay then. I'll tell her to get on home. How long will we be?'

'Half an hour.'

He hurried off. The small scene intrigued Ronnie. Here was this lad who, only a short time ago, was creating a strong, sensitive character on stage. Now he seemed flattened, nervous, bereft of confidence.

Asher Grey returned and, together, they crossed the road to a corner pub, active with regular patrons of the rep arguing a little too loudly about the production. One or two members of the company were also there. It was a large, bare, unattractive place: all that is worst in public houses, shirtsleeved publican and fag-in-mouth wife; no sense of display; a room in which you could buy and drink booze without particular comfort. But it was obviously the local for members of the rep and their audiences.

They found a quiet corner and Ronnie ordered the drinks. Asher opting for the familiar pint of bitter.

'What's on then?' the actor asked after taking a long pull at the beer. The coyness and uncertainty had gone. Ronnie wondered if Julia Philips had something to do with it.

'Well, you know that I'm with the Shireston Festival Company as stage director. You know what the Shireston is?'

Asher laughed. 'Aye. I know about the Shireston. What're they looking for? Someone to play Titania?'

It was a reasonable reaction. When Ronnie had joined the company, two years before, it was pretty run down. Now it was only thought of as the kiss of death. Some members of the company referred to the theatre itself as 'The Last Chance Saloon', and the current season had been an object lesson on how not to cast plays.

'Did you know there was going to be a new policy and a large injection of money. They are appointing a new director.'

'They bloody need to an' all.'

'Yes.' Ronnie agreed, deciding that it was time to stop messing around. 'Can I talk to you in confidence?'

'It's dangerous, but if you must.'

'Douglas Silver's the new director.'

Asher gave a low whistle and began to look interested.

'He's been given a large amount of money to mount a spectacular season. Shireston's making an all out bid to get up there with Stratford and the National.'

'So you're draining the reps of likely lads to be walk-ons and back-up men eh?'

'No. Douglas's in America for a few days trying to sign someone big. But he wants to see you as soon as he gets back.' Though it was not strictly true, Ronnie felt it justifiable. 'Can you come down and see him? And would you be prepared to audition?'

'Come down to Shireston?'

'Or London.'

Asher hesitated. 'It's a bit difficult. You know what it's like in rep. I'm playing Orlando, rehearsing Xavier in *Orpheus Descending* and learning Captain Keller for *The Miracle Worker*. It's tough at the top.'

'I know. I've had some.'

They haggled for a while about the possibility of Asher coming to London. Ronnie could not pin him down. In the end he said, 'If it's out of the question I suppose Douglas might get up here.'

'Sure he wouldn't spoil his pretty hands?'

Though he had shown interest when Douglas Silver's name was mentioned, Asher's attitude throughout had been diffident. Ronnie had yet to play his trump, the size of the role being offered, but Asher's last remark infuriated him.

'You obviously don't know Douglas and you have no idea what this could do to your future. I think you're being pretty stupid.'

'Aye, I'm well known for my stupidity. That's why I'll end up on top, Mister Gregor.' The eyes blazed. Then, just as quickly he seemed to take hold of himself again. 'If the Shireston's throwing money about, could they buy me another beer?' He grinned shyly: infectious and generous with warmth.

Ronnie went over to the bar. Asher Grey was one they would have to watch. There were tender areas in his character, the makings of temperament, the sign of deep talent. As he got back to the table a brace of girls, moddy dressed and shielded with thin raincoats, were passing the table. One of them laid a hand on Asher's shoulder.

'Smashing Orlando, Asher. Smashing.'

'Good. Glad you liked it.' The grin was a beautiful thing to see, embracing both the girls, making them prettier.

'Hey,' he shouted after them. 'See you at the party, Saturday.'

'Sure,' the girls chorused back, leaving the pub twittering.

Asher sighed. 'There's some smashing birds around here.'

'I thought you and the girl? Julia?'

'That's just it, isn't it? There's so much around it makes you want to cry.' He stopped and the face became serious again. 'What does Douglas Silver want me for?'

'I think he wants you to play Romeo.'

'Me?' The man's jaw dropped. 'Play Romeo at Shireston?'

Ronnie nodded. 'It's going to be quite sensational. You'd be playing opposite a black girl.'

Asher thought for a moment and laughed. 'That makes

sense. You can justify it artistically and it'll bring in the crowds. Hey, you're putting me on, aren't you?'

'No. Douglas has asked me to find the right Romeo. I think you're it.'

'If it's all going to be so sensational why doesn't he get a name?'

'Because for this he wants an unknown. There are going to be a lot of names in the company anyway.'

'Such as?'

'I'll have to trust you. It mustn't go any further. Jennifer Frost's going to play Desdemona.'

'To whose Othello?'

'That I can't tell you. But I'll give you another couple of names. Conrad Catellier and Maurice Kapstein.'

'That's okay for starters, isn't it?' He closed his eyes and sucked air in through his teeth. 'Christ, sorry I went off like that just now. About getting to the top and all that crap. Sometimes I really believe it myself. Then I think, what the hell, I've been at this end of the world since I left RADA I've never had another offer. I wonder in the night what I'll do if one comes along. Three years here and I'm cock of the walk. You get frightened of leaving, don't you? It's a bloody rootless profession and you stick around at one place and grow false roots. I want to say yes, but there are problems.'

'I can understand your feelings but I think you'd be crazy to turn it down.'

'I'm crazy. Can I have some time?'

'To think?'

'Yes.'

'No long. Douglas'll be back in a few days and he'll expect me to have someone lined up.'

'Till tomorrow? Can I have until tomorrow?'

'Tomorrow night. That's as long as I can possibly leave it.'

Asher Grey could be close when he wanted to and tonight he wanted to. He could not really face a searing shouting match with Julia, yet she would not stop.

'But what did he want, Ash?' She had pestered him from

the moment he arrived back at the bedsitter they called the Chamber of Horrors. Now she was still nagging at it as they stretched out in bed: looking at the cracked ceiling, illuminated from outside by courtesy of the street lighting. As Asher often observed, their hovel was early John Osborne.

'Come on, Ash, what did he want?'

The only thing he could do was slip her into laughing. She might bypass the whole business that way.

'They want me to do this washing powder commercial for the telly, love.' He grinned in the darkness. 'It's going to be with this gorgeous spade dolly, and we have to sing this jingle together. Well, actually we do a jingle together.'

'Liar.'

'Me, lie to you, darling? Never.'

'You're a bloody liar. He wasn't from television and there's no washing powder. . . .'

'I'll get some first thing in the morning.'

'What did he want?' She was getting angry: out of patience.

'He wants me in the movies.'

'What movie?'

'The one they're making from this novel they've just bought.'

'What novel?'

'You know. The one with the long title. The funny one. In fact he said they were thinking of using the title instead of a script.'

'What is the title?'

'It's called *The Night You Talked Me into Dining at the Dragon Room and I Got Left with a Sweet and Sour Waiter* You see it's all about this girl, she's going to be played by Meryl Streep, and she's a secret agent who spends all her time going round Chinese restaurants looking for the fortune cookie that has a message in it for the Prime Minister. She eats Lobster Balls and. . . . Hey, you're supposed to say lobsters haven't got any –'

'I know. Ash, for the last bloody time. What did that little bugger want?'

'Wants me to go to Shireston.' He knew he should not have said it and she knew that she had the truth at last.

'Well, why the devil didn't you tell me to start with. That graveyard. You said you wouldn't go?'

'No. I'm phoning him tomorrow.' Under the sheets, Asher clenched his fists tightly. For the past year, since he had been living with Julia, he had constantly gone out of his way to avert confrontations with her over myriad things: standing up to the director; his drinking habits; family; ambition; even, on one occasion, his choice of breakfast cereal.

Julia should never have been an actress. Ideally she should have been understudy to his mother. In many ways she already was understudy to his mother.

In the first instance, Asher had become an actor mainly to escape his mother. He had certainly taken the scholarship to RADA in order to get away from her. They were facts that plagued his conscience as much as anything. Plenty of people did not get on with their parents, the generation gap and all that crap. Plenty of young people openly despised their parents, you only had to talk to some of the boys and girls in the company. But most of them did it with good humour. Asher actively hated the couple who spawned him, especially his mother. His father he could accept as the gutless drunk every Friday, lazy soldier of industry. There was a despair in the man that he could appreciate, and which, sometimes, he thought he even shared.

But his mother was a different matter. She had neither the intelligence to accept the situation, nor the wit to find a way out by offering assistance to the wretched man she had married and vilified from that moment.

Only the other evening one of the older actors was talking about his childhood: one of seven, he drew a picture of Christmas that would have warmed the heart of Charles Dickens; you could smell the turkey and feel the glow.

Asher's early Christmas memories were epitomized in being wakened by the screech of his mother as she assaulted his father's ears, demanding to know where he had been until this hour. Not pausing for an answer, the nag shrewed her way right through the day of peace, joy and goodwill to all men. All the Sunday School pictures of the baby Jesus and his loving mother and father were shrunk to this undersize woman, if woman she was under the paint and nail varnish badly and thickly applied, screaming at his fuddled father.

And now, Asher clenched his fists against the barrage coming from Julia's pert honey mouth.

'. . . ask anyone. Christ, Ash you should know by now. After all I've tried to do for you. I suppose it's an escape. You're tired of me so you leave here and get rid of me at the same time. Well, it's not going to work, because I'm not going to let it work. It would be suicide. . . .'

'As it happens it wouldn't be suicide. You don't even know the deal.'

'What sort of deal can you get from a broken down place like that?'

'Well, this isn't exactly a shop window of the arts.'

'It's safe. It's secure. We're all doing what we want to do. Anyway, that's not the point.'

'It's very much the point. Shireston's going to be big, as big as any of the others, and I have an important chance of being part of it. . . .'

'And what about me? Just because we're not married doesn't mean that we have to forsake all moral obligations. You took me, I look after both of us, cook the meals, help you, let you fuck me when I'm dead tired and have to work on top of it. . . .'

'You always gave the impression – '

'Impressions? Asher, I'm not going to let you throw yourself away.'

'Look, love, when it all boils, down, I've got no moral obligations to you, and you know it. I'm a big boy now. I must make decisions.'

Then the tears. If there was one thing he could not stand it was tears. The comforting and baby talk. The half promises. Whispers. Confidences half-shared. If he got Romeo at Shireston he would make damn sure that Julia would be there as well. Yes, of course, he would. That was a deadly promise and he knew it. Deep down at the tip of the emotional and unstable bond which held him to Julia, Asher was painfully conscious of a situation that equated him with his father.

For over a year he had taken the line of least resistance with this girl: the easy way; the way that would quieten her, pacify her.

Whispers again. Then the soft, rhythmic creaking of the bed.

In the year 1810, Miguel Hidalgo y Costilla, parish priest of the little village of Dolores, Mexico, got up one September morning, rang his church bells and shouted, 'Long live Religion. Long live our Most Holy Mother of Guadalupe. Long live Ferdinand VII. Long live America and death to bad government.'

With that Cry of Dolores, Hidalgo began the revolt of the peones against their cruel and tyrannous Spanish overlords. Within a year he was captured and put to death.

Those are undisputed facts. Even now, on every September fifteenth Mexico's President rings a bell in Mexico City and repeats the *Grito de Dolores*.

The script for the movie, *Hidalgo*, used the facts as a loose framework. After all, the story was a natural for spectacle and box office in these times when revolution and change are the breathing air.

It was also an easy matter to inject into the historic bones some other aspect of box office: the beautiful daughter of a high-ranking Spanish officer, for instance. A junior officer. Love and Mexican moonlight. The young officer siding with Hidalgo and the revolutionaries. The lady joining her lover in the struggle.

Jennifer Frost was playing the beautiful daughter. She had taken the part because it was offered to her at a time when she felt the need to work again. It was also a bit of a joke between Douglas and herself. Douglas kept referring to her as 'Daughter of Cisco', and would constantly end sentences with a movie Mexican 'I theenk'. Jennifer had never been to Mexico either, which was a good idea on its own.

But the script that Jennifer had signed on was subject to much alteration. Now they had shot all the location sequences, which had been fun, she began to realize that she was mixed up with a dreadful script and a debased motion picture. The original idea had presented a wonderful opportunity for the examination of revolution in historic depth. With a clever director it could have been wonderful. But now the original script had been ripped asunder, all the thought-provoking material kept at arm's length and a banal emotional love story moved into the foreground. The whole thing was twenty years out of date and had nothing to do with the professional cinema as known by Jennifer Frost.

Tonight she felt useless, despairing almost; hot, dirty, tired. They had spent the whole day shooting a three-minute scene with one page of dialogue.

The action called for her lover, played by Richard Royal, an actor as phoney as his name, and herself to visit Hidalgo (Henry Frensham, one of the old school). The setting was a disused hacienda, the living area of which had been designed to look exactly like a Californian split-level dwelling done up by a faggy designer whose obsession was late nineteenth-century Mexican.

Henry was on one of his burbling days. Doing line five when line four was called for. The director was difficult, searching for chi-chi camera angles among the bric-à-brac, and Richard found it quite beyond his talent to get a move combined correctly with dialogue.

'You've got to be real patient with him, 'cos he's so good out in the great big spaces surrounded by nothing but horses and a pop gun,' an assistant cameraman said, a shade too loudly and with a sidelong glance at Jen. There followed a full shouting match which nearly turned into a brawl.

Should have known better, she thought, leaning back against the padding of the studio car. Should have known better. She had few real friends in LA any more. Who had in this business? Oh, they should tell all young star-struck girls of the hazards and commitments, the mental rape of the star: obscene outdated word. But then, she supposed, young girls were constantly being told in the headlines. Only they still kept coming.

Jennifer closed her eyes, hidden behind dark glasses, and longed for some mental and physical stimulation: longings which boiled down to needing Douglas. Perhaps he would call tonight. She laughed out loud. That must be a line from some women's magazine story. Perhaps he would call tonight. Perhaps . . . he . . . would . . . call. . . .

The noise of the engine, the rush of traffic outside. Outside in the heat and cloud. She began to feel detached: the pictures flashing at her in bright colour from far away.

Jennifer Frost, leggy schoolgirl walking through Esher, the end of the suburban world, where daddies took off each morning and rattled into the city to earn their daily bread and rattled back again in the evening to read the *Standard* or the *News*, watch television and tiptoe to bed. Cornflakes and bacon or kippers for breakfast; the boy called Gavin at the tennis club dance; dark hair and a darker sports car and a NO said firmly because she believed all that Mummy told her.

Jennifer Frost, long sexy legs, striding through the woods, caught smiling and healthy in the lens for every glossy magazine, selling clothes vicariously to middle-aged mums who all thought the clothes would transform them into Jennifer Frost, model girl, beautiful, untouchable.

Jennifer Frost, tear-streaked from the screen in technicolor because a director had been genuine when he said, 'I could use you in my next movie,' and was not put off when she declined a polite invitation to visit his apartment.

Jennifer Frost, instant success after several years and a lot of bloody hard work. And then Chichester. 'This is Douglas Silver. Jennifer Frost. Miss Jennifer Frost. Miss Frost . . . Miss Frost . . . Miss Frost. . . .'

'Miss Frost, we're here.' She felt the warm blast of air hit the inside of the car as the chauffeur opened the door. It would take ten minutes for the air conditioning to right itself after he had closed it.

There, in all its glory, God help her, was the Beverly Hills Hilton.

The senior desk clerk became alert as she approached, leaning forward to speak in a low voice.

'I don't want to worry you, Miss Frost, but there's a man over there, came in a couple of hours ago. Claims he's your husband.'

'Does he now.' She turned to look in the direction indicated. About twenty yards across the lobby Douglas sprawled in a deep leather chair, a battered suitcase beside him. He looked unkempt and was fast asleep. The desk clerk obviously regarded him as an affront to the Hilton.

Jennifer's impulse was to dash across the lobby and grab him. Her tired depression fell away as she turned back to the clerk with a half smile.

'Do you think he's dangerous?' she asked.

'I shouldn't think so. Look I'll get him out, don't worry.' He signalled to one of the doormen who came over and joined them.

'The guy asleep over there, Mike. Get him out nice and quietly.'

The doorman was large and looked very fit.

'No,' said Jennifer, wondering now if it had really gone too far. 'I'll come over with you. I want to find out what he thinks he's doing, posing as my husband.'

They moved across the lobby in a procession, Jennifer holding back the laughter as the doorman shook Douglas's shoulder.

'Come on, bud. Wake up. Come on. This isn't the international airport.'

Douglas came out of the sleep slowly and uncomfortably.

'Jen. God, how long have I been asleep?'

'The lady wants to know why you're posing as her husband.'

'Posing? Jen. You tell them.'

She managed to keep a straight face. 'I'm waiting for an explanation.'

'Tell them, Jen. What is this?' He was on his feet, six inches from her.

'Come on, Mister.'

She could not keep it up any longer. With a giggle she threw her arms round his neck and fell forward.

The doorman grinned when she said she had been playing a joke. The desk clerk did not seem to find it funny.

'You idiot.' Douglas wrapped an arm round her. 'I ought to spank you.'

'Might be worth it at that. But why are you here? How long have we got? Did you ring Mummy? . . .' She took his hand and they headed for the elevators with a boy in tow carrying Douglas's suitcase.

After a shower, shave and two hellish Martinis, Douglas began to see life at its correct tilt again.

The time change had caught up with him on the aircraft from Vegas that morning.

Joe Thomas had been quieter on the trip down, but Douglas, in his state of fragility, found it an effort to remain sharp enough to cope with the silky lawyers during the short breaks that Joe could find in the midst of the frenetic recording session.

Eventually, when the whole business had been settled, fatigue, coupled with the drinks, which had started coming early, caught him at the Hilton. When they refused him entrance to Jen's room, he had all but passed out in the chair in the lobby.

'Now come and tell me what you're doing here. It's super. Oh Douglas, it's . . . it was really so unexpected.'

He had refused to talk or tell her anything until he was clean. Now, clad in a towelling robe, he sat on her balcony, holding her hand, swamped with the realization of his true feelings for her. Carol paid a quick visit to his thoughts. Sitting here he felt guilty; very guilty. Sometime before the opening of the festival he would have to tell Jen. He also had to break the Desdemona thing to her. That must come first.

Quietly he complied with her wishes and filled in the gaps about the Shireston Festival. He told her about Catellier and Kapstein and, finally, Joe Thomas. Her attitude was one of bewildered disbelief.

'You've got Thomas to play Othello? Douglas, you're mad.

69

Look, I've worked out here among these people. I could tell you stories that –'

'Would make my hair curl. I know. I've heard. Everybody says so and I've seen a little for myself; I've been with Joe Thomas since late last night. I've spent almost the whole day with him. And, right or wrong, I'm stuck with him.'

'I mean, I think the *Romeo and Juliet* idea's fabulous, but Joe Thomas as Othello. Yuck. Who the hell are you going to get to play Desdemona?'

'You want to go inside?' he asked quickly. Now, when she was so strong against Thomas, was the wrong moment to tell her what he planned.

'I thought you'd never ask.' She rose. 'I've been needing old Long John Douglas all day and every day.'

They stripped and began to make love. Then the telephone rang. Before showering, Douglas had put through a call to Ronnie Gregor in London.

'Now the call has come,' he whispered.

Ronnie sounded bright. 'You all right, Douglas? You seem short of breath.'

'I'm fine. Had to come running from the bathroom, that's all.'

Jennifer stifled a giggle.

Douglas gave Ronnie the news about Joe Thomas and then listened to Ronnie's report. He hung on to the instrument with some impatience as his stage director relayed a whole pile of messages. Revill Sutcliffe wanted him to call urgently; both Catellier and Kapstein had been bothering the office, demanding to know the date of his return. Kapstein had signed his contract, but, Catellier, while in agreement, was holding back until he talked with Douglas.

They already had a schedule for most of the important casting: it only needed Douglas's okay.

Ronnie kept the best news until last. Briefly he detailed his meeting, and feelings about, Asher Grey. The young actor had called confirming that he wanted the role and that he would come down to London any Sunday. He had even fixed it with his director.

'Hold everything then, Ronnie. I'll see the boy next Sunday Tell Catellier and Kapstein I'll be back in a couple of days and the first item on my schedule is to lunch with them. I'll call Revill from here. Okay? . . . Then, see you.' He cradled the telephone at last.

'You're drooping again.' Jennifer put on a sad look.

'Not for long.'

Sex with Jennifer, from the first moment, had been more than the physical need, enjoyment and the act of love. Though it had been all of those things, when they were together, naked and alone, everything between them was stripped clean. It was a time for true contact. A meeting point as well as a great romp.

So it was this time, except for the pinpoint worry in the back of Douglas's very secret mind. The guilt he felt over Carol Evans. He would have to talk to her as well, when he got back. Be honest with her as well as Jennifer.

Later, 'So what about your movie?' he asked.

She laughed, stretching her body out on the bed, breasts lolling beautifully. '*Hidalgo* is without doubt the worst movie that has ever been made.' She told him of the fights the director had been having with Richard Royal, and of the actor's incompetence.

'That's an idea,' she said, 'Get Richard to play Romeo.'

'I think we got lucky with Romeo.' He grinned. 'Ronnie just told me. I need a good Mercutio though.'

Jen doubled up at the thought of Royal playing Mercutio. '*O, then, I see Queen Mab hath been with you.*' She mimicked Royal's thick Texan drawl. Then, suddenly, amidst all the laughter she caught up with the fact that Douglas had not answered her about Desdemona before they came in.

'Desdemona, Doug?' It was one of those freak tricks of the mind which happen to two people very close to one another.

He could read her face. 'Yes. What about Desdemona?'

'It's me, isn't it? You want me to play Desdemona opposite Joe the schmoe.'

'Good question.'

'Isn't it?' She took his wrist and started to twist it like a

71

child. He pulled back and gave her bottom a playful slap. They fell back laughing.

'When will I learn how to fool you, Jen?'

'You bastard. Who shall we get to play Desdemona? Let's get Jen. She's a sucker for anything. You clever, Machiavellian bastard.'

'When you think about it logically, who else is there left to play Desdemona?'

'You really want me?'

He stretched out a hand to her thigh.

'No, you fool' She was serious now. 'Want me to play Desdemona?'

'I can think of nobody better. It could be quite something.'

'I'd be working with you. But Joe Thomas.'

'Jen, I mean this, I think he could be quite something as well.'

'I'll demand a clause in my contract promising that at no time am I to be left alone with the leery Joe Thomas.'

'Done. You will play it, Jen? You will?'

They stayed naked on the bed until ten that evening. Douglas booked a call to Revill which came through just as they were getting dressed.

Adrian Rolfe had been non-committal but certainly ready to meet Douglas for lunch at any time.

They finished dressing, took the elevator down to the main lobby and went out to Trader Vic's.

Douglas insisted that they start with a drink called Rangoon Ruby. 'Because it sounds more like a whore than an aperitif.'

He took a jubilant delight in the complicated and fulsome menu.

'We will begin with Lomi Lomi.' Then, in a confident way to Jen, 'That's raw salmon marinated in lime juice and served with a coconut cream sauce.'

'How do you know that?'

'It says so here.' Tapping the menu.

They ordered the Indonesian lamb roast to follow, with Chinese pea pods, sliced waterchestnuts and Papeete rice,

72

completing their meal with a Flaming Tahitian ice cream.

'It's better than a flaming Howard Johnson ice cream,' said Douglas. 'You know, this menu has a certain rustic charm.'

Jennifer laughed. She had almost forgotten how good it was to relax with Douglas.

Over coffee he began talking about the season at Shireston. She had never seen, or heard him, as enthusiastic over anything before.

'Come home soon, Jen,' he said as they left the table. 'I really need you.'

His voice had been backed by urgency. For some reason he really did need her close. It was disturbing to her and she found herself worrying a little.

'Let's see what *The Late Show* has to offer.' Douglas switched on the built-in television and they plonked themselves on the bed, shoulder to shoulder.

'Phew, I'm so full. I must have put on pounds. I'm a pig.' Jennifer blew out her cheeks.

'Oink-oink.'

The picture came on. They had picked up a late newscast.

Douglas leaned over to kiss her, then something caught his attention on the newscast. Joe Thomas's name.

There was Joe on the screen, waving and doing little hops as he walked out to the Lear Jet in which they had flown down to LA that morning.

The newscaster was speaking. 'The surprising news that Joe Thomas announced was that next year he is giving up all club and movie engagements to take a few months off being a Shakespearean actor. Mr Thomas has signed an agreement with Douglas Silver, long haired British director of the Shireston Festival Company in Hampshire, England. Joe Thomas says he will spend most of next year with the Shireston Festival and is to play Othello.'

'Jesus God.' Douglas sat bolt upright and grabbed the telephone. 'The stupid, self-interested bloody, sodding amateur.' Amateur was about the worst thing Douglas could call anybody.

He tried to get through to Joe in Las Vegas but Mr Thomas

was not receiving any calls.

For a second he thought about trying Tommy Carr, but Carr was far from being on his side about Joe coming to the Shireston.

'For God's sake, Doug. Is it so bad?' Jen came and knelt at his feet.

'Yes it is so bad, Jen. You've just agreed to do Desdemona, right? Well, think about it, if you were going to be a lead with any other company but mine.'

'Well?'

'Christ, do I have to spell it out? The whole thing's supposed to be under wraps anyway. My appointment, though it's common knowledge, hasn't even been announced. It was going to be a big piece of package publicity. My directorship, the plays, the company, the big names. How do you think Kapstein and Catellier will feel now Thomas's jumped the gun? The board could easily blow up in my face. To start with they're scared of any personality cult. Then there's my chance of getting Adrian Rolfe. He's not going to be keen on a publicity situation that's already gone off at half-cock.'

He stabbed at the telephone dial, calling reception. Out loud he said, 'Jen, I'm sorry, I'll have to get back.'

'Joe Thomas,' said Jennifer, making the two words sound more obscene than any other in the English language.

CHAPTER FIVE

It was Wednesday evening before Douglas got back into London to a pile of messages waiting at the flat; there were more, like a paper Pisa tower, on his desk at the office in Rupert Street. Would he call Ronnie Gregor, Sir Basil, Revill: a dozen more.

There were also press cuttings. Douglas had taken care to cable all interested parties, making certain that a 'no comment' attitude was preserved, but the London press had been astute in picking up the items from America. The stories were printed exactly as Joe Thomas told them and the British papers only added single lines indicating that Douglas Silver was out of the country and that the Shireston Festival Organization was, as yet, making no statement on Mr Thomas's revelations.

Also, before leaving Los Angeles Douglas had been sharply in touch with Thomas's lawyers, asking them to use whatever pressure was available to stop Joe talking to the press about the Shireston deal. Now there was a cable waiting for him at the office.

SORRY I BLEW IT STOP LIPS SEALED YOU ARE THE BOSS MAN STOP JOE STOP

At least that would make it easier to explain to Daley. Douglas called him first. It seemed the most sensible action in the circumstances.

'I see you've got Joe Thomas.' You could almost see the thin smile on Sir Basil's lips.

'I'm sorry about that.' Douglas took a long drag at his cigarette. 'It happened very quickly: right out of my hands. But I think I've killed it now. Thomas won't say anything else until we've done a release.'

'What's he like?' Daley did not seem worried about the news leak: like most people his reaction was basic. Douglas had touched a legend, now Daley was reaching out to touch Douglas.

'Between ourselves, just like the rumours. There is one bit of news we've got to keep far from the press though.'

'Yes?'

'Joe's only doing it for the experience. He's only charging expenses.'

There was a pause: three or four seconds.

'And how high are the expenses going to be?' Sir Basil obviously thinking out all the angles.

'Well, he's not bringing a retinue. Just himself.'

'How did you manage that?'

Douglas pushed down the desire to be smart and take the credit. 'I don't really know. The whole thing was accidental and the timing happened to be right. I still find it hard to believe.'

Daley chuckled. 'You're a clever boy, Douglas. That'll cool old Dempsey's ardour.'

'He being difficult?' As he spoke, Douglas knew that he was being presumptuous, but Daley took it as a matter of course.

'No more than usual. I sometimes think he'll only be really happy if this whole thing falls flat on its face.'

'Well it's not going to fall on its face or anywhere else. We've already signed Kapstein and I'm seeing Catellier as soon as possible. I gather he's agreed money but there are other problems. Oh yes, my wife will play Desdemona, that's confirmed.'

'More good news. It all sounds very exciting.'

They talked for another ten minutes, then Douglas called Revill. While money was no problem with Catellier, the actor was becoming anxious. Revill felt that he was holding back because of a series of doubts – about his ability to play Richard and anxiety regarding the way the season was shaping. Revill thought it would be best to get hold of Catellier as quickly as possible. Douglas also had to talk with Kapstein before the week was out, and there was young Asher Grey's audition on Sunday.

During the next hour, Douglas talked with Ronnie Gregor, fixed lunch with Catellier for the following day and with Kapstein for Monday. Friday was free so he called Adrian Rolfe, apologizing for the hour and arranging lunch for that day. Only then did he cable Jen to let her know he was back safely.

Going through some of the other papers, the enormous responsibility of the situation began to sink into his mind. If they managed to sign Catellier and half a dozen middle billing actors for whom they were angling, the Shireston company would number around forty. Forty actors and actresses, of different age groups, different backgrounds, black and white: living together with nerve ends exposed and all the hopes, fears, hatreds, superstitions, difficulties, egos and sex drives all lumped together under one roof. Forty individuals of whom half a dozen were great and pampered talents. They would be difficult enough on their own, but slotted into a company of actors learning to play together as one unit their weakest points would be on display within the privacy of the unit: so, it followed, their defence mechanisms would easily come into force – all the sublimations of sex, drink, temperament, drugs.

For a moment, sitting there in the tiny office, alone and with the night noises of Soho drifting up from below, Douglas Silver wondered if it might be in excess of his ability. He sighed wearily and picked up the diary, noting that Ronnie had pencilled in a meeting for him with Tony Holt, who was to design the plays, at Shireston on Saturday. Life was going to be far from empty.

He thought of the apartment in Elton Court: their apartment, his and Jen's. It had seemed lonely and unwelcoming without Jen's presence when he had dropped off his suitcase earlier in the evening; now there was no desire in him to return to the place. He looked at his watch: a quarter past eleven. Like an automaton he picked up the telephone and dialled Carol's number. It rang for what seemed a long time before the familiar throaty voice came on the line.

'Hello.'

'Hi, it's Douglas.'

'Hey, when did you get back?'

'Earlier this evening.'

'How d'you make out?'

'Great.' He was almost lost for words now. 'Great. Hope I didn't wake you.'

'No. I was just mooching around. Reading a little. Spending a lazy evening doing a bit of work.'

'Working at what?'

'What do you think? The excellent conceited tragedie of *Romeo and Juliet* as it hath been often (with great applause) played publically. . . . I'm reading Granville-Barker's *Preface*.'

'Good God.'

'You sound shocked.'

'Not shocked. Surprised. I didn't know actresses still went in for that kind of scholarship.'

'I don't. I just thought I'd better know something about –'

'Well, forget it.'

'Douglas?'

'Oh not Juliet. Forget reading things like Granville-Barker.'

'Why?'

'Because I've done the Granville-Barker scene and I want this to be *my* production. I don't want a load of intellectual actresses giving me second-hand academic theories.'

She laughed and paused. 'So you had a good time over there?'

He nodded at the instrument. 'Yep. Can I come round and tell you about it?'

Silence in his ear.

'Now?'

'Of course now. When else is there?'

'Okay, come over.'

'See you in half an hour.'

It took longer. Cabs were scarce and it had started to rain. Douglas's watch showed almost midnight before he pressed the bell. Carol told him to come on up, the door was open. She sat in front of the gas fire, legs tucked under her, cosy on a black and white goatskin rug. A Penguin Shakespeare copy of *Romeo and Juliet* was lying nearby with another book, heavy and in a plastic clear jacket – the Granville-Barker borrowed in good faith from the local library. Carol wore a dark blue housecoat: thin material, silky, showing the curves where it touched.

'Hi there, sexy Carol Evans.' Douglas closed the door behind him, realizing as he did so that his reason for coming to see her was not what he had first supposed. He had begun to become involved in work again and did not require, or need, a sexual stimulant for living. He needed friendship now: a human wall against the void of loneliness; he could not bear the thought of isolation, reaching out in the night and feeling himself alone, or turning in the room to catch only his reflection in the window glass or mirror. He needed a kind of constant communication when he worked. Jen gave him that, and with her there was no need, at those times, to explain the sudden impotence. Now, Carol would be puzzled if he did not take her and provide the love thrust.

'Hi yourself.' Carol grinned, tilting her head on to one shoulder, obviously pleased to see him.

Douglas bent down and kissed her gently on the forehead before sinking down to join her on the rug. She had lolled her head right back, expecting the kiss to enfold her lips. Carol looked up at him, puzzlement around her eyes merging slowly into understanding.

'You saw your wife over there?' She asked as though the problem was that simple.

'Yep.' He nodded.

'You had her.' Statement.

Again Douglas Silver nodded, not looking at the girl's glowing dark skin. 'Yep, I did. Isn't that what's supposed to happen with wives?'

It was her turn to nod. 'And it was good and you felt very guilty about me.'

'I reckon so. It's always been good with Jen: and with you

the few times.'

'I just wanted to get the picture.'

In the silence he saw himself, over-dramatized, romanticized, standing alone on some beach with the moonlight flirting with waves and blue night licking at his profile. He smiled: the picture was secret, a small conceit of self-pity.

Aloud he said, 'Let's see what happens, Carol. I don't know. Tonight I just wanted to see you. I was alone and wanted to see you.' He reflected that it all sounded like something from a late television movie.

Carol gave a small sigh, lifting her hands and dropping them back on her knees. 'What's it matter anyhow?' She seemed to shake herself, like an animal waking. 'The newspapers say you got Joe Thomas.'

'I got Joe Thomas.'

'And . . .?'

'Period. I got Joe Thomas but don't ask me how. I got him, then I went on to LA and saw Jen.'

'And how was the good old US of A?'

'As ever. On the point of explosion. The movie Jen's doing has gone to seed. It's just like the old days. They tell you Hollywood and the studio system's dead; I only wish they'd tell one or two people out there, because they're still acting like it's alive.' He gave a quick smile. 'But what about you? In work?'

'I've got a couple of television spots. They'll carry me through until January I guess.'

He gave her a sideways look. 'Any problems and you only have to ask.'

'I'm not the asking kind. Actions speak —'

'With a higher volume than dictionaries, I know. Did I tell you that we might just have a Romeo for you?'

Not just the eyes, but her whole face lit up. 'No. No. Who?'

'Young actor. Unheard of. Unsung, doing his thing in the provinces. I'm auditioning him on Sunday, you won't be offended if I don't ask you along?'

'Mortally.'

80

'Pity. I wanted a live Juliet: for the bulk of the play anyway.'

Carol made coffee and they began to talk about the theatre. Inevitably the conversation shifted to *Romeo and Juliet*.

'Is it just a gimmick, Douglas?' asked Carol.

'The racial thing? No. Sure, some people are going to see it that way. As far as I'm concerned the racial thing will in some way serve to make the play more immediate: more comprehensible to the kids who haven't seen it before. It'll also bring it right into the present and that's what Shakespeare's about. It's about now. I want you and this boy and all the others to give us a great hymn of language and love. That's not a gimmick, it's realistic direction.'

Carol raised her eyebrows: almost a cynical look. 'Any other startling suggestions?'

'The love scene.' He lifted his head, looking straight at her. 'You averse to playing it nude?'

'It's the only way, isn't it?'

'Good.' He nodded.

As Douglas was about to leave, around two in the morning after they had talked much, Carol laid a hand on his sleeve. 'Douglas, some of them are going to knock hell out of you: you know that?'

'I know. They'll say that you and your Romeo constitute a theatrical gimmick which isn't necessary because Shakespeare's language is enough, and if I get Catellier to play Richard they'll call it tricksy casting; Kapstein playing Shylock sounds all right, but they'll probably have a go at the sanctity of Shakespeare: some of them did when George Robey played Falstaff and Jay Laurier played Launce and, for that matter when Frankie Howerd appeared as Bottom.' He grinned, lifted his eyes, rolled them and made a grimace. 'God knows what they'll finally say about Joe Thomas.'

The first hint of real criticism came from within the profession and on the following day. Conrad Catellier had insisted they should meet on his own ground, in this instance the Savile.

People in the profession often wondered why Catellier had never been given the accolade of a knighthood: in his late fifties the man stood undeniably among that knot of British actors which protruded, from the feet upwards, from the top talent. True, Revill Sutcliffe's comment that Catellier was a 'raging old queen' might have had something to do with the absence of a knighthood, for scandal had hovered close to the actor on three distressing occasions; but ability, a tremendous understanding of the theatre, the knack of judging the best way he could interpret a role, plus an extremely wide range, had carried Catellier to the summit. He was also a man of private means, tracing his ancestry back to the Norman invaders, a fact which his publicity had, over the years, used to no mean advantage.

Douglas Silver had met Catellier on four or five previous occasions: a tall grey man, grey close-cropped hair, grey suit, slim, almost thin, body which, strangely, gave one the impression of great physical fitness as though you could sense through the man's clothes the fact of a firm athletic body.

On stage you could not detect any homosexual proclivity, unless the role called for it; it was only when one was close to the man in private that the slight veneer of effeminacy showed through, and even then it was only apparent in the odd mannerism, or the way in which he used his voice. As far as professionalism went, Catellier was a hard coiled spring with almost the attitude of a big business executive. Douglas could feel the toughness as they shook hands in the hall of the Savile.

Catellier smiled, not much warmth about his eyes, but the facial muscles did all the right things. 'Douglas, how good to see you. Are you well?'

The grip was very firm. 'I'm fine, Conrad.'

Catellier raised an arm, the palm of his hand flat. 'Let's talk over lunch then. Unless you want a drink first.'

Douglas shook his head, he seldom drank during the day and in any case they both knew that time was limited and it was necessary to talk.

In the dining-room, Douglas was conscious of the presence

82

of a well-known comedian and a couple of familiar publishers. They had a table to themselves and Catellier refused to be drawn into any conversation until they had ordered.

Catellier signified almost regally that he was ready to talk, raising his eyebrows and giving a short nod.

'I believe we have some difficulty in persuading you to join the Shireston next season,' Douglas began.

Catellier ignored the comment. 'Is it true that you've signed Joe Thomas to act Othello?' he asked.

Douglas did not hesitate. 'It's true.'

'And that you've signed Maurice Kapstein to play Shylock?'

'Yes.'

'And that you are contemplating a production of *Romeo and Juliet* with black actors playing the Capulets, thereby making it partly an essay in racism?'

'Not through any inference within the production. I'm not making it an explicit controversy on stage.'

Catellier gave the director a quick, nervous look. 'You're being explicit by casting it like that. You –' He stopped short, hunching himself into silence, then, with a change in his voice he quietly quoted –

> '*It seems she hangs upon the cheek of night*
> *Like a rich jewel in an Ethiop's ear;*
> *Beauty too rich for use, for earth too dear!*
> *So shows a snowy dove trooping with crows,*
> *As yonder lady o'er her fellows shows.*'

Douglas remembered that some twenty-five years ago Conrad Catellier's Romeo was reckoned to be definitive.

'How does your Romeo say that about a black Juliet?' Catellier asked.

Douglas shrugged and pushed back his soup plate. 'I suppose he says it with a smile.' He tried to grin but Catellier did not respond.

'Why have you asked me to play Richard?' the actor asked.

'Because you have never played him and because I think that an interpretation by the two of us could be explosive and fit into what is going to be an explosive and sparkling season.'

Catellier made a sound that Douglas could not translate. 'Your season of juggled Shakespeare.'

'Juggled?'

'Three tragedies and a comedy, conjured, juggled with contrivance, slick casting, every gaudy trick and artifice that you can raise. Fairground Shakespeare. I thought better of you, Douglas. Your season will not glitter, it will be shoddy. A season of faded parchment overlaid with plastic paint.'

The speech was so violent and extravagant that Douglas was silenced for a moment: for almost the count of ten.

'You've got it all wrong, Conrad.' When he spoke his voice was soft in contrast to Catellier's last eruption.

'Have I? What if I did play Richard for you? Who'd be my Buckingham? And who my Duchess of York?'

'Steady, Conrad, you really have got it all wrong. A lot of people have got it wrong and we haven't announced the season yet. My appointment has yet to be announced. My job, Conrad, is to put the Shireston back on its feet. They are giving me the money to do it and I must do it my way, which is not the way of gimmicks.' He tapped the table lightly, mentally willing all his enthusiasm towards Catellier, beaming it into him, hoping that some of his own static would penetrate the actor's mind.

'Consider what I have to do in return,' he continued. 'My theatre is in a rural setting. The rail service is inadequate; the setting perfect, but forty miles from London. I can't compete with the Royal Shakespeare at Stratford. They have an ensemble: a company with its own picked leads, people used to working with each other. They also operate in a town geared to tourism: the Bard's birthplace; people flocking for seats to see Shakespeare's plays in the town where he was born. I've got none of that, yet in one season, six lousy months, I've got to rouse enough people to make the trip down to Shireston from all points. And those people have got to take a message back with them: they've got to say it is memorable so that they'll want to come again, bring their friends and tell others. Think what that kind of operation entails?' He paused as the waitress brought their lamb cutlets.

Catellier said nothing, pausing with almost a studied patience for Douglas to complete his argument.

'Just think, Conrad, what it takes these days to get people up off their asses and away from the small screen when the living theatre is within easy reach. I have to lure tourists from their hotels and computorized dinners and easy entertainment; people from their homes after the long hot day at the office; kids from their schools. And when I get them I've got to provide them with a unique service. I have to give them nights they are going to remember for the rest of their good, bad or indifferent little lives so they'll say to people and to each other, "The night we went to Shireston to see Fred Bloggs in *The Taming of the Shrew*, that gave us as much as the five package holidays on the Costa Brava. That was the night we touched life again."'

Catellier gave a little smile, like a grandfather patting a child's head because the child is showing enthusiasm. Douglas went on:

'The facilities have got to be unblemished. Their journey to Shireston has to be free from anxiety, their arrival uncluttered. They must see the lawns and the house, the theatre to the best advantage. There must be food, served with elegance before they are given the big treat: and remember some of them don't regard Shakespeare as a treat to start with.'

Catellier's smile went thin and dry: it was not unpleasant. 'You're an idealist, Douglas. The way you tell it makes everything smooth and glossy: like the colour advertisements. Come to the Shireston Festival. Travel in one of our superb streamline coaches that will whisk you effortlessly into the countryside, through the green lanes that are still part of Britain's heritage. Stroll on the lush lawns and watch the day die in splendour, once only available to a chosen few. Visit our Shireston restaurant and experience the delights of living like a gourmet. Then have the great experience of magnificently performed drama. This you will remember all your lives.'

Douglas smiled. 'We'll pay you for the advertising copy.'

'But,' Catellier held up a hand, 'when you take the trip, dear boy, the coach is crowded, the hostess has bad breath, you're stuck in traffic jams and it's pouring with rain when you arrive at Shireston and the gourmet dishes are rubberized plastic. Is that why you want to stuff *Romeo and Juliet* full of the racist problem? Why you want a sixty-year-old Jewish television folk hero playing Shylock and a smart coloured nightclub entertainer giving his tiny impression of the great Othello? How do you want me to play Richard? In clown costume?'

Douglas sighed. 'I know all of these things can go wrong. That's why I've got to have back-up schemes. I have one idea about combating the weather problem, but it is in the theatre itself that the final memories have got to be planted and it's there that I have to draw them in any way I think fit as long as it produces good theatre. I know I'm an idealist, but I still must have drawing power. That's why my *Romeo* has got to create a talking point; I'm aware of that even if I'm not prepared to make any distinct racist point within the direction: the casting's enough. As for Maurice Kapstein as Shylock, Kapstein's a diabolical comedian full of horrendous sick jokes, that's his appeal and I think that's casting William would have approved.'

'Joe Thomas?'

'Joe Thomas fell into my lap. Sure, wherever he goes people queue up at nightclubs to see him, and they'll queue at the Shireston. But I didn't get him for that reason alone. He's what they call a good marquee name, a good name at the box office, but that name only remains good if he can turn in a great performance. Think back, Conrad, did you ever see a couple of films – *The Talking Man* and *Under the Trees at Akron?*' His head was thrust forward, daring Catellier to remember.

The Talking Man had been made around ten years before; *Under the Trees at Akron* a year later; both of them long before Joe Thomas's meteoric rise as the all-singing, all-dancing black ball of fire. In those days he had been trying to make his name as a straight actor and had all but succeeded in the supporting roles he had played in the two movies: a cunning, psychopathic killer, masquerading as an Uncle Tom, in *The Talking Man;* and the sergeant in *Under the Trees at Akron,* a film concerned with the basics of fear: a patrol, during the Korean war, pinned down for one night in an area code-named *Akron,* and in particular the mental agony of one young soldier. A standard plot, but superbly done. Joe Thomas had been outgunned in both films simply because of magnificent lead performances.

Catellier remembered. You could see it in his eyes as he sat staring down at the table. Then his head moved, imperceptible at first, into a slow nod. 'Yes,' he said at last, 'yes, I give you that. It might just work, but don't forget that a lot of water, and even more applause, has run under Joe Thomas's bridge since those two films.'

'I know,' said Douglas. 'Only too well. I've been close to him and it's terrifying.'

'Perhaps because he's terrified.' Another pause, as though Catellier was switching his mind to matters closer to himself. 'I do see your problems, Douglas, even if I don't quite endorse your methods.' His eyes lifted, trapping Douglas who could see in the deep blue of them the marks of high intelligence and a certain concern. 'You haven't answered my question yet, Douglas. You talk about me making a fine Richard, though for the life of me I can't think why; it's a role I've never even contemplated playing. How? How do you want me to play it?'

'It's not a matter of how I would want you to play it. I believe you would make an exceptionally magnetic Richard simply because you're not the most immediate, or natural, choice; you're not a man for melodrama, but I think there are times, with great talents like your own, when one should go against the grain. We'll do it any way you want, Conrad, though I would suggest that we forget about the melodrama inherent in the play and do it straight. The unsubtle push to power played with subtlety. Point down Richard's physical deformity, after all, William only used that to colour the deformity within –'

'That's why the play's top-heavy and over-melodramatic.'

'Quite, so let's do it within your particular talent.'

'Wouldn't the downgrading of melodrama reduce the impact, somehow emasculate the play?'

'I don't think so. Reduce the obvious on stage and replace it with a revelation of Richard's mind. First we make Richard's hump almost imperceptible, the limp slight and the withered arm almost unnoticeable; that in itself would make the scene before the coronation more horrific – the meeting of the Council. . . .'

'Richard's accusation of Hastings?'

'Yes.'

'Look how I am bewitch'd; behold mine arm
Is, like a blasted sapling, wither'd up:'

'I thought you'd never considered Richard.'

'I know my Shakespeare.'

Douglas grinned, lifting his glass and taking a sip of wine. 'I know a woman who met Hitler twice. The first time was accidental: he was on his way to Berchtesgaden and broke his journey at the hotel where she was staying. She happened to be the only English woman in the place and he asked if he might talk to her. She spent the evening alone with him and told me that he was one of the most charming men she'd ever met. This was a cultured woman, Conrad, a woman who is no fool. She met him again in 1939, officially this time at some social function in Berlin, and she said that, in spite of the different atmosphere, her impression was the same: a man of charm, wit, intelligence and character. When the truth emerged she found it difficult to reconcile what she had experienced with the facts. Conrad, could you play Richard like that, with both sides visible to the audience?'

He took a long time to answer. 'It's certainly the right approach for me.'

Douglas leaned forward, one hand still on the stem of his glass. 'There are many facets. You could, for instance, do it with a slight hint of homosexuality.'

Catellier's head came up. For a moment Douglas thought he had lost his man, but when the actor spoke he was calm.

'What about the wooing of Lady Anne?'

'Expediency?'

'It's expedient already, but it would strengthen the point. Good thinking. That helps remove melodrama. Good.' He settled into his chair. Douglas had the distinct impression that the man was itching to get home to the text and start work. It was the moment for him to start pulling the threads together, 'There are other ways of ironing out the melodrama, we can suggest the rise of political despotism through the music and the way we use crowds, the soldiers, the Court . . .'

'Jackboots.'

'Peter Hall virtually did that in the Histories at Stratford, but there's no reason why we shouldn't try it again.'

'What about my supports? My Buckingham's got to be strong.'

'Trust me, Conrad. I'll give you a strong Buckingham. My wife's playing Desdemona and I'll try and get her to do Lady Anne as well, it's only small but it would be a start.'

Catellier smiled. 'A very pleasant start.'

'Then you'll do it?'

'I'll talk with my agent. He'll call you tomorrow.'

Catellier's agent did call: at ten-thirty on the following morning as Douglas was wading through a pile of casting lists and innumerable incidentals with Ronnie Gregor. Catellier would play Richard and Douglas felt he could now leave the small print of the negotiation safely in Ronnie's hands.

It was a tiring, necessary and fiddling morning, leaving Douglas edgy as he walked up Shaftesbury Avenue and into Dean Street to Gennaro's for his meeting with Adrian Rolfe, very conscious of the fact that Adrian's willingness to lunch was far from the real crunch of getting him to work at Shireston.

Adrian Rolfe was sipping what appeared to be an innocent tomato juice when Douglas arrived, and the director was relieved when Rolfe tipped back the drink and rose to meet him. Time was always against them, and Douglas, who envisaged a long haggle in any case, did not want to be pushed into small talk.

They were shown straight to their table, the one by the window corner where, if you sit with your back to the mirror, facing the big pillared painting of Christ casting the moneylenders out of the Temple in muted colours, you hold a dominant view of the place. If you face the mirror you have the same view reflected, so winning either way.

Rolfe was in his early forties, a short man with a slightly affected voice, trim clean good looks and closely cut hair which curled naturally near to the scalp. His smile, which was practically constant, irritated Douglas who saw in it that superior element which tends to display itself among the class conscious or highly competitive professionals. Rolfe was smiling, almost a smirk, now as they sat down flanked by attentive waiters.

'Nice to see you again, Douglas.' The timing held perfectly before he brought in memories of their last eruptive association. '*Peer Gynt* seems a long way off, especially now that you're such a grand person – director of the Shireston Festival.'

Douglas held himself in check, remembering that it was not so much what Adrian Rolfe said as how he said it. 'Adrian, one thing before we go any further. You were right about the *Peer Gynt* programme and I was wrong. I'm sorry. Can we forget that ever happened?'

'Of course, Douglas, of course. I never bear grudges.' He opened the long blue menu in which he appeared to become quickly engrossed.

It was at this point in the preliminaries that Douglas became aware of an added disadvantage, one not usual in this restaurant. Their first few sentences had been exchanged during a lull in the conversation from the next table. Usually the quiet atmosphere and careful service at Gennaro's overcomes any tendency towards loudness on the part of its clientèle; but, in the present instance, nothing – atmosphere, a book of printed instructions on decorum, the advantages of a Cistercian convent – would have dissuaded the gaunt, grey and elderly American lady who was entertaining a middle-aged couple at the next table.

Douglas opened his mouth to make some suggestion regarding choice of food and was shrilled into silence by the mannish bray which came from his left.

'Of course I'm used to the English now,' the American lady bawled at her companions. 'The trick is in understanding their sense of humour. Icky has it. Did I ever tell you about Icky and Alice when they first came over here in 1959?'

Douglas felt himself hunch against the outlandish volume and caught Adrian's eye: a mildly amusing frown.

'Well you know Icky, straight to the bar as soon as he gets on the plane,' continued the unbelievable grandmother. 'They get to Heathrow and the customs man asks Icky if they have anything to declare. He just looks around and points at Alice and says, "You'd better ask her, I'm loaded." The English love that kind of thing.'

The anecdote dipped into temporary silence as its narrator took a final mouthful of cream cake and they were able to give their orders. Once the waiter departed, Douglas leaned across the table.

'Can I plunge straight in, Adrian? What's your availability?'

The irritating smile again, lifting a little to the right like a sneer. 'For Shireston? Not available. Sorry Douglas but I've had the theatrical scene. It's just so much sweat and routine. In any case the best publicity story you're likely to have blew up in your face.'

'No.' Douglas put his hands palms down, firmly on to the table. 'No, I mean how are you fixed contractually? Can you get a release?'

'Oh I can get a release. Any time I want. But I don't want the Shireston, chum. Can't you tempt John Goodwin from the RST or David Fairweather from Chichester?'

'I want *you*, I understand your reticence but will you listen for a few minutes?'

'I'll always listen.'

The conversation was broken again. The male partner of the couple being entertained at the next table proved to have a voice at least equal in strength to his hostess.

'When the kids started growing up,' he announced to his female companions, 'Paul came to me and said, "Pop, I want a car." So I told him, "You want a car, so go out and work and get money and buy yourself a car." Almost all my friends said, "Jack you're a son-of-a-bitch doing a thing like that. You could buy that kid twenty cars." But I think I did the right thing.'

Murmurs of assent from the ladies.

'Mind you it was bad when he went on drugs.'

It was a natural punch line. Uncharacteristically, Adrian's shoulders began to shake and Douglas saw a determined waiter approaching the American trio with a bill. It was impossible to converse properly until the party had left on a trail of explanations of the British system of tipping imperfectly understood by the elderly lady.

'You still listening?' Douglas spooned pasta fagiole into his mouth.

'Go ahead.'

'First, a question. What is public relations work in the theatre about.'

Adrian did not pause. It was like a tennis volley. 'It's about actors and directors with inflated egos claiming they aren't getting enough publicity; it's about soothing over bad publicity and keeping some stories out of the papers and some stories in the papers; it's about advertising and programme layout and press calls, and picture calls, and after a while it becomes a complete drag.'

'Wrong.'

'Douglas.' A warning implied in the note of his voice.

'You *are* wrong, Adrian. You're wrong because you worked for too long with the same outfit and the whole thing became automatic. It lost its challenge. Public relations in the theatre is about getting people into seats every night of the week, and I have the biggest challenge any PR man could be offered. It's not just concerned with keeping actors and directors happy. Whoever takes over the PR job at Shireston will have widest brief anyone in theatre PR has had this century.'

Rolfe pushed some of his fish hors d'oeuvre around his plate and slowly shook his head. 'You always were one to be carried away by your own enthusiasm. I hear you've done a dodgy bit of casting that will catch a few votes, but it'll be hell for anyone handling the publicity scene. Quite something to have the great Joe Thomas at Shireston. But Shireston's clapped out, Douglas. They'll laugh.'

'Was clapped out, Adrian. Was. The trustees are putting up a great deal of money to make Shireston a viable proposition again. I'm going to see that we do it, and, while the plays, productions and performances are the obvious end product I have to start selling Shireston on its environment: on the theatre and its setting, the grounds, the natural beauty, the house, the restaurant which I'm building up from scratch.' Douglas was totally wound up within his subject now. He talked for fifteen minutes about the kind of advertising and the quality his project would mean, and about the kind of service that would be required: a tie-in with some luxury coach service, the link with continental package holidays to Britain, and hotels in the major cities, British Rail, charter flight companies, schools and organizations.

Slowly Adrian's attitude began to change, the mocking smile turning to one of concentrated interest.

'What about the end product though, Douglas? What is the real final weight of the company going to be?'

Douglas slid his hand into his breast pocket and drew out the, so far incomplete, cast lists, handing them across the table.

Rolfe put on his glasses and began to study the lists carefully, making comments and asking the occasional question. 'You've definitely got Catellier?'

'This morning we finalized, yes.'

'And Edward Crispin for Buckingham.' Crispin was a good solid middle billing actor with plenty of experience in the Theatre and a lot of recent television exposure as the lead in a twelve episode serial on the scale of *I, Claudius*.

'Crispin is another we only got this morning, I haven't talked to Catellier about him yet but I think he'll be acceptable. You'll see he's also going to play Iago.'

Rolfe's eyes flicked up in a look of understanding then returned to the lists. 'Who's Carol Evans? Isn't she a coloured . . .? Oh yes, I see you've got Thomas marked in to play Capulet . . . and Felicity Durrant as Nurse? But she's –'

'White,' said Douglas, clipped and sharp as though the casting should be obvious.

'No Romeo?'

'Auditioning a good unknown on Sunday. Hope he'll double as Lorenzo and Cassio, but he doesn't know about that yet.'

It was a grin this time instead of the smirk from Rolfe. 'It looks very good, Douglas. You directing the lot?'

'Yes.'

'Designer?'

'Tony Holt.'

'Well, you know him and he's got a fair range. Music?'

'We've commissioned Raymond Leggat.'

'Mmmm.' Rolfe mused to himself. 'It'll be hummable stuff anyway, none of your twelve note chromatics from him.' He leaned back. 'It's a big operation, Douglas. Needs wide vision and a large staff for the PR department. I presume that whoever took over would have total control of Public Relations for the entire project: theatre, environment, restaurant, company . . .?'

They talked about the casting and the difficulties of catering for such a wide variety of temperaments for half an hour or so. Then, Douglas said, 'There is one more area we haven't discussed.'

'Yes.'

'I've mentioned selling the environment. The grounds are exceptional, and they ought to be; we employ a permanent staff of fifteen gardeners.'

'Who are helping you to weed the permanent administrative staff I presume.'

Douglas let the frivolity pass and replied seriously. 'No, but I'm bringing in an executive director to take care of that. Fifteen gardeners and the grounds look fabulous in the summer. However, with our weather you can sell them the grounds and all they see when they arrive is sodden turf and dripping trees.'

'*And the rain it raineth every day.*'

'Quite. We have to offer them something else, if only as a diversion between dinner and the play.'

'Such as?'

'You remember the Shakespeare centenary exhibition they put on in Stratford for the fourth centenary celebrations?'

'Shakespeare's life and the plays, yes. Exhibits, set pieces, statuary, models, jewels, paintings, music, speech, light. Splendid. There was a marvellous London street with the street cries and noises, and a representation of the Globe with Gielgud doing Prospero on tape –'

'And Larry as Othello and Peggy and Paul doing a snatch of Lear and Cordelia.'

'Great, it had great style. Stays in the memory.'

'Right. I want to mount a similar exhibition at Shireston. A permanent section, not just about Shakespeare, but setting out the background to his time; yes, a London street like the one at Stratford, and a Long Gallery, do you remember that? With its view of London?' Rolfe nodded as Douglas went on, 'Those kind of things and more: how they really lived in Elizabethan England, attitudes to religion, superstition, what they ate – with the smells, the good smells not the bad – dress, adornment, language, the texture of life; and we could end with something like the Globe thing at Stratford, but keyed to the productions at Shireston. I also want a permanent section on the Shireston Festival and its history, its past, present and future.'

The conversation became even more animated, inspiration and the ideas flying. The change of key was notable with Adrian Rolfe talking about 'Us' and 'the festival' and '*We* could always . . .'

By three-forty-five Douglas knew he had sold him the idea. It would take Rolfe a month to clear from his other job, but he would start in on engaging people straight away and drawing up preliminary plans. 'How soon do I get an office down there?' he asked.

'I'll see your offices are ready within a week, so that you can start moving people in. I'm going down tomorrow and I know we already have a team decorating and renovating the offices and living quarters before they start on the theatre itself – that's got to have the full treatment. But I'll make your offices a priority.'

This quickly shifted them on to the question of salaries and budget. They ended back in the Rupert Street office, talking, planning, working until after seven. By then they had a magnificent vision. Carried away by their imaginations they saw Shireston as a beautiful image, the smooth velvet lawns and shading conifers, the house rising among crunched drives and walks bordered by vivid flowers; the restaurant efficient, a gourmet's haven, the exhibition teeming with visitors experiencing a new dimension; droves of elegant people arriving on clean, well-staffed Pullman trains or sweeping up the broad drive in purring coaches: the theatre, white and shining in the evening sun, and performances which stunned the imagination. When they parted, on that particular evening, neither Douglas nor Adrian were taking into account the individual complexities of men, the clash of temperament, lust, greed or crass inefficiency.

After Adrian left, Douglas Silver dialled Carol's number, waiting a long time before resigning himself to the fact that she must be out. Irrationally he felt annoyed, like a lover who expects his girl to be waiting for him to call and is ruffled and offended if she is not there for his convenience alone.

The sensation remained with him all evening, and there were still traces of it in his mind as he drove down to Shireston on the following morning.

'That's your problem. We'll have to lift the pros.' Douglas stood at the back of the auditorium of the Shireston Festival

Theatre pointing down at the stage and the proscenium arch, to which he had been referring. He had never been a great lover of picture-frame stages and this one was worse than most, the arch diminishing the size of the stage and almost forming an invisible barrier between stage and auditorium.

'You can move the sidepillars a good three feet and lift the arch four and a half to five.' He said. 'It needs some kind of decoration as well. Something like that thirteenth-century swan they used for Stratford and the Aldwych.'

'Would a cygnet do?' Tony Holt was beside him, tubby with a head that looked top heavy, shoulder length hair and a small beard; the big, aquiline Alec Keene, the theatre's house manager, was with them, also Wilfred Brownhill, in charge of property maintenance.

It had been a hard and detailed day. Autumn was already beginning to topple into winter and the grounds of Shireston looked less inviting, more bleak and threadbare, than they had done on Douglas's last visit. But Tony had been waiting for him, bursting with ideas and agility.

One of Douglas's first actions on accepting the directorship was commissioning Tony, not simply to design costumes and settings for the four plays, but to convert the stables into a modern and workable restaurant, and advise on any refurbishing, both inside and out of the theatre and house.

They spent most of the morning going through the house and stables where a labour force of forty or fifty men were already working. The house itself was fascinatingly ugly, a grotesque mixture of styles and odd additions: a combination of all possible excesses of mock gothic architecture: red weathered brick clashing with stone, small turret windows appeared in the most unlikely places, a pair of stubby castellated towers rose from the centre section from which the whole building seemed to spill out in all directions.

Douglas was amazed to find that the original conversion work, carried out in the late twenties, had not only been done intelligently, but also with a fine standard of craftsmanship: now, apart from a lot of painting, only small adjustments were called for, a number of new telephone lines were being brought in, minor alterations in plumbing and some general patching up. On the whole the condition was good.

The central section and west wing were made over entirely to administrative offices, the property department, wardrobe and living accommodation for office and theatre staff; while the east wing had been broken up into quarters for the company: some thirty single bedsitting-rooms, fifteen small double flats with their own kitchens and bathrooms, and ten larger apartments.

The director's accommodation was among the latter, with a high-ceilinged sitting-room overlooking the lawns, a large bedroom, bathrooms, kitchen and, for want of a better name, breakfast room. Jen would not care much for the shabby furnishings but they would be bringing a fair amount of their stuff down from London. Douglas lingered in the flat for a while, aware of the fact that this would be his home for the bulk of at least three years if everything went well, and trying to envisage what Jen would do to these rooms. There was a long bow window into which their leather buttoned settee would fit. But where would she decide to hang the Bratby or the David Arnot collage? A moment of longing as the wind hit the wide leaded window: trying to picture Jen in the room, the atmosphere tinted with her particular scent, her movement, the essential parts of her. Then Tony called him, and Douglas had to move on and look at something else.

Right at the beginning, after he had first visited Shireston, Tony Holt had written to Douglas suggesting that the Victorian atmosphere of the house's interior should, in some way, be made less powerful: he argued that there were areas where it became depressing and overbearing. They might even camp it up a bit with framed playbills and objects selected from the property department. Tony had, in fact, already started to put his ideas into practice by having a mural painted on one wall of the company restaurant, once – aptly some thought – the servants' hall, by making some discreet changes in the appointments of the green room, originally the large family dining-room.

'The place looked like one of those fading political club rooms you find in the provinces,' he said. 'I expected to find dead old actors under the dustcovers clutching yellowed copies of *The Stage*.'

In the stables they were already well advanced, the interior gutted, leaving the bare slatted wooden walls, some of the wood flaking old paint. The new parquet floor was being put down, the smooth area ending abruptly, half-way across the building, in a squarely serrated coastline. While the exterior was to remain unaltered, except for a paint job and new fitments, Tony designed false walls and ceilings for the interior, with one wall entirely made up of mirror to add a sense of spaciousness. They had already worked out the major essential statistics – that the main dining-room would seat eighty people at one time and, as far as the design was concerned, no one person should have to take more than an hour over dinner.

They lunched quietly in the permanent staff cafeteria, an undistinguished meal, soggy and overcooked without any style. Douglas made a note that this was another area which needed attention quickly: you could not expect staff to work properly if they were being fed slop. A further thought struck him: if this was the normal standard of food, the administrative people were probably a pretty dull lot to accept it. The need for an executive director was even more apparent.

Over lunch they looked at Tony's first draft designs for the productions. The Venetian settings for *The Merchant* and *Othello* were exciting, suggesting the city by subtle innuendo rather than doing a straight job of pictured realism, while the Cyprus sets for the later action of *Othello* were light and sunny, using a lot of white walls and creating the idea of hard reflected sunlight. Verona, for *Romeo and Juliet*, was complicated, worked out on three, sometimes four, levels; streets winding off into narrow stairways, balconies and small windows clustered overhead. He had been least successful with *Richard III*, a standing set of wooden scaffolding that reminded Douglas of early Sean Kenny. The ideas which had emerged during the conversation with Catellier called for

99

something more positive.

'A standing set by all means,' he told Tony Holt, 'but I need to express change. Up to the second scene of act four, the coronation, the court has got to be in a kind of decaying decadence. We must feel it, shredding velvet, grubby silk and worn rugs. After Richard becomes king there has to be complete change: a military dominance: you know, the outward signs that the régime is working. The whole fascist dictator thing. You can suggest it in the costumes as well.' He went on to talk about the costume designs for the other plays, having found Tony's first drawings too classic for his conception of the season.

Tony did not take the criticism well, remaining slightly sullen for the rest of the day. Douglas added yet another mental note to his growing list: that he would have to revise his instructions to Raymond Leggat regarding the music for *Richard III*.

After lunch they went over to the theatre where the real depression set in for Douglas. The exterior alone was in need of a great deal of repair, he did not need Alec Keene and Wilfred Brownhill to point it out. The façade, with its Spanish cloister running the length of the frontage, had become reminiscent of some old, peeling and impoverished Mexican hotel. Inside, the auditorium was even more cheerless.

'Like a 1920s cinema that nobody's thought of renovating,' Douglas observed.

He got the details settled about the proscenium arch, and Tony agreed to look for some suitable symbol for them to use above the arch and in front of the theatre: something they could reproduce on posters and programmes, some instant identification with Shireston.

'God alone knows what we're going to do with the auditorium.' Douglas looked about himself, raised his arms and let them drop slackly to his sides. The walls and ceilings were filthy, the lighting inadequate, the seating looked in bad shape and the floor coverings were threadbare. It was no wonder that the festival had gone downhill. Douglas thought for a moment.

'How long to get an estimate for new carpeting, seating and lighting?' he asked, turning to Keene and Brownhill.

They looked at their feet and muttered together. Douglas felt his irritation rise, realizing that, so far, he had probably been too easy going.

'About a month,' replied Brownhill at last.

'One week,' snapped Douglas. 'And a realistic estimate in one week, or both your resignations on my desk. As for the rest, we'll have to make do with a good paint job.'

The remainder of the afternoon was spent discussing the possibility of the exhibition with Tony.

'I can't take that on, not on top of everything else,' Tony protested. 'Christ, Douglas, I'm up to my eyes already.'

'Yes, I can see that, but I've got to have some other diversion for the customers. I didn't reckon on having to find another salary for an exhibition director, we're going to leap over budget anyway if I'm not careful – especially if I've got to refit the whole bloody auditorium.'

'Never mind, mate, you might save yourself something on Alec and Wilf's salaries.' Tony grinned.

'Could be yours as well, chum.' Douglas did not smile, his cosiness had departed during the day, the anxiety of running a project like this starting to gnaw his secret nerves.

He drove badly on the way back to London and found himself taking unnecessary risks. Once in the apartment he mixed a stiff whisky and soda and slumped into his favourite armchair. Saturday night and nowhere to go. Nobody to go with either. He dialled Carol's number but, once more, she was not home.

At last he decided to assuage his anxiety and rage with work. He got out his notes, clip board and copy of *Othello* and started to plot the play, using a square of cardboard as the stage and coloured counters for the actors. But the day came between him and the text. The long mental list compiled at Shireston ticked itself in his mind. Just one day at Shireston had shown him what was in store, and he had yet to have a proper meeting with the finance people; there was also the exhibition and the need to get help for Tony: a hundred minor points and decisions blundered through his mind.

When he finally gave up and went to bed, the anxieties still churned – and there weren't any actors there yet. He smiled, cynicism on his lips in the dark. Actors would bring a bundle of trouble with them. The fabric; decay; the gardens; the exhibition; the house; restaurant; auditorium; kitchens and cafeteria; executive director; Christ, who needs actors? Tomorrow, he remembered, he had to see an actor.

CHAPTER SIX

It was warm, dark and comfortable. He was Asher Grey; in his mind there was recognition of himself: the knowledge of the morning; and it was warm, dark and comfortable. He was content: the first stirrings, a pinpoint of consciousness, a tip of light in the centre of Asher Grey's mind: the light containing the necessary things, all surrounded by blackness and warmth.

Something else: pleasurable, making him turn on to his back and wriggle against the sheets and go on writhing the small of his back and his buttocks into the mattress beneath him: a hand, small and light, stroking his genitals. Julia Philips's hand. That was nice, and not usual: Julia, his little cross, feeling him up in the wee small hours. She did more than just stroke now, the hand kneading him into an untamed erection. He moved close to her, moved his body as she moved, the pair setting up a rhythm they had learned long together. Pleasure, warmth and satisfaction fed the light until it grew more brilliant at the periphery, taking other facts into the pattern of consciousness.

Douglas Silver . . . Silver and gold. . . . *I am not covetous for gold*. . . . That was something, somewhere from Shakespeare. Douglas Silver. . . . Christ. . . . Sunday. London.

'What the bloody hell's the time?' Asher Grey grunted. 'I've got a train to catch.'

'Shshshsh.' Julia did not falter in her movements as she soothed. 'It's early yet. Only about half past three.'

Reassured, he took up the rhythm again, thrusting towards her; but she reached over his body and gently flattened him on the bed, her hand moving still, the other

103

parting his thighs as a man will ease a woman open before mounting her: then, thigh against thigh, she was kneeling inside his legs, holding him with both hands. He groped upwards to feel the soft nest of hair and part her wet lips as she lowered herself on to him, her hands guiding the stiff centre of his being towards its natural place; lips parting, the passage giving away and sucking him into her belly. Julia slowly straightened her body on top of his, legs lifting astride him and moving with assured strokes, the roles reversed, she playing the male dominant. The flash of comprehension like a great magnesium flare in the mind. He saw his mother at the foot of the stairs goading his father, lips moving in soundless flow; the picture on the wall, some fancy unnatural print of cows going to be milked over plastic green grass and false mud. Cusha bloody cusha calling. Cows all of them. His first woman ever, Anthea at RADA lowing him to her room. He had turned in the act of undressing and seen the stained dirty underclothes and she reminded him of his father, not a young lively girl. Scheming cows with red mouths which opened and closed incessantly with whines and threats and, once in a while, cold comfort. The cheap barometer. His father, hands flat against the wall trying to gain his balance late on a Saturday, viewed from the top of the stairs with his mother prancing down in worn slippers, a yellow thin housecoat billowing and patterned, a Viking raider in full sail ploughing down the stairs in curlers to ravage the drunken Saxon. Fish teas, cold meat on Sundays with the floral decorated bowl erupting with lettuce and the saffron eyes of hard boiled eggs. A whole stink of memories overridden with melancholy.

It was then that he realized what Julia was doing: when it was too late, when he could neither stop her impaled jogging nor his own wild flailing reply. This was the climax which had started two nights before.

He had played the matter with care, the closeness learned from childhood: making the arrangements and saying nothing until Friday night. They were paid in the afternoon and after the evening performance Asher took Julia over to the pub. Several members of the Stanthorpe repertory company were there and it developed, as it often did, into a small party. They got home, back to the Chamber of Horrors, late and elated. He was in bed first, leering while Julia, a shade tipsy, pirouetted around the bed as she undressed.

'Do you think I'd make a good stripper, Ash?' She stood, legs apart and arms raised wearing only bra and pants. 'Eh? How about this?' undulating her hips and reaching to unclasp the bra clip. She had a reasonable body on her. Asher had to admit that.

The bra came away displaying the well-known full breasts with great discoloured rings around the nipples. Strange how he loved to suck those nipples when he was all bunched up close with her after they had fucked well. She was good at that too: in spite of the peevishness and yatter, she was bloody good at it.

'You look good enough to eat,' said Asher tracing his thoughts into the hard line of words. 'Come on, get your knickers down, we've got to make up time. Won't have our usual Sunday morning of debauchery; I'm off to the smoke on Sunday.'

She stopped, frozen, half bending towards the bed: the long blonde hair hanging, falling across her face and the swinging breast, fingers at her waistband.

'What for?' Arrogance: straightening up, worry slapped over the pudgy bright face.

'My audition, stupid. I'm auditioning in London for Douglas Silver on Sunday.'

She grinned. 'Great. I haven't had a day in London for years.'

'I'm auditioning. Me.' He pointed, stabbing his chest. 'I am going to London on Sunday.'

'You don't want me to come? You don't want me there.' It began as simply as that and continued with rising hysteria all through the Saturday. He was trying to put something over on her, going up for the audition by himself, sly; and if he got the job he would not keep his promise to her, to make it a condition that she should also come to Shireston. It went on, like a toothache, the unrelenting pummelling stretching of

105

the nerves until his brain became dead to the clatter of her tongue and the stagnant spew of words, until after the Saturday night performance when she suddenly seemed to have come becalmed, like a potential suicide who has made up her mind that the pain of living will end at a definite point in time.

Now, at three-thirty on the Sunday morning, with his body arching towards climax and Julia on him, humping with more concentrated effort than he ever recalled, Asher Grey knew what was in her mind. She knew him and she knew how he could be thrown. This one plunge would tire him, drain him so that his body would be conscious of it for the next twenty-four hours and his mind would remain aware of the succulent delights; there would be no more sleep tonight and he would arrive in London washed out and exhausted, certainly in no fit condition to give of his best for Douglas Silver.

The rhythm was stronger, settling down into the rapid rise to its conclusion; faster now and their breath coming as one, panting: her vagina round him tight, gripping and the tingling, low down at the base of his spine, the swirl and pattern which engulfed the universe so that he could stretch out a mental arm and pull down the stars or bring the wise philosophies of a thousand years clear and absolute into his mind. The pressure building like a wall, a dam about to break, building until he could not bear it.

The choking at the back of his throat and the automatic, 'Now, Julia, now.'

She made some noise, shaking her head in a violent nod and increasing the burning motion of her thighs, pulling away to the fullest extent and then plunging back on to him again.

The dam burst.

Gouts and throbbing spasms as the world and its orbit cracked and erupted, all knowledge made free and spinning in a glare of colour and comprehension. Then the relaxed panting, the entwining of arms and legs, the sudden weight of Julia's body heavy on him and the diminishing throb of life in his slackening organ as it slid from her.

'You bitch,' Asher panted. 'You whoring, intriguing bitch.'

She laughed, a high bray.

Pushing her away, rolling her body from him, Asher brought up his right hand and slapped her full across the cheek.

The afterburn of gloom settled uncompromisingly on Asher Grey as the train ploughed south. Emotionally he was numbed: dull post-coital depression combining with the vapour trail of hysteria which had followed in the wake of his violence. His knuckles were bruised where he had brought the hand back across Julia's mouth, while his words, hissed in uncontrolled violence, now seemed unreal to him.

'You stupid, ignorant woman. I have work to do. I needed rest and all you think about is screwing me up, tiring me out to save your lousy skin so that we can both rot in this excuse for life.'

The hand paddling back and forth and a scream forming way back in Julia's throat. She had tried to scramble from the bed, but he pinned her down, an arm hard over the small of her back as she twisted and kicked and he showered her buttocks with blows until they were scarlet. At least, after the first moments he had been controlled enough not to hit out indiscriminately.

'Now stop bugging me.' He pushed the flapping, writhing, flailing girl from him. 'You'll get a job. You'll be with me: if that's what you want. Just don't be so bloody stupid.'

Then the recriminations, the pounding on the bathroom door while he shaved, the pounding of a neighbour on the wall. The hysterical and nonsensical shrieks.

Now he was conscious of fatigue and the fact that the train was carrying him away from her. He was also conscious of the trap: he would have to return: again take the line of least resistance and all would be calm on the surface until some other fear, real or imagined, blew the girl's mind. She would never forgive him for the physical assault, he knew that; it would be brought up against him at every moment of conflict.

Fatigue and the sound of her voice bruising the early morning. 'All right. Leave me. Leave me, you sodding lousy actor. Leave me . . . Leave me. . . .'

For two and a half hours he waited in the slow changing dark until the first Sunday bus grumbled into life; then again the interminable stretch of time at Manchester, the station sleepy and lethargic as it automatically went through the motions of its Sunday routine. The *News of the World*; all life was here in tiny uncoloured dramas; the *People*; a girl red eyed and tottering, hampered by her coat through which one glimpsed a flash of thigh, her face knotted in worry and the body sagging. A long and arduous illicit night? Children, blinking the sleep from their eyes, gleaming and awed to be out and doing something different, spent parents shepherding them into some small adventure. The *Sunday Mirror*, cracked in the washroom giving him a haggard reflection: *O Romeo, Romeo, wherefore art thou Romeo? The Sunday Times* ticking the minutes towards the 10.15, the conveyor belt that would bring Douglas Silver, Romeo, Shireston at least within his grasp. The *Observer*, regulation beat, pausing to look at him sitting idly on a station seat; other passengers, suspicious as television spies, and the waiting and walking and sipping coffee the colour of brown ale and the colour supplements sweeping their little piles of litter, the spoor of travellers, or taking tickets, carrying bags, overseeing, sharp shod trotting for trains.

The compartment on the London train was grubby, the feel of ingrained dirt in the seats, his companions uninspiring: a young man in crumpled, stained grey suit and with raggedly cut hair who resolutely picked his nose behind a newspaper; a girl of around twenty-five, dark hair and skin uncared for, a sullen mouth and hands constantly active, at war with the hem of her little skirt, pulled down feverishly each time she crossed and recrossed her hopeful legs.

There was no real sense of release, freedom, if only for the day. Just the depression bordered by the pinpoint of hope. If success. . . . He closed his eyes and thought of what that could really mean. Julia would still be there, but perhaps the problem might be easier. The fact of working among established names, a routine with people who knew what they were doing, people he could respect, the washing away of the dull grind of getting experience by performing one play each night, rehearsing another and learning a third by day; if success . . . then a comparatively clean and civilized way of life . . . the country . . . the passing countryside . . . cuttings . . . escarpments . . . telegraph poles . . . the whizzing silent cars . . . trees, sheep and cattle . . . far away houses . . . the roll of the carriage and the train noises . . . floating . . . away from reality . . . her voice subsiding as though it had never been . . . only the bumping and jarring of the train. . . .

When he woke it was one o'clock and they were less than an hour out of Euston. Asher washed and tidied himself in the cramped lavatory, the floor swimming in water and the paper towels all gone.

Arriving in London was the first exhilarating sensation of the day since the bursting orgasmic pleasure. The smell of London and its feel brought pleasure more solid than any sexual thrill. It was to this clawing, brutal, beautiful, ugly city he had first escaped from the guerrilla warfare of home, and it was here that he had dreamed the unfeasible dream while people taught him about acting. London had always been the imagined springboard for Asher, who, during his time at the Royal Academy of Dramatic Art, had never doubted for one moment that natural talent would fly him with immediate accuracy to the top of his profession; indeed, it had come as something of a shock, once he left RADA, to find himself out among that great amorphous mass of actors collectively 'resting'.

The rehearsal rooms were within walking distance of Euston Station, above a double-fronted reach-me-down ready-to-wear tailor's establishment off the Euston Road and Asher had a good half an hour until two-thirty and his appointment with Douglas Silver, so he set out in the watery sunlight, taking deep breaths, clearing his head, trying to will the remains of fatigue from his body and concentrate on the important matter: his Romeo.

Access to the rehearsal rooms was by a narrow flight of stairs to the right of the tailor's shop. A small card, attached to the wall with Sellotape, just inside the door at the foot of the stairs, informed prospective clients that this was the gateway to *Sampson's Rehearsal Rooms. Available to professional and amateur theatre companies. Also wedding breakfasts, committee meetings and social functions of all kinds. For Bookings Phone D. W. Sampson 378–4929.*

For a brief moment Asher's stomach clenched and turned over as he began to climb the stairs, remembering other decisive moments, climbing stairs in a far from outstanding career. Stairway after stairway: to agents who asked what work he had been doing and told him to come back when he had got some experience; to managements who said they had nothing for him; a week of hope with a movie producer, shattered in a few seconds; then the final one, the audition for Stanthorpe Rep on a grey afternoon with twenty other hopefuls.

Now this, like a gallows climb. Ronnie Gregor had told him of all the plans, and the money that had been made available to Shireston, and it crossed Asher's mind that they should be using more salubrious quarters for their auditions. He quickly blotted out the thought, recalling that he had read an article about the Royal Shakespeare Company rehearsing in a church hall and that the idea of glamour in the theatre was a myth he should have exploded by now.

The door at the top of the stairs was firmly closed (a further Sellotaped card reiterated that this was Sampson's Rehearsal Rooms). Below it a list of bookings for the month. He hesitated, not knowing whether to knock or walk straight in. He knocked, only loud enough for a person of acute hearing to detect. There was no reply so he pushed open the door.

It was a long room, the walls lined with tubular chairs, not of recent design, a black upright piano, grey-green oilcloth covering the floor, the faint smell of powder and stage make-up.

110

Two big windows at the far end of the room, in front of which stood a table around which three men formed a silhouetted tableau: two sitting with their backs to him, the third, whom he vaguely recognized, perched on the table itself. Far gone in conversation they did not notice Asher's arrival, and it was only when he began to walk slowly towards them that the figure sitting on the table raised his head. Asher recognized Ronnie Gregor.

'Here he is now.'

The other two men turned so that Asher had to walk a good ten paces under their gaze. He felt uncomfortable; not self-conscious, that was a luxury which actors soon learned to do without, but he was aware of his appearance, knowing that he should have taken more care, had the worsted suit cleaned and pressed, chosen a shirt instead of the turtleneck that he had grabbed in the middle of the brawl with Julia.

One of the seated men rose, a tall well-proportioned man with thick curly black hair, eyes which seemed to take in everything, restless, and a smile which, while tentative, had the makings of real warmth.

'Hi. Asher Grey? I'm Douglas Silver.' He extended a hand and Asher felt a strong firm grip.

'You know Ronnie Gregor,' said Silver, 'and this is Art Drays, our production manager.'

Asher and Art Drays exchanged nods and Douglas Silver indicated a chair. 'Sit down, Asher, Ronnie's told us a lot about you. You have a good journey?'

A nervous smile, he was trying to sum up the famous cultural whizz-kid. 'You know British Rail.'

'I try not to.'

'You should have come down by air like I told you.' Laconic from Ronnie.

Asher could not recall Ronnie mentioning the possibility of making the trip by air. Why didn't they get on with the real business? Asher felt the kind of tension he could not ever remember experiencing, not even before the most difficult first nights. But Silver was inclined towards petty conversation. Asher tried to cut through the words, forcing his mind

111

away. The oilcloth on the floor with the light making it appear to be a map of seas and rivers, land masses shaded with mountain peaks and smooth plateaux; papers on the bare wooden table and a couple of books, half hidden; a deep brown circle stained into the wood, the careless work of some tea-drinking committee member, amateur or professional; the tiny black burn, a cigarette left balanced precariously on the table edge and then remembered, snatched quickly away to save the deeper scar; a motor-cycle burning it up in the street below, shaking the windows; Romeo burning it up in Asher's brain, somewhere right at the back, behind the thrusting prominent thoughts which still took in the presence of this trio of neat men, who, on the surface at least, seemed calm and assured, self-possessed, controlled.

But Asher was not going to be allowed to settle down, to take in the landscape and then retreat to prepare his Romeo. Douglas Silver was relaxed and comfortable. He chatted on amiably, then, suddenly, began to insert questions, making Asher Grey turn from that particular point of clothing himself in the character of Romeo to the general terms of his real self, his abilities and his personal attitudes as an actor.

'Why on earth did you ever become an actor, Asher? It's a godforsaken profession. Why choose insecurity at a time when there's so much going on outside the arts?' Silver's question was phrased uneasily: like a question in some set examination paper.

'I suppose I wanted to communicate.' Tentatively, not wanting to go too deep.

Silver laughed. 'But as an actor you're communicating other people's ideas. They're other people's words you have to speak. You have to clothe yourself with other people's personalities, characters.'

'I suppose that part of it is escape.' The actor stretched out his long legs, accepting the inevitable and trying to take the question seriously. 'I had to get away from a pretty horrific home environment. I used to fantasize a lot at home, so it seemed the natural thing to do, to become a professional fantasist: and, no, I don't agree that the actor only communicates other people's ideas. His way of communication is his own way, it belongs to nobody but himself.'

'You see yourself as a star performer?' Silver did not smile.

'I don't like the word *star*.' That was a sentence which Asher Grey had instilled into his consciousness over the past few years. 'We don't look for star actors in the theatre any more, it's a sloppy way of thinking. We only look for great actors.'

'You see yourself as a great actor then?'

'If you mean a technically responsible professional actor then I'm trying to learn to be that, yes. I'm not interested in the phoney stuff.'

'Phoney?' Silver raising an eyebrow.

'Opening fêtes, laying foundation stones, being seen with the right people. I want to be known simply as an actor.'

Douglas Silver made a quizzical gesture with his head. 'And as yet you're not even known as an actor.'

Ronnie Gregor looked up sharply. Douglas was showing a cruel streak.

'Okay,' said Silver. 'What about working in repertory? Have you found that a dulling experience or has it been worth while?'

Asher made a throw-away motion with both hands. 'It's all experience. Nowadays we need all the live experience we can get. Older actors and directors have always told me not to throw away opportunities, but there've been times when I've felt it was a waste.'

'You get anything tangible from it?'

'Oh, of course. Acting's like driving, you don't really begin to learn until you're out there alone on the road with the others. I've learned a lot about technique, and I've forgotten a lot of crap I used to believe about the feel of a part and inspiration.' He paused, realizing that he was about to move into inner thoughts: thoughts he normally did not share with others. 'I've learned that the curtain goes up at eight o'clock and you have to be there and do it right. I think I've learned to listen: to the other people on the stage and to the audience. Occasionally I've touched the power, known how to regulate a performance; I've sometimes felt the wonder of a game of emotional tennis.'

'You think there's a future for the theatre in our age?' asked Silver, backing away from the personal involvement.

'As long as we don't get bogged down in trying to do things we are not equipped to do. Television and the movies are always a threat, just as they're another way of earning a living: but the theatre's got to be different. It can't rely on having to create realism, because audiences get that sort of realism on the box or in the cinema, which is the natural medium of our time. Our job is to convey emotion . . . Truth . . . the great senses, in a different way. . . .' He was wallowing a little and could see that Douglas Silver detected it.

'What about the British classics then?' The director eased the situation. 'What about Shakespeare? Does he have any relevance to the present day?'

'Complete relevance.'

'Why?'

'Well, language for one thing, the poetic beauty, but, most important to me, his characters are set and established living beings. Man doesn't change much, as far as basic emotions and reactions are concerned. The great Shakespearean figures are figures for all time, from whom we can learn, interpret and re-interpret. Then, of course, there are the classic patterns of history. . . .'

'Okay,' Silver held up a hand. 'You just convinced me.'

'Asher?' It was Art Drays, the silent unassuming man, smiling now and speaking quietly. 'How do you stand with directors? What do you think is the function of a director?' It was no accidental, stray question. This one was a sniper for Douglas Silver.

Asher knew that he could not fake it. 'The director is the overall controller of a production,' he began, searching for the right words, the ones that would not offend a man like Douglas Silver, yet would communicate his feelings. 'The director is the eyes and ears of an audience. He can tell me, as an actor, what he hears; what he needs to hear; where I should go, on stage, and what I should do. He can give me a central focal point: how he sees the play and the character I am playing within that conception; but that of the character which is within me is mine, and the director must not meddle with it.' At least, he thought, he had been honest.

Silver leaned forward. A solemn look. 'Ronnie's already told you something of our plans for Shireston?'

'Yes.'

'Is there anything particular you'd like to ask me about those plans?'

'Not at this stage. If I was offered something then naturally . . .'

Another motor-cycle and some catcalls in the street: Capulets and Montagues having a go in the Euston Road.

'Great.' Silver rocked back in his chair. 'Have you got anything you'd like to do for us?'

Now the moment had come, Asher's mind cleared, leaving one item uppermost. The approach had been almost casual, but he knew this was the crunch.

'Ronnie said something about Romeo, so I've prepared the death soliloquy. Is that okay?'

Silver smiled, nodding. It was ideal, the one passage that would tell him what Asher Grey could do; how he could handle the text and make an audience feel, command them to listen to the words, see the poetic images, conjure emotion. The director indicated the centre of the room.

Asher Grey stood alone, mind drained and empty for a few seconds, his back to the trio. When he turned Douglas Silver had some intimation of the strength that the young actor possessed. Asher's face had lost colour, seemed to be thinner, taken on a strained, haggard look, a surfeit of shock.

Silver softly spoke the dying words of Paris which are the cue lines for the soliloquy.

Asher did not see the bare room or the three fixed faces. He looked down at his hands trying to perceive the hands of Romeo, then up and around him, slowly. The setting body of Paris. Drugged Juliet. The blood-soaked Tybalt. Feeling the cold oppression of the tomb, the thoughts of shock and resolution, conveying the feelings as he spoke.

115

Asher Grey's voice, though pitched low at the start, contained the quality which directors long to hear: the timbre, accent, texture which makes a voice theatrically different. It contains the very heart of potential greatness, and one hears it in the voices of Olivier, Gielgud, O'Toole, Scofield, a dozen more. It is something which holds the listener, captures the ear and, at the same time, brings total comprehension.

Douglas sat very still in concentration, noting the technical tricks, appreciating the skill which was here.

'A grave? O, no, a lantern, slaughter'd, youth,
For here lies Juliet, and her beauty makes
This vault a feasting presence full of light.'

The romantic tragedy took on form and meaning. Douglas glanced quickly towards Ronnie who gave a tiny tilt of the head.

'Death, that hath suck'd the honey of thy breath,
Hath had no power yet upon thy beauty:
Thou art not conquer'd, beauty's ensign yet
Is crimson in thy lips and in thy cheeks,
And death's pale flag is not advanced there.'

On the line, *Death that hath suck'd the honey of thy breath*, Asher seemed to single out the word *suck'd* so that it took on the gruesome form of a death rattle, while the sequence about Juliet not yet having her beauty transformed by the ravages of death became a poignant statement, at one and the same time personal to Romeo and the individual members of his small audience.

Asher looked up, staring at a point some three feet in front of the table –

'. . . Ah, dear Juliet,
Why art thou yet so fair? Shall I believe
That unsubstantial Death is amorous,
And that the lean abhorred monster keeps
Thee here in dark to be his paramour?
For fear of that, I still will stay with thee;
And never from this palace of dim night
Depart again: here, here will I remain
With worms that are thy chamber-maids; O, here

Will I set up my everlasting rest;
And shake the yoke of inauspicious stars,
From this world-wearied flesh. Eyes, look your last!
Arms, take your last embrace! and, lips, O you
The doors of breath, seal with a righteous kiss
A dateless bargain to engrossing death! —'

Even with a stage, and the full complement of actors'
bodies, the speech is difficult, for he who plays Romeo treads
the delicate bridge between great emotion and pure ham.
Asher walked it firmly and with confidence, holding the
natural pauses for the exact amount of time, playing down
the gestures and indications with hands and head and eyes.
He knew that he was doing it well, his actor's sense told him
and he could feel it even from the audience of three. As he
went into the last soft moment, in the final five lines, he
caught the look on Douglas Silver's face and knew that he
had won: Silver's look was that of a man who had just struck
gold.

'Come, bitter conduct, come unsavoury guide!
Thou desperate pilot, now at once run on
The dashing rocks they sea-sick weary bark!
Here's to my love!'

A dangerous, half raising of the imagined cup: the hand
curved up level with the shoulders, head tilted down in a
flashing smile, on and off: a gesture of almost Errol Flynn
romanticism.

'. . . O true apothecary!
Thy drugs are quick — Thus with a kiss I die.'

The last words all but whispered, yet whispered in a
manner that would carry them throughout any good
auditorium.

There was a pause and silence. Ronnie Gregor moved as
though to start applauding, but Douglas restrained him with
a careful and quiet gesture of the right hand.

'Good,' said Douglas Silver as though the performance had
been commonplace. 'Anything else?'

Since Douglas's departure from Shireston on the Saturday

117

evening, Tony Holt had thought about little else but the symbol he was supposed to find as a trademark for the festival. His first reaction was one of surprise that nobody had provided such an obvious device before. But, on examining the festival records, which consisted of twelve thick bound volumes of newspaper cuttings, programmes, letters and photographs, he found that nobody had anticipated them. The most obvious choice for a symbol was, naturally, the Longwell family's coat of arms, but Tony thought it too dull to capture the imagination: an *argent* shield with a *sable* Bend Sinister and two *martlets*.

Tony Holt was, professionally, a solitary man. At Shireston he had four chosen female assistants, but he only achieved a reasonable happiness when working alone. It was the secluded search for ideas which intrigued him, and once his imagination was caught he could usually see quickly how a particular idea could be translated into action; the interpretation being, to him, a mere detail, almost a mechanical matter which, as often as not, could be left to others.

He spent the Sunday morning again perusing the festival records to see if anything in them could spark him, but nothing came. Early in the afternoon he decided to take a walk into the town itself. Since his arrival at Shireston House there had been little time for sightseeing, his only trip so far being a quick car ride to the Blue Boar for dinner: the food ordinary enough and the hotel giving off a pedestrian atmosphere.

About a hundred yards down from the main drive of Shireston House, the road dipped into a gentle slope from the top of which you could see the whole town spread out a mile or so below: the long straggle of main street cut in the middle by the market square from which four roads ran away into the country, disintegrating, at their outset, into narrow winding streets. By the shading and colours of the rooftops, and those buildings visible from the rise, it was plain that the centre of the town was its oldest area, the crux from which the community had grown; there the majority of buildings were either grey weathered stone or plaster, gently refurbished and kept in good condition by owners or the local council. The rooftops which sprang away along the main street all bore the solid grey or red tiling of Victorian builders, while the outer periphery of Shireston was already well scarred with the plain new bricks, concrete paths, blue, red, yellow doors, metal window frames, identical living boxes and the segmented uninspired geography of small housing estates.

It was a chill bright afternoon, well lit, but, as he walked towards the town, Tony Holt felt the vague uneasiness of a perpetual city dweller thrust into a rural situation. As he approached the almost empty main street he found himself anticipating a wealth of hostility, feeling that he was walking, unwanted, into a small tight and closely packed society which reserved a barrier against strangers. Perhaps, he thought, this was due to the history of the festival: the townspeople of Shireston had never really given it a wholehearted welcome and, going through the records, he had been struck by one or two occasions when there had been an almost violent hostility between actors and townspeople. He would have to mention that to Douglas, because at one time the town had sponsored a Shireston Festival Society which acted as a go-between and a repository for information: maybe the society was not quite dead, or at least it could be within the bounds of resuscitation.

Along the main street, Palmer Street it was called, so presumably pilgrims had walked that way at one time, there was only the occasional piece of interesting architecture: a chemist's shop with original bow windows, a couple of carved oak front doors, a beautifully preserved and renovated ornamental clock, picked out in shining gold above *George Harvey and Sons Jewellers and Watchmakers* who, with the inevitable rumble of progress, now displayed only cheap and mass produced watches in their window. For the rest, only a thin film, new and vulgar, spread across the fronts of middle-aged buildings: the cheap transparency of little supermarkets with tinned goods, refrigerated meals and packets of coloured lavatory paper glared, whorish objects dressed gaily to catch the shining new pence. *Maynard's Mod*

119

Shop, outdated name with outdated clothing, staving off the advance of progress in pastel shades. Radios. Televisions. Gardening supplies. One bookshop with the window dressed full of romantic fiction, the feeding drug of the dull housewife. *Shireston Gazette: Founded 1892*.

The area around the market square was a different matter, with buildings dating from a whole range of periods, all certainly before the time of Victoria. The brashness of a new age had not been allowed to pollute here, even so the dead hand of a country Sunday flopped over the scene: a pair of arm-locked lovers, he in best blue and she in Sunday coat, shoes and hat, marched in step across the square, not pausing to glance at the seventeenth century gable ends of buildings, the targets of Tony Holt's eye, while a policeman bent the knee in watchfulness at the corner.

Tony was undecided about the direction he should explore, his tic of intuition telling him that somewhere here there was a find waiting for him.

The silence of the square was broken by the noise of children who came bubbling in a small flock, school caps, boots, yellow and pink flowered dresses, bully boys and prim little girls, from a narrow side street to the right of where he stood: hands clutched at Sunday School stamp books, telling the year from Advent to the horror of Golgotha.

To Tony this was a clue and he set off in the direction from which the children had come: narrow pavements, barely room for one person to walk, the little street flanked by cottages which Tony could swear were original Elizabethan. He walked the fifty or so yards up the street to where it bent sharply to the left, turned the corner and suddenly came up against the church.

It stood within its own small square of green graveyard, well filled, a squat building, dark-grey stone, its outline full of the heavy Norman style but with a more slender tower than usual, making the total picture one of imbalance. The churchyard itself was surrounded by a low brick wall in which a dark wooden lych-gate was set, certainly much later additions.

Tony pushed open the gate and walked the neatly weeded gravel path to the West door. The door had been much repaired, creaking to let him into the atmosphere of old age, the scent of damp and successive flowers; death. For a second, Tony remembered the tiny Norman church he had discovered in Kent where some lack-humoured cleric had inscribed the altar with the text *He is not here*.

The interior of Shireston church was small, but made to seem smaller by the large archway, six concentric half circles upon small pillars, the circles ornamented and the whole arch standing between the main body of the church and the chancel. From a position just inside the door one could see up through the arch into the darkened chancel to the altar and what Tony took to be a constantly restored East window depicting the Ascension, Christ in a loincloth being levitated on a sturdy cloud to the wonder of apostles whose hands were raised as though threatened at gun point. But his attention was quickly drawn away from the deep colours of the window and fastened outside the chancel, to the font which stood before the pillars to the right of the arch.

The font, he thought, as he approached it, was probably the most unique item in the church, as it had been fashioned from a large upturned bell, its headstock sunk into a thick square of stone and the marble piscina of the font itself fitted neatly into the rim of the sound-bow. The bell stood some four and a half feet high, the metal boisterously ornamented with leaves and branches, while around the outside of the sound-bow the inscription 1564 *Elizabeth Regina* 1564 was repeated several times.

A strengthening band of brass was clamped round the bell's waist, and, on examination, Tony saw the reason: almost directly opposite each other, along the rim of the sound-bow, were two jagged V-shaped tears where the metal had been broken away. From the breaks, hairline cracks traced down either side of the bell. The whole line of the bell, its shape, the decoration, the cracks, the unusual use to which it had been put, made an instant appeal to Tony Holt who examined it for several minutes before he caught sight of a large glass picture frame leaning against the pillars. The frame contained photographs and drawings of the bell, together with two pages of neatly typed folio which told its ironic story.

In the year 1563 the Lord Bishop of Winchester received, from Queen Elizabeth I, a gift of *church plate, silk, and other materials including monies and precious metals, both of silver and gold, to be used in the restocking and refurbishing of churches within his jurisdiction.*

Certain churches in the diocese were then asked to state their most immediate needs and requirements. The Parish Church of SS Peter and Paul, Shireston, was single minded in its request. The church tower contained a small bell chamber but, for some obcure reason, the tower had *for all living memory lacked a bell.*

The request was finally granted and, after much going back and forth between the parish and the Bishop's palace, it was decided that the bell would be cast in the churchyard at Shireston.

The narrow steps leading up to the bell tower being too difficult to negotiate, it was also decreed that the bell would be winched up to the top of the tower from the outside, and from there lowered into the chamber.

The whole business became an excuse for several days of planned feasting and revels in which the entire town would play a part and the date was set for early June in the following year: the bell to be cast on a Friday, consecrated by the Lord Bishop himself on the Sunday and winched into position on the Monday morning.

All began well enough in fine warm weather, with Shireston the focal point of the local countryside. The bell was cast and marvelled at for its beauty and good tone. There followed, however, a certain amount of drunkenness and lewd behaviour on the Saturday night, a fact commented upon by the good Bishop in his consecration sermon: he had rather been in the thick of it for he stayed the night at the local inn, which stood, so the typescript maintained, *where the Blue Boar stands today.* The Bishop departed on the Sunday even-

122

ing, after consecrating the bell, leaving the townspeople, workmen and their guests to lapse once more into their behaviour of the previous night – a reason held by many for the tragic events that were to follow.

On the Monday morning a large crowd gathered in the churchyard to see the bell hauled up the tower. The winching tackle had been secured to the top of the tower on the Saturday and work began at around nine in the morning. But, after three hours the bell was only half-way to the top, some suggesting the cause of the inefficiency was the sluggardly state in which the workmen found themselves following the previous two nights of revels.

By late afternoon the crowd had become restless, a large number drifting away to find more satisfying pleasures. However, just after five o'clock, the bell reached the top of the tower amidst *great cheers of jubilation from the populace*. The cheers were turned to shrieks of horror seconds later when the tackle broke and the bell came plummeting down, striking the side of the tower and bounding outwards, *with much clamour and force*, into the crowd. The impact of the bell killed no less than three adults and one child, Jane Bloodwell aged seven years; her mother Alice Bloodwell; Thomas Dumfries, a farm labourer and William Berry, an apprentice tailor.

Indeed, the unlucky bell must have scythed its way through the crowd with considerable force for *there were many wounded in its journey, Master Bride, the local surgeon, reporting that he attended to four broken arms, three broken legs and a multitude of gashes and bruises, some of serious matter*.

For over three hundred years the bell stood inside the church door to remind the townspeople of the disaster, until 1892 when an ingenious vicar, the Reverend Mr Whitelaw, decided that it would be more proper to put the bell to good use, *the font being damaged beyond repair*; and it was this reverend gentleman who brought craftsmen to the church in order to *convert the bell to its present use*. So the bell, a gift of the queen, cast to call the faithful to prayer, became *an instrument of death and then one of rebirth as the means to baptism.*

Below the typescript was a drawing dated 1565, ringed with an uneasy circle and showing the bell in minute detail, tilted sideways to display the fragmentation and cracks. *The drawing*, said a note below, *was intended to be converted into a mould for a Parish Seal, but the work was, to our knowledge, never carried out.*

Tony Holt looked from the drawing to the upturned bell. Unless some obstacle prevented it, the drawing could become the symbol for the Shireston Festival. The story of the cracked bell of Shireston contained so many elements of life and death that it was a fitting enough sign for drama itself. His hand brushed against the metal of the bell and he made his way anxiously from the little church in search of the vicarage.

Asher Grey did the balcony scene, after which Douglas Silver asked him to read Lorenzo's *In such a night* with Ronnie Gregor reading for Jessica.

When he finished, there was a long silence in the room. Asher felt the onset of nerves: the bodily quiver and droop; he had given his best, particularly in Romeo's death soliloquy, and he should have had Silver eating out of his hand, at one point he was certain he had; but the man was like a brick wall. The edges of Asher's earlier depression once more began to ease forward into his consciousness.

Douglas Silver stared down at the floor: at the oilcloth. This boy, Grey, was impressively good; he could not remember when he had heard the death soliloquy done so well, even taking into account the fact that Grey was doing it as a set piece and not as the culmination of two and a half hours concentrated performance. Douglas knew he could do things with Asher Grey: he could lead him, mould him even, but a warning in the back of his mind told him to beware. Asher Grey had a supreme talent, the kind of talent that could be ruthless and turn easily on the hand that fed it. In plain thinking, Asher Grey's talent might turn out to be more bother than it was worth. Yet he could not afford to let it slip

124

away. Douglas Silver decided to ignore the omen in his brain.

'Do you think you could leave Asher alone with me for,' Douglas glanced at his watch, speaking to Ronnie and Art, 'for ten, fifteen minutes?'

They nodded, smiled at Asher and wandered from the room. Douglas offered Asher a chair which he took, sitting down politely; upright; tense; feeling the pressure building at the back of his neck, certain that Douglas could sense it.

Douglas lit a cigarette, offering one to the actor before he began to speak.

'You're very good,' he said at last. 'Did you know that? You have a very special sense of theatre; you know how to handle your body, your face, your eyes; you have a good voice – no, you've got a distinctive acting voice and you know how to use it. Did you know all that?'

Asher had the feeling that it might be a trap. 'I know I'm not a bad actor.'

Douglas gave a tiny smile, quick as a snake's tongue. 'No, you're not a bad actor,' he paused, pursing his lips. 'But you *could* become a bad actor. Any actor at your stage of development can become bad, totally worthless. You're already slipping into tricks. Another year in a rotten environment, the kind where you would be the best actor in a mediocre bunch, and the tricks would be the only thing left; you'd rely on them; you'd start taking short cuts: walking it on your own good looks and your presence. . . . I don't have to tell you.'

Asher did not speak.

'Asher, do you think you could work with me?' Douglas spoke in earnest now. 'I mean really work with me? Trust me? Go through a little hell? The purifying fires?'

'What do you mean exactly?'

'Ronnie's already told you that we're trying to pull Shireston up by its boot straps. A lot of people are going to have the knives out. They're going to scoff, sneer, snarl, call me a gimmick man, a sensationalist, a spoofer. But the proof will be in whatever success we make of it.' He quickly outlined his plans, telling Asher more about Joe Thomas, Jen,

Catellier, Maurice Kapstein, Carol Evans and the general order of things. 'It's going to be a hard year, hard as a diamond, and as brilliant as a diamond. As well as four major productions to direct I have massive executive and administration problems: the organization has been allowed to run down, the whole place has gone to seed. So I've got all that on top of four productions and a large company; a lot of talent to look after. What I'm trying to say to you is that there's going to be no time for temperaments. Asher, I'm going to offer you the biggest chance you've ever had: if you louse it up not only do you damage your own career but a lot of other people's. So if you've got any qualms for God's sake say so now.' Five seconds slipped by. 'I'm going to offer you the role of Romeo in what will be the most publicized production of *Romeo and Juliet* since the Zeffirelli movie.'

Asher Grey opened his mouth to speak but Douglas went on. 'I am also going to ask you to play Lorenzo in *The Merchant of Venice* and Cassio in Joe Thomas's *Othello*. Do you need time to think about it?'

'I'll . . . I'll have to talk to my agent.'

'When can you do that?'

'I can call her in the morning.'

'No fancy prices, Asher. You're young and unknown. We both take risks. Who is your agent?'

'Veronica Turnbull.'

'Well, if you want to do it, tell her the contracts are all Equity and no messing around. You get board and lodging for the entire season, beginning the first week in January. Normal rates, half salary during rehearsals. *The Merchant* and *Othello* go in during the first week in April. *Richard III* and *RJ* during the first week in May. But we start work as a company in January.'

'I'll talk with her first thing tomorrow. There won't be any difficulty.'

'Then I take it that you agree in principle?'

'Of course I do, Mr Silver, I'd give —'

'Your eye teeth, I know. Just give me a first-class Romeo. I'll expect Veronica Turnbull to call me tomorrow then?'

'Yes, I'll tell her.'

They both turned as the door opened: Ronnie Gregor had returned, raising his eyebrows in query. 'Okay, Douglas?'

'Okay, Ronnie, come on in.' The director was suddenly in an expansive mood.

'Art's gone back to the office. He didn't think you'd need him again.'

'Right. Meet our prospective Romeo.'

'Splendid.' Ronnie grinned at Asher. 'I'm very glad.'

Asher's train did not leave until eight so Douglas asked if he would care to eat somewhere with Ronnie as he had to go on to another meeting.

Asher still could not find the right words, he grinned, mumbling his thanks, and Douglas left feeling very happy and pleased with himself.

Douglas Silver got outside and began to walk, looking for a cab, when suddenly there was the unexpected leap in his loins: the spring of sensuality. Asher Grey's sample Romeo had been good but it should not have this effect, he smiled to himself, especially when he was so jammed full of work and problems. Then he realized the complete aim of the desire and the victim of the urge. The Romeo had brought Douglas back to Juliet.

He found a telephone booth and dialled Carol Evans's number. It rang four times and then she answered.

'At last,' Douglas put warmth in it, a shade mocking.

'Who's that? Douglas?'

'Who else? I've been calling you for the last couple of days.'

'I've literally only just walked in. I've been away, filming. On location for TV.'

'Very grand. Where?'

'Would you believe Brighton beach? It was supposed to be the Persian gulf. In this heat.' She chuckled.

He laughed. 'I've got your Romeo.'

'The one you told me about?'

'The same.'

'Lemme see.'

'No. Not yet, but I'll come and tell you about him.' There was a specific tone in his voice.

A long silence.

'My place?' asked Carol, throaty.

'Yes.'

'I don't know, Douglas. I thought you were off coming to my place.'

'I've missed you. Even three days.'

'Isn't it just a case of "What's she got that I haven't? Nothing, but she's got it here"?'

'It may well be. But. . . .'

'I've missed you, too, Douglas. You coming now?'

'Straight away.'

She opened the door wearing a woollen dress, bright orange with a high neck line; patent lace-up boots ending just below the knee, and she came into his arms as he stepped over the threshold. Douglas locked her close, and within seconds, as the sliding tongues met, her breathing changed to the quick nasal pant.

Douglas scrabbled for the zip at the back of her dress and tugged right down below the waist. It slipped from her shoulders and she stepped free: the glistening coffee-coloured body with a texture that seemed as deep as some dark sea, smooth and welcoming.

She went to the bed and fumbled, unlacing the boots as he undressed, her fingers wrenching at the laces. In the end she heaved each boot in turn from her feet and threw them from her, rising for him to help her with the tiny white cotton pants and her tights. She wore no bra and his desire was raging: a fester of coloured pictures in his head which all spoke of his need and the wish to bury himself in her.

When they were both naked, Carol turned from him and dropped face downwards on the bed, turning her face from him as she opened her legs.

'Like this,' she whispered.

He climbed on top of her back, the tight hard buttocks

moulding into his stomach; her hand feeling for him, pulling him; their legs and bodies adjusting for her to take him into her. This way she was tight and clutching as a virgin; his hands on the breasts, nipples hard as pebbles; the pleasure frantic and all consuming.

'In some countries they'd put you in jail for that,' she said as they lay together, on their backs, naked and holding hands, the glow subsiding.

'No, it's the thing with the mouths they . . .' Douglas began and then realized she was talking about race and colour. 'South Africa's a long way off, baby.'

'Is it? I don't know. Douglas. What are we going to do?'

'We're going to give them the most spectacular *Rome and Juliet* of all time.'

'Not that. You know I didn't mean that, and I know I started it, out in Malta when I said if two people wanted to and needed it they should go ahead: but things have changed for me.'

Douglas propped himself on to one elbow and looked down at her.

'Tell me.'

'Well, that's how I've always felt about sex. I'm not promiscuous, Doug, I promise you, but I've always thought that if the right guy comes along and you fancy him, and the opportunity's there, then you should go ahead. What do they say? Lie back and enjoy it?' She closed her eyes, turning her head away, voice dropping to a whisper. 'Then you should go on your way rejoicing. That's how I thought it would be with you; but the other night, when you came over and I saw you again, I just wanted you so much. I've never felt that big physical thing before. I was soaking wet for you, Douglas. Then you came in and it was like I had nothing between my legs. You'd had your wife in LA and that was like slapping me in the face.'

'But Carol, love, I thought –'

She put up her hand to check him. 'I know what you thought, and you're quite right. I've no hold on you. I'm not going back on my word either: not asking for favours. But

129

I'm in trouble, Douglas, because I've got to come down to Shireston and work under you, and I know that half the time I'll want to be screwing under you. You. Your wife'll be there, you'll be harassed half to death.' She turned back to him, almost violently. 'What I'm trying to say, Douglas, is that I don't know if I can give you even a good Juliet, because I'm totally involved with you in the most basic way a woman can be. I don't know if I can do it.'

She did not sound, or look, hysterical, but Douglas felt the fear strike in his guts. As a professional his reputation was at stake with the festival. Things were too advanced to make major side steps and alterations. His own sexual irresponsibility had brought him into this situation and he felt abnormally guilty. There was, indeed, abnormality here, because usually when he became involved in work he did not either need, or desire, sex. No purpose would be served by making light of Carol's physical and emotional feelings, but, on the other hand, he did not want to upset her any further by lecturing on professionalism.

'I'm sorry,' was all he said. 'Easy words, baby, I know.'

'They're bloody easy. Like saying I love you. They should ban those two phrases – I love you and I'm sorry.' She continued to talk, but Douglas only heard her with part of his consciousness: Asher Grey's potential Romeo, which had temporarily slipped to the back of his mind, now came clawing through and he saw, on the screen of his perception, this beautiful black girl and the gutsy Asher Grey melting stone with the romantic lasers of Shakespeare's tragedy.

Asher Grey did not mention Julia until it was almost too late. Ronnie Gregor had been friendly and very complimentary, urging Asher to talk about himself and his work, at the same time, filling in pieces of information about Douglas's plans for Shireston. They had a light meal together and Ronnie came back to Euston, queued up with Asher, and went down on to the platform to see him off.

There were only five minutes left before departure when Ronnie said casually, 'I almost forgot, Asher, we'll need to

130

know what kind of accommodation you'll be wanting. A single bedsitter or . . .?'

All right. Leave me. Leave me, you sodding lousy actor. Leave me. . . . Leave me. . . . There in the middle of the leave taking, crammed platform, the rush to catch a train north, the clatter and the tired lovers, strained after a week-end and each wanting the other to be gone, the porters, aggressive travellers, the worried, sad and happy, Julia's voice plunged through Asher Grey's head, a crimson streak of discord, the sound of cacophony from which he knew he would never be free.

'Well there is this girl . . .' he began.

Ronnie's face registered the memory.

'This actress,' Asher fumbled, 'you might remember. Julia Philips. . . . We live together. . . . Is there any chance of . . .?' He did not even like to frame the question.

'Any chance of what, Asher?' Ronnie remembered Julia Philips and her dull Phebe in *As You Like It*. 'We can probably let you have one of the small double flats we've got at the house if that'll keep you happy and contented.'

Asher clenched his teeth. 'There wouldn't be anything going for her? For Julia? In the company I mean.'

Ronnie frowned, thinking for a few seconds. 'We still have to fit in some supers. It would only be a walk-on. I've got to be honest with you, Asher, I couldn't recommend her for anything else.'

Asher nodded tightly. 'I know. I couldn't recommend her for anything else either, but if she doesn't come down, and if she's not working, I can't promise that I'm going to be left in peace.' He looked up. 'Could you really fix that for me?'

'Yes, I think I can do that. But she'll have to behave and I think you should talk to Douglas about your personal situation before we start work.'

The journey back to Manchester seemed to take twice as long as the trip down, and, while Ronnie's offer helped to quieten his fears, Asher still sensed a pre-battle dread, not knowing to what he would return, aware that, even if he had gone back with some plum role for her, nothing would be

131

truly right or satisfactory for Julia.

The train was half an hour late into Manchester and it was almost midnight by the time he reached the bedsitting-room. It was in darkness and he left the door slightly ajar so that a crack of light would partially illuminate the room yet not disturb Julia. But when he reached the bed, Asher realized that Julia was not in it. He whirled in a moment of fear and apprehension, a flash in the mind that Julia might have boiled into real violence and was about to strike. But there was nothing except shadows and the wedge of light shafting in through the door.

Asher went over and switched on the main overhead light. The room was tidy, only the wardrobe doors swung open on their hinges showing him that Julia's coats and dresses were gone. She had left only one trace: scrawled in crimson lipstick across the dressing table mirror two words: FUCK YOU.

By Monday morning Douglas Silver had made up his mind about Carol and the immediate steps he should take. On the previous evening she had pulled his mind back on to her problem and he was forced to talk gently to her, asking if she did not think he could get a better Juliet from her because of their more intimate knowledge of each other.

'I would have thought it might have been better if I felt this way about the young man you've got to play Romeo,' she retorted. 'Anyway, you can start really worrying when *Othello* goes into rehearsal. What's the tradition? All great Othellos sleep with their Desdemonas. What chance your beloved Jennifer, Doug?'

He bypassed that particular drop of venom and their conversation continued. In the end, Carol seemed more quiet and able to accept the situation, but desire again warmed, boiled and flooded. Douglas tried to resist, but he was no match for his own sensuality and they made love again: a hard, throbbing contest taking them up to the mutual peak of satisfaction where all problems were dissolved for a few leaping moments.

'There's only one thing, Douglas,' Carol said as he was

leaving. 'Keep Jennifer as far away from me as you can. Please, love and I'm sorry this had to happen.'

After a night's sleep, Douglas decided that the obvious and only course was the simple remedy. Keep Carol working as hard as possible once she got down to Shireston.

As soon as he arrived in the office, Douglas went over to the casting chart which covered almost one entire wall and showed at a glance who was already signed and to what roles; which roles were still available, and the names of possible actors and actresses free to join the festival company.

'Who's Julia Philips?' he asked Ronnie Gregor after looking at the chart for a few seconds.

'Court lady, servant, attendant, citizen. She's Asher Grey's bird. Plenty of experience: I thought you'd want to keep him happy, she's playing middle roles at Stanthorpe with him. Okay?'

There was something about Ronnie's manner which disturbed Douglas: just a feeling, nothing concrete, only those tiny emanations which carry coded messages and symbols. There was an unease coming from Ronnie, as though his action regarding Julia Philips was wrong and he knew it; but Douglas left the matter and returned to the board.

He looked for several minutes before tracing out exactly what he wanted; then he turned back to Ronnie and asked him to telephone Carol Evans's agent to see if she would countenance playing Nerissa in *The Merchant* as well as Juliet.

'Tell her it's a personal request from me,' he said, 'I'll call Carol tonight to talk about it.'

Veronica Turnbull, Asher Grey's agent, came through during the morning and Ronnie Gregor quickly went over the details of the proposed contract with her. Naturally, she said that she needed twenty-four hours to think about it and talk with Asher, but she was a sensible woman, not pushy, knowing what was best for her client: there would be little argument from her.

Around noon Tony Holt called Douglas with his story

133

about the Shireston bell and the news that he had spoken to the vicar and the diocesan authorities and there seemed to be no problem about the festival taking a copy of the original drawing and using it as a symbol. Douglas told him that he could not obviously commit them before he had seen a copy, and also he would have to discuss the matter with Adrian Rolfe. He did not dare leave Adrian out of a matter like this.

'You'll get copies in the morning,' chuckled Tony, 'I've already had it photostated.'

Douglas had to meet Maurice Kapstein for lunch, predictably at Rosenberg's, the only place Kapstein ever lunched when he was in London: Soho's famous Jewish restaurant where celebrities had chairs named in their honour – names emblazoned on the high backs.

Maurice Kapstein certainly had his own chair: Maurice Kapstein was undoubtedly a celebrity. For nearly fifty years Kapstein had been in show-business, originally as a stand-up comedian, exploiting Jewish humour in the London music halls long before it became fashionable in the United States (for years, Maurice Kapstein's catch-phrase was, 'Don't trust anyone: not even your own father, yet.') He worked in radio and, for at least twenty years, played small solid supporting roles in British films, ranging from low comedy to high drama. In this way the public was ready to accept his face as a known commodity when he starred, as a wily prize fight promoter, in the pilot of a proposed television series titled *The Game Game*. The series took hold, and Solly Jacobs, the character played by Kapstein, became a household name, the scripts containing all the aspects that are supposed to appeal to the regular television fanatic: sport, crime, violence, a tincture of sex, big business, politics and a spray of humour. Kapstein's success was total.

When Douglas arrived at the restaurant, Kapstein was already installed at a centre table, the sole attention of two waiters and the proprietor. Seated, one would take him for a short man, for Kapstein's height was in his legs: in fact he was a strangely proportioned man: long legs, the short, stout body and a magnificent huge head with features which looked as though they had been moulded quickly with rough hands from clay, great dark eyes overhung with bushy brows, a large aquiline nose and sensuous lips, the whole topped with a mane of white hair. The impression was one of immense appetite and strength.

'Douglas Silver.' He called loudly. 'I'm over here, come and join me.' The voice had strong melody touched with a carefully fostered accent. Douglas smiled and went over to the table. Everything Kapstein did seemed to be orchestrated with extravagance. The actor rose and held out his arms in a wide gesture. 'At last we are to work together. My boy, I can't tell you how long it is that I have wanted to work with Douglas Silver. It's a happy day, huh?'

Douglas nodded, knowing that he would not get much of a chance to talk until Kapstein had winded himself. He extended his hand which was immediately taken in both of Kapstein's paws, held with an unexpected gentleness.

'Nice to see you, Morrie,' murmured Douglas, extricating himself from Kapstein's grasp and taking his seat.

'Good, huh?' beamed Kapstein. 'The menu you don't need, I've already ordered. I arrange it all, yet: the herrings in sour cream with apple, okay? Then a little salt beef with a stuffed chicken neck, potato latke? Sauerkraut? That is good?'

Douglas nodded like a buddha, knowing that it would be churlish to snub Kapstein's hospitality. 'Good, but rich, Morrie. Very rich.'

Kapstein nodded and leaned back. 'Now you want to talk to me, huh?'

'It'll keep.'

'No, we can eat and talk. No problem. What you want to know? You want me to tell you about the Shylock I'm going to give you? That will be a performance, Douglas, ah-ah.' A loud guffaw before going into an absurdly overdrawn characterization. '*Ships are but boards, sailors but men. There be land-rats, land-thieves – I mean pirates. . . .*' He pronounced it pie-rats and bellowed with laughter again. '*Three thousand ducats . . . for three months . . . Antonio shall become bound.*

135

. . . How about that, Douglas? You like me to talk about Shylock?'

'I think it'll wait until we start rehearsals, Morrie. I only thought it right we should meet.' He shrugged. 'So that I could make sure you're happy about the season and the company. To make certain that you're going to be there.'

The herrings arrived, Kapstein grinning between mouthfuls. 'Happy? You ask if I am happy? Now your Ronnie Gregor, a smooth one, huh? That one'd have a Christian nun's knickers off before she'd know it. A smart boy you got there, Douglas. Too damned smart. Had me signed, sealed and stamped before I could make any terms in my own favour.'

'Your agent said you were happy.' A twinge of alarm in the back of Douglas's mind which must have shown on his face for Maurice Kapstein laughed loudly once more.

'Don't take me so seriously, Douglas. All the time I'm getting people around me who take me seriously. Television? On the set they take me seriously: I pretend to go into great rages, this is not right; that's not right; the make-up is bad; the lighting's wrong; the script is terrible. They all believe me and do everything I ask. People are strange, I think they must be a little frightened of me.'

'I'm not frightened of you, Maurice.' Douglas said it with gravity.

'Ahh,' as though it revealed much. 'There is one thing though, Douglas.'

'Yes.' Wary.

'At your Shireston Festival will there be room for my concubines?'

'Your what?'

'Don't tell me Ronnie didn't say anything? This is one of my conditions, Douglas. If I come to act for you, out there in the country, away from civilization, from all the niceties of life, then I need at least twenty concubines. Young, good ones, I don't mind if they're not all kosher, shiksas I don't mind. Heey. . . .' he grumbled a long laugh, rising from the stomach. 'Don't worry, Douglas, I'll provide my own con-

136

cubines from whatever materials you've got down there. They all come flocking to Morrie. Boy, you're looking at one of the great yentzers. You know what a yentzer is?'

'A sexual performer I guess.'

'You guess right. That's me, Douglas. At my age. Sixty-five and still going strong: I am a great consolation to the middle-aged, because it is the young ones who come to me. The beautiful young ones, ripe as peaches, they come and enjoy or I spank their little tochas then they enjoy and go away happy. They say, "I have been with a man of sixty-five years and he's more powerful than any young man; he is like a bull." Bless their little hearts. That's how I stay young, Douglas. Like a bull.'

Like an old ram, thought Douglas: like everybody else in the profession he had heard stories about Kapstein and knew the man's reputation as a lecher, but he had never heard the actor boast about it.

Douglas suddenly felt swamped by other people's problems. Why, in this particular profession, did they all become screwed up? He had once heard a psychiatrist say that you could not tell which were the worst, the so-called aristocracy or creative people. They gave so much yet they were like children and their private lives were a morass of difficulties. If it wasn't women then it was men or boys, or pills, or drink, or, with women, women. Douglas knew also that he was within the reach of temptation. So much wasted time, worrying, fighting, mistrusting, hating, screwing, searching, guilt. Escaping? Yes, creative people lived for escape. Actors, directors and writers never escaped in their work, even in their fictions, because, strangely, their work brought them too close to reality and the pain of life. For an actor to really get inside a character was to bring himself hard up against life. One needed another form of escape; another tunnel: into the glass, the vagina, the rectum, the mouth, the ear, the armpits, the breasts, the hand, or the bottle-top leading to the capsules.

Douglas swung round towards the actor, face set in uncompromising severity. 'Morrie, I'm the director of the

Shireston Festival. By rights I should be able to say, "Treat me like a father. Bring all your troubles to me." But it isn't like that any more. I'm a young director and in many ways that's tough on you older and more experienced people. My job is to form a company: a group of actors and actresses who are so welded together that they work as a unit for the whole season. I understand that the leading actors in that group are more talented, and more experienced than anyone else, but I'm in no position to pander to prima donnas. Prima donnas are yesterday.'

'Prima donnas: prima schmonnas,' smiled Kapstein, unbelievably glib.

'No, I'm serious, Maurice.' Douglas held up a hand. 'Things have changed. You will get the respect your position grants you, but you must be willing to work as a member of the ensemble. I can't build that team if any one person is going to bug the works with temperamental or private demands.'

'Douglas.' Maurice Kapstein spread his fingers, the palm so his hands downwards, his face taking on a half smile, a hurt look. 'Douglas, you don't think I'm going to be difficult? I understand your problems. Any trouble, you just come to me. Okay? I know what a weight this must be. Forget it, Morrie Kapstein won't let you down.' He gave a great tensing movement, hunching his shoulders, then relaxing with the big smile which turned his lips up sharply at the corners. 'Now we talk about my Shylock, huh?'

'No, I think we talk about your Shylock when we've got the whole company together.'

Douglas felt more than usually depressed returning to the office: a depression spawned by the clash of personalities and the ensuing chaos that could result. Back in the office there was a message from Carol asking him to call her. As an act of defiant cowardice he postponed the call until the privacy of evening, telling Ronnie that he was out if she rang the office.

Eventually he got through to her around seven-thirty.

'Douglas, what're you playing at?' Her voice faintly

aggressive.

'What do you mean, playing at? I don't play at anything, love.'

'Nerissa, that's what I mean. I get these odd messages from my agent. Mr Silver would take it as a personal favour if you would play Nerissa as well as Juliet.'

'Didn't you get a message that I'd call you tonight?'

Silence. Clicks on the line, the constant backdrop of Telecom sound effects.

'Yes,' said Carol, 'yes, I got that message.'

'Then trust me. I've called you.'

'And?'

'And I'd like you to play Nerissa as well as Juliet. A lot of people are going to double up. Joe Thomas is going to play your papa in *Romeo*, Jennifer's doing Lady Anne in *Richard III* as well as Desdemona. Many others. I thought you'd be pleased.'

Again silence. Then –

'Come over and talk about it, Douglas. Please.'

'I don't really think. . . .'

'I know what you think, and I know it isn't wise, darling, but I need . . . I want . . . Christ, Douglas please come over.'

Jen's voice whispering in his head, *Doug sweetheart, it's mine isn't it? Only mine? nobody else. Please nobody else.* That was, oddly, a thing of desperate importance to her. Even Jen, with her liberated mind and large intellect, needed his sexuality to be hers alone. She would tenderly place a hand on him and whisper, *It's like owning some secret precious object, darling. Just knowing that nobody else can look, touch or have its pleasure helps keep away the evil spirits.*

Jen was far away and this could not possibly hurt her. This was different, it was a question of the coming season and the foundation of the company. Jen need never know: need have no fears. He slid a curtain of darkness around the figure of Jen within him.

'I'll be around as soon as I can get a cab.'

He did not even hear Carol Evans's harshly breathed 'Thank you'.

They did not hesitate: going to her bed within seconds of his arrival, Carol's body far more awake and aware than his, yet her skill swiftly goaded his passion and ability so that their sweating pleasure returned again and again: white on black, black on white, her body wet with him and his with her, drooping then erect, her nipples changing to his touch, her mouth around him encompassing his being, and his tongue within her belly: then, side by side, lips locked, bodies fastened close, mounting to a culmination again . . . to saturation point.

The light was still on and she was asleep, the need appeased, the sleep deep and rhythmic as their acts. Douglas saw the room in flashes as he moved his eyes: the paper-backed books on the shelf: *Stalin. Mao Tse-Tung. Going to the River. The Pillow Fight. Mountolive. The City Boy.* Others whose titles he could not read at this distance, squashed as he was in the narrow clean-sheeted bed. The lampshade, white, now cream where the nicotine of broken nights had changed its colour, the stand itself a single ionic column; near the base an ashtray, a heavy piece of stone with a smooth bowl, a filter of ash and a pile of ugly ends. He could see their last pair, smoked before the night's final bout and, like a harsh sudden jagged cut, he remembered a blue ashtray and a pair of cigarette ends. In Paris? Rome? London? It did not matter because they belonged to Jen and himself, not long ago when the night had been as seething and splendidly wild as this, if not more so (he could not make comparisons: the man was wrong who said it was the same thing with different bodies). Guilt, as painful as fire, terrifying as a near miss, flooded home and he wanted to leave the sleeping girl. A sentimental lyric, half-heard, swung through his mind:

And I looked at you a long time
Before I left,
Thinking how beautiful you sleep
And so I wouldn't waken you I dressed in the darkness,
And covered you against the morning cold.

Soon Jennifer would be back and, however he tried to convince himself, the folly with Carol would be out in the open desert: a matter of choice.

Julia Philips was not on call during the Monday, but she was there for the evening performance. In fact Asher did not see her until she was on stage, an incident which threw him slightly so that he fluffed a line. But she was there, waiting in the passage near the men's dressing-room, when he came out after the performance.

She looked terrible, as though she had gone without sleep for days, which was ridiculous because only one night had intervened; her complexion had taken on a dirty grey look and the eyes were ringed, violently red. Asher tried to read some meaning behind them but they were dead, the dead eyes of a fish. She spoke almost in a whisper as he approached.

'Can I come home?'

The question most longed for and most dreaded. For a day he had languished in that terrible limbo of needing her yet hoping, in the small background of his consciousness, that she was gone for good. Now those withdrawal symptoms had to be exorcized.

'Of course you can.' Hesitation. 'If that's what you really want.'

She nodded, a dumb shake like a nervous affliction.

Asher took her arm and led her out of the stage door.

Back at the Chamber of Horrors they did not talk, Julia going through the automatic actions, putting on the kettle for coffee, getting something to eat, opening a tin of meat which looked like a solid wodge of pink blotting paper. They sat opposite one another: coffee, luncheon meat and sauce, bread and butter, half a tomato each.

'Would you like me to tell you what happened?' Asher asked at last.

The nodding again, it seemed to have taken over from real communication and he felt the first risings of irritation, nevertheless he went on to tell her about the audition and the following talk with Douglas Silver, spinning it out and saving the final glory so that it was blurted in an unexpected spurt.

141

She nodded again.

'Can't you say anything? You haven't spoken.'

'No. I knew you'd get it. I knew. You're bloody good, Ash.' A long sigh, self-pity, or at least that was how it sounded. 'And me?'

Asher chose the words carefully, putting the accent on the fact that they would have good living accommodation rather than the grimmer news that Julia would only be walking on.

'Anyone who's in this season will be at an advantage in the future, no matter how little they have to do. I promise you, love.'

Yet again the nodding, followed by a quivering lip and the whole relished dissolve. 'Asher, you're so good to me and I've been such a cow. You should beat me.'

'I did, yesterday, or have you forgotten?'

Between the sobs. 'No. You should take your belt to me like my father used to. Hold me, Asher, hold me close . . .'

He knew that he had returned to the old treadmill, that he was being used as an emotional sump and that, in spite of it, he wanted her.

During the following weeks, Douglas Silver virtually moved his office down to Shireston. The development of the season began to take a more definite shape and the transfer to the theatre, and Shireston House, had the value of removing Douglas physically from Carol Evans's immediate orbit; though there were the constant business trips to London which led, inevitably, to telephone calls, meetings and bodily satisfaction, always at her apartment.

In the offices at Shireston House things began to stir. Tony Holt's bell symbol looked fine now that it had been printed up on dummy posters and programmes on instructions from Adrian Rolfe who was now installed in the house and working like a beaver.

Douglas showed the dummies to Sir Basil, who was both pleased and impressed, promising that there would be no artistic or financial difficulty with the board of trustees.

Casting was all but complete, and, apart from the main

leads, they had gathered together a sparkling group of actors and actresses. Elizabeth Column, known internationally as a highly successful and brilliant actress, was to play four roles: Portia, a part which, at the age of thirty-five she had not yet acted, Emelia in *Othello*, Queen Margaret in *Richard III* and Lady Montague in *Romeo and Juliet*.

The young, very up and coming, actress Rachel Cohen was cast as Jessica, Bianca and Queen Elizabeth (in *Richard III*); while well-known names like Murray Fleet, Peter Berger, Laurence Pern and Ronald Escott were all taking on important roles.

Douglas had also solved his largest problem, that of appointing an executive director. It happened almost by accident on a chilly November evening. Douglas had gone up to London to see Sir Basil and decided to postpone his return to Shireston until the following morning, mainly for the old reason of seeing Carol.

He called her from the flat in Elton Court and, as usual, she was overjoyed to hear that he was in town.

She came straight into his arms as he walked through the door.

'Sorry, baby,' she whispered, 'my timing's off. The curse started ten minutes after you phoned so we'll have to be ingenious.'

'I don't only come to see you for that.' Douglas's voice gentle at her shoulder.

She laughed, 'Don't let us kid ourselves that this relationship raises itself much above the navel, sweetie. Sure I'm crazy about you; you think I'm a reasonable actress but I know my mind can't get a quarter of the way up yours, while you can get all the way –' He stopped her with a kiss.

They decided to have dinner out and it was half in Douglas's mind that he might drive down to Shireston in the early hours, a thought quickly rejected for its callousness.

Normally he was careful about the choice of restaurants with Carol, never taking her to places where he went with Jen: it was not simply an act of intrigue but one of respect. Tonight, however, his guard dropped and Douglas ordered the cab driver to take them to the Campagna in Marylebone High Street, a small and exceptional Italian restaurant which he seldom visited with anyone but Jen.

Douglas realized that he had made a mistake the moment he stepped inside the long narrow room; Umberto, the head waiter, allowed his eyebrows to raise a fraction of an inch and it was enough to warn Douglas that the visit with someone other than Jen had been noted. The other reason for Umberto's lifted eyebrows did not at first make itself apparent.

They were seated at a table on the left-hand wall of the room, side by side facing the line of tables which stood along the opposite wall. Douglas glanced up and took in the fact that three of the tables were occupied: turning back to the menu, which Umberto had handed him, he was also vaguely aware of someone rising from one of the other tables. The next moment he looked up into the face of David Wills, a man he had not seen for the best part of three years.

At the age of thirty-seven David Wills was a man who had stood at the threshold of success in British theatre on at least four occasions during the last decade, but triumph had eluded him, one of those strange disappointing quirks which so often beset talent in the precarious world of the arts. It was a sad story of near tragedy, for David Wills combined a keen penetrating mind with endless enthusiasm for any project in which he became involved.

'Douglas Silver.' Wills smiled down, hand outstretched: a tall thin man, lean-faced with alert eyes that looked, at this moment, tired and wary.

Douglas half rose. 'David,' the echoes of surprise at their unexpected meeting. He introduced Carol, and Wills explained that he was dining with his agent. The conversation became stilted and fragmentary.

'What are you doing at the moment?' Douglas's question about David Wills's work was completely innocent but he detected a bleak look crossing David's face.

Wills shrugged. 'Nothing, old chum. Bloody nothing. To be honest, my agent's giving me dinner. It's been a bad year.'

144

The idea flared in Douglas's mind, but discipline held it back. 'Could you give me a call tomorrow afternoon at Shireston?' He gave Wills the number.

So it happened. That night, sleepless in the afterglow of Carol's ministrations, Douglas gave the matter a great deal of thought. David Wills was a good director and his methods were neat and orderly. It followed that he would be neat and orderly as an executive. David also knew the theatre, he knew drama, particularly the Elizabethans, which would be a great asset.

The main details were settled on the telephone the following afternoon. Within two days they had lunched together and spent twelve hours in each other's company at Shireston. David Wills was excited and stimulated by the idea of being Douglas's executive director, for one thing it might give him a possible stability for which he had long sought: he was ready to take up the appointment immediately and part of Douglas's mind became eased, knowing that some strains would now be reduced.

The question of a restaurateur was settled by Adrian Rolfe who found an Italian with the startling name of Emilio Benneto right on the spot at Shireston.

Benneto had come to England shortly after the Second World War, worked hard and finally set up his own restaurant in London only to watch the profits slide off to a protection firm. Eventually the restaurant itself slid away and he was forced into the more mundane area of running a coffee shop in Shireston, from whence his English bride had come. But Benneto was an enterprising and experienced restaurateur, a man whom, Adrian told Douglas, they could happily leave in charge, allowing him to deal with the major problems, the hiring and firing of staff and the general running. Douglas took it a stage further, authorizing Benneto to take control of the whole of Shireston staff catering as well as the new restaurant. The Italian was hesitant at first but finally agreed and was due to take up his appointment in the second week of December.

Adrian Rolfe's first major press release went out in the last week of November – a bulky dossier filed in an elegant grey folder upon the flap of which the new Shireston Festival bell motif was printed, crossed with raised silver lettering in sixty point Gothic proclaiming

SHIRESTON 81

The preliminary hand-out began in traditional Theatre journalese: *For his first season as director of the Shireston Festival, Douglas Silver has gathered together a company which is unique in modern theatrical history . . .*

Other features dealt with the major members of the company, while there were news stories about the refurbishing of the auditorium, the new restaurant, the personalities behind the company, a personal article by Douglas Silver in which he wrote of Shakespeare's validity in the present age of change, revolt and a new stabilization. The dossier was completed with photographs of the leading players, a couple of Tony Holt's rough drawings for costume designs and a plan of the new Shireston which Tony had done for Adrian with the idea of reproducing it in the programme.

In all, the press release dossier went out to all major newspapers, national and provincial, specialist papers and magazines and some selected weeklies such as the local *Shireston Gazette*. Adrian had also slipped in a section on getting to Shireston, having already done half a dozen deals with coach and tour operators: this in itself guaranteed a lot of free publicity, particularly from the tour operators.

The opening of the campaign was a block buster, with the London evening papers devoting entire pages to the new Shireston structure. The dailies were also generous with space and Douglas suddenly found himself in the middle of a publicity floodlight with precious time being taken up in television appearances and broadcasts.

The mists of November settled into the harsher coldness of December with its rain and threatening snow. The heating system of ancient hot water radiators at Shireston House had to be supplemented with a few electric fires, but it was still deplorably sub-standard and Douglas passed a memo on to David Wills asking if they could take some temporary steps towards an efficient heating system, at the same time costing out something more permanent and modern for the following year. He was worried about people like Joe Thomas having to spend a first winter in the depth of the stark English countryside with little but neat brandy and an available female walk-on to keep him warm. A bad winter might make life intolerable for the whole company living in the huge house with such atrocious heating.

The days moved swiftly on, then, two weeks before Christmas, Jennifer arrived back in London unexpectedly.

CHAPTER SEVEN

Against her wishes, Jen had stayed on in Los Angeles to post-synch a few scenes from *Hidalgo*: location sequences where the microphones had not picked up her voice clearly, or a jet had suddenly pushed a scene ludicrously into the present. She spoke to Douglas twice a week and had sadly told him she saw no chance of getting back until immediately after Christmas. Then, out of the blue, she discovered that her schedule was all wrong and that she had only two small scenes left to complete. She prayed that, during the next couple of days, Douglas would not telephone her, for it was always much more exciting to surprise him with her presence, even if she was in London and he at Shireston.

Jennifer got a seat on a direct flight and finally landed at Heathrow in the cold misty drizzle of a late midweek afternoon. In other circumstances the weather would have been depressing, but Jen had a facility for day-dreaming about future events. During the flight she had gone over her arrival a hundred times: the cab to Elton Court, the breathless telephone call to Shireston, Douglas either dropping everything, dashing up to town, or sending a car to speed her down to Shireston. The whole business was drenched in the rosy glow of emotional sunlight, for, while Jennifer was a gifted and controlled actress, her one emotional blind spot was Douglas Silver. Even so, she still managed to keep just within the bounds of reality. She knew the demands made upon Douglas by his work and the moods he underwent: her day-dreamed romances did not include Douglas sweeping her off her feet, with a background score of a hundred strings, lifting her in his arms and carryng her to a cushioned

148

bed upon which their mutual passions could explode in sweating climax. She knew Douglas too well for that. The moment would come, but, if he was hard at work, it would have to be her doing and at this moment she could not deny that her needs within that area were most explicit: she needed Douglas as a stimulant for her mind; he was always the motive force behind her life, and the sensuality, never far below the surface of her consciousness, was inevitably roused by his nearness.

The flat at Elton Court had a stale feel to it, tidy enough, but that was the work of the cleaning woman who came in at least twice a week when they were not there; now there was a sourness about the air, mingled with something else which Jennifer could not quite define.

Out of habit she dumped her suitcases in the bedroom, turned on one of the fires, lit a cigarette, dropped into a chair and picked up the telephone. She had not even bothered to take off her coat. With the pressure of the instrument against her ear Jennifer could hear her heart tripping. Stupid, like a schoolgirl, she thought, or one of those women's paperbacks, opiate for the housewives who never even got as far as 'O' Levels. She smiled to herself and began to dial.

The impulses clicking on the line: the final whirr and then the ringing tone.

'Shireston Festival Theatre. Good afternoon.'

'Douglas Silver, please.'

'One moment.'

Click. Click. The switches and the little lights.

'Mr Silver's secretary. Can I help you?' The voice was heavily overlaid with middle-class county vowels, the kind which, at one time, had been the complete horizon to Jennifer's life.

'Could I speak to Mr Silver, please?'

'I'm not sure if he's in. Who's calling, please?'

Jennifer did not often use her married name, but the smug voice of the secretary-to-the-big-man gave her the nudge.

'Mrs Silver,' she said with as much edge as she could muster.

There was a pause.

'Mrs Douglas Silver or Mr Silver's mother?' The protective instinct of the unseen secretary rose to the occasion.

'Mrs Douglas Silver.' Acid on the line.

'Just one moment, Mrs Silver.'

Jen smiled to herself, there had been a slight change of note in the final sentence.

'Putting you through.'

'Thank you.'

Douglas was on the line, over-anxious. 'Jen? Surprise. You all right?'

'Fine, darling.'

'What's the weather like out there?'

Christ the eternal conversation piece, the meterorological situation. *Chilly day. Looks like rain. Red sky at night is the shepherd's delight.* . . . It took her a few seconds to realize that Douglas thought she was making a transatlantic call. 'Not good,' she said loudly. 'Nasty drizzle.'

He laughed. 'Snap. The same here.'

'Well I'm not that far away. I'm phoning from the flat.'

'The . . .?'

Jennifer was intrigued: the sudden stop and silence did not have the right feel.

'Jen? Where are you?'

'I told you, darling, in London. I'm back, Doug, back for good.'

'You're in . . .?' Douglas was thrown badly. He had been looking over a complicated memo from Adrian dealing with advertising: not really a memo, more of a report from a fact-finding commission, breaking down types of advertising and going into minutiae like the idea of providing picture postcards of the house and theatre for hotels and tour operators. Immersed in this, Jen's unexpected call put everything out of perspective. The whole wide screen business of living and working moved to tilt. He had even shelved the problem of Carol in the knowledge that there was plenty of time to work it out before Jen's return. Now the time had shrunk and life was altered dramatically.

'What's the matter, darling?' Again the flash of illogical apprehension for Jen.

'Nothing.' Douglas recovered balance. 'Nothing, love. It's all so. . . .'

'Sudden?'

'That's a good word, sugar. You have the advantage of me.'

Jennifer grinned to herself, allowing a pause before, 'Hey, Douglas Silver? Are you having an affair?' She tried to smile with her voice.

'A what?' Douglas clutched the telephone close to his ear: mind filling with questions and the stomach roll of guilt. Tiny uncleared incriminating things left at Elton Court? Indiscretions?

Jen was still talking. 'An affair, Doug? An illicit relationship with your secretary.'

'What are you talking about?'

'Joke, sweetheart. Your secretary was incredibly rude to me just now: asked me if I was Mrs Douglas Silver or Mr Silver's mother.'

Douglas fought himself out of the sudden fluctuating panic. He swallowed and allowed a small laugh of relief. 'That's the fair Deborah. She can be rather trying.'

'She'll be trying when I get down to Shireston.'

'I really should speak to her, but she's great at keeping people at bay. But, Jen, what're we going to do about you being back? It's great, baby. I still can't believe it.'

'Oh, the relief. . . . clowned Jennifer. 'What are we going to do? Your place or mine?'

'I don't know, baby, all I know is we can't go on meeting like this.' That was the old Douglas.

'Well, are you coming up here or do I come down to you?'

The pause was longer than she expected. Then –

'Look, Jen, I haven't really got our flat organized here. It needs your touch. I was leaving it for you to play with.' Douglas had a picture of the Shireston House apartment bright in his mind and the mental note that someone would have to get in there and clean, fast. He had only been using it

151

for sleep, leaving the home-making aspect as something else to be dealt with when Jen returned: like the other thing: black on white, white on black, white on white. 'I've been slumming: really needs a woman's touch. I think you'll have to come down here and take a good look, decide what you want to get moved and how much of our stuff should be brought from town. Look, I'll tell you what, I'll come up to London now.'

'Can't wait.'

'Then I can bring you back here tomorrow. Okay?'

'I just said: can't wait.'

'Be with you in a couple of hours then.'

'Super. You all right, Doug?'

'I'm fine. Why?'

'I don't know. I just. . . .' She let it trail off, the vague thought in the corner of her brain that Douglas was not the man she had left, not the man to whom she dreamed of returning: the timbre of his voice: something guarded. 'Oh it's me, love, and the journey, greeting you on the telephone. Be careful driving. I'll be waiting.'

Ten minutes after Douglas left the office Carol Evans telephoned. Deborah, who was blonde, twenty-two years old, a keeper of secrets and self-appointed guardian to Douglas Silver, director of the Shireston Festival, knew Miss Evans like she knew a lot of other voices on the telephone. Deborah worked strictly within the bounds of those things that were familiar and known to her. She had not known Mrs Silver so her guard had been up. With Carol it was different.

'I'm sorry, Miss Evans, Mr Silver's gone to London.'

'He has? Okay, I'll probably get him there. Thank you.'

Deborah did not have time to say anything else. In London, Carol smiled, rubbing the palm of her right hand up and down her cheek. Douglas said he might possibly make it this week; tonight would be admirable.

An hour later Carol called the Elton Court number. Jen answered and a shaken Carol quietly replaced the receiver without speaking: she had never met Jennifer Frost but knew her voice immediately.

Jennifer was unnerved, she did not like kooky telephone calls, even though in her profession one learned to live with them. She had been idling away the time waiting for Douglas to arrive, just sitting, relaxing, trying to come back to normal after the hours of travel, letting her thoughts skim over her consciousness at not too deep a level. The telephone call jolted her into action, injecting a restlessness.

She shivered after putting down the telephone, stretched and then smiled before walking slowly into the bedroom to prepare herself for Douglas. Maybe Douglas did not need her so much when he was working, but they had been apart for a long time and that always sharpened his appetite. Jen felt the longing inside her. Douglas's need for her? What about her need for Douglas?

Jennifer had already made a start on Desdemona: like many actresses she found that, when tackling a difficult classic role, it was best to get the words well into her head before dealing with the more difficult job of sorting out meaning, innuendo, dramatic intent or emotion. She preferred to have a foundation on which to work, the words firmly entrenched in her mind. Now she bathed, put on fresh clothes, choosing for Douglas's pleasure, unpacked as far as possible, restarted her make-up before picking up her copy of *Othello* and beginning work again. She was concentrating on the text when Douglas turned his key in the lock.

A tiny blister of concern flowered in her mind as he embraced her. A nervousness or lack of passion? Uncertainty in the way he held her? She dismissed the quick-flooding questions as part of her imagination, knowing that she was tired and Douglas was in the middle of great works.

Douglas whisked her out to dinner, extravagance at Prunier's, and talk, a stream of conversation, mainly concerned with Shireston – the festival as a whole, then the detail: the casting and its inherent problems, the publicity and promotion angles, the theatre itself and the changes he had inaugurated, the idea of an exhibition, the lures they were setting to bring people down to Shireston, the problems that were going to hit once the whole operation got underway

153

and the company was settled into Shireston House.

Jennifer made a mental note that throughout all the talk Douglas hardly mentioned his true function, that of directing the plays.

Later she brought the matter up, feeling her way gently, tactfully. Douglas reacted violently, cursing the lack of time and the yoke of administrative difficulties. Even with David Wills in the executive chair he found it almost impossible to make time for the most essential end product.

'You're going to have to make time, sweetheart, otherwise the company will arrive with you unprepared. What's happened to the director in you?'

Douglas knew what had happened. His sudden interest in the project as a whole; the infusion of power on a large scale, and lust for a beautiful black actress, had taken away the time. Jennifer was right and he wanted to react to her, yet, now she was here he seemed to have developed a strange negative feeling towards her. She was unquestionably the woman he loved, but the sacramental outward passion was transferred. He could envisage Jen as his wife at Shireston; see her in their apartment there; on stage as Desdemona or Lady Anne; being a wonderful hostess and companion; but in bed it was Carol who devoured and itched away within him. The guilt rose in conflict, quivering in his head.

They talked on – about the apartment at Shireston, Jennifer agreeing to come down with him on the following day and take over the organization of setting up their new home.

'Christmas in a new home, Doug,' she reached out and placed her hand over his, flat on the table. 'How about that?'

'Yes, how about that?'

She was conscious that he had moved his hand, and even though it was to grope for a handkerchief there was an unaccustomed clumsiness in the action.

The same kind of ineptitude was there in bed that night, disturbing Jennifer. Her own desire had grown throughout the evening, being close to Douglas bringing her own need into warm and firm perspective, yet she had to make all the moves: her hand had to caress him into readiness, her fingers first finding the erotic points. She pressed her crotch hard at him, when they kissed his lips remained closed so that it was her tongue which had to force them open and jab into his mouth; she was aware, in the heights of her passion, that he did not return her kisses with his usual panting and licking ardour. When at last they were locked and sliding together he worked with his normal vigour, though Jennifer sensed a detachment, resulting in her reaching an orgasm before him: Douglas straining on long after her pulse of pleasure had died.

'What's wrong, love?' she asked in the darkness as they were lying together.

'Oh the usual, Jen. Sorry, baby, I'm loaded with problems. Tired as well, I guess.'

'So am I.' She did not mean it to sound like a criticism.

'Sure. I know. But with men, well . . . I didn't expect you. Bodies often fit into mental patterns. I just wasn't prepared.' He gave her hand a little squeeze, as though to make up for the inadequacy. Jen had expected the squeeze to be elsewhere: it always had been before. Christ, she thought, I'm being bloody neurotic. This is ridiculous.

The following afternoon, at Shireston, Douglas found time to make a safe and private call to Carol who had wholly taken over his mind. She sounded hysterically distraught.

'Your wife's back. I called your apartment last night and she answered. Why didn't you tell me she was back?'

'I didn't know myself. She called me late yesterday. It was unexpected.'

'You said she wouldn't be back until after Christmas, Douglas, you said. . . .'

'That's what I thought.'

Their voices seemed tunnelled on the lines, disembodied, wrapped in thin gloom.

'Is she in London now?' asked Carol.

'No, she's come down here to look at the flat.'

'What're we going to do?'

'Just what I've always said.' A pause before he spat out the

155

words. 'I'm sorry, Carol.' He felt that, in spite of all his good resolutions, he had, to a certain extent, come to depend heavily on Carol, her ways with him and his with her; this was a terrible destructive thing for him to do.

'You won't see me again except when I come down to work?

'Don't you think . . .?'

'That it's best? No. Douglas, I've got to see you. Please. Please, baby, I must, even if it's just once, alone. I have to talk with you.'

Uninvited, Jen's eagerness to please him on the previous evening leaped into his mind. The sweating smell of their union and the feel of her body, then over this was the whisper of the silky black girl and Jen diminished, vanished, so that it was white on black, all sense of dimension gone, sweeping as a single unit, one motor working perfectly carrying them to the plane of emotional, physical and intellectual pleasure – *Douglas, I love you . . . I love you . . . I love you. . . .* Urgency growing in the throat.

'Okay,' he said quietly. 'I'll call you in a day or so. I'm sorry, love. . . .'

'I'm sorry, but I love you, Douglas.' The last words wasted on the air because Deborah had tapped on Douglas's door announcing David Wills who had a meeting with him at three o'clock.

Archie Swimmer was fifty-eight years old. He had been part of the permanent staff of the Shireston Festival since it first opened in 1928. In that season, aged sixteen, he was a junior stage hand. For the past eleven years he had been the stage carpenter. There was not much that Archie did not know about the Shireston, particularly when it came to its secrets, the private scandals, the real triumphs and failures. Archie was a close man, which was a good thing for the reputations of many actors, actresses and directors. He saw much and said little, though his memory was long and, if tapped, could have been the basis of a Sunday newspaper serial that might run for ever.

This afternoon he stood on the stage looking at the wreckage that was once the auditorium. Scaffolding ran up both sides of the proscenium and across the arch, which was in the process of being raised and lengthened, while the side pillars would be pushed outwards.

The auditorium itself looked as though several bulldozers had run amock in some violent barn dance, ripping the rows of seats from their cast iron moorings and tearing up the floor covering. Even the walls, and the jutting balcony, were not safe: scaffolding everywhere, growing like some obscene creeping disease, crawling with germs, men, stripping away the once gold wallpaper, removing light fittings, displaying the cracked and dirty nakedness of the plaster.

Archie remembered the shining auditorium as it had looked on the first night back in April 1928. On that evening the stage staff had been allowed to peep into the auditorium through the spy hole in the stage curtain. All those ladies and gentlemen in their evening clothes; he had thought that wonderful. The dresses and winged collars, the colour and glitter. The stage manager had pointed out Mr James Agate with some awe, though in those days, Archie did not know if James Agate was a stonemason or a butcher.

He glanced up, now, with apprehension at the men working on the proscenium. The alterations also meant adjustment to the grid, over which all the suspension gear ran. His eye took in all the familiar dimensions of the grid and the catwalk, his vision going up into the fly tower above. His boys, together with the chief electrician's men, had spent much of the day clearing the grid, lowering the suspension lines and the long four-colour battens of lights, stripping away the remaining equipment.

Stephen Sultan. Christ, why think of Stephen Sultan now? He was Orlando that year, 1928; jet haired and having it away with one of the girls from the booking office, Gladys Williams, a local girl, married now with three grown sons; saw her the other day down. . . . Stephen Sultan, tall with fine looks, frenzied in the Forest of Arden searching for Rosalind: that was Emma Duncan, she was fine as well. Archie grinned.

He had given it to Emma Duncan in the prop room one rainy Sunday afternoon that season. Sixteen years old and she must have been all of twenty-five; taught him a trick or two though, up the wide lace legs of her French knickers that afternoon. He could still smell the sharp odour of paint on canvas which pervaded the prop room that day, and the rain dripping down from the trees outside.

'Sad day for you, eh, Archie?' Archie drew himself back from the pleasant past as Wilf Brownhill, head of property maintenance, advanced across the stage with Alec Keene, the house manager.

Brownhill and Keene had just escaped Douglas Silver's wrath by coming up with a reasonable budget for the refurbishing of the auditorium: a budget based mainly on Wilf Brownhill's long-standing contacts within the building trade.

'Sad day?' queried Archie Swimmer, hitching his trousers around a stomach running speedily to fat. His red face broke into a wide grin which deepened the many lines, forming abstract patterns at the top of his cheeks and around his eyes. 'Sad day be buggered. It's about time someone ripped the bloody place apart. I hope Demolishing Duggie goes on and does something about the fly tower and back stage.'

Brownhill sniggered at 'Demolishing Duggie'. 'You think Mr Silver's on to something then, Archie?' he asked.

'Spendin' a lot of money, isn't he? That's what's been needed here an' all. Some of the locals are shouting about what the newspapers say he's going to do this season though; but they always used to shout in the old days. If anyone did a play of William Shakespeare's without the whole cast being got up in Elizabethan gear they went hairless. Now he's got a pop singer playing Othello and a nig-nog as Juliet. Race riots we'll have down here. Very conservative the locals.'

'You're a local, Archie.' From Keene, winking broadly at Brownhill.

'Ah,' Archie laid a finger to his nose. 'I'm a local, but I'm theatre, Alec, so they don't really trust me.'

'Oi up,' muttered Wilfred Brownhill, 'here comes the

scoutmaster.'

Douglas appeared at the far end of the auditorium with David Wills, the two men picking their way through unfamiliar rubble.

They had spent an hour that afternoon discussing what small steps David had managed to make with the exhibition; now David had persuaded his chief to come over to the auditorium.

Douglas stood and looked at the wreckage which faced him. For a few seconds his nerve nearly gave way. He was responsible for this, he had okayed the estimates and the financial people had added their agreement, but to see the interior under the wrecker's hammer was another matter. Certainly he was conscious that the refurbishing would be to their advantage, that out of the ripped flooring and cracked plaster a more pleasant and comfortable atmosphere would be born. But what if he, Douglas Silver, could not bring his chosen actors to the high state which the situation demanded? What if their corporate efforts did not prise people from their armchairs and bring them into this theatre?

He had screwed up his private life in a manner likely to explode into the company. It would be all too easy for him to screw up the whole project so that, at the end, the Shireston Festival would lie, a wreck like this auditorium, at his feet.

It was a difficult afternoon for Emilio Benneto. He had taken up his appointment on Monday and the week was spent sitting in his little office, bright and brand new, interviewing possible restaurant staff. Emilio was an enthusiastic man, though courage was not one of his particular virtues. He would, for instance, have preferred to have good Italian boys as his waiters, but Mr Rolfe had put it to him that Shireston had it fair share of young girls looking for jobs. Good girls whom he, Emilio, could personally train as waitresses. Emilio capitulated because he had learned long ago that, in the end, you could not argue with men like Mr Rolfe; and he really should be arguing with Mr Wills or Mr Silver.

On top of this he knew all about waitresses: he knew about

boyfriend troubles which erupted just when you needed the girls most; he knew of the small discomforts which, with young girls, could be exploded into major hysterical dramas; he knew of their moods and their dangers; it was all very well Mr Rolfe talking about the male patrons liking to see pretty faces and pretty legs, he knew about the female patrons. But he still interviewed the first few girls.

He was also seeing some chefs, which helped take his mind off the girls and brought him nearer to his goal. In fact Emilio thought he had found a chief chef and possibly one assistant. If he completed the arrangements with the chief chef by next week they could get down to the real planning, the part he liked best, the kitchen organization and preparation of menus. Next week would be good.

But he was now faced with this afternoon, the afternoon he had dreaded all week. Each morning, Emilio's wife, Doris, a dark-haired woman of twenty-nine, still a firm-boned beauty and ten years his junior, packed a neat cold meal, consumed by the restaurateur at his desk and washed down with half a bottle of wine. That was each morning until today, for today he had lunched in the permanent staff cafeteria, and this afternoon he would have to face the permanent staff cafeteria manageress, Mrs Doul, a lean razor-faced, forty-year-old widow who had once supervised the catering at a well-known boys' preparatory school and never forgot it.

For Emilio, the lunch in the permanent staff cafeteria was all kinds of hell and he knew at once why Mr Silver had told him that he never ate there. To begin with, Emilio deplored the idea of collecting your own food from a greasy self-service counter. To have lunch pushed at you, with hardly a second choice, and by people whose enthusiasm was barely subliminal, had been the depth of humiliation. He had grabbed the badly typed menu from the counter and demanded, 'What is da soupa da day?' his usually perfect English lapsing into caricature, ice cream man, Italian as it always did when he was nervous or angry.

The large white-grey overalled woman, who was serving behind the counter and hot plates, eyed him up and down, then shouted to a colleague who could not be seen.

'Lil, is the soup of the day the same as yesterday? The veg?'

Lil responded in the affirmative and Emilio asked for the tomato juice. He also chose the lamb which arrived dry and cold, trying to fight off the swash of soggy mashed potato and cabbage. Two mouthfuls told him all he needed to know, though the taste and memory lingered with him as he sat at his desk, one hand on the telephone, the other on the little typed cardboard list of internal telephone numbers, checking, for the tenth time, that Mrs Doul, permanent staff canteen manageress, was 456. He took a deep breath and dialled. The ringing tone came on and continued for some time until someone picked up the instrument and said, 'Yes,' sharply.

'Ah. Mrs Doul?' Emilio asked nervously.

'Mrs Doul speaking.'

'Ah. Mrs Doul, this is Emilio Benneto.'

'Who?'

'Benneto. Emilio Benneto. I am the theatre restaurateur.'

'Oh yes. Yes I heard you were coming up here. You used to run that little coffee place in Mead Street, didn't you?'

The tone was patronizing and a tiny flare of anger flamed and burned Emilio. 'I used to do a lot of things, Mrs Doul. But now I am the theatre restaurateur.'

'Yes.' Without interest.

'I wonder if you would be good enough to step over to my office. It is at the back of the new restaurant.'

There was a pause which Emilio recognized as one of shock.

'Well, Mr . . . er . . . Mr Benneto . . . I'm rather busy at the moment. My orders you know. The food for tomorrow.'

'I would still like to talk with you. It is a matter of some importance.'

'So are my orders.'

'With respect, Mrs Doul, I am in charge now and we have to talk.'

Again the shocked pause. 'In charge? In charge of what and whom, may I ask?'

161

'I am in charge of all catering at the Shireston Festival, Mrs Doul, and I must ask you to come over to my office.'

'It's the first I've heard of it. I don't think you understand the way things are done down here, Mr Benneto, I . . .' She paused, this time to make an impression. 'I am the permanent staff cafeteria manageress, and as such I am answerable only to the executive director, Mr David Wills. Until two weeks ago I was answerable to Mr Alec Keene, the house manager, but that's been altered. You, Mr Benneto, have never been mentioned, so I presume that I am still only answerable to Mr David Wills, and from Mr David Wills I will take my orders.'

'But. . . .' Emilio Benneto clutched at the telephone in frustration.

'And Mr Wills has, so far, seen fit not to interfere with the running of the permanent staff cafeteria. Good afternoon, Mr Benneto.'

There was a thump, followed by the dialling tone. Emilio looked at the instrument as though it had personally assaulted him. The small confrontation made him angry. It also showed that there were flaws in the organization. Emilio Benneto did not like flaws. He was asked to do a job and part of that job had been explained to him as a very difficult task, that of reorganizing the permanent staff cafeteria: to do this he needed backing and authority. Either Mrs Doul had not been made aware of his authority or she was flouting it.

Emilio dialled Adrian Rolfe's number. Mr Rolfe's secretary came on and said that he was with somebody, so Emilio told her that it was most urgent. At last –

'Adrian Rolfe.' Whatever his mood, Adrian had long acquired the habit of answering the telephone with a soft, calm voice.

'Mr Rolfe, it is Emilio here. Emilio Benneto. I have great difficulty.'

'And I have someone with me, so if you could make it quick.' Rolfe flashed a smile at his visitor, a tall, white-haired man with a thin moustache and a suit which suggested shabby elegance. The visitor, who had only just been seated, returned the smile with a nod meant to convey that he quite understood about the interruption.

'Mr Rolfe,' said Emilio with as much Latin charm as he could muster on the telephone, 'when I talked last with Mr Silver he ask me if I will take over reorganization of the permanent staff cafeteria. I say yes, and you tell me that I have overall charge of all catering staff and arrangements at Shireston Festival. Right?'

'Right.' Rolfe still quiet, though he now had a rough idea of what was coming.

'Today I eat at the cafeteria, Mr Rolfe, and it is a terrible experience. So this afternoon I call the manageress to my office: I call Mrs Doul.'

'Uh-huh.'

'She refuse to come. She say I have no authority and that she is answerable only to Mr Wills. How can I work like that, Mr Rolfe? I am right, am I not? I have authority?'

'You're quite right.' Rolfe spoke quickly now. 'The fact of your position and authority here has obviously not been passed down the line. Where are you speaking from?'

'My office.'

'Someone will call you. Just sit tight. It'll all be ironed out. Okay?'

'If you say so, Mr Rolfe.'

Rolfe replaced the telephone and with a shrug excused himself. In the outer office he hissed to his secretary, 'Get the director on the phone. If he's not in his office track him down, but get him; and when you've got him, call me out, I can't talk in front of journalists.'

His secretary was already dialling as Rolfe closed the door on himself and his visitor.

Adrian Rolfe had a special interest in this particular visitor whose name was Hedley Moir.

A couple of weeks before, Tony Holt had mentioned the existence of the Shireston Festival Society. Holt had been digging around and discovered that the society still held meetings, even though their contact with the festival had, in the last six or seven years, become merely nominal. They had, Tony said, a reputation of being difficult and their chairman was a man named Hedley Moir.

Adrian recognized the name at once, for Hedley Moir was also the editor of the *Shireston Gazette*, the little weekly newspaper which still operated, serving the area well, even though it was engulfed in a large, centrally operated chain of newspapers.

The *Shireston Gazette* had devoted half of its front page and a double page inside spread to the festival's plans, so when Moir had called Adrian that morning the chief of publicity had arranged a meeting straight away. Adrian Rolfe knew well enough what use both the local newspaper and a festival society could be. He was prepared to smooth any edges and iron out any bumps for Mr Hedley Moir.

'I'm sorry about that,' Rolfe resumed his seat behind the desk. 'I'm afraid I might get called out again in a few minutes. Reorganization has its problems.'

'Yes indeed.' Moir had a clipped manner. Like his moustache, thought Rolfe.

The publicity man leaned his elbows on the desk and smiled pleasantly. 'I'd like to say, first of all, Mr Moir, that you and any members of your staff are always welcome here. Now that we have a young administration at the Shireston we hope to make a lot of friends in the town and among local people in general.'

Moir let out a long sigh. 'That's really what I wanted to talk to you about.' He placed his briefcase on his knee and began to open it. 'You are aware of the chain to which our newspaper is tied?'

'Yes.'

'Then you will appreciate that we are bound by certain group policies.'

Adrian nodded, neither of them needed to mention the Sunday newspaper which was the cornerstone of that particular group: it was a paper noted for its in-depth, news grubbing and its drilling to the core of small sensations, blowing them, if it felt necessary, into vast and important issues.

'Then you will understand that I am absolutely obliged to

164

send certain stories direct to London.' Moir was looking up over his eyelids in a vaguely unpleasant manner. Adrian was conscious of intrigue.

'What is it, Mr Moir?'

Moir began to remove papers from the briefcase. 'Nothing of great import, Mr Rolfe. We gave you a pretty good spread last week, yes?'

'As did most of the nationals. It was big news for Shireston.'

'Quite, and I don't suppose the nationals received any correspondence like this.' He passed a small pile of papers across the desk. Adrian took them and settled back to see what was obviously making the newspaperman feel so smug. The man's attitude was becoming more and more apparent to Adrian, as though some bad odour had seeped under the door with Hedley Moir's advent, so that the smell now built up to considerable proportions.

Adrian turned his attention to the bundle of papers in his hand. They were letters, about a dozen of them, on a varied array of notepapers: azure, white, grey: expensive, cheap and thin, lined and unlined. They were all addressed to the editor of the *Shireston Gazette* and the one on top of the pile spoke for the rest, even though it was the shortest and not the most intelligent.

Dear Sir,

While it is always good to hear that the living theatre is to have an injection of much needed financial aid, there are some disturbing elements regarding the forthcoming plans for the Shireston Festival, published by you in last week's issue of the Gazette.

As one who has known and loved the Festival for the best part of my life, I would like to ask who Mr Douglas Silver thinks he is to foist tasteless, experimental productions of the Bard's great works on Shireston? True, we have yet to see Mr Silver's work in action, but, it would seem obvious from his casting and the ideas so far made public, that we are to be treated to a display of gimmickry and red herrings in which William Shakespeare will come off a very poor second best to the whims of the director,

165

coloured actresses, scene designers and actors. Can nothing be done to stop this travesty before it is too late?

Yours faithfully,
Norman Myles

Adrian looked up with a laugh. 'Norman Myles. You aren't taking this seriously, Mr Moir, surely?'

Moir nodded, grave faced. 'I take it very seriously, Mr Rolfe. There are twelve letters there. In all we have had thirty-three.'

'But they're crank's letters.' Adrian began to sort through the pile, 'Racist even. God there's one here complaining about casting Maurice Kapstein as Shylock. Listen to this – *Mr Kapstein has no place in the legitimate theatre. He is a lowbrow and vulgar television comedian. It is a blot upon Shireston and its Festival to be even linked with his name. The genius of English drama must be turning in his grave at such an insult.* My dear fellow, that's just intolerant ignorance.'

Moir looked at him coldly. 'As a newspaper editor I have to be objective. I felt you should have some warning. I must publish a selection of these letters and I must also pass the story on to London.'

'What story? *Local Objections to Shireston Festival Plans? Colour Prejudice in Shakespearean Season?* It wouldn't get three lines at the bottom of page eight.' As he said it, Adrian knew he was wrong. If handled properly it would be a wonderful news story. It would also drag in the TV cameras.

'I beg to differ. It will be most harmful to your image.'

Again Adrian laughed, trying to show an attitude of sophisticated, liberal disbelief. 'All publicity is good publicity, you know.' Then, in spite of himself he added, 'Except ignorant critical publicity.'

'There has always been a certain element in Shireston which has fought for true Shakespearean productions.'

Rolfe got it, suddenly the fact slid into his head and the puzzle was solved. 'You've told me what you think about it as a journalist, Mr Moir. Now tell me what you think about it as chairman of the Shireston Festival Society.'

Moir visibly preened himself, but at that moment the

telephone rang and Adrian's secretary was telling him that she had Douglas Silver on the line in the outer office.

Adrian excused himself with as much courtesy as he could muster. Outside he hissed into the telephone, 'Douglas, someone has made a balls. I passed Emilio Benneto on to you. You gave him full authority to get on with putting the catering problem right, but apparently nobody has bothered to tell Mrs Doul, the arch-priestess of the permanent staff cafeteria. We have some evil tempers flying around. Emilio's in his office. I suggest you get on to him there, and that somebody tactfully breaks the bad tidings to La Doul.'

'Oh Christ,' moaned Douglas standing at the Prompt Side telephone to which he had been called. 'It's bloody David. Okay, I'll see them both later on. Leave it to me, Adrian.'

'I'll have to, I'm up to my eyes, mate. The local vigilantes are out in force. Save Shakespeare for those who understand him and don't monkey with the plays by casting nasty television performers and spade singer. I didn't think that kind of muddle-headed intolerance existed.'

'Oh it does, Adrian. You should hear some of the things they told me at. . . .' He stopped short as hammering in the auditorium almost drowned him out. 'Look, drop into my office later this afternoon, would you. We'll talk then, okay?'

'Okay, Doug, but please get that catering business sorted.'

'Don't worry.' Douglas sounded weary.

Adrian Rolfe made a face at his secretary and returned to his office and the smooth Hedley Moir. The man was smiling and began to speak as soon as Adrian closed the door.

'You asked me what I thought about these protests in my capacity as chairman of the Shireston Festival Society, Mr Rolfe. What do you know about the society?'

'I know of its existence; I know that you are its present chairman, and I know that its aim is broadly to establish a link between the festival and the town.'

Moir steepled his hands, tips of the fingers resting on his lips. 'Was, Mr Rolfe.'

'I beg your pardon?'

'I said, *was*: its aim *was* to establish a link between the

167

festival and town. You have not researched the history of the Shireston Festival as well as you should.'

'No? Well, you tell me.'

'There were many keen students of Drama in Shireston long before the festival. Some of our older members, Mr Norman Myles, for instance, and one of our most respected medical practitioners, Dr Michael Archer, were close friends of the late Richard Longwell, earl of Shireston, whose untimely death began this whole business. His lordship had a way of infecting people with enthusiasm and there are, as I say, many who studied the theatre in general and the Elizabethan dramatists in particular with Richard Longwell. Some were very close friends, and were surprised not to have been included among the Shireston trustees.'

The picture became even more clear. 'But they must be old men now?'

'Old men and women,' corrected Moir. 'Yes indeed, but the membership of the society stands at around sixty or so and most of them are middle-aged or young.'

'You were going to tell me about the society's aims.'

'Yes indeed. The founders of the society started out with the good intention of bridging the natural gap between town and theatre; but it did not take long to discover that the commercial side of the festival was outweighing the artistic: the producers, or directors as you call them nowadays, were staging Shakespeare's plays for their own benefit and not for the enrichment of the public. The society began to see that it had a more important role to fill. We try to be guardians, Mr Rolfe, guardians of tradition, a word that is not popular these days.' Moir seemed to swell visibly.

'What do you call tradition?'

'We protest at any production of a Shakespeare play which warps the original by overlying it with gaudy stagecraft or vulgar acting techniques. It is the poetry and wisdom of the plays which we seek to protect: anything that detracts is unworthy.'

'I see.' Adrian saw clearly enough and he wanted to know why nobody had warned him that these biased extremists

168

were active around Shireston.

Moir still droned on. 'We protest, quite peaceably I promise you, whenever we find this kind of dramatic sacrilege:
Stratford, London, Nottingham, Shireston.'

'Particularly Shireston?'

'Yes.'

'You are concerned about the coming season? I mean
personally concerned?'

'Most. It seems to me that Mr Silver is bent on giving us
trivia and not grandeur.'

'And as editor of the *Gazette* you're going to make a lot of
noise?'

'As editor of the *Gazette* I shall remain objective.'

'But you'll publish these letters.'

'I shall be selective.'

'Well at least that's a starting point. How would it be if Mr
Silver replied to the letters which you publish by writing an
exclusive article for your newspaper?'

The editor frowned. 'Well, it would depend. If the article
is constructive and –'

But Adrian had heard enough. 'Listen, chum,' he barked,
'I can show you letters from the editors of two Sunday heavies
and a couple of national weeklies, pleading for articles by
Douglas Silver. I also spend part of each day cooling features
writers who want to come down here and interview the man.
When the company arrives it will get worse, the pressure will
really be on and all we'll have time for will be one press
conference. After that it will be selective. I'm offering you a
unique chance because I think our local public relations are
important, but it'll be like a drop in the ocean once we really
get started; and your little society can howl its head off while
nobody listens. We are professionals, Moir, all of us, so get
that into your head. We're running a living theatre not a
memorial or a museum. I'm sorry if you don't like the way
we're doing things, but it's the way that makes most sense to
us. Now, do you want that article?'

'I've –'

'Never had this kind of treatment before? I bet you

haven't. Well you're dealing with the cream now. Mr Silver will read the letters and there'll be an article for publication, not more than two thousand words, on your desk a week on Monday. You can play it from there.' He paused, as though studying the man. 'When I deal with provincial journalists I always ask myself one question. Is this guy in his job by choice, or did he never get any further up the line because he wasn't good enough?'

Adrian rose to indicate that the meeting was at an end.

David Wills was full of apologies when Douglas came off the telephone and explained the Benneto-Doul fracas.

'One of those things, David.' Douglas shook his head. 'I'd better sort it out now, but you're going to have to deal with these matters by yourself from here on in. We cannot risk this sort of internal aggravation. Get hold of Mrs Doul and tell her I want to see her in fifteen minutes.' He turned away abruptly and crossed the stage towards Archie Swimmer. Douglas knew that he was going to rely heavily on his stage staff and that he could get to them through the stage carpenter, so he made a point of always spending a few minutes with Archie whenever he was in the theatre.

Mrs Doul was already waiting for Douglas when he got back to his office. At first she was inclined towards truculence, so Douglas quickly took a hard line.

'Look, Mrs Doul. I won't play games. I think the staff cafeteria's a disgrace. You've been running it like a soup kitchen; the organization's terrible, the food's disgusting and the standard of service is appalling. There are going to be a lot of changes around –'

'Well, if you don't like it I shall have to go elsewhere won't I?' Douglas detected the note of the hysteric.

'I hope not, Mrs Doul.' It was going against his common sense, but he felt a kind of pity for this thin, easily bruised woman. 'A lot of dead wood is going to be chopped away, but we don't really think of you as dead wood. We must have change, and Mr Benneto is an experienced man. Can't you even try to work with him?'

170

It took half an hour to convince her, and a further half an hour, with Emilio present, to get them both on the right track; it was well after five by the time Douglas got them out of his office, actually smiling and looking as if they might tackle the job in harness. By then Adrian Rolfe was waiting with his tales of local intrigue and Shakespearian intolerance, briefing him about the letters and the article he would have to write for the *Gazette*.

'Draft something would you, Adrian? Just a skeleton. I'll put the flesh on it.'

It was long after six before Douglas could even think of going up to his flat in Shireston house. He had almost forgotten that Jennifer would be there waiting for him, and the fact of his memory slip worried him more than all the problems of the afternoon. In the far back of his mind there was the question – did he want to forget?

Jennifer was enchanted by Shireston, even at this depressing time of the year it had a strong natural beauty about it which made her feel that she might find truth and the eternal values in this place. She loved the apartment, the views over the lawns, the high ceilinged rooms and leaded windows. As Douglas predicted, she was horrified by the shabby furnishings, and straight away set about making lists and taking measurements, planning what had to go and what she needed to have brought down from Elton Court.

By the state of the kitchen it was obvious that Douglas had done little more than make himself the odd cup of coffee there. Jennifer needed to stock the larder from scratch, so, late in the afternoon she took the car, which Douglas had left for her, and drove down into Shireston with a list of necessities ranging from herbs to dish-cloths.

She was back by five-thirty, checking her lists like a newly-wed and preparing a chicken casserole for their evening meal. The kitchen already had its standard number of pots and pans, yet, even doing a simple meal, Jennifer longed for her own familiar equipment from the London flat.

Douglas came in just before six-thirty, looking tired and

distracted. The curtains were drawn and the flat was warm, mainly from the big electric fire which had only been installed a couple of days before. Jennifer poured drinks for them and prattled on about what she intended to do.

'If your people here can move out some of this junk, and I can get the stuff ready to come down from London, I think I can get the place straight by Christmas, even though it's only a couple of weeks. What do you think, Doug?'

'You'll have to. We both start working for a living the first week in January.' He forced a grin. 'So, Jen, you'll have all of your time cut out being a little home-maker.'

'Can we play house? Mothers and Fathers?'

'Watch it. That kind of talk can lead to trouble, you might even end up giving Othello something to be really jealous about.'

'A preggy Desdemona. The critics would go crazy. But seriously, Doug, I'll play house and I'll make this place good for us: get it really straight.'

Douglas lounged back in the threadbare armchair, took a sip of his drink and smiled. 'I'd better hire a car for you, so that we can move around independently for the next couple of weeks. I'm going to be dashing to and fro as well.' The picture in his mind was Carol; the tongue moving wet along her lips; standing naked, her back to him, peeping between the curtained window of her snug rooms near the Bayswater Road; the movement of her hips and the sway of her buttocks; their hands playing, turning her hand so that it was flat, palm upwards on his stomach, forcing open the fore and middle fingers and running a stiff forefinger up their apex in steady hard motion; her nails in his back; her tongue in his ear; his hand in the coarse black triangle between her legs; his mouth open against her stiff nipple.

The picture cleared and there was Jen, the beloved face smiling at him in innocence as she sprawled in her chair. Her breast moved under her shirt and Douglas caught the line of her thigh under the long black skirt as she shifted a leather booted leg. Just a few short weeks ago that movement would have enticed him, now he glanced away.

But Jen had seen his look and misinterpreted it.

'Now?' she asked, glancing towards the bedroom.

'Let's eat first. There's a great smell coming from the kitchen. This place really feels like home at last.' It was a half lie, for he remembered what he felt about the flat the first time he entered it.

A minute or so later, Jen called from the kitchen. 'Sorry I'm not properly organized yet, love.'

'We both have a lot to do,' he replied.

'We'll spend all our time leaving messages for one another. Let's try and meet once in a while.' She had come to the kitchen door.'

Douglas looked up at her. 'Most of the time we'll be in the same place. It's only a matter of days after all.'

They ate, and Jennifer still went on talking: about how she intended to put the leather buttoned settee into the bow window, as Douglas had thought she would, and how she would have to get new curtains made up if they were going to be there for three years.

In the bedroom, later, she asked Douglas about the bed. Just after they had married she had seen a big brass four-poster, a Victorian design, hung round with thin white curtains. It was in Harrods and it appealed to her. 'Just imagine,' she said, 'it would be like sleeping in some plush tent, like an ancient Arabian princess, cut off from the world.'

'You've been at those cheap romance paperbacks again,' Douglas had laughed. 'And who am I supposed to be? The ancient prince?'

The bedroom at Shireston was huge, with a large fireplace, two long windows on the outside walls, and the ten-year-old double bed seemed dwarfed. Now Jen recalled the brass four-poster. 'It would be ideal here, Doug. Can I get it, please?'

'It's going to cost . . .' he began.

'Let me pay for it. Let it be my treat. I've just made a movie, remember?'

Douglas shrugged and reached out to her, closing his eyes. 'If that's what you want, Jen.'

'This is what I want now.' Her hand went down to him, slack and unaroused. She locked her lips on to his, pulling him towards the bed, fumbling at his buttons and zip.

For Douglas it was the same problem. The magic did not work, the drive and passion of what had been seemed to have dissolved. They stretched out, naked under the covers, and Douglas lit cigarettes for each of them.

'Sorry, love,' he spoke into the darkness, staring up at the ceiling, blowing smoke against the burning red tip of his cigarette. Jen put her hand out and squeezed the upper muscle of his left arm.

'What is it, baby?' Repeating her question of the previous night.

'Work. Non-work. I'm too involved with non-directorial trivia. I told you that already, but today's been an object lesson.'

He outlined the events of the afternoon: his discussion with David about the exhibition, his doubts when he saw the auditorium in ruins ('I talked with the stage carpenter, a character, you'll like him, Archie Swimmer. He wanted to know when I was going to spend an equivalent amount on the stage and back stage.' He laughed aloud. 'I must say all that does worry me. There's a barn of a rehearsal room at the back and I think we're going to be stuck in that for weeks. I can't see them finishing the auditorium until towards the end of February.'); the sudden blow-up with Emilio and Mrs Doul; Adrian Rolfe's concern over the local newspaper and the Shireston Festival Society.

'Poor love,' said Jen. 'You're up to your eyes in it. Seriously, Doug, how much plotting have you really done on the plays?'

Douglas was silent for a full fifteen seconds. It seemed a long time in the darkness. At last he said, 'The first two scenes of *The Merchant* and scene one of *Othello*. That's how bad it is.'

'Well you're going to have to delegate more of your authority, aren't you? David Wills must take over more and more.'

She was right. Ronnie Gregor and Art Drays were due

174

down tomorrow. Once more it swept in on him that not only the festival but also his whole career was at stake. This time there had to be complete ruthlessness; there was no room for sentiment or emotion. Tomorrow he would see Carol and change that relationship, or at least alter its foolish, suicidal direction. If she could not face coming to Shireston on those terms then he would get another black actress to play Juliet: it was as serious as that. In his private life Jennifer had to be reinstated. As though suiting the action to the thought, Douglas reached out for Jennifer and she moved her body closer to his. They fell asleep holding hands like young lovers, though Jen's mind was filled with unaccustomed thoughts of rugs and curtains, furniture and the fabric that would surround them at Shireston.

Douglas, in spite of his resolution, could not ward off the erotic pictures of Carol, the many poses of their sexual combat weaving through his dreams so that he woke in the early hours, erect and clinging to the deep slumbered Jennifer. Even in her sleep she turned for him and opened her thighs in need. Douglas lifted himself over her and felt her close compass him. She groaned as he reached his climax, pushing her belly towards him, oblivious to the fact that, in the unseeing eye of night, her skin had changed colour and her face was not that of Jennifer Frost.

The winter sun trying to brighten the whole wretched business as it flooded in through Carol's window, picking up the dust spots and ending in a wan burst on the carpet near to where they sat.

Douglas's mind was held in a vice, as it had been since his arrival an hour before; and now Carol was crying. Not an hysterical outburst of self-pity, but a small volcano of genuine sorrow: for what they had done and for what they meant to each other.

Douglas thought about what he had done to the unknowing Jennifer. It rose like some baroque monument in his mind, over-dramatized into figures of treachery, the stab in the back, the betrayal. Could a few loving fucks be a betrayal? That wasn't really the question, it was the mental involvement, the love, solace, comfort, stimulation that was the betrayal.

From the outset, Douglas had been gentle with Carol, while staying true to his decision.

'It's for all our sakes: for you and Jen as well as for myself. I've taken on an important job, Carol, and I have to see that through: I have to put it first. I thought there would be time for us to straighten out our relationship before Jen came back. But that hasn't worked and I have to put our personal and physical desires to one side. I have to be realistic.'

'It's not just physical. It's a longing for your presence as well.' The last word coming up in a long wail of distress, a choke.

'Of course it isn't just physical. But I've got the hardest question yet for you to answer.'

She looked up and then away again, covering her eyes. Douglas went on speaking.

'Under the present emotional stress, bearing in mind we will have to work together without really being with each other, and allowing for the fact that Jennifer will be around, do you still think you can give me a Juliet?' There was a silence in which all the unsaid things hummed between their minds. 'I have to be horribly professional about this, love.'

'You mean you'd even get somebody else?' The voice bordering on incredulity, as though the shock was just starting to hit.

'For all our sakes I'd have to get somebody else.' He was conscious of repetition – *For all our sakes*. Douglas struggled for the right words, new words, different words, but there were not any new or different words. 'Don't you see that? Don't you see that I have no other real choice?'

'I see nothing but my love for you and my need for you, Doug. It fills my nights and days; like the song says, it's my reason for living, so I've got to cling on to some small hope. If not now then maybe some other time.'

Suddenly Douglas wanted to break up the heaviness, he had the urge to be frivolous and say, melodramatically, 'some

176

other place'.

But Carol was still talking. 'Christ knows, I seem to have said it a million times, I didn't mean it to go this way, but it's as though you've crawled inside me and made your home there. You pervade my atmosphere.'

'Pollute it.' Douglas had yet to get used to the slime of guilt which had seeped into him.

'No. No, never that. Human love – real love, not the romantic swash, or infatuation – real love is bloody terrifying: it . . . it's so demanding . . . so crippling.'

'I know.' Ice cold. 'I know this is something that should never have happened. The thing with bodies shouldn't have turned into the tangling of minds.' With half his conscience, Douglas was aware that it would be the physical side that would, at first, be the maiming blow to Jennifer. If she ever discovered. With this knowledge also came the unreasoned sense that discovery was inevitable. He turned back to Carol, reaching out with his hands. 'I know, love, I know how you feel. I bear it as well.'

'The body pull's still here.' She touched herself and seemed to be speaking to herself. 'I want you, Douglas. All the time I'm wet for you.'

'I know. I know.' A meaningless litany.

'I want you now.' It was then that she really began to cry, the great tears soaking the long black lashes and running down her face like thunder rain. It went on for what seemed to be hours, only a few minutes, but who really understands time; and Douglas felt helpless, squatting there uncomfortably, with one arm round her, not knowing what to say.

Then, without any warning, Carol straightened up violently. 'Shit.' Running the backs of her hands over her eyes, sliding the tears away with her forefingers in almost balletic movement. 'This is no way. You're quite right, Doug, we've got to be professional, but that won't stop me trying to make you every chance I get. Yes, I'll play Juliet, and I'll give you the best Juliet you've ever seen, or that you're likely to see.' She tossed her head in the standard gesture for shaking away the last traces of grief. 'We're very resilient, us spade ladies.'

Douglas knew that he was watching the enforcement of hard professional discipline. If she could do this she could do almost anything with Juliet.

Completely under control, Carol looked up at him, breaking out a small shy smile. 'And now, Mr Silver, will you, for the love of heaven, take me – just for old time's sake?'

The afternoon winter sunshine was also crawling across the book which Jennifer held lovingly on her knees. She crouched, in neat symmetry, feet tucked under her, in the middle of the living-room floor at Elton Court. Around her were books, boxes (one big cardboard monster marked in black stencil, *Bristol 188 Jet Plane Each In An Ind Box Quan ½ Doz G.W. 9 Lbs.*), two large old fashioned leather suitcases and an assortment of odds and ends: photograph albums, a cuttings book, a large pile of neatly folded clothes (blacks, whites, reds predominant; cottons, rayons, wool; on the top a small pile of clean and laundered underclothes, blacks and whites predominant: the whole topped with a note. *For the Family Service Unit. To Be Called For*). There was a tin box spilling trinkets, a sheaf of papers, a little bundle of letters, and the book on her knees.

In the midst of her sorting and packing, Jennifer had come across her old Address and Telephone Number book, the edges of its leather binding beginning to wear and the gold lettering on the front looking patchy.

The book, oblong, around eight by six inches, dated back to Jennifer's pre-Douglas days: she smiled, flicking through the pages, memory grasshoppering over days, months and years, gone like the last summer. Of its kind, the book was a biography, one of the few things which she retained from the time when she was a young sylph model girl: a patchwork of the threads which made up her life at that period and since. It also gave the lie to any idea that she was an organized person – a public image which she always tried to present, even to Douglas.

The light blue frontpapers were alive with notes, drawings, jottings, names, all twisted about with swirling tendrils from which sprouted flowers, leaves or stick men. Names, long forgotten, grew from this unchecked vine which spread across two pages, as did dates and numbers to which she could now put no reason, name or face.

The organized part of her life was most discernible in lists of numbers: thirty or so under *A* listing agencies, and, with a quirk of humour, a dozen photographers under *F*. Her brow creased as she came across a telephone number slashed on to the page in a brilliant purple. Jennifer could not recall ever possessing a purple pen. It amazed her also to see how often she had obliterated what must have been really important telephone numbers by elaborating them with stick men or neat twirled elongations.

There were also the mindless mysteries: the name *A Prothero*, written neatly and with no note, certainly no memory, of who or what *A Prothero* was. She smiled also at her own small pomposities, such as listing people she liked under their christian names, while business numbers, and the people she had not cared for, were solidly planted under their surnames. In this there were special cases, those with whom, for one reason or another, she had become disenchanted, could be found listed twice, the first time under their christian name, then shifted into the surname category. There were whole pages like the front papers, with numbers barely discernible amidst the squirls and twirling flowers of doodles, while special males had particularly ornate decorations, sometimes incorporating advice to herself: *Be intellectually aware or you will be physically undone. Do not drink champagne and brandy. Armour plating.* Under the *D*s there was Douglas's old number and address, wreathed with strange bulbs and tubers, the meaning of which was only plain to her now, at a distance in time. It was the only number on the page, and next to his name Jennifer had written. *Five Star de Luxe Glory. I shall marry this man.* A little lower down, in smaller, neater hand, *12th June 1978 Married him. Six Star.*

She rifled on through the pages, this time giving herself a tiny stab of pain: a number came spinning out of the past to set up aches around healed emotional scar tissue. The name did not matter, she saw his face more clearly than she had for a long time, and heard his voice: the man with whom she had been closely entangled when she first met Douglas: obsessed with him to the point of almost giving up her virginity. She shook her head, thinking, Christ, what horrible tortures and eruptions of pain we bring upon each other. She remembered how Douglas had wafted the beloved from her brain like a fresh wind blowing at mist; the sudden transference and the need for Douglas; the bright love for him giving her a hard ruthlessness which, in retrospect, she now even despised.

Her mood changed, a natural continuation of her thoughts, which swiftly centred back on Douglas: amazing, in this day and age, and with her opportunities, her freedom, that she had gone to her bride bed a virgin. The thought pleased her, because she had been able to give something unique to Douglas, a romantic thought maybe, but it had worked, as a pair they were equally matched lovers, she always knew and had that thought: the one constant thing in their relationship was their coming together. There were patches, like the one at the moment, when it seemed as though retrogression had taken the place of progress and exploration; but that would pass and the wonderful natural voyage of discovery would take hold again. That was the wonder of being Douglas's woman.

She continued to flick through her book, past doctors, dentists, a couple of solicitors, girl friends (not many of those, not for people like Jennifer Frost), car hire services, studio numbers, home catering services, plumbers, electricians (she could never mend fuses), handymen, boring people, happy people, sad and selfish people with their lives chock-a-block with what? Certainly not what she had with her, husband, father figure, joy, delight.

As though on cue, she turned on the floor as Douglas came in, her mind barely taking in the fact that he looked flushed and would not hold her eyes in his. She closed her book tightly, making a gesture of partially hiding it under her body, it was so close and private a thing.

'Hello, darling,' she tried to sound winsome, the word

actually came into her head, then she got lost trying to remember if it meant what she thought it meant. 'I'm sorting things out.' The forthright voice annexing the winsome.

'So I see.' Douglas could not help laughing; he knew too much about Jen's sudden enthusiasms, her passions and quicksilver. Last night, when she had gone on about getting the flat organized, the truth had flared briefly and he remembered to make a quick silent prayer asking for the mood to last until she finished the job. The only thing about which Jennifer was consistently enthusiastic was her work, outside that, life was lived in sharp and radiant bursts which blossomed and faded like beautiful fireworks. Her intellect rose above it all, but Douglas always remembered Jennifer's doting Mama showing him a school report which read, *Jennifer's passage through the fourth form has been paved with good intentions*.

Jennifer giggled, the sharing of their secret. 'Well, don't you think I'm good? Look at the stuff I've cleared out already. Just look at it.'

'Looks a good haul. What're you hiding?'

'Nothing.'

'Lies.'

'Only my old telephone book.' Then quickly, 'Harrods are picking up the things from here on Wednesday. Oh, and they're putting the bed on as well. I bought it. Such a lovely bed, Doug.'

'I remember. Ugly. Brass.'

'With a very firm mattress, my darling, so that when all the plays are in performance and running smoothly you will be able to ride me on a soft, yet unyielding surface.' He did not reply, so she added in a small voice, 'Or I can ride you on a soft, yet unyielding surface?'

Silence.

'All right, have it your own way.'

They both laughed this time. Then she went solemn. 'You really okay, love?'

'Yes.' Douglas nodded. 'I've just dealt with one bit of casting that was looking dodgy. You want to come back to

181

Shireston with me tonight?'

'Have you got to go tonight?'

'I really must get down to plotting first thing in the morning.'

'Drive down early, huh?'

Douglas capitulated.

'By the way,' Jen in bubbling mood again, 'I telephoned your nice Mr Brownhill today. If I let him have a list of the junk we want moved from the flat he'll get it out by Wednesday lunchtime. Will you take a list down to him tomorrow?'

'Anything you ask, ma'am.'

'I'll make the flat super for you, Doug. A real home; and I'll be a real wife to you.'

'You always have been, Jen.'

She gave him a quick, pinched smile. 'No. Not always, love. Me going away. It wasn't good, was it? I shouldn't have gone.'

'Jen, you. . . .'

'We're together now.' She saw that Douglas was not looking at her, and she did not even try to understand the way he held her when she arose and went to him. It was as though he was saying good-bye and hello at the same time.

With Jennifer seeing to the flat and very firm orders given to his executive staff, Douglas Silver was at last able to give some thought to the direction of the four plays.

Tony Holt had provided models of the sets for *Othello*, *The Merchant of Venice* and *Romeo and Juliet*, but was still hung up on *Richard III*; this did not, however, hamper Douglas in his job. The first plays to go into rehearsal would be *Othello* and *The Merchant* on which he eagerly started.

His method of preparation rarely varied; he would work quickly through the text of the play, simply getting the feel of how he wanted actors to move on the stage, making sharp notes of difficult points as he went. Douglas was a firm believer in the director as an audience, allowing the full development of the play to come from within the actors, but to do this, one had to provide them with a safe ground plan.

Once he had plotted, Douglas would usually allow himself a little time to think about the play in its entirety, trying to find the keys to his own production, filling the skeleton ideas with flesh.

He started working alternately on *Othello* and *The Merchant* but after three days found himself strangely drawn and immersed in *Othello*. It was an odd sensation which he had not expected. He knew the play well enough and the plotting was quite easy, but one specific point began to weave into his mind. He always thought of the plot of *Othello* as a fairly straight road, a line drawn from the eloped marriage of Othello and Desdemona to their deaths, the road marked tragically by Iago and his complex plans to crack the Moor's mind and fill it with mad jealousy. Certainly the characterization was difficult, but normally this was something which came when he was working with actors on stage. Yet at this point, Douglas was beginning to see the actors and the way in which they should naturally move. As he plotted, he could see Joe Thomas as the bewildered and passionate Othello; and he could see the tall, handsome Edward Crispin as Iago: the matador, as a lot of people thought of the character. Douglas thought of it now: Iago the matador running rings around Othello the bull; poisoning Othello's mind with hot lies, corrupting him against the innocence of Desdemona; Iago with his vocal passes, his *Veronicas*, *Quites*, *Naturals* and *Estatuarios*, running *Othello* through a whole *faena* until they reached the *estocada*, the moment of truth.

There, with the little model of Tony Holt's settings and the coloured counters he always used for plotting, Douglas became most aware of the way in which he could make the play work as a kind of vocal and physical *corrida*, a bullfight. His subconscious must have been nagging away at the production ever since he had hooked Joe Thomas, for the visual flashes came upon him in heavy detail, like the quick and carefully edited scenes one sees in trailors for movies.

He saw Crispin's Iago, constantly wearing a short scarlet-lined cloak which he swung and used as the *muleta*, the cape with which the matador makes the passes, bringing the

bullfighting analogy right into focus. He saw Jennifer, cool
and radiating virtue as Desdemona, heard her speaking her
plea before the Senate, asking to go to Cyprus with her lord
Othello –

So that, dear lords, if I be left behind,
A moth of peace, and he go to the war,
The rites for which I love him are bereft me,
And I a heavy interim shall support
By his dear absence. Let me go with him.

In hearing her voice, the scene seemed to set itself, the
coloured counters taking up the most natural and dramatic
positions under Douglas's fingers.

Then he began to hear more. Not Shakespeare's words but
the noises which enshrined the central moods and action of
the play, so that the focal points began to express themselves
in sounds which might well counterpoint the poetry of the
play: the sound of muttering, growing and spinning a web on
intrigue; giggles, two voices, their conversation indiscern-
ible; whispering, kissing; the soothe of flesh against flesh; the
noise which might depict the festering jealous thoughts taking root in Othello's mind – the scream of a high-pitched
violin, or was it the scream of a man as he plunged down some
gaping crevasse opened within his own brain? The chink of
money; flesh on flesh; the murmurings again; then the wild
roar of a crowd; the bray of trumpets, tin-like, not the clear
brass of an Elizabethan fanfare; and once again the whispers,
the sighs and moans, the fleshly noises.

Douglas heard all this and knew how to knit his production, how to start the company, how to spin Joe Thomas,
Edward Crispin and Jennifer and all the others, into that
incredible dance which sparks immortal theatrical magic and
produces moments which are burned into the memories of
those who watch and listen.

On the third day, Douglas telephoned Raymond Leggat,
whom he had commissioned to provide the incidental music
for the three productions, most conscious that he should,
long since, have held a productions meeting. Leggat agreed
to come down towards the end of the week, so Douglas

notified Art Drays, Tony Holt and Ronnie Gregor. Knowing that time was short, Douglas forced himself to shift quickly on to *The Merchant* so that at least he would have some basic outline about which he could talk to his productions team.

Once more, looking at Tony's Venetian settings for *The Merchant*, which had the same roots as those used in the Venetian scenes of *Othello*, Douglas found that his imagination was already well primed.

The Merchant of Venice was a brilliant romantic comedy to the Elizabethans, and maybe to other generations since, but what was it to audiences of today? That was Douglas's first question and to him the answer was obvious. In spite of its inherent romantic themes and comedy, *The Merchant* stank of romantic decadence. The central plot, of Shylock and Antonio, the loan and the percentaged pound of flesh were motivated by greed and racial despisal; each of the three love affairs had about them an unpleasant quality – the ludicrous choice of a husband for Portia hanging on the right man choosing the right casket; Jessica and Lorenzo have one beautiful poetic orgy, apart from that their orgies are of a different nature, showing complete contempt for Jessica's father, Shylock; while the coupling of Nerissa and Gratiano is purely comic. The trial is blatantly rigged, though dramatically brilliant. In short, Douglas felt, there was not a single character in the play whom one could respect: all were motivated by gain of one kind or another.

The first key, for Douglas, was to ask Leggat for a straight score of almost rapacious link music, romantic melody gone wrong, debased. So by the time they gathered in his office for the first productions meeting, Douglas had managed to plot two-thirds of *The Merchant* and was able to give Leggat an indication of how much actual music was needed.

'I want the production to speak of human corruption, even in its moments of high comedy, romance or drama,' he told the composer, a short hunched bespectacled man who looked more fifty than his thirty-five years.

Douglas's voice boiled with enthusiasm. 'We've got to drag the audience into the circle of the play as though it was against their will; and their laughter has to be made uneasy; they have to see man at his basic worst, hung up with greed and power and corruption and lust. You name it, this play's got it. It has to appear brittle and witty on the surface, but we have to load it with contemporary suggestions: comment on contemporary values if you like.'

They were sitting in Douglas's office, the small model theatres which housed Tony's settings for the plays ranged in a half-circle on the director's desk. Leggat listened to Douglas, nodding from time to time, he had done enough composing for films and theatre to know what was required.

Naturally, Art and Ronnie wanted a great deal more than this, they always needed to be passed technical information long before the director was ready. Douglas held them firmly at bay, telling them that, in this case, the production had to be developed in rehearsal. After all, they were dealing with a known quantity, Maurice Kapstein, who, whatever else, was a good old professional. The director then pointed out that he was more concerned, at this point, with *Othello*. Joe Thomas was a very different kind of pro and they had to be ready for him, if necessary even be prepared to catch him should he fall.

The director centred the first setting for *Othello* on his desk and began. 'I want to go through the production skeleton in some detail.' He waved a hand towards the first set, an impression of houses cobbled on to each other, a street slicing through the dark mass of rooftops, drunken windows and long balconies through which some giant machine had cut a path. Downstage was a paved open space and one definite structure (for Brabantio's house) on the OP side.

'The scene starts,' continued Douglas, 'with Iago fussing around Roderigo and it ends with Roderigo leading Brabantio and his men off to the Sagittary to find Othello and Desdemona. Now keep this premise in your minds. Iago is the matador. Roderigo is a little fighting bull; Othello a big and important fighting bull. On each occasion that Iago meets and makes intrigue with either Roderigo or Othello he is engaged in a *faena*. . . .'

'What the hell's a *faena*?' asked Art quietly, giving a puzzled look which lifted his eyebrows into a comical twist.

Leggat answered him, a touch of disdain in his voice. 'A bullfighting term. The *faena* is the series of passes made with the *muleta*.'

'The *muleta*?'

'The red flannel cape. You know.' Leggat made a not inelegant gesture with his hands, as though moving the cape in a *natural*.

Douglas looked from one to the other. 'I'm sorry,' he smiled, 'anyone working in this production who's unfamiliar with the terms of the *corrida* should rectify the matter as quickly as possible; that will be the first real note to the company. I see Iago physically making the classic passes at distinct moments in the text.' He looked sharply towards Tony Holt. 'Will you make a note of that? You'll have to alter Iago's costume. I want subtle hint of the suit of lights. Nothing elaborate, just a touch, and if you plan changes for him he must always have something on him or nearby that he can use as the *muleta*. Okay?' His manner was already changed, complete confidence, the style of a tycoon, a professional who knew exactly what he wanted and how to get it. This was the Douglas Silver that most of the acting profession knew: the rock hard activator with the quick tongue, yet quite approachable.

Tony Holt was writing quickly, a pad balanced on his knee. He nodded furiously.

Douglas switched to Leggat, raising a finger, half stabbing at him. 'I'd like you to work closely with Art and Ronnie on the tape. The full business will be worked out in rehearsal but you all have to grasp the technical idea now. Most of the Iago exits and entrances will be covered by a few bars of a *corrida pasodoble*.'

'In Venice?' From Ronnie.

'In Venice,' Douglas hard. 'It's in the audience's mind. There will also be the hint of a crowd of *aficionados* behind the music, but, like the costume, it all has to be subtle. I don't want it to stink of Spain, it simply has to get the idea across

187

and then maintain that idea in dramatic terms without abusing the action or poetry of the play.'

He turned back to his working copy of the text, which was in fact made up of two copies of the play so that each page could be pasted on the left-hand sides of a large stiff bound exercise book, the right-hand pages of which were already scattered with notes. 'Okay, as they say, from the top. Act one: scene one. Houselights down. Stage in darkness. Raymond, I now want a fifteen-second fanfare. Drumroll and trumpets, no clean: a good cheer bray, like you hear at provincial *corridas*, you know what I mean?'

Leggat nodded his bullet head. 'Like you would hear at . . .' his brow wrinkled, one hand prescribing a circle in the air, . . . 'at San Feliu de Guixols?'

'Just right. Tourists, blood, forty-one guys in the ring trying to kill one little bull, hot dogs and everything cheap. Okay, after the fanfare the tape comes up, high volume with street noises, and I don't mean the old-chestnut horses and carts. I want this tape to be so different that the audience is going to sit bolt upright when they hear it; I want the hairs to tingle and a cold shudder go through everyone who listens to it, every time they listen to it. Experiment, let me hear what you come up with; but I have to hear a whole lot of things: night, intrigue, lust, the works, and I've got to hear the right sounds on every cue. Okay, street noises, then, above that, louder, echoed, we have Roderigo's first speech –

Tush, never tell me; I take it much unkindly
That thou, Iago, who has had my purse
As if the strings were thine, shouldst know of
this –

Stage lights up to night plot, Iago and Roderigo walking slowly from upstage. Iago speaks his first lines from the stage.'

Ronnie raised his eyebrows and looked happy. 'A Douglas Silver socko opening,' he observed, off key for Douglas took no notice and went on speaking. 'Now, down to Iago's exit –

Lead to the Sagittary the raised search;
And there will I be with him. So farewell.

Fifteen seconds of *pasodoble* ending with a shout which, in turn, dissolves into Brabantio's search party returning.'

'An olé?' From Ronnie.

'Not quite, but it could be. Got it? Now, end of scene one and the opening of scene two. Brabantio's line –

On, good Roderigo; – I'll deserve you pains.

High volume on the tape, sounds of intrigue.'

'Sounds like a group.' Art wrote as he spoke. 'You want muttering, whispering?'

'Yes, but like the night noises, different. Scratching at the scalp.' Douglas returned to Tony's setting, probing like a surgeon, removing Brabantio's house, pushing a little coloured cardboard watering trough on to the Prompt side. 'Trucks on and off. Muttering dies. Now, two loud bars of the *pasodoble* as Iago enters with Othello.'

Over the next three hours, Douglas took them in heavy concentration through the key technical moves and sounds that would knit scene to scene, or dissolve one scene into the next: the basic structure of the production. The whole team was impressed by the style and brilliance of the director's conception. They talked long about individual ideas – the high-pitched noise to create the idea of jealousy behind the Bard's words, the kind of sounds they could use. As they were leaving Leggat solemnly asked 'How does one represent in sound a hand stroking a nude buttock?'

Art, standing by the door, grinned. 'You get some recording gear and a naked woman.'

For the next few days Douglas worked on, locked inside himself as the first two productions grew clearly in his head. At night his mind was lanced by characters, mixed and leaping from play to play, Shylock and Othello walked through his dreams with Antonio and Desdemona, Portia and Brabantio.

But, while Douglas worked, Jennifer had been far from idle. In a matter of ten days she had righted the Shireston House flat, changing it out of all recognition. Her enthusiasm did not flag, as Douglas had suspected it might. Each time he returned to the apartment there was something new to see.

One day the kitchen appeared to have been transformed, bright where before it had been dull: plates, cups, jugs, dishes and pans gleaming. Somehow there was the feel of unreality about it all, like the glossy ads in the thick magazines, an unused look.

Other things altered, like the new light fitting replacing the old single flex bulb and lampshade illuminations which hung like odd party decorations in each room and hallway, relics of the early thirties (one lampshade actually had patterns of coach houses and shops with great bow windows printed around imitation parchment, the windows glowing when the bulb was turned on). But Jennifer's ingenuity, and the enticement of a stage electrician, changed all that, and now converted oil lamps swung on gleaming chains and the small standard lamps, which Jen had brought from London, were strategically placed.

The new bed was installed early in the process, though Douglas merely noted that it was comfortable to sleep in: Jennifer had more sense than to even attempt goading him into using it for the other pleasures, he was so obviously well inside the skin of work.

Slowly, books began to line clean shelves, favourite pictures and ornaments took on a fresh and different appearance in new settings.

Douglas, involved in the complicated mental process of plotting and rediscovering first two and then four plays, lost all track of time. The days ran into each other. One evening, he returned to find small golden angels decorating the fireplace, a silver tree, festooned with coloured lights, rising five feet or so in one corner and the smell of mincemeat hanging round the flat.

Jen was in the kitchen.

'You like the decorations, darling? Tidings of comfort and joy.'

'Christmas,' said Douglas lamely, his consciousness crammed with flashed pictures of thick wrapping paper, blacks and gold, regency striped, tumbling with Santa

Clauses, coaches, holly; the afterburn of turkey, the taste of Christmas pudding and a couple of erotic poses: Jennifer and himself left alone in her parents' house three years ago on a Christmas afternoon; Mummy and Daddy had set off to walk down the heavy meal; he remembered that Jen wore a velvet back dress, he could even recall the little lacy black pants underneath and the explosion between them – something memorable about that; her skirt pulled up around her waist, eyes closed and hair spreading out over the rug a mass of tendrils, the moments of long loving climax under his palm, with her hand around him, flashing colours and the awareness. That was why he remembered all the Christmas sights and sounds and for a few minutes in the afternoon they had touched their first abandoned time where bodies were discovered with eyes and fingers. In the evening they sang carols and he had looked across at Jen who blushed because, she said later, *I knew you were thinking about me, down there and I could feel it, sore from your hand . . . well, you were energetic.* The Holly and the Ivy. Once in Royal David's City. Carols. . . . Carol. . . . The black mass.

'Only a week, darling.'

'I don't care what star you're following you're not coming through my garden on that camel.'

'And we haven't planned a thing.'

Douglas slumped into one of the velvet covered armchairs.

'We haven't planned a thing for Christmas.'

His hand on the velvet arm. *I love that colour*, Jennifer said long ago, *it's like the bottom of a pool.* Someone changed the main feature in his brain and the guilt clawed at him, the abstract idea changing to a picture's reality of detached animal and bird nails rending and tearing inside him.

'I'm sorry, sugar.'

'Don't worry,' Jennifer came over and smoothed a hand through his hair.

Dark fingers ran down his chin, Carol's fingers, tickling his neck: down through the tough undergrowth of hair on his chest to the thick pubic hair in which the long fingers raked and probed; the backs of her nails stroking his erection, her

191

lips coming down on his, the fusion and their tongues hard inside each other's mouths; his mouth dry, detaching itself, feeling downwards for the nipple, further, lapping over her black silk belly, then his nose embedded in her thatch, his tongue, long and flexible feeling her secret. Another flash, the reason why he would not relax and open his mouth to Jennifer's kisses: because of where his mouth had been in the time between; and all it meant; and the guilt, the foolish tension.

'You've been too busy, Doug. Anyway, I've organized things. . . .' Her hand stopped stroking, fingers dovetailed among his hair as she realized he was saying sorry for some other reason and that it had nothing to do with Christmas, or cards with robins on them, or the decorations, lists of groceries, smart cards with silhouetted holy families, gift wrapped nightdresses, cheap crackers, children's luminous faces and, out of the mulch of images, her own small bed, when she was a child, and a lonely stocking hanging in readiness.

Douglas was still with a mixture of guilt and the faded memories of Christmas, another Christmas with Jen. Last year? They had argued for nearly two days, a logical game of intellectual ping pong which began with the existence of God and ended with man's social responsibility.

'I'm sorry, sugar.' He did not speak, but Jennifer heard it again, the tone and manner. It was like having ice injected into her bones.

'Sorry for what, Doug?' Jennifer slid down to a sitting position at his feet, a theatrical pose, looking up at his face, tired, the eyes not looking back at her, strain bunching the flesh at the corners.

'Sorry about what, Doug?' She heard herself and was conscious of the vocal pitch being out of control, too high.

He moved his head so that their eyes met; Jennifer felt the unaccountable fear move, like a reptile in her intestines. Then Douglas smiled, just with his mouth at first, then it grew to embrace his eyes. 'People say private sorries sometimes.' The smile faded. 'I'm just saying sorry for a lot of bad

192

things.'

The black hand in his head went out of focus, replaced by the face, tears, the streaked cheeks in close-up so that he could see the skin texture and watch the liquid globs running down leaving their trail. *Like it says in the song: you're my reason for living.*

She had lain in his arms and talked of so many things until she seemed to have always been a part of his life.

'Something in particular, Douglas? There's been something wrong ever since I got back.'

He looked straight at Jennifer again. The face he loved. The face he had loved? No, loved: the mind behind, and the body, the person he loved; had cheated. Carol whispering in his ear. Christ, he needed her and her body, his brain was awash with her.

'Tell me, Doug.'

Jennifer, on whom he had bestowed everything, shared all things, given his body and taken hers, and offered his mind in collective exchange of thoughts, ideas, revelations. Even her name evoked the cause of his existence. Carol's breasts, her thighs. Carol as a person, loved, satisfied. Jennifer. Carol. Carol. Jennifer.

Against his will, Douglas nodded, signifying yes, there was something in particular, hoping a miracle would change the direction.

'Tell me.' Jennifer's voice warm, loving, the voice of a woman trying to help her man: the mother in her. Her brain ticking through the possibilities: money? the job at Shireston and its responsibilities? family, relations? some friend in distress? The obvious question flicked into place and was rejected, but she asked nevertheless, 'Is there someone else?' Knowing it was impossible and that there could be only one answer.

'Of course not.' She even heard it, then above it his voice saying, 'Yes, there has been.'

She should not have asked the question and Douglas knew that he was at fault for answering it, but there had always been honesty between them, even at this moment when he

193

knew there was a kind of moral right in hiding the truth from her.

Within Jennifer the pain was complete: physical and blinding; mental and bewildering, horrid malformed animal figures scurrying within or skulking, the whole shock starting low in her stomach and raging in a great wave which submerged her.

As though she had not heard him she groped blindly, hoping that it was all a nightmare, a horrible sick joke. 'You've . . . someone else . . .? You've had . . .? No . . .' No, it was not true. Not Douglas. The mind refusing to accept. Who? Who is it?' A small index of friends, the mental finger of her brain running down the list, pausing.

'Don't, love, it's all over now, finished, you don't know her. Please, I'm sorry.'

Jennifer reached out, trying to focus on sanity. There was one of the little gold Christmas angels in her hands, a cone of gold card, embossed thick paper wings and arms, a pert little carved face.

St Mary Magdelene
Pray for us
St Agatha
Pray for us
St Lucy
Pray for us
St Agnes
Pray for us
St Cecelia
St Catherine
St Anastasia
Pray for us.

She had once played a nun in a very bad movie stacked with religious sentiment. Christ, she'd even played this part before, the wronged wife. Aloud she said, 'But that was in another country and besides the wench is dead.'

'It really would be better that way.'

She stared at the paper angel. 'Better for whom? Why, Doug? Because I wasn't here?'

'Something like that.' He could feel her pain mingling slowly with his guilt.

'I should be terribly cool, that's the fashionable way isn't it? To take it all, to understand, shrug one's shoulders and say, what's a fuck between friends?'

'Please, Jen, it wasn't like. . . .'

'It wasn't like that? Well how the hell was it, Douglas?' The two bodies moving like one, Douglas, whose body she knew so well, every inch, each area known to her. She remembered that once when making love with him she had realized that this was the true biblical meaning of knowing a man, not just the bodily experience or the satisfaction and pleasure, but the real knowledge: the map of his physical and mental terrain, fully explored and fully conquered. Now, sometime in the night, when she was unaware, disabled by absence, he had given his body and mind away: that which had been so completely hers had become a bright new country for someone else. She saw his nakedness and the white gleaming nakedness of the other, young, writhing under him and usurping, her face ill defined.

'It was a thing that happened and got out of hand.'

'Out of hand? I only hope she was good; that it was worth it.' The tears forming in her eyes, of anger, hurt, bitterness, misery, failure and all the things any woman feels.

'Jen, darling,' Douglas half rose, his arms going out to her, 'please don't, it's not worth it. It was nothing, I promise you, nothing.' The lie echoing within him, shifting *his* pictures of the lovers: black on white and white on black, turning, weaving, floating in a peace and harmony he thought that he had never known before. But the truth lanced into the lie; for a second the bodies changed and it was Jen who looked at him from the bed.

'Was she?'

'Was she what?'

'Was she good? What else?'

'Don't, Jen I promise, love, it was different.'

'Better?'

'Look, Jen. . . .'

195

She had one weapon and, paradoxically, she needed to use it now. Reconquer. She rose, standing in front of him, a most uncharacteristic attitude for Jennifer Frost, legs apart, planted firmly, hands on her hips.

'Let's see if she was that good,' a pause of no less than two beats before she turned, heading for the bedroom, 'or if I can do any better.'

From the bedroom she shouted, 'Come on, Douglas. Or are you a coward as well?'

Tired and rattled with the day, Douglas did not at first grasp her meaning. Jesus, he thought, women, I shouldn't have let it go . . . never understand why . . . coward? Coward as well? He walked to the bedroom door. Jennifer was naked by the big brass bed.

'Come and see, Doug. Then you can make up your mind which of us is best. Because that's really all there is when you boil it down. Nuts to your beauty and poetry, it's the pair of bodies and what goes between.' She took a step forward and put her arms aggressively around his neck, clamping her mouth to his, leech like, ungiving and, for a moment, unforgiving, her hands moving down reaching firmly and expertly for his clothing.

Later, Douglas wondered at his body's immediate response and the urgency of what followed. His skin tingled in a way he had rarely experienced. Jen worming herself over him with an enthusiasm and concentration unique to his knowledge. It was as though each part of his frame was, in turn, ravaged, satisfied and then given a delicious after pleasure. When they finally sank into the ease of tender, playful and quiet post-combat she whispered, 'Better than that?'

'You know it couldn't be.'

Jen smiled, then the smile changed, a realization of sadness, her eyes moving away.

'Sorry, Jen, truly sorry.'

'Tell me about it.'

He shook his head. 'No torture. Not yet. It really isn't worth it.'

She returned the nod, the other bodies coming back into

her mind, the woman's face still out of focus.

Three days to Christmas and Douglas drove to London in the morning leaving behind him a trail of questions in Jennifer's mind.

She need not have worried. Douglas, cramped with his personal load of blame, arrived in London with one thought of getting some gorgeous Christmas present for Jennifer: maybe to appease his grinding guilt.

He found what he wanted after a slow irritating journey up, and the grind and frustration of elbowing through the crowds intent on stripping the shops in a last minute buy-about.

On the pavements and in the stores humanity grappled with the season of peace and goodwill: a river of people flowing multi-coloured along the main thoroughfares, branching off into tributaries which became seething lakes among the merry floorwalkers, their faces sprayed grey with fatigue. Everywhere the loaded, useless magnets of Christmas commercialism brayed, hung about with gold, red, silver and purple tinsel, bows and ribbons, while in the big store windows a hundred Santas overshot a hundred rooftops, sleigh and reindeer defying gravity.

Douglas found the ring in Harrods: a chunky wide modern setting carrying an inch long oval moss agate. It sat on black velvet crying out for Jennifer's finger, and Douglas knew that this had to go back to Shireston with him. There was a mental double-take when the saleslady, black dressed and oozing creamed sweetness like a crushed meringue, told him the price; yet he did not really have to think twice about buying it.

With the ring boxed and gift-wrapped, lying snug in his pocket, one gloved hand covering it against the possible pickpocket, Douglas began the long push towards the nearest entrance. Then, above the sea of bodies, about ten yards away, he caught the glimpse of a dark head tilted at a familiar angle. He struck out through the crowd, frantic, as though fighting a monster under-tow, shoving towards the girl, drawing near and realizing that it was not Carol after all: the desert opening up inside, a long mental wasteland.

The immediate effect of the incident caused Douglas to press himself back into the store, a wandering aimless fight, part of his mind sure that Carol was somewhere near, the other part wanting to buy her a beautiful memento, an act which might give them both a handful of hope. Or maybe it was just a salve to his conscience. In the end he purchased a luxuriant nightdress, heavy with four or five layers of flimsy material, high at the neck and encrusted with lace and bows, ordering it to be gift-wrapped and sent to Carol with a card on which he wrote – *With Love. Douglas* – the L of Love turning into an elongated squiggle as his arm was jogged by someone in the bobbing throng.

Only later, in the car, did he remember that Carol had no use for garments like nightdresses. Jennifer adored things which were considered feminine, while Carol had an austerity about her clothes which rejected even the tiniest lace trim; Carol relied wholly on her body, her femininity, she thought, needed no gilding: things like nightdresses did not come near her scene of living.

Why then a gift like that? And why the sudden violence? He had fought to get near the girl, mistaken for Carol, pushed hard with his shoulders and even handed off people. Perhaps, he wondered, this was the difference between obsession and love. Obsession with Carol and her body, love with Jennifer and her whole self.

Women tend to pry, especially when their security seems to be threatened. But the prying did not make Jennifer feel any better, she hated herself, going through Douglas's pockets, examining the contents of his briefcase, going through the glove compartment in the car. It was worse because she knew that Douglas would never do the same to her, she could not see him turning out her handbags or examining the laundry.

Out of all Jennifer's sifting the end product was one small clue, laid bare across two pages of Douglas's pocket diary, five, six weeks before: neat clear writing, unmistakably a woman's hand: three lines –

For the Chinese it may well be the Year of the Ram,
Or the Bear, maybe the Tiger.
For me this week has been the Week of the Small of your Back.

She could not even ask him about it because that would make her guilty also, yet it did not stop the clear pictures of jealousy projected inside her: the girl lying naked writing over the pages, her face brimming with love, adoration and physical satisfaction.

'What happened? Did you just stop loving me, like dying stops you?'

'I didn't stop loving you at all, it was something else, Jen, I can't really explain a thing like that. I'm not gifted with the use of the right words.'

'Did you find the words with her? Did she find the words for you?'

'What do you mean?'

'I mean did you have a language? Are there special phrases you recall?'

'Jen. . . .' stumbling around his mind for the phrases, yes of course he remembered what she had said – *You want to make a circle? When you fill my body you also fill my mind, and when you've left my body my mind is still full of you. Dangerous Douglas Silver* . . . But there were also phrases, sayings that only he and Jennifer knew. 'Jen, must you? It is over, finished. . . .'

'I have to understand. It isn't as though we didn't get along. Or if we constantly quarrelled. If you loved her and wanted her you must have put me out of your mind. I want desperately to get back in there.'

'You were away, I needed someone to . . . someone I could turn to, physically. It progressed further than I thought it would. You never left me though. I didn't stop loving you for a second.'

'She was good for you though, I see it in your eyes and feel it in your. . . .'

Jennifer would not let it rest. If Douglas had caused the

first damage it was Jennifer who spread the infection, her mind wriggling with dark fantasies that could well contain truth. The unfound face and the nameless name playing havoc with her confidence, crumbling her inner self: the destruction of knowing that, for a time, she had been unwanted, not needed; the despair of seeing for herself that whatever terrible thing had lurked in Douglas's immediate past there were traces of it still there, crouching, waiting to destroy the trust and that happiest encoiled relationship which they had known. Or was even that a myth in her mind? Had she lived a dream alone all the time, imagining what she felt: Douglas leaning across the table, grasping her hand; the smile radiant (through him she had come to know the meaning of that word); Douglas whispering, *Jennifer Frost, you don't know how much I love you*. There had been safety in this thing, now the roots of safety had been ripped out by . . . By whom? No face. No name.

So she picked, probed, prodded at Douglas who genuinely wanted to ease his smarting conscience, simply to rid his mind of what had been between Carol and himself. At times he even wished that Jennifer and he could be promiscuous people, able to shift partners and return to each other, embroidering their own intimate moments with close muttered tales of what he had done, or how she had reacted, and so spark anew their own private flame. But their feelings were so entangled that all Douglas could sense was the real agony of the inner gnaw, the grind of the rats' teeth at his guts and the need to purge himself so that it could be sane again; so that he could face the company when they arrived; so that he could meet Carol on a new and professional level.

There was only a handful of people at Shireston House over the holiday; most of the stage and office staff lived locally and the few others departed for friends and relatives. Of those who remained, Ronnie Gregor had already installed his current blonde, nineteen-year-old girl-friend, Stephanie, in one of the double apartments with Douglas's blessing; Adrian Rolfe's wife and two young daughters, little dark girls with mean eyes like their father's, now regarded Shireston almost as their birthplace; Art Drays was an anywhere-I-hang-my-hat-is-home man, so he had bedded himself down in one of the unused flats and settled in, comfortable and self-reliant.

'I haven't noticed a turkey walking around. Or nuts. We not celebrating the Winter Solstice this year?' Douglas asked on Christmas Eve.

'Discovered,' sighed Jennifer, relaxing for a moment in ordinary things, her subconscious blessing the fact that Douglas could still make remarks like this to her. 'The grub's ordered, darling, and they're bringing it up from the town this morning.'

'Bringing it up from the town, eh?' Douglas assumed his country dialect, 'Yer, Jack, this lot be for the big 'use. You git 'im up there sharpish.'

'But we won't be having turkey.'

'Scrooge.'

'There's a quarter of humbugs.' A tentative grin.

'I want my turkey.'

'Oh does he want his turkey? You'll get it, darling,' she smooched at him. 'Shall I tell you a secret?'

'You shouldn't tell secrets.' He saw it was wrong as he said it, the sudden lowering of spirits, the words misunderstood and placed in the context of his infidelity, her face becoming frozen, hard, dead with unspoken hates and pain. 'I'll give you a kiss for your secret,' he said, longing for the magic to flash between them.

Jennifer gave a small switched smile. 'It's worth more than a kiss.'

'Name your price. I can be very generous.'

'You can't pay it. Not yet.'

'Give me credit. I'll pay soon enough.'

Her smile widened, not the screen smile known to a million seat-paying clients, but the one she reserved for Douglas and private moments. 'Okay,' she took a deep breath, raising herself on tiptoe, arms straight at her sides, like a small girl trying to get some indiscretion off her chest. 'There's going to be a Christmas party here. I fixed it all with Emilio; his chef lives alone and had nowhere to go on Christmas Day. So we're going to christen the new restaurant, Christmas night, tomorrow night: turkey, plum pudding, crackers. . . .'

'Figs?'

'Plenty of figs, and nuts, dates, celery. The works.'

'Can we get a little drunk and come back here to make abandoned love?'

She looked at him, all serious eyed, 'That would make a beautiful Christmas present . . .' a pause and giggle, '. . . but who's going to be the little drunk? Adrian?'

Douglas pulled her to him and smacked her bottom lightly. 'You and I, my darling, will share a bottle of champagne and eat sparingly. We will do our duty as the director and his lady, then we will steal away to this our chamber, there the deep art of sexual combat to apply.' The last words spoken in his Olivier *Richard III* voice.

The party was one of those strange bits of organized spontaneity which worked in spite of all things being against it. Christmas Day was cold, gusty winds blowing at the stripped branches, ripping at tiny pieces of garden litter, pushing at the house rattling the windows and creating moans along the empty passages. It was very much the kind of day for staying indoors, a situation which made it difficult for people to pull themselves together, struggle out of lethargy and head for the restaurant which had been decorated and made attractive for the occasion.

Emilio had given up the entire day to making a success out of the small affair, while his chef, the newly appointed Dominic, grinning, red faced with a long drooping Mexican moustache and an almost traditionally fat body, came out to greet the guests and see they were happy with his work. Emilio buzzed around, refusing to sit with his colleagues; his wife, the pert and bright Doris, assisting enthusiastically with the serving, but with eyes for nobody but her husband. Douglas noted with a secret pride that Emilio had persuaded the thin Mrs Doul to help, and that she actually looked happy.

You could tell that the Rolfes would much rather have remained at their own fireside, and that Ronnie and his girl, Stephanie, had been clutched to each other, coupling and uncoupling all day.

Douglas and Jen had spent the holiday in mutual good humour, both of them taking trouble and care to push their double problem far below the surface, Jennifer entranced with her ring.

'It will be my Desdemona ring, Doug. I'll wear it all the time and it will bring luck to your production.'

At first, when everybody gathered at the restaurant, they sat around the long table, decorated with holly and Christmas roses, like members of a family who had been separated for a long time, not ready to reinstate each other back into full confidence, but, as the food and drink began to circle the table, as crackers were pulled and the paper hats put on with that everlasting self-conscious bravado, they stopped being stiff individuals, relaxing, beginning to share. Turkey with chestnut stuffing, roast potatoes, carrots and swedes, thick slices of white meat, Christmas pudding with the brandy flames electric blue, the dry bubbles of champagne lighting other fires deep inside.

Of his own volition, Art Drays had fitted up one of the big tape machines and amplifiers so they could eat to modern standard Christmas music like *White Christmas* and all its derivatives right down to *Little Donkey*, and, as the evening moved on, more pop beats emerged and people began to dance.

Douglas, as director of the company, did his duty and danced with each of the ladies in turn. It was as he danced a slow blues with Ronnie's Stephanie (who prattled about her chances of getting a job with wardrobe and what did he think?) that Douglas looked up and caught Jennifer's face, her expression begging him to leave.

They slipped away just after eleven and, in the big brass four-poster, again knew joys that, Jennifer at least, had not known since their honeymoon.

The individual members of the company were due to

arrive over the first three days of January and the week between Christmas and New Year's Day passed in a tunnel of preparation, a sense that they were all just beginning.

'Good Christmas, Archie?'

'The usual, you know. Quiet.'

'Yes, always have a quiet Christmas nowadays. Pissed most of the time though.'

'Ah. Sitting in front of that bloody box watching it all happen without you.'

'Ah.'

'She's incredible, Art, I've never known a girl like her. Never satisfied.'

Ronnie, you always say that. It's you that's never satisfied.'

'You don't partake, do you?'

'Sex?'

'Yes.'

'No sex, Ronnie. I haven't the need.'

'Not for anything? Anyone?'

'Only once. A long time gone now. Come on, how about some work, chum?'

Romeo and Juliet 216/217
Link III: 4/5
Exit Paris. Exit Capulet through door.
Lights slow black.
Fly doorway and window.
Drop in interior window.
Trucks on with bed etc.
Sound: the dawn chorus horribly mutilated (like a conman might hear it).
Lights up to dawn. Romeo and Juliet in bed.
Movement and sexual sounds.
Lights slowly up to daylight during next five minutes.
As dawn chorus reaches crescendo overlap with electronic whoops turning to long screech and silence.
Romeo and Juliet very still then Romeo disentangles himself

and slips out of bed moving to the window. He is naked. Juliet begins first speech (*Wilt thou be gone?*), leaves the bed and joins him close at the window. She is naked.

'Oh, Ash, just a few more days and we'll be there.'

'Right in the sweat, love.'

'I'm not thinking about the sweat, I'm thinking about being down there in the country, with a proper, decent flat to live in and really big actors to watch.'

'Good-bye to the Chamber of Horrors.'

'The Bloody Tower.'

Internal Memo
To: Douglas Silver.
From: Adrian Rolfe.
Date: 28th December 1980.
Subject: Reception for the Company.
All arrangements have now been made for the reception for the company to be held in the green room at 8 p.m. on 3rd January. I have instructed the catering staff that you will be speaking to the company and their wives at about nine o'clock. May I suggest that you make this speech one of informal welcome as the press will be present. Matters of company policy should be kept until the company meeting at 9 a.m. on 4th January in the rehearsal room.

'Hello?'

'Adrian?'

'Yes.'

'Douglas. I just called to ask you to watch the wording of your memos in future.'

'What's wrong with my wording?'

'Nobody, but nobody, tells me when I should make statements on company policy.'

'I didn't know I had.'

'Well read that last memo carefully, Adrian, and don't presume again.'

'How do you describe love, Doug?'

'Human love? Two people?'

'Yes.'

'I don't have the facility, I interpret. I don't write, though I suppose you can do it with sounds. Music describes love for some people doesn't it? Objects, trinkets acquired on the journey.'

'For me it's words. I suppose some people think it's sentimental but do you remember the passage from *As You Like It* where poor, moonstruck Silvius descibes love?

It is to be all made of fantasy,
All made of passion, and all made of wishes;
All adoration, duty, and observance,
All humbleness, all patience and impatience,
All purity, all trial, all deservings –'

'They're the big, straight simple statements aren't they? The trinkets touch me more. Try this one.' He leaned back on the pillow, eyes closed, willing memory, voice just on the right side of emotion not to make it sentimental.

'There is no loving without losing.
You lose yourself to become part of somebody else,
That's just how it is.
I didn't expect to remain the same, but,
Oh I guess I didn't know what to expect.
It's different every time though.
A new language invented,
A new system stumbled on,
Different from the old one.
What I have gained from being with you,
Besides a belly and a deeper beard,
I guess I couldn't get anywhere else,
And I'll be damned if I'll ever try.'

'I didn't know you went for McKuen.'

'Neither did I.'

'You learned that with her, didn't you?'

'Yes, but that's all over now.'

'I'm glad.'

206

'Hey, Emilio, you're putting on weight.'

'I could do with a few pounds.'

'It's all that food you steal when Dominic's not looking.'

'Nah, it's the spaghetti I teach you to cook, Doris. A wild English rose like you, yet you cook spaghetti like you came from Milan.'

'The new job's good, Emilio, you're really happy again. For the first time for. . . . Oh I don't know, for years, I see you happy.'

'I told you, it's your spaghetti.'

'No, dear, I go down to Shireston on the second. It means almost a whole year out of London, simply nobody will remember me, but I believe I'm doing the right thing. I mean the chance to work with Douglas Silver and all those people. You did know that Conrad's going to be there? What do you mean, Conrad who? You camp old bitch, you know as well as I do, that's why I'm going down a day before I have to, I don't want to get trampled under foot trying to get at him. I'll be there already. . . .'

Douglas Dear,

Thank you for your Christmas gift. I did not dare to telephone you, but I've marked this Private For Mr Silver Only. I hope that is all right.

About your present: are you trying to tell me something about the future or the lack of something in the past?

I am longing just to see you again, though dying with fear because of the circumstances.

Sorry. I can't help loving you,

C

'Jen, your hair?' Shouted, face in shock, from the doorway. 'What have you done to your hair?'

'I've cut it off, darling.'

'I can see that. But why? Your lovely hair.'

'It's better this way. It'll be better for Desdemona.'

'What do you mean it'll be better for Desdemona? You

should have consulted me on that. For Christ's sake I am your director.'

'You're also my husband. First you're my husband.'

'Sure, first I'm your husband. So?'

'What do you think about it as my husband?'

A long, long pause during which Douglas cocked his head on one side and allowed a smile to touch the corners of his mouth. 'As your husband I love you any way. I'd love you without any hair at all. You know that. It's great.'

'And as my director, for Desdemona?'

'You look like a butch St Joan.'

'It is rather drastic, isn't it?' She peered into the mirror, face close, turning her head.

'It's bloody drastic and . . .'

'And?'

'I was going to say that Desdemona was not the reason for cutting your hair.'

'No?'

'No.'

Joe Thomas was due to arrive on the afternoon of the second. He came into Heathrow, unannounced, late on the afternoon of the first.

CHAPTER EIGHT

Gentlemen. Ladies and gentlemen. I would be stupid – a nut – if I tried to hand you some line about being honoured and privileged to be here. Hell, those are the words you hear people use, but I want to find some other way to tell you. Like, I'm knocked out to be here: but unconscious. I can't believe it's me here, in England steppin' out to act Shakespeare. On a personal note, my own thoughts at this time go straight back to my old father, who, in his long and hard life carried only two books with him: the Bible and the works of William Shakespeare. . . .

Shit, thought Joe Thomas, he couldn't do it that way, it was phoney as a seven-dollar bill. Sitting there in the wide cabin of the 747 bound for London, a shiver of apprehension trickled from the base of his spine, rising to the back of his neck. You could get away with the flip talking, like this last imagined press conference speech, when you were dealing with the brittle world of show-business and clubs: there you could use the tinsel town talk, but put it next to the enduring classic theatre and you were dead.

Joe Thomas had spent a lot of time with the classic theatre, *Othello* in particular, during the past few weeks. His contractual obligations at Vegas finished at the end of October and, with inherent professionalism moving his reflexes, Thomas cut loose from the shiny halters of his work and dropped out of sight. In fact he was holed up in a rented villa just north of Sacramento, his only companion being a thirty-year-old professional boxing trainer who had him out doing road work at five every morning and again after dark each evening, with a couple of indoor sessions during the day.

The rest of the time, Joe Thomas grew a beard and studied *Othello*, working on the text, consuming every book he could find about both the play and the Elizabethan Theatre: he had a fixed intention in his mind to go to Shireston with a full working knowledge, a fact which would have disturbed Douglas Silver had he known.

Early in December, Joe Thomas's natural urges got the better of him to the extent that he sent the trainer off on a long week-end and called in two trusted girl friends from Los Angeles, an excess for which he suffered when the trainer returned.

Over Christmas he became restless again, anxious to get started, a feeling which was mixed with the occasional twinge of uncertainty. In the end he returned to Los Angeles, spent a couple of days catching up with accumulated paper work: putting letters on tape, finalizing matters with the now blatantly sulky Tommy Carr whom he tried to appease with good spirits and half promises.

'Come on, Tommy. Christ, man, you're getting paid while I'm away.'

'It ain't just that, Joe, it's not simply the money. I think you're mad; I think you've been conned, baby. You're going to spend a whole year in some English hick town with people you don't know: they're not like us you know, Joe.'

'I'm going to get me a year's culture and training, Tommy. Hell, Smiley'll be comin' over later, then, once the play's on maybe you can come as well; perhaps fix up a couple of recording sessions, you know the clause in that KDM contract gives the okay to do two a year for another label.'

'Maybe. Maybe we can do something like that, but, man, I still think you're crazy.'

Smiley packed for him and, without thought of any pre-arranged plan, Joe boarded the first jet he could get – eight suitcases, heavily overweight, but, he thought to himself, there would be no big journalist problem at Heathrow if he arrived unexpected, unheralded.

Now, high above the Atlantic, with the anxious flicker of uncertainty superimposed against pictorial images of Shireston (which he had never seen), the festival, himself as the Moor, Joe Thomas leaned back and tried to ease his mind. He put on the headset and switched it through to *Popular Music*. Frank was ripping up the seats with *You Make Me Feel So Young*. Thomas had the immediate and immature reaction of why the hell isn't that me? I did a deal with this airline only three months ago. They've got three tapes of mine, so why ain't I on now? But that was always his way – the ego, the talent, the necessity for constant and instant admiration, success, adulation. The chill feeling within him increased.

Back on the ground again he was even colder: inside the terminal building at Heathrow he could feel the drop in temperature, making him shiver through his topcoat and suit. He collected his pile of luggage and found a porter who gave him a surly, 'All this?' pointing at the bags.

'Sure.'

'I'd better get someone to help.' The man walked away with a slow lope, disappearing for ten minutes before returning with an equally weary colleague, the pair making a great deal of display about the number and weight of the cases.

At customs he did not fare any better. It became increasingly obvious to Joe that he was either going unrecognized or had happened on some very race conscious Englishman. The customs officer was abrupt, almost rude.

'All these yours?' he asked in a manner suggesting that there was something very wrong for a black man to be travelling with so much luggage.

It was with the customs officer's first query that Joe Thomas realized how far he had been shielded, privileged even, within the racial tensions of his own country. It had been wrong and foolish of him to come over alone and unheralded. When Joe Thomas said jump they jumped: Joe Thomas was proof that black was beautiful and successful, but only when he had the symbols with him. Now he was very much alone and among people who had mixed ideals; people who said they deplored racism yet had hard fixed thoughts and beliefs in their hearts; frightened people and

211

lethargic people.

Joe did not fully comprehend the rise of turmoil in his body, but one decision was certain, if difficult. He simply nodded slowly at the customs officer signifying that it was all his baggage: cooling his arrogance was the better way. It would be easy to blow and make a big noise, but, whatever his personal problems, Joe Thomas still clung on to his firm base of professional discipline.

The customs officer had a blotchy complexion and moist eyes which spoke of fatigue. 'Have you read this before?' he asked pointing to the familiar card that proclaimed what was needed by way of a customs declaration.

'Many times.' Joe could hear the dullness in his voice. Many times and in so many different circumstances, different countries and different states.

Can you read, boy?

I'm going to read this for you and you'd better listen.

Open that case, boy, then put your hands against the wall.

It had been a long time since anything like that had happened, but, when they wanted to, they really had the edge on you when it came to insults; all of them; the uniforms might be different but the looks and words always seemed to add up to the same thing. You did not expect it in liberal Britain, yet there it was deep behind those watery eyes, the prejudice and look which said black was not beautiful, black was dangerous, black was inferior.

'Where have you come from?'

'Los Angeles through New York City.' Surprised, baby? You think I came from Pakistan? Or the jungle? I ain't wearing my loincloth. Or maybe you think I just made it in from South Africa? No, sir, you don't catch me in that neck of the woods. That would be great: Joe Thomas starring at the Starlight Room of the Johannesburg Hilton.

'Are you here for pleasure?'

'I figure living is pleasure, but if you want to be accurate, I'm here on business.'

'You plan to work here?'

'I do.' And I know you've got plenty of vacancies on the

212

London subways, and the buses and there's always street cleaning.

'You have a work permit?'

That was enough. Joe Thomas leaned against the counter, making the movement an overtly exaggerated gesture. 'Is this some kind of put-on or do you really not know who I am?' He looked straight into the man's filmy eyes.

'Are you travelling on a United States passport?'

'That's already been checked out, by the gentleman back there who deals with passports. Now, take a good look, do you still not know who I am?'

'No, sir,' the 'sir' was drawn out, 'I do not know who you are. I simply asked if you were travelling on a United States passport. I also asked if you had a work permit.'

Thomas felt the blood rise, but he still held himself in check: there were vague, half-known facts about the English Race Relations Act fanning around his mind. The controlled and unroused part of him tried to be subjective: the officer could claim that he was perfectly within his rights; on paper the questions would look nothing, the insults being in the nuance, the tone, the attitude.

Slowly he reached inside his breast pocket and removed his passport, tossing it on to the counter, another flamboyant gesture as the flat little book spun against the wood, stopping the right way up and pointing towards the customs officer who reached lazily to lift it from the counter. He slowly leafed through the pages, flicking his eyes up to Thomas's face and then down again at the document.

'You look different with a beard, Mr . . . er . . . Mr Thomas. That's a Welsh name, Thomas.'

'So is Davis, as in Sammy Davis. I am an American citizen.' He was too big to get uptight about it. Who was he talking at anyway? Some little official with a spit of power who probably really did have no idea who Thomas was: the man might even be an opera buff.

The customs man nodded at the passport. 'An entertainer? We usually have to ask you gentlemen to open one or two pieces of baggage.'

In spite of the internal rage, Thomas smiled. 'Rogues and vagabonds?'

'Something like that, sir.'

Maybe he had been wrong about the man: there was no way of telling. Pictures filled his mind, flashing out against the mental retina: the sea of faces and crash of applause, the band backing him, blaring, his hands outstretched as though taking the audience to him; his ability to captivate, to lift, to create a small happening of mass hypnotism; the pleasure which he obviously gave to them and the stimulation he felt when he was giving; and the contempt he so often felt for large numbers of his fans. It was just possible that there was one lone cat in British Customs at Heathrow Airport who had never seen or heard of him, who had never been exposed to him. Yet, in the next second he knew it was not quite as straightforward as that.

'Have you anything to declare?' The officer's face insolently blank, as if he knew something of which Joe Thomas was unaware.

'I'm only carrying my personal effects.' As he said it, Joe realized why he had been disturbed. It had nothing to do with colour, simply the unconscious worry that customs men detect like radar scanners. Personal effects. His dressing case and what Smiley had said at the airport before he left.

'I put a little in the soap container, boss, just in case you need relaxing a shade when you get over there.'

He was thinking of something else when Smiley had said it and the whole thing only registered vaguely, but it must have been heavy in his subconscious and now he knew why the customs officer seemed to be hammering him. It did not feel good.

'Only your personal effects?'

The pause was too long. 'Yes.'

'And you have nothing to declare?'

'Nothing.'

'Then you've no objection to our looking through your luggage?'

Joe Thomas shrugged. 'Do I have a choice?'

The man tipped his cap on to the back of his head which he shook, slowly. Another, younger, officer had joined him. 'Okay, we'll start with the small stuff.' Unerringly he indicated the briefcase and dressing case.

Joe Thomas pulled out his slim gold key chain and began to unlock the larger cases.

'No, sir,' the officer's hand on the dressing case: it had been a Christmas gift, a couple of years ago, from a grateful executive for whom he had done a couple of contractual favours: a handsome oblong black leather box which opened out flat, displaying brushes, bottles and containers: ivory, glass and silver.

The second man busied himself with the briefcase while the first began unstoppering bottles sniffing at their contents. Fascinated, Joe watched him move from the bottles to the cordless electric shaver and on to the electric toothbrush and then the soap container. He did not speak until the man lifted it from its leather holding strap.

'Okay,' Joe's voice low, almost a whisper. 'Okay, I'm busted. It's in there.'

The customs' officer gave him a quick sidelong glance and then returned to opening the soap container. Once more Joe felt the rise of anger. Why was this happening to him, Joe Thomas? The anger was mixed with a terrible feeling of isolation, loneliness, hatred for this white bastard. As if down some long cavern of memory that was not his own he could hear the baying of dogs. That was his grandfather's memory passed on at childhood, but it was real enough.

The customs man had unwrapped the small packet. 'This all you've got?' he asked. They both spoke quietly.

'Every little bit. I don't use it that often. My man put it in at the last moment in case I needed relaxing after the trip. Where do we go from here?'

'I'm afraid we'll have to check the rest of the baggage. I'll personally take your word that there's no more, but they'll still order a search. If you unlock everything, then we'll go to some less conspicuous place. Okay?'

Joe nodded, moving automatically, unlocking the cases

against his instincts which were telling him to raise all hell. As he opened the last case the customs officer quietly motioned him to follow and together they crossed the wide hall.

Joe kept his eyes to the front, seeing nothing, nobody, only the man's uniformed back. At one point he thought he heard someone mutter, 'Hey, isn't that Joe Thomas?' But he could have been wrong.

At last they moved into a long empty passageway, stopping at a door. The officer knocked lightly and opened as a voice bade them enter.

It was an ordinary, small office: cream paint and inexpensive standard furnishings. The man behind the desk was stocky, middle-aged and with a greying moustache. He wore the uniform of the customs' service and was obviously a senior officer.

'Mr Joe Thomas, sir.'

The senior officer rose, did a genuine double-take and swallowed perceptibly. 'Mr Thomas? Oh . . . yes. Come in Mr Thomas.' Eyebrows lifted in query towards the other officer.

'A small quantity of marijuana, sir.'

The older man's face cleared itself of the smile, his lips pursued and he emitted a quiet 'Oh.'

'Mr Thomas admits that it is his and that it is all he is carrying.'

'How much?'

The man who had initiated the whole business was still clutching the soap container which he now opened, drawing out the marijuana wrapped in greaseproof paper. 'I haven't had it weighed or examined yet, sir.'

'Go and establish it then, and make sure there's no more.' The older man turned to Joe Thomas, 'Please sit down, Mr Thomas.'

'What now?' Joe Thomas perched on the edge of a hard stand chair, wrapped in an air of unreality as though the whole business was some warped dream.

'Have you had problems with the police before?'

216

Joe shook his head, again the crushing sense of loneliness, aridity he had not felt like this since he was a child. 'Sure,' he laughed, 'I raise hell from time to time. I know what my reputation is and there's no smoke without fire.' Another laugh, stuck in his throat. 'I don't smoke dope very often though, so it's what you might call ironic. I only use it when I need to relax a little and always by myself.'

'Well,' the senior customs' officer shrugged, 'there has to be a charge I'm afraid. The police will come here with Hodges, the man who found you in possession, and you will be taken to Uxbridge Police Station where they will take statements and formally charge you. Can you get a solicitor – a lawyer?'

'I guess so. Can I make a call?'

'You haven't been charged yet, but I'll have to stay in the room. Anything I can do to help, Mr Thomas, you have only to ask.' He waved his hand towards the telephone.

Joe Thomas stretched out his arm to the instrument. 'What happens after they charge me?'

'Probably your solicitor will guarantee your appearance in court, possibly tomorrow morning. If you are as open there as you have been with us then there should be no problem. You only get real trouble in a case like this when the person concerned is truculent and uncooperative. I should imagine the court will fine you.'

'And a lot of mess in the newspapers.' He sounded glum.

'It needn't be that bad, not if you're reasonable.'

Joe had his leather address book out; he found the number and code and began to dial.

Douglas felt not unlike a headmaster on the first day of term. The day began for him with his two new young assistants, Frank Ewes and Robin Alvin, being brought up to the office by Ronnie Gregor and Art Drays. Douglas had met both Ewes and Alvin only once previously, when the appointments had been made in London two months before: likeable men in their early twenties, they were both graduates with a little practical experience in repertory companies and their new jobs were chances of a lifetime for each of them.

Hands were shaken and they all muttered things intending to communicate their mutual pleasure in being part of the Shireston Festival.

'Your real work doesn't start until we get into production,' Douglas told them. 'In the meantime, Frank I want you in this office at eight-thirty every morning. By that time you will have read *The Times*. While I'm dealing with the morning's mail you will give me a rundown on what's happening in the world – the leaders, politics, the international scene, the arts, correspondence. Okay?'

Frank, shock-haired with the face of an intelligent pixie, nodded enthusiastically.

'Today,' Douglas continued, 'you can both make yourselves useful to Art and Ronnie, they always need spare hands. You'll be meeting members of the company for the first time so let them know who you are. Don't be self-important, you're only glorified office boys, but remember that sometimes you will be an actor's only route to me, so always listen when they want to talk to you and don't show any favours.'

The rest of Douglas's morning was spent greeting first arrivals and making sure that the whole organization started to take up the slack and pull together.

Most of those who had come on the first day were supers: the younger actors and actresses who would play soldiers, court ladies, attendant lords – 'Spear carriers', as Ronnie called them, enthusiastic and longing to be at work. There were, however, one or two important exceptions among those who arrived early. Asher Grey got to Shireston around noon with Julia Philips who, for once, seemed to have made the effort to look happy, her pudgy face carefully made up and hair in decent order. Douglas made a point of inviting them to lunch in the new theatre restaurant together with Edward Crispin who had also come early.

Until the season started it had been arranged that the theatre restaurant would cater for the director and executives and their guests only. Once the season began, in April, the general public would be admitted, but this three months' run up would give Emilio a chance to get his staff working properly and provide much needed experience for them.

From the outset of lunch, Julia Philips managed to annoy Douglas. During the meal she constantly drew the conversation towards herself, embarrassing Asher and straining the ever courteous Edward Crispin. Douglas, on the other hand, sat fuming, making mental notes about the girl and trying to show his disapproval by ignoring her.

Even taking the bulk of Julia's behaviour into account, Asher seemed more shy than Douglas remembered him; eventually, by consistently pushing Julia to one side, the director was able to get and hold the young actor's attention.

'You've managed to give some thought to Romeo since I last saw you?' queried Douglas.

'I've thought of little else,' Asher looked up from under his eyelids. 'Old Shakespeare really knew what he was at, didn't he?'

'You mean the "love story" formula?'

'Yes. I've never examined that play in depth before. William really knew how to do it though, the whole compulsive inevitability of the thing.'

'I think that's one of the problems.' As he said it, Douglas realized that far down within him he was quite frightened of *Romeo and Juliet*. If taxed with it he could not have been explicit about his fears: not knowing if it was some sense of awe, or the fact that he was going to direct Carol Evans (still a dark sensuous pulling fact in his mind), or simply a rooted knowledge that he had never yet seen a satisfactory production of the play on stage. 'It's a long piece,' he continued, 'there's so much to be sustained. . . .'

'And the audience knows exactly what's going to happen,' interjected Asher.

'Ah well, that's one of the great difficulties with all the classics.' Douglas smiled, 'That's why we knock ourselves out trying to make them fresh and new every time we do them. The poetry is of paramount importance; so are gripping performances, but it's always a good rule to approach William's plays as if each one is a new work.'

'It's the question of conviction that worries me . . .'

At the other side of the table Julia was loudly telling a now thoroughly bored Crispin about her interpretation of some character recently played.

'. . . and my Miss Hoyden in *The Relapse* brought the house down. . . .'

Douglas stopped himself from murmuring a vicious line concerning type casting but caught the look in Asher's eye. 'Conviction?' he repeated wrinkling his brows.

'Love.' Asher sounded bleak.

'It's the key and it's difficult. You have to convince even the most cynical person in the audience that you are totally a slave, enmeshed in the emotion of love and desire. Shakespeare found all the right words but they don't do the trick by themselves, particularly with a twentieth-century audience. To some extent you have to create an almost visible volcanic emotional and passionate area between you, a state of need, reliance, lust: the whole thing as thrilling as hurtling along at some unimaginable speed, knowing that disaster has the edge on you.'

From across the table the loud monologue continued. '. . . but then he's such a fabulous director, so inventive and willing to take risks, to take everything from the Noh Theatre, the Mexican Flying Festivals and the Kathakali Dancers down to beat music and heavy groups and fusing them, using them. . . .'

'What did you say his name was?' Crispin, like Asher Grey, had a distinctive voice; the man was a natural for Iago, Douglas thought in the brief moment of distraction; short in the body, swarthy, black-haired with Italian good looks, a natural, Douglas had been convinced about that from the start: Crispin was a man who could 'play deception with absolute conviction' as Zeffirelli once put it.

'What's she like?' asked Asher.

Douglas had the feeling that it was a repeated question, that he had done the unforgivable and switched his mind from their conversation. 'Sorry, Ash, I got carried away. What's who like?'

'Juliet. Carol Evans.'

'Carol?' The sleigh ride down a rainbow; she was earth, fire, air and water; the soft well-oiled gate to paradise; every poet's perfection; the adored one in all beautiful ballads; the dark lady of the sonnets.

'She's a nice girl,' he said aloud, part of his mind fragmenting, the shattering mirror. With firmness of will, Douglas pulled himself into the present and reality. 'A very strong actress. You'll get along very well.' Somewhere, in colour, behind his mind Douglas saw and heard Sinatra singing *I Get Along Without You Very Well*. 'You two should make a singular commixture. If it works you might just blow all the fuses.'

Asher Grey gave a pleasant grin which faded as Julia's stridency made itself once more apparent. Douglas switched topics as a prelude to leaving. 'Your living quarters okay?'

'Splendid.' In the one word it was obvious that the accommodation provided by Shireston was the best that the young actor had ever enjoyed. There was no need for Douglas to probe any deeper. He looked up and spoke in a louder voice. 'Your accommodation all right, Edward?'

Crispin looked relieved, as though the Fifth Cavalry had arrived. 'Great, Douglas. I've never been here before but it looks as though you've got things organized.'

'Our apartment's fabulous,' Julia cut across the conversation. 'You should have seen the hell hole we were living in; this is a palace compared to that. We're so grateful, Mr Silver,' she had started to gush without a trace of sincerity. 'You have no idea what difference it makes to actors when they have pleasant surroundings in which to live and work.'

'I have every idea, and I know it from bitter experience.' Douglas's tone was effectively rude and brought the conversation to an ultimate standstill. He dabbed his lips with his napkin and asked if he might be excused.

'I have a lot to do. No doubt you have as well.'

Outside it was overcoat cold, but with a blue sky and a bracing atmosphere. There were more people about than usual and across the lawns the theatre building seemed to stand out in glistening clarity. The director caught the spark of activity and realized with a singing of nerves that it was all about to happen. The plans, the expense and the care that had gone into the last few months' work was about to have its first test. Under the clump of tall conifers which rose from the lawn to the right of the theatre he caught a glimpse of Conrad Catellier, alone and aloof, walking with a measured pace. He is going to have to learn to mix with the rest of them, thought Douglas as he headed back to his office. Catellier might well be one of the larger personality problems which would have to be fixed here at the start of rehearsals; if there was one thing Douglas had to accomplish quickly it was the establishment of a team where each person pulled with the same amount of strength. He could not expect quick miracles with members of the company working together, anticipating each other's moves with instinct: you only attained that kind of ensemble acting through the creation of style, and style was usage, the linking of actors' minds and bodies over a long period of live performance. Yet if this was to be his final goal they had to start with equality; Conrad would be difficult on that score, so would Kapstein, maybe others.

It was late in the afternoon when the call came. A crackle on the line and then Joe Thomas's familiar voice, 'Douglas?'

'Joe? Where're you calling from?' Since the episode with Jennifer, Douglas left nothing to chance.

'I'm at Heathrow, Doug. Look. . . .'

'But you aren't due until tomorrow.'

'I know, Doug, but, look, listen, I'm sorry. I've goofed again. I'm in trouble.'

'What kind of trouble?' Douglas immediately alert.

'I'm with the senior customs officer at Heathrow. They found me carrying.'

'What?'

'A little grass.'

'How little?'

'A half ounce maybe, but they have to take me to . . .' A pause while he obviously checked with someone, '. . . to Uxbridge Police Station, to charge me with being in possession. It's a police matter.'

Douglas swore inwardly, a moment of fury towards the man.

'Among other things I need a solicitor,' continued Thomas.

'All right, Joe,' Douglas pressurized the calm into his voice. 'Don't worry, it'll be fine,' wrestling with a confusion of thoughts. 'Whatever else happens stay cool. Right?'

'I am being cool, man. So cool it'll freeze your ass to come near me.'

Douglas did not know whether to chuckle or sob, the mixture of emotions clashed in his throat. 'Stay put, Joe. I'll be over with a solicitor as quickly as I can.'

'I ain't got much option about staying put, man, but you'd better come to Uxbridge.'

'All right, to the police station, but don't you say anything. No statements, nothing, not until we get to you. Right?'

'Right.'

It was a definite crisis, a situation that could rock the whole festival. Douglas sat quite still for a couple of minutes, thinking the matter out before taking any action. The Trust used a big firm of London solicitors for their work, but there might be complications about getting somebody over to Uxbridge at speed, and speed was essential. In the previous week he had been introduced to a local man, young, lucid and, on the surface, a bright man, called Robert Hughes, junior partner in his father's firm. Adrian had invited several professional men up to drinks: local doctors, a dentist, two architects and Hughes. Douglas had spent the best part of the evening with the man: an instant rapport which he trusted. Now the decision was fast and he was through to Hughes in a matter of seconds, not waiting upon the niceties of social chat.

'How are you on drugs, Robert?'

'How bad?'

'You know who Joe Thomas is?' Stupid question, they had talked of Thomas during the party.

'Naturally.'

'He's being charged with being in possession at Heathrow. They're taking him to Uxbridge now.'

'They usually do. What was he carrying?'

'I gather a nominal amount of marijuana.'

'Has he talked?'

'I think he's played it very cool. Can you handle it?'

'Do we go in your car or mine?'

'Mine. I'll pick you up within the next half an hour.'

Hughes gave him directions on how he could get to the office and Douglas had the phone down and up again, calling David Wills and Adrian Rolfe to come over to him fast. Once that was done he called Jennifer at their apartment.

'. . . and whatever else you do, don't talk to the press if they get on to you,' he told her after outlining the situation. 'I'll come through to you as quickly as I can, but if the press start on you transfer them to Adrian as quickly as possible and take the phone off the hook.'

David and Adrian reacted calmly, like the professionals they were; young Robin Alvin was called in to sit at Douglas's desk and deal with the simple things which might come up, and in less than his calculated half an hour Douglas collected Robert Hughes and they were on their way, ploughing against the homebound traffic, heading for Uxbridge.

A small knot of men outside the police station told them that the news had already been leaked to the press, and flashbulbs exploded as they left the car, Douglas being quickly recognized. In fact it was the press whom Douglas feared more than the police or a court decision, and he feared them for the sake of the Shireston Festival and nothing else. If they wanted to do so, the national press could splash open a smear campaign that might condemn the festival before it even started, and the very thought of that made Douglas shiver.

Inside they were greeted politely by a uniformed inspector who took Robert Hughes off to see his client while Douglas was asked to wait in the inspector's office. It was an experience which he did not relish. Like most law-abiding citizens, Douglas felt nervous, ill at ease, sitting on the edge of his chair and pondering what kind of men had sat in this plain utilitarian office before him. A young policewoman brought him a cup of coffee and the general worry on his mind began to grasshopper, first to Joe Thomas, then to the ill fortune of the incident's timing, back to the daily running of Shireston, what he had to say on Sunday night at the reception for the company, what he would have to say at the first company meeting on Monday, rehearsals, technicalities, personalities, Jennifer, Carol, who would arrive tomorrow or on Sunday.

It was a good hour before the door opened to admit the inspector followed by a smiling Hughes and Joe Thomas looking most subdued.

'Sorry, man, it was a stupid mistake.' The black singer offered a large palm which Douglas grasped with warmth; there was no mistaking the equal amount of affection and gratitude which passed through Joe Thomas's hand to Douglas. It had obviously been an unpleasant and tricky time for the man.

'We are releasing Mr Thomas on his own guarantee that he will present himself at the Uxbridge magistrates court at ten o'clock tomorrow morning,' the inspector said, the voice of a junior executive. 'I would add that Mr Thomas has impressed all of us here.'

They shook hands and spent a few minutes working out whether it would be better to smuggle Joe Thomas out (in the end they decided against anything like that), and what their next move should be. The police and customs had released the luggage and it had been brought down to the station in a Land-Rover, two tall policemen now transferred it to Douglas's car.

'Shit, of all the stupid, silly damned idiotic things to happen. Doug, baby, I really am sorry.' A flaming violence, almost as though he was inflicting a wound upon himself.

They had come down the police station steps at some speed, avoiding the clutch of reporters and refusing to make any comment. Joe Thomas began his outburst before they had hardly drawn away from the curb.

'Don't worry, Joe. I'm sure nobody here's averse to a

225

mature man like yourself using a little grass. Tell me what actually happened?' Douglas did not take his eyes off the road ahead.

'That's what's so stupid.' Joe went on to tell how Smiley had put the stuff in his soap container, how he had hardly registered the fact when told, and woke up to it only while being questioned by customs.

'I shouldn't get too worried,' young Robert Hughes leaned back behind Douglas. 'The police seem anxious enough to play this one down. That's certainly the impression I get.'

'I thought they liked to clobber people like me.' Thomas swivelled round in the front passenger seat.

'Oh certainly there's the influence on the public bit, but in your case they don't want to mess up relations with the public or with the whole Shireston Festival scene I should imagine; they seem concerned that you shouldn't appear a raving red-eyed junkie.'

'How are you going to handle it?' asked Douglas over his shoulder.

'On those very lines. To show that Joe isn't a junkie; that he was completely honest and courteous and co-operative with the police and customs; that he is a man of good character; that the small amount of marijuana was provided by somebody else in an attempt to keep him relaxed at the beginning of what might be a very difficult time for him.' He went on to outline exactly how Joe should behave in court.

'You got me a dandy lawyer here, Doug.' Joe smiled when Robert finished.

'I think I have,' Douglas grinned back. 'I only met him last week but I reckon I've probably got a new solicitor for the company.'

'Your people use big guns from the Smoke,' said Robert shaking his head in the darkness.

'The trustees do, but we always need somebody around to deal with individual matters within the company. You fancy that?'

'We aim to please.'

'Then I think we're going to see a lot more of Mr Hughes

around Shireston.'

There were three magistrates on the Bench at ten o'clock the following morning: two men, both slim, moustached, in their fifties, and one younger woman.

'Wilson, Kepple and Betty,' Douglas whispered to Art who had driven over with them. He was conscious of his own nervousness being the spur to frivolity.

The court was unusually crowded, the fact that the legendary Joe Thomas was appearing on a drugs charge having flushed coveys of reporters from Fleet Street as well as the major television companies.

Even though they had made an early morning start from Shireston, Joe looked rested and meticulous. On the previous evening Jennifer (having sought Emilio's assistance) had welcomed them with a meal, after which they got the singer to bed as early as was tactfully possible.

The case was the first to be heard, and the chairman of the Bench, the slightly more military-looking of the two male magistrates, carefully explained to Joe Thomas that he could have his case dealt with straight away, but that he was within his rights to choose a trial by jury which would take place at the next quarter sessions. On Robert Hughes's instructions Joe elected for a decision by the magistrates and pleaded guilty to being in possession of 13 grammes of cannabis leaf at Heathrow Airport on the first of January Nineteen Hundred and Eighty-One.

The first evidence, called by the police, came from the customs officer who had discovered the drug: a simple and straightforward telling of facts. Then Robert Hughes rose.

'Did my client appear to be in any way truculent either before or after you detected the small amount of marijuana?'

'No, sir, quite the contrary. He did seem a shade nervous at first, and I must apologize for not recognizing who he was.' The man looked over in Joe's direction, 'I'm sorry, sir, I've heard a lot of your records but I'm really not one for the television.'

Robert smiled. 'What about when you found the drug?'

'I didn't really find it,' the man looked shamefaced, 'he told me, Mr Thomas told me it was there. I picked up the soap container and he said, "Okay, I'm busted".'

There was general laughter.

'And he behaved in a normal manner?'

'Well it depends what you call normal. A lot of people get angry and shout a bit when we face them with this kind of evidence.'

'Mr Thomas did not do that?'

'No, sir, as I said, he behaved with dignity: in a most responsible manner.'

Those same words, 'in a most responsible manner', were used by the police inspector who concluded the prosecution evidence.

Robert told the magistrates that he only wished to call one witness: Joe Thomas himself.

'We have all heard what happened yesterday afternoon at Heathrow, Mr Thomas,' Hughes began, facing Joe Thomas, 'but would you tell the court exactly why you were at Heathrow.'

'Certainly. I am here to work with the Shireston Festival Company. I am playing Shakespeare's *Othello* and Capulet in *Romeo and Juliet*.'

'This is the first time you have acted any Shakespeare?'

'It is. I'm not really an actor by profession. I've made a couple of movies but basically I'm a song and dance man.'

More laughter.

'Can you tell us why you're playing Othello if you are really what you call a song and dance man?'

'The director, Mr Douglas Silver, talked me into it. He seems to think I can do it.'

'Do you think you can do it?'

'I'll give my best, but I'm no judge of my own talent.'

'I'm sure we all wish you well in this venture.'

'Thank you.'

'Does the prospect make you nervous?'

'Very nervous.'

'You have in fact been very nervous about it for some

228

time.'

'That is true.'

'Do you regularly use drugs?'

'I use alcohol and nicotine, but I very rarely use grass: only occasionally to relax me.'

'Would you tell us why you were carrying the marijuana that was found at Heathrow.'

'Sure, a friend of mine came to help me with my baggage at Los Angeles. As I was leaving to board the plane he told me that he'd put a little grass in the soap container in my dressing case. I didn't hardly think about it until I got to London. He said it might help if I was going to be under strain after I arrived.'

'Is there anything else you would like to add?'

'Yes. Thank you, I would like to apologize for any inconvenience I have caused to Her Majesty's customs service, the police and this court. I'd also like to say how well and politely the customs officers and the police have dealt with me.'

Robert Hughes summed up, telling the three magistrates that it was obvious to everybody that Joe Thomas was not in any way a drug addict and, if necessary, he could bring medical evidence to support this; that Joe Thomas was an entertainer of extraordinary calibre and, as such, was often under an unnatural strain; those facts together with the evidence they had heard should be enough to move their worships towards leniency.

The trio of magistrates did not even leave the Bench; they muttered together for several minutes and finally composed themselves in obvious agreement. At last the chairman addressed Joe Thomas.

'Joseph Thomas, I want to make it quite clear to you that this court is not normally inclined towards leniency in cases of this kind. We always view the possession of drugs, particularly when it concerns someone like yourself in a position to influence the public, as a matter for the highest concern. However, the evidence laid before this court makes it clear that you are acutely aware of what you have done. You are fined the sum of two hundred pounds – and this Bench wishes you the best possible fortune in your appearances at the Shireston Festival.'

The relief was clear on Thomas's face. Douglas, sitting at the back of the courtroom, let out a long sigh.

That evening the television newscasts all had fleeting references to the incident together with brief snatches of film showing Joe Thomas arriving outside the court.

On the following morning the Sunday newspapers had their mild fling, but Douglas need not have been so alarmed; there was no smear campaign. The *Sunday Mirror* carried a picture of Joe coming down the steps inside the court, shoulders at a tilt and one foot poised to descend, hand stretched out: a splendid, fluid moment frozen and captured in black and inky grey. A big banner headline proclaimed JUST A SONG AND DANCE MAN, while the story gave only brief and simple facts. The *People* and *News of the World* played it in a similar manner and the *Express* only mentioned it in a small paragraph. The two heavies, *The Sunday Times* and the *Observer*, gave impartial treatment to the story, both using it on the front page and adding facts about the festival. In all, the affair had been a matter of publicity for the festival and nobody had taken out axes.

By lunchtime on Sunday, Shireston was fully alive, the house resonant with activity and noise as the final members of the company began to occupy their apartments, settled in, started to explore and get themselves domestically organized before the official reception which was to take place at eight o'clock in the green room, now bright with flowers, the long tables ready to bear the cocktail food and drinks lovingly prepared by Emilio, his chef Dominic and their assistants.

Adrian Rolfe had taken a great deal of care over the reception, seeing that name labels, complete with small silver safety pins were distributed well in advance, and that the press invitations were limited to one by-line columnist and one photographer for each invited paper or magazine. He knew from past experience that general invitations would result in little parties arriving, from London or the larger provincial cities, freeloading and then not filing any copy, or worse, features writers turning up and pinning down people like Joe Thomas or Conrad Catellier for an hour at a time. The party was primarily for members of the company to meet each other together with the executives, stage staff and administrative chiefs: the press was there partly as a concession and partly because Adrian was loath to let any occasion pass without press coverage; but they were there as observers and not as probing minglers.

As he returned to his apartment in the late Sunday afternoon, Adrian realized that he had developed a strange possessiveness towards Shireston, feeling twinges of indignation because he now had to share Shireston House with all these actors. The sense of the place taking on new life was apparent in every small noise that wafted through the corridors; the far away bang of a door, footsteps as yet not absorbed into the pattern of familiarity; voices calling, laughing, talking, sounding like murmurs. So many talents and individual lives enveloped within this particular set of walls. Adrian, being very much a man of moods, held on to the passing thought: how many of these lives would be changed by the experience of the next few months? How many talents would be broadened, re-found, fully expressed? How many minds would be enriched? How many stifled?

Conrad Catellier viewed the scene with a mental bleakness. At first he had been angry at having to wear a label with his name on it: *Conrad Catellier* written in a neat tight hand in blue ink on an oblong of card and pinned to his lapel. It was unnecessary, he felt; whimsical; trivial: if people could not recognize him by now then it was too bad. But the sharp Adrian Rolfe had told him that it was only right that the big names should wear tags as it helped the unknown members of the company. He did not explain how or why and Conrad was certainly in no mind to ask or argue with him.

Unknown? Catellier queried in his mind, we're all unknown in the long run. He looked down at his glass, still half full, then out at the crushed scene. The noise was horrific, but you could only expect a rising crescendo of gabble if you put forty actors and actresses together with forty assorted people, including the press who, up until now, he observed, seemed intent only on getting their fair share of the food and drink, though, he grudgingly realized, he had noticed a number of flashbulbs directed at him. Young Crispin had come up and said politely that it was going to be nice working with him again; and Pern was deferential, but they were well-tried actors who knew how to behave. Catellier was not so certain about the black singer, Joe Thomas, who appeared to be holding court at the far end of the room. Perhaps, Catellier thought with a desperate melancholy, it had been foolish of him even to think about joining this kind of company: it was not really his style, most of these people did not know about his nerves and the internal chaos he had to support in preparing a role. Or did any of them really understand the absurd loneliness of an actor in his situation? Not just the sexual thing, that could easily be settled here, only yesterday two of the young walk-ons had approached him separately, leaving no doubt as to their proclivities: he had but to beckon and they would come, both of them well-built, good-looking boys but neither with the intellectual stimulus which might act as a flint to spark some deeper relationship. There were not so many of those in life, and, he supposed, he could count his on the fingers of his right hand: in his mid-twenties there had been the Italian boy. He still could not bring even his mind to speak the name for it had engrossed his thoughts and body for the whole of those seven years, remembered still in detail: through his rise to fame as an actor, the Italian was a spur, then suddenly, just when things seemed to have settled, inched into a stable life style, he was gone. There one day, laughing, happy, sparkling with a rare wit and intelligence; the next day, gone, a nothing crushed between metal as two cars squirmed together at speed on a wet road near Florence. Only memories, and they did not go easily from the head. Since that, there were three he could really count, and each of those had ended in turmoil. It was better to immerse oneself in work, to become a more proficient actor, a great interpreter of roles. Yet the thought of actually doing it did not act as a balm to the fears; few people would ever guess at the anxious twist of true stage-fright which was a constant guest of Conrad Catellier's being; as bad, he sometimes considered, as Lord Nelson's seasickness.

The same nervousness of public appearances was present even now as he stood, pressed against the wall, looking out across the bobbing heads, his eyes acting like camera lenses, zooming in on the holes of moving mouths, the tricks of fingers playing together, or with another's hand or body; panning on to examine the clothes worn carefully, or carelessly, covering hard and soft bodies, gross bodies, thin ungiving, rounded and erotic; hair, heads turning; smiles; laughter; glasses tipped back; quips, almost visible, hurtling across the room.

'Conrad.' Elizabeth Column, tall, dazzling in something scarlet and expensive, placed her lips firmly against his cheek. Out of usage, Catellier lifted his arms to embrace her, forcing a smile; she was not one of his favourite people.

'It's so nice to see you again,' she mouthed, the eyes never still, looking across him into the throng. Catellier thought he knew what he was searching out: Elizabeth Column was still far from the sere and yellow, yet even at thirty-five rumour had it that her taste eased towards very young men.

'So you're doing Portia at last,' he said in an attempt to hold her, keep her there, at least as another human being with whom he could talk on reasonably equal terms.

'Yes.' She looked up at him with a broad grin and made a purring noise. 'She's such a nasty lady really.' She gave him another grin, patted his arm and began to disengage herself. 'Do excuse me, darling, I must have a word with our director. So many people.' And she was away into the fringes of the clutching crowd.

Catellier sighed and returned to sipping his drink.

'It's going to be an education, this season. You know what we've got here? We've got an actors' kibbutz.' Maurice

Kapstein swallowed a mouthful of his third gin and tonic, leering opening at the young female journalist who was giving a convincing performance of hanging on to his every word.

'What newspaper did you say you were from?'

'I'm only on the local rag,' said the girl, head cocked, her pencil poised. 'The *Shireston Gazette*.'

'Don't knock it, kiddie. You live locally then?'

'Yes.'

'Well, you let me have your address. There are a lot of things Maurice Kapstein could do for a young girl like you.'

'Thank you, Mr Kapstein. You talk about this being an actors' kibbutz. Aren't there dangers in putting all these people under one roof?'

'What kind of dangers? Plenty of people live in communities.'

'Yes, but, well, actors and actresses.'

'You think all the men actors are going to leap on all the lady actors?'

'I mean temperamental dangers. The clash of personalities. It's always been a local feeling that it's a danger to have so many artistic talents crammed together.'

Kapstein shrugged, his whole bulky body moving as he let out a wheezing laugh. 'These people are professionals. Of course the younger ones will have a rave up now and again, but who can blame them? No, there will be no such problems like the clash of personalities, as you put it.' He leaned forward and whispered behind his hand, 'As for girl actors being leaped upon, they've put me in rooms surrounded by married couples or ladies of uncertain age and sex. I suspect they're limiting my field of operations.'

The girl laughed, holding back her closest feelings, that this man was an unpleasant member of the species, warming herself with the thought that she was getting quotes from him which would please her editor, Hedley Moir.

The Joe Thomas drugs story had come as a divine gift to the newspaper, even though they had to wait for a week to make their comment. But Moir, who did not want to use this one gun on its own, had been explicit in his instructions to the girl, Janet Ridley, twenty years old, a protégé of the editor and a Methodist, alive to society's problems and rooted in the belief that even the smallest example of permissiveness was a pathfinder towards decadence. If the local newspaper could link the drugs case with hints of orgiastic happenings among the Shireston Company a large area of public opinion, within the town and its neighbourhood, would become irritated.

'Getting all you want?' Adrian Rolfe appeared at Janet Ridley's elbow. He had been anxious about the *Gazette*'s representative from the moment Moir had written to say that he was unable to attend the function himself, but would be sending Miss Janet Ridley. Yet Adrian had allowed this to slip his mind, among all the other tiny anxieties which hailed down on him in the consuming rush of a hundred things to do once the reception got under way. Spotting the girl with Kapstein and noting the actor's intimate movements had, from the far side of the room, alerted him, and he had made his way, weaving through the groups and couples, until he could place himself strategically beside them. Now he smiled grimly down at the girl, his mind telling him that he knew exactly what she was at.

'Miss Ridley?' he asked, knowing well enough that it was her.

'Yes.'

'Just making sure you're getting everything you want. I'm Adrian Rolfe, in charge of publicity. Would you like to come and meet somebody else?'

'We're enjoying ourselves.' Maurice Kapstein was unsmiling.

'You've had quite a while with Mr Kapstein,' Rolfe addressed the girl. 'The press have to circulate,' then looking at Kapstein, 'so do you.' He had the girl's elbow in a firm grasp and was pulling her steadily away towards Jennifer Frost who had just emerged from an intense conversation with Peter Berger, an old friend from her first acting days.

Adrian settled the Ridley girl with Jennifer and quickly returned to Maurice Kapstein.

'I should warn you, Maurice, the local press here are difficult.'

'I am like dripping honey to all of them, you know that, Adrian.' The wide maddening smile.

'I know it, Morrie, and I know the quality of your honey. All I'm telling you is that the local newspaper drips poison. They're out to get us, so be bloody careful.' He turned away abruptly, leaving Kapstein looking into his drink before swilling it back, refixing the smile and heading towards the bar. Adrian Rolfe was a small, bumptious man, he thought, Adrian Rolfe was above himself: just the kind of job Morrie Kapstein enjoyed, cutting a man like Rolfe down to his true size, all in good time, in good time. . . .

Felicity Durrant had been in the theatre for forty-two years, since she was twelve years old, so the pace, laughter and fury of the reception did not fool her. She knew exactly what strains lurked behind the smiles, what shimmering nerves and fears, what hopes. That, she supposed, was one of the snares which lured you into this profession: the danger and insecurity. It was a paradox, but with some truth to it: all actors were gamblers with their talent. Some went on to the end, knowing they would make it with the chance of one more throw; others made it early, put all their winnings on the turn of a card and then dropped from the public gaze; some made it and stayed; some came to a compromise, realized exactly what talent was theirs, made use of it and moved steadily on from one similar job to another. Such a person was Felicity Durrant. She had done just about everything – comedy, tragedy, farce, the classics, music hall, musical comedy, straight theatre, cinema, television: never as a great blinding star, but always good, steady, dependable, turning in workmanlike performances, a mistress of technique. Each new part was, to her, a job, a task to be undertaken with responsibility. Certainly the two roles for which she had been cast in the current season were demanding: the Duchess of York was a nice challenging piece of fire, and Juliet's Nurse was something in which many very great ladies of the

236

theatre had excelled; but Miss Durrant was under no illusions about the depths she could bring to either role, she would play them within her range and scope, no director in the world could take her further.

The thought of being Nurse to the black child appealed to her as she watched Carol Evans threading her way through the party, alone and looking, Miss Durrant thought, a shade lost. As Carol came within her reach the older woman put out a hand and touched her on the arm. 'Carol Evans?'

The girl nodded shyly, her lips together in a close smile.

'I'm going to be your nurse. Felicity Durrant.'

'Of course. I knew your face. . . .' Carol thought she looked a comfortable woman.

'But you couldn't put a name to it. That's the problem people like me have to live with.' Felicity Durrant laughed, a pleasant ring.

'It's nice to meet you.'

'I hope we have a good season together. Have you met your Romeo yet?'

'No, to be quite honest I was looking for him. You know, lurking around and squinting at likely men's labels.'

'Come on, he's over here.' Still with her hand on the girl's arm, Felicity Durrant moved to where she had left Asher Grey talking with two other actors, and his young woman, a few moments before.

'This one here?' whispered Carol as she identified the group they were approaching.

'With his back to you, dear.'

She saw the back and took in the fact that there were two other men, one of them she vaguely realized was Murray Fleet, whom she had worked with in television, and a girl with soft pastry-textured cheeks. Then Felicity Durrant spoke again.

'Asher, come and meet your Juliet.'

Asher Grey turned and Carol was looking into dark eyes and a face transparently lived in. For some unaccountable reason she shivered.

'Hello.' His hands extended. Carol had the sense that she

was being publicly stripped: not a simple sensual disrobing, but a wrenching away of the protective covering of her mind: it was, she reflected later, a purely emotional reaction.

Their hands locked; a firm grasp.

Asher felt the unfamiliar tremble within him, deep in the gut. What had Douglas Silver said? *You two should make a singular commixture. If it works you might just blow all the fuses.* Deep in the centre of her eyes he could dimly detect moving figures, and through the touch of her skin a burning.

'I'm Julia Philips,' the girl with him brayed, but Carol and Asher stood transfixed. Carol began to identify with the character of Shakespeare's Juliet: a production she had once seen: was it the Zeffirelli? Where, at the lovers' first meeting at the ball, everybody but Romeo and Juliet froze as their eyes locked.

A flashgun flared and died, those near applauded the theatrical moment, behind the small knot the party babbled on, oblivious. Carol relinquished Asher Grey's hand and turned to where Julia Philips had spoken. But the girl had gone, so she brought her eyes back to Asher's face and was puzzled to see it livid with rage. Felicity and the others melted away.

'What on earth's wrong?'

'I'm sorry. I must apologize for my friend. She was here a moment ago.'

'Julia Philips? The girl who introduced herself? Oh, I'm sorry, I must have seemed terribly rude to her. I didn't mean. . . .'

'It's all right.' His face lined with what could have been anxiety or fury. 'I'd better go and find her. Can we. . . . Can we talk later?'

'Of course.'

He moved away and Carol turned, scanning the faces for Felicity Durrant. Conscious of the foolish, girlish sensations, she needed her nurse, but, as she moved, all she could see was Douglas Silver a half a dozen paces away, Jennifer Frost beside him.

All day Carol had put off the moment, creeping into Shireston and then into the house, finding her rooms and staying in them, unpacking and hanging up clothes, stacking the bookshelves, bathing and dressing, eeking out the time until she could not prevaricate longer and had to show her face, knowing their meeting was inevitable.

'You've met your Romeo then?' His voice sounded incredibly calm and unemotional. Carol had the flash in her mind, picturing their last meeting: her tears, the farewell intimacy which had left her spent and wretchedly alone; the minutes and dragging hours since when her whole body seemed full of him and he was not there. Now she looked and wondered because she felt nothing. She opened her mouth to speak and it was like a fish gasping, she could not believe that such emotions and feelings could alter with so complete and sudden disintegration.

Douglas was speaking again. 'Then meet my wife, Jennifer Frost. Carol Evans.'

My wife. . . . My wife. . . . Repeated in a descending scale within her head as though from an echo chamber.

'I'm so glad to meet you. I'm sure we're going to be good friends.' Jennifer with her hand extended.

Carol shook hands and at that moment the situation was broken by Adrian Rolfe at Douglas's shoulder.

'Time for your speech, Doug.'

Joe Thomas had found himself a place near the bar, and after a few drinks, and some adoration, was feeling much more his old cocksure self. The press spent some time with him: Thomas either glittered or glowered when the press was about: tonight he glittered; but his most natural attraction was for the other black actors whom Douglas had cast. Sylvia Kostamore, a tall, lithe young black woman with striking looks who, among other parts, was to play Lady Capulet, made a straight line for Thomas early in the evening and introduced herself with, 'I hear we're going to play at being Momma and Poppa Capulet.' To which Joe had made the most obvious and crude response. Sylvia had laughed delightedly and never left his side for the rest of the party. Lonnie Barnes, a big and handsome Jamaican actor, came up and introduced himself with little Tom Soota. Later they were joined by William Ontora and the thin Adam Domine, both of whom had made their mark on British television. Others came and went, paying their respects to Joe Thomas, but the black faction stuck together.

'You're not going to circulate, Joe?' Ontora asked after they had been in the same spot for the best part of an hour.

'Nah, man. Why should I? Let them come to me. There's enough of us here to form a Shireston branch of the Black Panthers anyhow.' He looked through the crowd to see Douglas and Adrian Rolfe were heading towards the small rostrum at the far end of the long and packed room.

'Hey now. The Man's going to talk. . . .' Thomas broke off and stared. '. . . And who's the sweet chick with Jen Frost?'

Lonnie Barnes replied. 'That's our Juliet. That's *Miss* Carol Evans.' Stressing the *Miss*.

'Is that right?' Joe spoke almost to himself. 'Maybe I will do a little circulating after all.'

There was a general shuffling, the conversation running down as Douglas mounted the rostrum.

From his vantage point, Douglas had a quick opportunity to judge how the party was going. Well, he considered, as they were taking a while to settle down. His gaze took in Carol and Jennifer standing just below him with Adrian. He had to look away, his feelings mixed and disturbed. To have had most intimate and passionate relationships with two beautiful women and then see them together for the first time was a strange experience: pride mingled with guilt and some sadness, which, he told himself, was probably sentiment. He lifted his head, looking out into the mid-ground of the crowd, which, from his viewpoint reminded him of those scenes they used to have in American big band movies: Glen Miller or Tommy Dorsey shot from behind with the dance hall clientèle jammed hard against the stand. But this crowd contained faces you just would not see in any crowd sequence in a modern movie: he felt the rush and glow of admiration as he picked out the faces which had made some kind of theatrical history: Catellier, Elizabeth Column, Maurice Kapstein, Joe Thomas tucked away in the corner, his own Jennifer Frost; and the faces known to millions even if they could not put names to them: Peter Berger, Laurence Pern, Edward Crispin, Murray Fleet, Mark Lynton, Felicity Durrant, the beautiful little Rachel Cohen. He could not spot the, as yet, unknown Asher Grey but he was probably out there somewhere. Sir Basil Daley was talking quietly to Catellier, and Douglas quickly rescanned the room to see how many more of the trustees were present. He spotted the sad-faced George Tupnall, and Rupert Crown, but could not see Dempsey, the one trustee the director had any cause to fear.

His audience were now quiet and waiting, faces looking up at him, full of expectancy, doubt and even, he seemed to detect, cynicism. Douglas cleared his throat and his mind. Public speeches were not the easiest thing for him, he did not like standing up and talking to a bunch of people, though the fact that he did not find it easy had long since forced him to adopt a formula. He preferred to think about short speeches a few days beforehand, not commit himself to paper but allow the thoughts to lie fallow, hoping they would come out fresh from his subconscious when the time came. It was a method which Douglas had found effective over the years and now he summoned all his charm.

'My duty tonight is to welcome you to Shireston,' he began. 'I wanted to do this with a quote from the Bard himself, but the only one I can think of at the moment comes from the Scottish play, and, quite honestly, though I'm a lucky man, I don't trust my luck that far. So I simply say to you – welcome.' Pause, before adding, 'And I would like to take this opportunity to make a public denial to the rumour that, since we announced the company for this season, the National Theatre is planning a takeover bid for Shireston.'

It was a weak joke, but there was laughter and loud applause. Everyone seemed to settle back and relax.

'Seriously for a moment. Around us we hear cries of gloom: alarms and excursions off. The theatre is in a shaky and fast dissolving state; the commercial theatre is, we are told, on the rocks; the cinema industry is in the grip of a slow fade,' he gave a quick grin. 'television doesn't look too good to me either.' He waited for the ironic chuckles to die. 'If all this is true, and there is no use denying that a large proportion of it is accurate, then we find ourselves in a unique position. We are a new company, a refurbished company, we're not so well established as the National or the Royal Shakespeare, but, thanks to the good management of the Shireston Trust, we don't have to go begging for money. Mind you, our source of supply is not a bottomless well, but we have certain advantages and I am convinced that these can be used to thrust a fresh injection of confidence into the theatre as a whole. We are going to present a festival this year which will explode like the biggest firework display ever known in the history of English theatre. It is going to make headlines all over the world, and I put it to you that we are going to draw record crowds to Shireston.'

Douglas paused, again looking out over the now intent crowd. He saw Ronnie and Art, both smiling, together with young Frank Ewes; Elizabeth Column was with them and David Wills hovered in the background. Douglas took another breath.

'Most of what I've just said was for the benefit of the press, who we're more than pleased to see here tonight. But, even though I'm saying it for the press to hear, I do not indulge in idle dreamer's boasting. We *are* going to have an exceptional season here.' He barked the stressed *are* as though making it a command. 'We *are* going to see a real company, an ensemble, emerge from this glorious mulch of talent we've assembled here; a company which will reinstate Shireston as a major theatrical festival and a natural focal point, both for visitors to this country and for people who draw their emotional, spiritual and intellectual reserves from the experience of living theatre. Our efforts here at Shireston will, I believe, be of value, not just to the theatre in this country, but to the country as a whole, and we should all feel proud that we have this opportunity to begin building for the future within the very changing, complex world of the communicative arts.

242

'I'll have more to say about that when we meet for the first time as a company at nine o'clock tomorrow morning. Until then – mingle and enjoy yourselves.'

For a second there was silence, then the warm blanket of applause wrapped around him. Douglas felt it was not a case of polite hand clapping but a true gesture of solidarity. As he stepped from the rostrum his mind quickly reflected on what he had just said, that he absolutely believed it all was incidental; he had pointed up Shireston, made a small humbling gesture towards the press, asking for their help and, without being tough or hard (as he would have to be in the morning) suggested to the company that they were going to be called upon to do some pretty hard work which could result in high glory. He desperately needed them on his side, from the big names to the smallest and most insignificant walk-on. At this moment they were with him, applauding, smiles of hope and success on the faces close around him. Douglas realized that he was walking towards Jennifer and Carol, and the emotionalism of the past weeks and months did not seem to matter that much, his personal problems shrank under the vastness of the project now fully set in motion. Someone, he presumed it was Adrian Rolfe, had provided music, now switched on for the first time and brought up from the applause and sea of conversation. He registered that if it was Adrian then the PR man had been very clever, the tune was *What the World Needs Now Is Love, Sweet Love*, and the opening bars, pounded out on brass, strings and percussion, were instantly recognizable as the first track on Joe Thomas's latest album: *Joe Thomas Loves*. There was a whoop from the corner, where the black faction were grouped as Joe's voice came singing out and the general noise level rose several decibels.

Douglas took a pace forwards and stretched out his arms across Jennifer and Carol, drawing both of them to him in an instinctive gesture of affection. He could see Joe Thomas bearing down on them, Sylvia Kostamore not far behind and Joe overtly pointing towards Carol, seeking out an introduction. Douglas found himself grinning back inanely.

Asher Grey missed the speech. He had stumbled away from Carol Evans, feeling foolish and like some idiot schoolboy. Julia's sudden disappearance had thrown him, pumping rage through his body as though it was mixed with his blood. Not only was she being excessively unprofessional but also she had provided acute embarrassment; if this was the way it was going to begin, he dared not think of the ending. One thing was clear, he had to put her straight on matters of public behaviour here and now. He searched through the crowd until Ted Crispin said that he thought he had seen Julia leave the party. 'Seemed a bit upset, old boy,' he added without malice, for already, following his short experience of Julia over lunch, Crispin felt a certain pity for Grey being saddled with such a plainly difficult woman.

Asher left the green room and headed straight for their apartment. It was the obvious place for the girl to go. She was out for an unnecessary row, a drama, one of the constant teacup storms that were entirely of her own making, so she would go to the place where Asher would most easily find her.

But she was not in the apartment, nor the deserted company restaurant, his second choice. Asher, bewildered and now uncertain about Julia's intentions, briefly returned to the reception which seemed to have turned into a small swinging party with people starting to dance. But Julia had not deigned to show her face back there.

Asher finally went outside, into the clear night, raw cold but with the moon bright, throwing buildings and trees into sharp silhouette. Across the lawns he noticed there was a dim light coming from the theatre, as though someone was in the auditorium with a torch.

He felt the grass wet with a frosty dew as he started out over the lawn, the sounds of music and party noise drifting out of the house behind him; a car engine came to life in the drive, and to his left Asher watched its headlights bob slowly away towards the main gate. The music grew more faint and the theatre lowered above him.

The main doors to the foyer were locked, so Asher circled

the building, trying each possible entrance in turn until he came to the small wicket set into the big swing doors of the scenery dock behind the stage. It was open, moving easily on its hinges. He stood for a moment, just inside, allowing his eyes to adjust to the dim light. He was also conscious of a noise, a drone, coming from the direction of the stage which also seemed to be the light source. Asher blundered forward and the drone became clarified, a human voice chanting, Julia's voice. He approached the stage on the Prompt Side and the sound became less diffused. He recognized some words, lines –

'*You must sing . . . down-a . . . that stole his master's daughter. . . .*'

Julia stood in the centre of the stage, above her the light came from two of the battens, but only the whites and blue gels were up, casting an eerie light on the small, lonely figure dressed in the purple dress and black boots she had bought, less than a week ago, especially for this night.

He thought of what it must have been like for the girl, only a few years ago, when she was a child. The fractured life; parents who left for a day-trip and then, with final, unbelievable suddenness, the aunt with the stricken face telling her: the road accident; both dead, and after, nobody really wanting her; no member of the family willing to take on responsibility.

'*There's rosemary, that's for remembrance; pray you, love, remember. . . .*' She chanted on, swaying slightly, one booted foot forward, her head thrust upwards. No feeling, no attempt to act or create. Simply a repetition of words: Ophelia's mad scene from *Hamlet* spoken to an empty auditorium.

'*. . . and there is pansies, that's for thoughts.*'

Her hands moved to the back of her head.

'*There's fennel for you, and columbines: – there's rue for you; and here's some for me. . . .*'

Asher did not at first realize what she was doing as her right hand moved down the back of her dress.

'*. . . – we may call it herb-grace o'Sundays . . .*'

245

Too late, he saw that the back of her dress was unzipped to her waist. Her arms dropped and the dress fell from her, a purple mound around her feet. Julia stepped forward out of the dress.

'. . . *O, you must wear your rue with a difference.*'

Asher knew he should do something about what was going on, but he remained still for a dozen or so seconds. It crossed his mind that a young woman standing alone on an empty stage in her underwear should look seductive, alluring. Julia simply looked a mess: black boots ending just below the knees, tights, black pants and a white bra. A pudgy, tatty, untidy mess.

'. . . – *There's a daisy: – I would give you some violets, but they wither'd all when my father died . . .*'

Her hands were going to the back of the bra and Asher now moved before she completed her strip.

'Julia,' he called softly.

Her body went rigid, stone still, like a reaction of sudden fear, then she turned her head towards his, peering to see him through the murky light.

'Ash?'

'Put your clothes on.'

She nodded and bent to pick up the dress as Asher took a pace forward.

'What the hell do you think you're playing at?'

She began to step into the dress. 'I wanted to be on my own, wanted to get the feel of the house.' Arms into the sleeves.

'So you come up here, recite the mad scene and strip off.'

'I was angry. I thought it might help to calm me. Zip me up Ash.'

'The mad scene calm you?'

'I often recite pieces to calm me. There's a lot you don't know.'

'I'll bet. Why were you angry?' He pulled up the zip.

'Because I saw all my fears coming true.'

'Fears?'

'You know exactly what I'm talking about, Ash. From the

beginning I've been afraid that we'd get down here and I would have to play second fiddle. . . .'

'Julia, this is old stuff. We've had it all before. This is the chance of a lifetime for me. . . .'

'Not your career. Of course I'll play second fiddle to your career. It's the other thing. The women. . . .'

'The fictitious women. The shadows in your mind, Julia. There are no other women.'

'I saw it. I saw the way you looked at that black bitch. . . .'

'For Christ's sake, she's going to play Juliet.'

'And what else is she going to do?'

'Julia,' he was calm, he even consciously put on a quiet understanding voice, unconsciously it was the tone he would have used had he been playing the role of a doctor with a difficult patient. 'You're a trained actress, you know about these things. I'm going to say it once, right at the beginning of our time here. I cannot cope with your silly unprofessional and jealous tantrums. If they persist I shall go to Douglas Silver and tell him that I cannot give of my best if you remain in the company.'

Her eyes had a hard insolent look and one corner of her mouth turned down. 'Make sure it's not me who goes to Mr Silver first.'

But Asher was not going to be drawn into argument or even discussion. 'Are you coming back to the party?'

She looked at him for a moment, then shrugged. 'There's nothing else to do.'

In his brain, Asher Grey repeated the question, Why this woman? Over and over like a litany. The folly of even allowing himself to be shackled to a person who could provide such nonsensical aggravation. To hell, he was not even legally shackled to her. The same old depression dropped round his mind, made worse as they walked into the green room and Edward Crispin gave him a knowing look, the kind of look men gave to one another, showing that they can feel a brotherly spirit for what is going on; that they too have had difficult wives, lovers, mistresses before.

David Wills felt quite flattered he had danced for nearly half an hour with Rachel Cohen, and now, flushed and clutching glasses of punch, they sat together on one of the big settees which had been pushed back against the wall. Rachel Cohen was a small girl in all senses of the word: slim to the point of looking frail, with calm clear-lined features, high cheek bones and startling dark eyes, thick shoulder-length hair and a personality which seemed to radiate from her before she even spoke. Now she leaned forward and examined David's name tag.

'David Wills. Executive Director,' she read in a voice which had a style of its own: clear, fresh but without any direct hints of having been trained, by instruction or custom. 'I'm with the top brass then.'

David laughed. 'You sound very military. The top brass.'

'I've got a military background. I used to go out with a lance-corporal. No, I've just done three episodes in a spy epic for the BBC and the scripts were loaded with that kind of jargon – "top brass", being put on a "fizzer", "getting your knees brown", "jankers".'

'Terribly masculine stuff.'

'Oh dead boring, yes, very butch; I think the sexiest expression in the whole thing was "Divisional HQ". But enough of that,' she said waggling her head like a sick robot, 'what does the executive director do?'

'Just about everything that has nothing to do with directing plays, which used to be my function in life.'

'Yes, I know, I recognized your name. You did a super *Miss Julie* about three years ago.'

'Four.'

'As long as that? What happened?'

'Fell on evil times, didn't I?'

'It can happen to any of us.'

'I know,' with a sigh which was not quite self-pity. 'But Douglas picked me up so I must be grateful. Actually he's been good, I might even do some directing next season. He's letting me organize some poetry readings this year, Sunday night things, but. . . .'

'But it's a bit of a comedown after *Miss Julie*.'

'Quite.'

'Well, apart from directing next year and doing the poetry readings, what does the executive director do?' She leaned back, eyes sparkling.

'I have to see that all departments are working smoothly, everything from props and the typing pool to stage carpenters and the restaurant; I make sure that everybody's doing his or her job; I deal with all the hundred and one minor problems when I can. . . .'

'Like Joe Thomas getting busted?'

'Oh no, the boss man did that one personally, though I believe I am responsible to the director for the morals of the company.'

'That could be amusing.'

David grinned and then realized that the grin was more of a smirk. 'The really interesting job at the moment is the exhibition.'

'What exhibition? Morrie Kapstein?'

'No. . . .' They both laughed, and David went on to tell her about the skeleton plans already made. After a great deal of thought they had decided to sacrifice the tennis courts, upon which a large oblong marquee was to be erected to house the exhibition. The marquee was to be divided into four sections: the first dealing with the short history of the Shireston Festival; the second with historic performances of the four plays of the current season, the third and fourth sections would cover a broad spectrum, presenting a long view of Shakespeare within his own period.

'There will be four separate tapes, one for each section, music and the spoken word, but I don't know if they're going to let me touch any of that.'

'Oh come on, David – I am allowed to call the executive director David? You're feeling sorry for yourself.'

'Now you're sending me up. Executive director.'

'Well, it's such a pompous title. I think that helps to get you down, holding a job with a great fat overblown appendage.'

'No, I don't care what they call me and I like dealing with the exhibition, it's only that Tony Holt and Adrian Rolfe both think they're doing the bulk of work on it so there's a bit of a leadership snarl-up.'

Rachel sensed it was time to get less serious. She swallowed the remainder of her punch. 'Come on, let's have another dance, then you can take me back to my quarters, as they say in military circles. At least I know I'll be safe with the executive director in charge of the company's morals.'

Elizabeth Column looked down at Frank Ewes. 'You seem terribly young to be assistant to the director.' Her voice plummy, almost as though the gastric juices were running wild over some choice dish.

'I'm only a glorified office boy, Miss Column.'

'Nonsense, you're assistant to the director, and stop calling me Miss Column. I'm Liz to everyone.'

'Yes, Miss Column.'

'We will get ourselves a drink and you can tell me all about yourself.'

Douglas Silver surveyed the scene from the doorway. The party spirit seemed to have exploded with a vengeance: even though the crush was starting to thin out the atmosphere was undeniably that of a successful evening.

Most of the press had got their pictures and stories and left; only a small rearguard remained: he noticed that the local girl, Miss Ridley, not as naïve as she tried to make out, was still in the centre of things pouting, preening among the knot of reporters as if she was Miss Provincial Journalist nineteen eighty-one.

Douglas flicked his eyes at Adrian, signalling that the press should be eased away, this was the danger period when someone could say or do something foolish. Adrian nodded in reply, also inclined his head towards Morrie Kapstein, now quite drunk and being very heavy with two of the younger girl supers: that was definitely a flash point.

There were others, notably a large group of the young

supers and lower billing people who were now starting to settle in for the evening, pair off and do their own relaxed free thing to the music. Douglas noticed that more and more members of the company were joining in and if that was allowed to develop he would have a heap of tired actors on his hands tomorrow. Give them a little bit of rope, half an hour, then he should turn it all off, he thought, his mind springing forward and checking off his list of items which had to be dealt with first thing in the morning; at the same time he continued to scan the room, trying to see who had settled for whom among the more important names.

Catellier was nowhere to be seen; Adrian had gone over to Kapstein and was doing his best to get rid of the girls without causing a scene; across the room he could see that the dancing group had swollen to include most of the black people: Carol Evans was in the thick of it, her face displaying the trance-like look of one totally involved in the music and erotic movement; Joe Thomas was near her and, for the second time that evening, Douglas experienced the sense of unease, a dissatisfaction in the pit of his stomach which had to be quelled with conscious effort.

Rachel Cohen was obviously getting sweetly linked with David Wills, and, a tweak of apprehension here, Elizabeth Column was head to head in conversation with young Ewes. If he knew anything about Liz, the lad would have a backful of painful scratch marks by morning.

'I've got the not so innocent children away from your Shylock and I think the message is penetrating the ranks of the National Union of Journalists.' Adrian was at his side. 'If you haven't got any other plans, why don't you take Jennifer and drop out, Doug?'

'Are you sure?' He spotted Asher Grey enthusiastically moving with his girl, Julia whatever her name was. At least she looked happier and they seemed to be talking a lot.

'You must have had enough of this,' Adrian charmed. 'Besides, if you went now, it would give the kids half an hour or so to let their hair down.'

'They've got it down already.'

'You know what I mean. How about it?'

'I think it's past my bedtime. I'll find Jen.'

'She's with my wife. You stay here, I'll bring her to you.' Adrian was gone. However difficult he could be, Douglas considered, Adrian was a most smooth professional operator: a man who cared for the people with whom he worked. The PR chief was laughing as he returned with Jennifer who looked flushed and beautiful.

'Here you are then, Miss Frost,' Adrian almost giggled, 'you wanted to meet the director, Mr Silver.'

Douglas laughed and took her hand. 'Seen all you want to see?'

'Yes,' she gave him a grimace, 'but I haven't done all I want to do.'

'Then it's definitely time for me to take you home.'

The music and dancing went on for an hour after they left, even though Douglas was unaware of it.

Slowly, almost reluctantly, Shireston House fell to silence.

Conrad Catellier stretched out uneasily on his bed; sleep was not the simplest of matters for him these days, a state which had to be induced with a little sodium amytal. Tonight, even that was not working as quickly as it usually did, keeping him hovering between consciousness and the dark, his mind crowded with words and images, fears and anxieties: a stage peopled with freaks and monsters, the audience unseen yet physically present: he could hear his own voice warped in the ear –

I pray you all, tell me what they deserve
That do conspire my death with devilish plots
Of damned witchcraft, and that have prevailed
Upon my body with their hellish charms?

Then a vision of himself among the monsters, his back horribly misshapen; a mirror, and his face pocked and rutted; he could feel his heart thud and the voice fade before thankful blackness took over.

Snug and warm, they were like two animals, Asher thought,

the world shrunken to a small burrow, and they two animals who only touched common ground when mating. He talked until there were few words left to say, attempting to turn Julia's mind from fantasies which her imagination weaved, constantly asking himself why he allowed it to go on: the repetitive depressing attacks, the questions and tantrums. Why? Now, as always, he had part of the answer: their rhythm together, something he had not known with any other woman, the strange animal mixture which came between the sheets or on the floor or wherever and whenever it happened (once, he would always remember, in a ditch during a four-day holiday they had taken in Devon a year before). Here and now it was like a pair of tiny things, voles maybe, crushed together in an earth tunnel, moving with an almost ritualistic violence towards the bursting of spring. Then the pictures changed as she whispered, 'Ash . . . Ash . . . The Glasgow to London Express. . . . Ash, be the Express . . . The Express. . . .'

Maurice Kapstein was naked, prone and fuddled, his hands moving like tired spiders crawling over the gross and wrinkled grey flesh. He had lost all sense of time and it seemed hours that he had been lying there, waiting; and now he could not even remember the girl's name, only that she had hurriedly promised to come to his room, when Rolfe began interfering, and the erotica of imagined moments, the lifting of her dress, touching, the act of undressing her. But she would not appear and even if she did, Morrie would not be able to accomplish anything. He belched, the flavour of alcohol filling his mouth and nostrils so that, for a second, he felt nausea and revulsion, saw himself as the dirty old man, sensed self-pity that it had descended to this: a man grown old and fat, eating and drinking over much and leching after young girls, using his position as a leading actor in order to grope at the young breasts and buttocks. Flesh oozed over the screen of his mind: buttocks, breasts, thighs, hair, all young, beautiful; it was as though he needed to touch young skin in order to rejuvenate his own. Acres of smooth flesh, nausea, the slow relaxation, the dark patch of fern, the thought of a ripe schoolgirl, the wink of action in his loins. Sleep.

Douglas and Jennifer, in the dark, having talked away the undressing moments, swapped impressions, laughed at each other's comments, flattered and aware of the venture in which they were involved, now turned to each other. Douglas put his hand down and patted her, holding her, cupped for a moment.

'You okay?' he whispered.

'I'm fine.' Her own hand to him. 'You?'

'No sweat.'

'Sleep?'

'Sleep.'

'I love you, Doug.'

'And you, love.' Pause. 'So much.'

The good night kiss held tight, the touching and shuffling of bodies into familiar positions, a sense of safety, warmth and normality. As she nuzzled into her pillow, Jennifer had one tiny anxious mental jump which came unsought, a fraction of worry in which she again saw Douglas and the unknown girl, but fatigue blotted it out, filtering away the unthinkable.

David Wills finished his third cup of coffee, replacing the cup carefully on the saucer before slowly getting to his feet.

'Tomorrow there is work.' He knew it sounded pompous.

'I told myself not to get involved with people in authority.' Rachel Cohen, tucked, legs under her, into a comfortable human mound at the end of the couch, pouted at him. 'I chat up a man, bring him back to my lodgings, feed him coffee and then he departs into the night without so much as a light kiss on the cheek.'

'I'm vaguely old-fashioned.'

'And very nice. It gives one confidence after all those ghastly young men who take one out, spend the minimum on you and then expect you to be interested enough to lay it all

254

out on a bed for them. Oh, now I've shocked you.'

'Far from it. Beds are close to my mind, it's just that it has been such a good evening I don't want to spoil it.'

She rose, coming to him. 'Thank you, David.'

'Thank you.'

Their arms wound around each other, briefly; one small, almost pecked, kiss.

'See you tomorrow?' It was a question and there were other queries in his eyes.

Rachel nodded. 'Tomorrow.'

The leave-taking at her door was simple, not a protracted, self-conscious business, but quick and friendly. When he was gone, Rachel set herself about the task of tidying up: carrying the coffee tray into the kitchen, rinsing cups and pot before heading for the bathroom. It was an automatic action, all done without thought. Alone again without having to smile, be bright, make light conversation, she asked herself what she had expected of David Wills. Part of her, she knew, had wanted him to ease her into his arms, force her down and open her; the other part held back, after all it was only six weeks. Six weeks and four days, Christ she knew that without having to stop and count. Harry with his non-stop clattering charm, their closeness and the sense of safety within the little flat, so convenient for them both. Their involvement in each other's work, the short, heady week-ends and their lives so locked together that she thought it could never end.

Then the cold evening, coming home to him after a day in front of the cameras, having had nothing substantial to eat, swilling coffee against a super meal with Harry and finding nothing but the oblong envelope, he could not even tell her face to face. Just the classic note and the crevasse of emptiness and disbelief.

It had lasted almost exactly two years; and in the bad moments which followed there were natural periods of self-accusation: she should have known, seen, should have pressed for a more satisfactory outcome. It was not as though she did not know that he had a wife, that he was sometimes troubled about her and the five-year-old boy; theirs had been so perfect a relationship that she had no doubts that one day Harry would announce the divorce and all would be straight and easy.

I cannot deny that I love you and you have given me more than any other woman ever will, but my greater responsibilities lie with my wife and child. Thank you, Rachel darling, for everything. I do not mean to hurt you but I know what this is doing to me so it must also be a deep wound to you.

Harry in the kitchen, Harry on Hampstead Heath, Harry shopping with her, taking her to the cinema, holding her hand, Harry in a restaurant or walking close to her, Harry in the bedroom ('A little touch of Harry in the night.' That had been an obvious joke, but a good one for them).

At the time it all finished she sometimes thought that death was perhaps easier than this present rending: at least with death all was removed; with life she would go about her jobs and the necessary things knowing that, somewhere else, Harry was doing the same, with someone else, while she was alone.

There had been the suicidal moments, overcome by reason and the inbuilt instinct for survival; and they had been followed by the natural desires. She knew the exact number of those as well: two, each different and giving her nothing except a kind of animal relief, guilt and a refusal to see either of the men again. After each small lapse there was the fall into desperate dreaming, the impossible hopes and longing. Then there was tonight and David Wills; brief, but the feeling of being alive again. She was wary about the emotion, approaching it with care as though it was a dangerous crossroad.

Rachel Cohen sighed: like a girl in some romance, she thought, sitting in her nightdress, the cotton wool in her hand oily with make-up remover and her mind far away in dreams. If David Wills came closer, all the better. She thrust out her chin, the defiant pose; whatever happened it was her career which counted at this place. Tomorrow she would start on Bianca and Jessica – she gave a little loud laugh. Bianca the whore and Jessica the spoiled, wayward daughter of Shylock. A lot of work tomorrow.

Joe Thomas was without sleep. Beside him Sylvia Kostamore groaned and stretched in a dream, sated, physically dried out in the dancing and sexual exercises which had followed. But Joe was uncompromisingly awake, his body still crying out for warmth, love and comfort with the image of Carol Evans high on the list.

Mingled with the lust there was fear, something he could not quite put his mind to, or realize in a definite shape: fear for tomorrow, fear of facing up to the enormous task which he had set himself. The others were actors, experienced in the art, while he was a singer of ballads, bouncy tunes, catches. Tonight, he knew that he had deliberately held himself apart from the others, played at being Joe Thomas the pop idol, but now, in the dark, the moment of reality drew nearer, closer. Tomorrow he had to stand up, catch Othello's many moods, be part of the company.

Frank Ewes was not experienced with women; true there had been a girl at Cambridge with whom he had slept a dozen times, and another about a year ago who had twice brought him to an unnerving passionate heat, but he rarely felt at ease, as though he knew he lacked the true ability to stimulate a woman's mind, which was the only real way to make a woman's body come alive.

Liz Column seemed a terribly mature person to him, almost a sacred object, an actress whom he had almost worshipped as a superb craftswoman, a lady destined to be a great person of the theatre, someone in a lofty position of awe. Yet here she was, this goddess panting for his kisses, her hand cupped around him while he blurted, 'Liz, you shouldn't. No, Liz. . . .' Like some girl being felt up behind the bicycle sheds at school.

She had given him brandy when they got to her apartment and he tried to talk theatre to her, seriously, wanting to know the process by which she had created so many of her outstanding performances, her Hedda and the fantastic Shrew he had seen her do at Stratford the same year as she had moved him so much with her Ophelia. But she only partially communicated with him, getting closer and closer to him on the couch: first a hand over his, then stroking his knee, and now the kisses and her hand on him. Frank was appalled, his mind not accepting the facts, his body reacting against his will. He gave a little scream of pain as her nails bit into him but she took it as a sign of mounting desire. For a moment he was free as her hands moved inside her dress, then he had to take his eyes from her, not able to look at this great lady struggling to get her underclothes off. He lunged sideways but she was again on top of him, her hand reaching towards him.

Then it was all over before anything really happened and Liz Column was being tender and cooing, 'There, Frank, never mind, I'll teach you. There's a great deal to learn, but you mustn't worry. There's plenty of time.'

Felicity Durrant dreamed of rose petals falling on her face; Laurence Pern did not even dream; Edward Crispin fell asleep reciting Iago; and the super who had promised to join Maurice Kapstein in his room (a thin girl called Eve Lester) lay awake worrying about whether she had done the right thing. Mr Rolfe told her she was to go back to her room, stay there and lock the door; but a fragment of her mind said that big rôles and success was not all talent, perhaps a notable actor like Kapstein might. . . . Then she thought how it would be with a man like that, fat and with the flabby skin, a slobberer. Eve Lester felt sick.

Carol Evans thought about Asher Grey: just for a long moment before sinking into sleep. She also thought about Joe Thomas and how, if she lifted a finger, she could have him, for a while anyway: and she thought how odd it was, this negative feeling about Douglas when he had once meant so much, the whole world, to her.

Frank Ewes did not find it either easy or intellectually stimulating to verbally lob his précis of *The Times* newspaper across the desk to a Douglas Silver who did not seem to be listening anyway. Heavy rain was striking the windows and the blonde secretary, Deborah, hovered in the background, interrupting, commenting all the time while Douglas gave her curt instructions.

The news was bleak, in character with Frank's own mood, disturbed and bewildered: strikes, impending strikes, industrial unrest, rising prices, government indecision, the eternal gloom from the Middle East; he stumbled through it while Douglas scanned the day's mail, gave Deborah letters she could answer herself and instructions about the taped letters he had managed to do in odd moments through the weekend. He also checked the diary to see the way his day was going to run.

At nine-thirty there was the first company meeting, at ten they started rehearsing *Othello* which would call for a lot of concentration, they would break at twelve-thirty when he had a working lunch with Adrian and a meeting directly afterwards with Adrian, David Wills and Tony Holt. The afternoon would be taken up with the first *Merchant* rehearsal until around five-thirty when he would have to get into the office and clear up the day's mail, taping replies to the letters which only he could answer. With luck he would have an hour for a meal with Jennifer before starting the series of personal interviews which he had scheduled for most evenings during the next fortnight: he wanted to spend a minimum of half an hour with each member of the company, if possible fitting them all in within the first two weeks of rehearsals.

Frank had got to the correspondence columns of *The Times* now and Douglas was glancing at his watch, eight-forty-five and the director felt low and a little apprehensive, which was not surprising as he had been awake since five, his mind already churning with the way in which he would handle the first real working sessions with the company.

Deborah had by now made her exit, but was gone only a moment before she buzzed through to tell Douglas that Robin Alvin, his other young assistant, was waiting.

'Wheel him in,' Douglas snapped into his squawk box, then lifting his head signalled Frank to stop. 'That'll be enough for today. We can only presume things are going to get worse before they get better.'

When Deborah had closed the door on the three of them, Douglas pushed back his chair and looked up at the two young men. 'All right,' he began. 'You should have managed to integrate with them all by now. Who are the Marxists in the junior echelons of the company?'

Robin tittered and was cut short by Douglas's abrupt tone. 'I'm not joking. That's the kind of information I need from you two. You're not going to tell me that the younger set are apolitical because I just won't believe you. Two things motivate the minds and actions of men and women, whether they're actors, on the shop floor, in government or doing flower arrangements for the Women's Institute: sex and politics. They operate in equal levels and in the same strength. In the young they are unpredictable, because the young will usually go for the highest ideals with the least choice. Hence the Communist Party and the Roman Catholic Church having so many young adherents. I know about most of the bigger guns in this company, or at least I can make intelligent guesses. It's among the young element that I'm going to find the idealists, the fanatics even, and if I'm going to be hung up in arguments involving Karl Marx, or even the Pope of Rome, I want to know who I'm most likely to be arguing with and who'll be on my side. You, my lads, are my secret police, my agents and if either of you have any political, moral or religious scruples concerning that part of the job you'd better declare them now. If we're not careful this place will be like a Tudor court within a week.'

'Do you really think . . .?' began Robin.

'Yes, I do really mean that. There will be intrigue, attempted assassination of careers, there will be petty squabbles and, if we're not careful, the Shireston corridors of power will ring to the axe and thumbscrews. Christ, you've both worked in rep, you know what that can be like if it's not checked – the whispering, tale-bearing, sackings, directorial favouritism. Magnify that in a big company like this, chock-a-block with prima donnas, would-be prima donnas and people who think they could do it all so much better than the man at the top. Yes, very like the Tudor Court, so I rely on both of you.' He grinned. 'Be my eyes and ears.'

Deborah buzzed to say that Art Drays and Ronnie Gregor had arrived. It was five minutes to nine. Douglas, unaware that his old directorial manner and authority was beginning to show through once more, told them that he planned to arrive in the rehearsal hall at about five past nine. 'Should give time for the stragglers to arrive.' Adrian Rolf, David Wills and Tony Holt should already be waiting for them. He did not have to explain that their entrance was meant to be an impressive show of executive force.

The rehearsal hall was exactly as Douglas had first described it to Jennifer, a great barn of a place, built like a cold gymnasium by an architect who must have favoured the mid-Victorian period.

The company had assembled quietly, some even subdued: Maurice Kapstein and Joe Thomas both looked mildly unwell and the whole picture was not one of unrestrained enthusiasm. The members of the company were seated like an audience facing a plain wooden table behind which eight chairs were ranged. In spite of the party hangover feeling, the director's entrance, followed by his entourage, was welcomed with some loud shouts and hand clapping from the younger element, while throughout the hall there was a general stir and buzz of conversation.

The rise of noise was quickly stopped, however, when Douglas reached his chair. Hardly pausing he turned and began to speak.

'Good morning, ladies and gentlemen. I'm not going to waste any time because we'll do enough clock fighting before the season is over. If you don't know it by now I am your director and my name is Douglas Silver.' He caught Jen's eye and winked, she was sitting in the front row between Joe Thomas and Carol Evans. 'You should know the other gentlemen here with me and if you don't then it is their fault

261

because they should have introduced themselves to you. In case any of them have omitted to do this. . . .' He proceeded to introduce Frank, Robin, Art, Ronnie, David and Adrian, adding the exact facts regarding each man's position within the organization.

'Last night,' he continued, 'most of you heard me say that we were out to make a company from this glorious mulch of talent. Now we're in private I can tell you that you don't look all that glorious, but that won't stop us making a company, an ensemble. This we have got to do, and we can only do it together as a team. I think I'm likely to be a bit of a disappointment to some of you as a director. I believe in a liberated and liberal society, but I also know from my experience that, in theatre, the classics can become travesties of what they should be when they are handled by an undisciplined company. So, in order that we can quickly achieve a unified style I have to operate like a dictator. My political standpoint, then, will hover somewhere between that of Marxist sheep dog and Fascist hyena.' There was some more clapping at this, followed by a short burst of laughter. Douglas held up a hand.

'I'm now going to give you the most difficult points in my doctrine. They are obvious things, which I'm afraid, will not please all of you.'

He stopped for a moment and took a long look around the hall. 'In order to act together as a unified group we have got to spend as much time as possible with each other. By this I simply mean that, from the outset, we must aim for a classless society here at Shireston. There are those among us who are big names in the Theatre, and quite rightly so: through talent and much hard work they have achieved position,' he looked towards the seats nearest to him, 'most of the big names are sitting in the front here. Well, even though in the natural order of things you are leaders we cannot have segregation of any kind. The general public can think in terms of big names, but here, on the ground, we must have total equality – that goes for you black guys as well, those of you who spent most of yesterday evening segregating yourselves. All equal and with an equal voice, that's how it's got to be. I want to see this company mixing together, talking together, doing what we used to call at school "spare time activities" together.' A couple of catcalls from the back, silenced with a freezing look. 'This, I know, will not appeal to you all,' a pause held for a count of five, 'and that's just too bad because that's the way it's going to be.'

Douglas took a step back from the table, buried his hands in his pockets, allowing the last words to sink in.

'As you know, from the numerous instructions I have had circulated to you, rehearsals start each morning at ten o'clock. But the whole company, and I stress the *whole* company, will meet here at nine o'clock each morning. On Mondays we will have our weekly company meetings when we can thrash out company problems, things we haven't got time to deal with during rehearsals: you can all have a good beef at me and I can have a go at you. On Thursdays we will *all* work at communal voice production; there will, of course, be individual voice coaching for those who need, or want, it. On the other mornings we'll exercise for one hour before rehearsals.'

He did not dare look towards Conrad Catellier who was already shuffling in his seat. Douglas cleared his throat and went on.

'What are the matters of urgency in the world today? I believe they are concerned with social order, that many-headed beast: the racial problem, pollution, violence, crime, famine, personal relationships on every level, greed, hatred, lust, want, common sense and true freedom. Now I also believe, as I know most of you must do, that William Shakespeare wrote about these very things: whether he knew he was writing about them is another matter. I believe that the four plays we are to perform this season make apt comments on the matters which are of most concern to us in this age. Some of these are obvious, others we will discover as we work together on the plays; and the plays have more to say than just comments on our problems: I would like, for instance, to put a little of the romance back into *Romeo and Juliet*.' There was genuine laughter now, a true sense of relaxation.

'Now, with regard to direction. I'm afraid there is no time

263

for us to have any magical mystery tours, to discover how best we can interpret the plays as we go along. But I'm not a cold and inflexible dictator; I expect actors to evolve characters, even though I will provide the ground plan, the working guide lines for each play; I will set the moods and give the technical aid to the extent that I will even be old-fashioned and plot your moves at the outset of each play going into rehearsal. That will give you more than a skeleton with which to work. Your task will be to provide the flesh, blood and nerves. So, we will have to rely upon each other, trust each other, set up links of collaboration which will create moments of theatre capable of shattering the minds of audiences: and this we can only do as a team. We must interpret Shakespeare so that the modern audience will understand with complete ease yet with a fresh insight; and this we can only do as a team. We must pull from our collectively stored theatrical knowledge all the devices and resources known to our art, smashing our critics with colour, style and brilliance; and this we can only do as a team.'

He paused again, letting the last words thud home before making the concluding remarks.

'I apologize for this bleak and barren hall in which we have to work, if it's any consolation I am assured that the theatre will be ready for us in a matter of two to three weeks, so that we can at least expect to transfer rehearsals to the stage in good time. Are there any questions of burning importance?' He did not give anyone time to develop a mental theme. 'No? Good. Then if those of you who are not concerned with *Othello* would be good enough to leave, and those who are concerned with *The Merchant* will note that they are to reassemble here at two-thirty, we can get on with some work.' He gave them the most dazzling smile he could muster, sat down and pretended to be busy sorting papers.

Adrian put a hand on his shoulder as he moved past, on his way to the exit. 'We meet at twelve-thirty?' Eyebrows raised.

Douglas nodded quietly and then cast his eyes round the hall. He was pleased to see that the *Othello* cast were shifting into a solid group at the front and that Jen was doing her best to react to his plea by splitting herself from the bunch of principals, going to sit next to a couple of supers. Edward Crispin, Liz Column, Rachel Cohen and Murray Fleet (who was to play Montano) were clustered together, and Joe Thomas was with Asher Grey, cast as Cassio, and Laurence Pern, their Roderigo.

During the following hour, Douglas talked about his visible and audible vision of *Othello*: Iago the matador, Roderigo the little bull, Othello the big fighting bull, the *faena*, the music and noises for the cinematic fades at exits and entrances, the noises of intrigue, the suggestion of a *corrida*. He went on to speak of the main issues within the play, of love and the devil jealousy, hatred, greed, ambition, personal and political power and the interrelation of the major characters.

By lunchtime they had walked through the rough plot of the first two scenes and were well into act one, scene three, the Council Chamber where, in front of the Doge and his senators, Othello clashes with Brabantio following the secret marriage to Desdemona.

There was a sense of headiness, an almost naïve camaraderie, as they broke for lunch; Douglas was fending off a stream of questions from the junior actors and shrugging into his coat when Jennifer came over to him.

'I've been asked to lunch with my Othello,' she announced, a half smile on her upturned face, as though she was asking permission to go. For a second Douglas felt disturbed: doubtless all the old theatrical legends of Desdemonas and their Othellos screamed silently round his mind, then the calm returned. He grinned at his wife, looking over to where Joe Thomas stood out of earshot.

'If you like that sort of thing,' he said quietly. 'Some prefer them.' In the rear of his brain there was a tiny image: Carol Evans naked and thrusting out towards him, reaching for him. 'Enjoy yourself,' he pulled a glum face. 'Me? I have to work. Lift that barge, tote that bale. I'm lunching with Adrian. A working luncheon.'

'You're moving like a politician, darling. Maybe my

lunch'll turn out that way as well. A working luncheon.' Jen wrinkled her nose.

'Watch it,' Douglas grinned again. Then, seriously, 'How do you think it went?'

'It's going to be great, but your Othello's in need of a lot of help,' her hand on his arm. 'He's not an actor, Douglas, and it's no good any of us pretending he is. He's a performer and you'll have to blast an actor's performance out of him. It's going to take a lot of work and patience.'

'Will you talk to him over lunch?'

She nodded assent.

'Then we can go over it tonight.'

'Okay, love, see you.' A wave of affection bubbling through her. His appeal to the company had been impressive, even inspirational, and Jennifer felt the least she could do was to give him as much assistance as her mind, body and professional knowledge was able to contribute. She did not marvel at her husband's brilliance when he gave out glimpses of his vision of *Othello*, or the company, but she was thrilled by it all, becoming excited about being part of the festival, an emotion she had not felt until that morning, although her doubts all too readily moved under the surface.

Joe Thomas's invitation had come as something of a surprise to Jennifer, who felt that the man was uncertain of his attitude to her; she did not particularly like him, even at their early meeting in his bewildered and downcast state during the drama of his arrival he seemed too wrapped up in the extreme fantasy creature that was the public and publicized Joe Thomas – ballad singer, owner of real estate, automobiles, a helicopter, countless women. He seemed to be limited in the amount of time in which he could be serious, professional and involved in the matters of the season and *Othello*, his mind slipping quickly back into the extraordinary other world which existed for him as a normal lifestyle. Strangely, Jennifer thought, it was that world which made him unpleasant. Was it that all the ballads, the beat songs, the sweet love sonnets arranged for this black man's hypnotic voice, set against milling strings, were so deeply equated with sex that he had become to believe in the music and the, often banal, lyrics as an ultimate truth? But this was only how she saw him, a vain singer stuffed with arrogance and little real culture. Was there more? Could she feel anything else? After all, creative people were always a prey to their own work, and Thomas was undoubtedly creative and professional within his particular field. Did she dislike him, resent him perhaps, because he was trying his strength in a more demanding area, acting? That was nonsense, and she quickly dismissed the thought, for it was Douglas who had persuaded the man to come, against his nature, to Shireston.

'I ain't organized yet, Jen. You got transport?' Thomas asked when she returned to him.

'Yes, Douglas isn't using the car.' She was surprised, automatically thinking that he had meant lunch in the company restaurant. She gave a little chuckle. 'You want to go off limits?'

Thomas flashed a smile. 'I always want to go off limits, ma'am.' He gestured towards the door. 'No, I just heard some of the boys talking about a nearby pub. Sounds a good place.'

'You mean The Bleeding Sheep?'

About half a mile up the road, leading away from Shireston, was the small and attractive village of Ledgerow. Bristling with retired army and navy officers and civil servants, it also sported the best country pub for miles, The Lion and Lamb, known traditionally as The Bleeding Sheep. The place had been an actors' haunt since the festival's early days, in fact the present landlord, who had been in charge for the past ten years and had therefore known Shireston's bleak years, was quick to cash in on the new surge of life which had been granted to the festival. While his steady round the year custom came from the locals, he knew very well that the company trade, and that of passing tourists drawn in by the festival, could be of great benefit to his books. In other years the actors' patronage had added a little colour to the place, a whisper of small scandals for the locals, but not an enormous amount of profit in the till. Now that there was an injection of power, money and big names up the road, the landlord, Jack Wedlock, had taken the step of circularizing the whole Shireston Festival Company and executive staff, sending each his specially designed brochure listing The Sheep's amenities and placing high on the list the fact that lunches and simple dinners were available, either from the cold buffet (*notable attraction of the house for many years*) or the grill.

At first, Adrian Rolfe had been furious over the circular, knowing that it was a direct threat to business in the company restaurant and possibly to the new theatre restaurant as well. Adrian even made a vain attempt to find out who had supplied Wedlock with such a complete and detailed list of the company and staff, but the task, he soon realized, was beyond him: too many of the permanent staff were long-standing customers at the Sheep.

'Competition's a healthy thing, Adrian,' Douglas told him. 'In any case I think it's good that there's at least one reasonable local where the company can feel at home. There is a tradition you know, and it doesn't hurt any of them to get out. After all, we don't want to make Shireston into a concentration camp for actors.'

Now, on the first day of rehearsals, the director's wife was going to become a customer in company with possibly the most notorious celebrity at Shireston.

Art Drays was waiting outside the rehearsal hall when Douglas emerged. The rain had stopped, but there was a cold damp feel to the air, clouds black-grey washing the sky.

'I thought I'd catch you for a second.' Art fell into step with his superior.

'It'll only be for a second. I have to meet Adrian.'

'Enough time. Douglas, I wanted to know if you'd come to any decision about Conrad's understudy. I know we don't go into rehearsal with *Richard* for a few weeks, but if it's going to be Asher Grey I think someone's got to approach him soon.'

The question had been difficult and one that Douglas had already shelved a dozen times. They were all conscious that Catellier's Richard III was going to be one of the most difficult performances to extract, and that it was of utmost importance that the understudy should be strong. Conrad was a highly professional man of the theatre but, everybody knew, he was also prone to nervous attacks, particularly if he found the role difficult or the production not to his liking.

Douglas, head down into the wind, gave a sigh. 'I know. I know. Asher's the most obvious, but I've got him doing Romeo, Lorenzo and Cassio; that's a lot for the boy to handle. I'm worried about him carrying an overload.'

'He's young and strong.'

'Oh yes, and I'm sure he'd be willing.'

They were on to the gravel drive now, in front of the house with only about a hundred yards left to get to the theatre restaurant.

'We've got to have a decision, Douglas.' Art making it sound like life or death.

They walked a few more paces.

'Give me until the morning.' Douglas stopped, turning towards his productions manager. 'I don't think Asher realizes how much of a key he is to the season. When he does discover how important he is, that boy is going to begin worrying and if he's overloaded he'll get distracted and maybe ruin the roles I've already given to him. By tomorrow you'll have an understudy for Conrad. All right?'

It was just one of a dozen or so decisions of some importance that were hanging over Douglas now that the company was gathered together and matters were moving inexorably towards productions being in performance. Now he had to face Adrian who undoubtedly would have another pile of problems which only he, as director, could untangle, veto or mark with his verbal seal of approval.

Adrian Rolfe was already seated in the restaurant, Emilio fusing round him with menu and wine list as though he was some tycoon with an externally extendable expense account. As soon as Douglas entered, Emilio switched his attentiveness to the director, seeing that his coat was taken, ushering him to his table, during which time Douglas observed that Ronnie Gregor and young Robin Alvin were lunching together (a good thing, he thought), and in the far corner

David Wills was hosting Rachel Cohen.

'Stirring words this morning,' Adrian greeted him with a smile. 'Had us all straining in the slips, blood pounding and all that. The company that prays together stays together: only I spell it p-r-e-y-s.'

'That's a pinch. It's a line out of a play.'

'I'm the greatest plagiarist since W. Shakespeare, didn't you know?'

'It's based on a line from David Turner's *Semi-Detached*.'

'How about that, I couldn't remember where it came from.'

After they had ordered, Douglas opened his briefcase. 'I suppose you've got a list as well?'

'Long as your arm.'

'You want to have first crack?'

'I'm cautious, let's hear yours.'

Douglas looked at the foolscap page he had withdrawn from his briefcase: it was covered with scribbled notes and had the scrawled heading *Adrian Rolfe*. 'I'm concerned about us making the maximum publicity push,' he began.

'Don't be.' Adrian spoke quietly but with his usual confidence. 'Everything's being handled. All your principal actors and actresses will get at least one feature in the national press or on the magazine scene before April. *The Sunday Times* wants to do a photo sequence for their colour supplement: that'll mean a day here and then a morning or afternoon with you. Got your diary?'

They fixed the date for early in February and Adrian went on talking. 'I have the ad layouts over in the office if you need to see them. The posters will be ready by the end of February but I haven't booked space until the middle of March. The brochures are ready now. . . .'

'They'd better be, we open the box office on the first of February.'

'That's another thing I have on *my* list.' Adrian looked grim for a moment. 'We're obviously overlapping on some matters.'

Douglas caught the apprehensive look on his PR man's

face.

'You're worried, Adrian? What's the problem with the box office?'

'Have you talked to anyone about the situation there?'

'No, the box office is David Wills's territory. I was quite specific about that.'

Adrian looked down his nose and pulled a face. 'Douglas, I know David's your protégé, and I speak low because he's sitting over there, but he's not the most on-the-ball executive director in the business.'

Douglas was aware of the lack of trust which had existed between Adrian Rolfe and David Wills from the moment of the latter's appointment, but it was now coming out into the open: the first intrigue of the season, perhaps; the first of the long knives.

'Tell me what's wrong in the box office.'

'I'm only your PR man, I shouldn't. . . .'

'And as my PR man you have to be very close to the box office. Your job is to sell the season, theirs is to sell the seats, and I need every seat sold for every performance. . . .'

'Otherwise you're a dead duck.' It was the kind of impertinence for which Adrian was famous.

'Not quite, Adrian, not quite. But I'll level with you because you're the sharpest man on the team. I'm running this place on a budget of £2 million, the bulk of which is already spent, or at least spoken for. The trustees know they'll not see all their money back, but they've put it to me quite plainly that I have to retain a minimum of three-quarters of the original investment, that's £1½ million, otherwise it'll be difficult for them to put money into a second season, and a second season has got to show profit. Now you don't have to be a great mathematician to work out the figures. A house full on one night represents a cash intake of £6,588. One week, with six evening performances and a couple of matinées brings in £52,704 – if every seat is taken for every performance. The figures are engraved on my heart.' Douglas thumped his chest. 'If the house is full for the entire season we take £1,397,400, a sum that is below that

271

which I have got to make back for the trustees; and it's going to cost me another £400,000 to keep this season propped up anyway, so that means I have to get every ticket sold throughout the season, and make around £600,000 over the top – out of the restaurant, from the exhibition, sale of programmes, odds and sods. So, Adrian, I rely on you to sell the season for me and to tell me when something is wrong at the box office even though it is the executive director's problem and he's my protégé.'

Adrian looked stubbornly at his plate. 'I can see why we had the happy ship is a good ship bit this morning.'

Douglas snapped back. 'We had it because I happen to believe in it.' He dropped his hands palm downwards on the table, looked up and gave a shy grin, 'In part anyway. I do believe the equality thing'll keep our political friends happy. There must be some comrades of Marx or Mao among the younger brethren and I don't want to waste time on side issues. Look, chum, when you open up a company like this you're starting a new society and the extremists are only too willing to get on to the band wagon. I don't like taking chances, so what's wrong with the box office?'

Adrian gave him a nervous smile. 'I'm making a big drama out of very little, Doug. But the present situation in the box office is one of utter inefficiency. I could be nasty and say that really you should have gone into the matter at the outset, but it's only just come to *my* notice.'

'I talked with Harper very early on.' Graham Harper was the box office manager and now Douglas realized that he had not seen him around the place much: a fat, sleek individual with darkening blond hair. 'He gave me all the right answers then. Seemed to know his way around; know what he was about.'

'I dare say,' Adrian said it quietly, without any hint of irritation. 'I dare say, but it's part of the old régime, isn't it? In a very short time here I discovered that, in practically all areas, the old régime was riddled with incompetence. Christ, Douglas, you did as well, and yet you've gone and taken the box office at its face value.'

It was true enough, the box office did not come into operation until the beginning of February, and Douglas knew deep down that he was guilty of simply assuming it would operate properly and efficiently, when his experience so far should have told him differently.

'Have you examined, I mean really examined, the staff situation in the box office?' Adrian asked.

Douglas shifted as though his chair was uncomfortable, a sigh leaking from his lips. 'No. No, I haven't.'

'Well I've seen it all this last week and I've been checking back. You want to hear what we've got?'

Douglas, tense across the table nodded.

'We've got Graham Harper, a man of forty-nine who was appointed box office manager here nine years ago and immediately brought in his girl friend as a number two. He is now uncertain and vaguely embittered, she is now forty years old, tired and fed up. She'd leave at the drop of a ticket. . . .'

'I know her, Elsie. . . .'

'I don't know her name and I don't want to know, it doesn't matter. Douglas, between the two of them they've run the box office, nice and quietly, with the help of a couple of girls who change from year to year. All they're interested in is keeping things ticking over, and nobody'll convince me that they're going to adapt to our bustling, booming new image. If any one person in the box office over the past nine years has gone out of his, hers or its way to sell a ticket then I'm the president of the Cube Shaped Earth Society.'

Douglas had been feeling reasonably pleased with the way things were shaping. The reception, his speech to the company, and the first rehearsal had gone better than he had dared expect, hence his buoyant sense of confidence. Also, in the weeks that had just passed they had, he knew, made a lot of headway with things like the mailing list, brochures, posters. Knowing Adrian's ability, Douglas had been certain of a good strong selling position; that part of his mind which held pictures of the future had retained a constant image of applications for tickets flooding in from the general public, agencies, tourist organizations and hotels, all being handled

273

with, he fondly imagined, customary efficiency: after all, once the season was fully promoted the actual sell was a simple, straightforward job. Now, to be jolted into the reality that the most important factor in the operation was not only badly staffed, but also ineffectual. His personal anger, bottled for a few moments, was natural enough and aimed at himself. 'Jesus Christ, Adrian, what a way to run a bloody railway. Are they really that bad in the box office?'

'Deadbeats, chum.' The PR man grinned. 'And I'm telling you that if all my arrows strike home they just aren't going to know what's hit them. They'll be up on their arses in applications for tickets and they'll think the roof's fallen in. Sorry to give you a shock, but I thought you should be warned.'

Douglas Silver played with his fork for a moment. 'They're going to think the roof's fallen in anyway when I get through with them.' He said coldly, 'Don't get mad at David, I'll put him in as a beater straight away; if he hasn't got them properly organized within a week then I'll go in with the guns. Now, what other terrors have you got for me?'

CHAPTER NINE

From the outside The Lion and Lamb was a typical picture postcard English inn: standing back from the road in its own garden, with a grey stone terrace which in summer was always filled with customers, the place looked like a large, expensive whitewashed country cottage complete with small windows set at uncertain angles, great hanging eaves and, one of its main attractions for tourist photographers, a beautifully kept thatch. It sported five double bedrooms and so qualified as an hotel, but it was the bar and grill which gave the place its reputation and drew regulars from thirty or forty miles away.

The bar itself acted as a natural room divider, being a large three-sided affair jutting straight out from the rear wall, the third, short side running directly parallel to the glass double-doored entrance.

Nobody could be quite certain about how much of the interior was original. Certainly the main cross beams, and at least part of the large open hearth, were seventeenth century, but for the rest it was rather like the broom that has had three new heads and a couple of new handles yet still remained the one great-grandmother bought.

To the left of the doors, the room opened up into the main bar parlour which was almost too much the English dream with its Windsor chairs and matched prints. Yet nobody could accuse it of lacking atmosphere, that strange blend of bonhomie and the sense of being a privileged member of a closed shop; plus all the more natural things, the smells and pipe smoke, the bursts of laughter from regulars and the non-stop clash of the till.

Straight across the bar in the parlour, one could see through to the other open section which, while still a bar, was mainly designed as a restaurant.

At lunchtime, The Sheep was usually quite full and Archie Swimmer eyed the scene from his almost legendary stand-point, the far end of the parlour bar. The Sheep had been Archie's local almost from the first day he began work at Shireston, and hardly a lunchtime went by which did not see the stage carpenter in for at least a couple of pints.

In the many years that actors had used The Sheep as their pub during the festival, Archie Swimmer had seen many men and women make fools of themselves in that bar parlour, but he could not bring to mind any big name who had brought himself to the brink of folly so quickly as Maurice Kapstein.

Kapstein had obviously been in the place since opening time and, while he was not particularly loud as yet, there were definite signs of alcoholic deterioration in his gait and speech.

It was amazing, thought Archie, how people reacted to television faces. Kapstein had a half dozen regulars around him, all obviously basking in the reflected glory of spending an hour in the pub with the live flesh and blood character they had all watched weekly on television in *The Game Game*. They were no more interested in Maurice Kapstein than in their local grocer, it was Solly Jacobs the ruthless fight prom-oter walking the corridors of sporting power, ousting vil-lains, pulling off half-million deals with intrigue, adroitness and underhanded skill, which interested them. It was also plain to see that Morrie was in his element, even reverting to character, his accent becoming thicker, in the vein of Solly Jacobs.

Now he had been joined by Ronald Escott, a character actor of much experience and of the same vintage as Kaps-tein. Archie had been watching Escott rehearse Brabantio, Desdemona's father, all morning (he usually sat in on some of the rehearsals), and he was much aware that Escott would be required that afternoon, as he was playing Old Gobbo, the sand-blind father to Launcelot Gobbo, the major clown in *The*

276

Merchant. Ronald Escott knew The Bleeding Sheep well, Archie considered, for he had been in at least two Shireston Festival companies since World War Two. Archie took a sip of his pint and tried to remember what Escott had played; he recalled a buoyant Touchstone in *As You Like It*, and one of the rustics, Snug the Joiner he thought, in *The Dream*.

There was a bubble of laughter around Kapstein and Escott, then a bustling with heads turning towards the door. Archie Swimmer shifted his position to see Joe Thomas and Jennifer Frost standing in the doorway.

Kapstein saw them a little later than most of the people in the bar, but as soon as the fact of their presence had registered upon him, the actor let out a whoop of recognition. 'Here comes more of the suppressed minority. Joe Thomas, you unliberated negro you, come and have a drink with one of the unliberated Jews.'

Jennifer felt Joe Thomas's body stiffen as Kapstein shouted. For a second she experienced the brief alarm, thinking that the black and legendary singer was about to head into some violent unpleasantness; but he replied in a cool voice.

'Hold it, man,' raising a hand to Kapstein, fingers spread wide. 'I got to get food organized.'

Jennifer had already caught the eye of the young woman obviously in charge of the restaurant and who had begun to advance towards them, when the landlord, Jack Wedlock himself, hurried across the room to greet the couple personally. A large, pleasant man, Wedlock seldom lost the opportunity of making people feel at home when they visited his hostelry; now he poured out a flood of effusive welcome; what an honour it was to have two such distinguished names under his roof; what a personal accolade it was to him; how good it was of them to choose this particular public house. In the end Joe stopped him, almost abruptly, by asking for the menu.

The head waitress, or overseer, or whatever she was, had been standing quietly behind Wedlock and now stepped forward with two large, blue and rather pretentious-looking menus.

They chose a simple meal: farmhouse soup, steaks, French fried potatoes and mixed salads, then excused themselves saying that they would be ready to eat in ten minutes.

'We'll be in the bar. If we're any longer than ten minutes would you call us through?' asked Joe.

The smart young woman nodded understandingly.

Jennifer could not figure why she was so surprised at Thomas's common sense or the tactics he had employed to avoid any lengthy involvement with Kapstein; to her, she supposed, it seemed out of character with the man she really only knew through his recordings, newspapers and magazine stories.

She realized now how much the force of publicity could create the image of a public figure, even on the minds of those who knew the profession well. At the same time she could understand that the tall black man might well be quite a hell raiser should the circumstances prove favourable: no person living under the strain of constant public appearances, riding in trains, boats, planes and cars, living out of suitcases, exposed to all kinds of incredible flattery, public and private adulation, could come out of it all unscathed. Looking at the back of his neck, as he led her through into the bar, she could well imagine how insecure and explosive he might be.

Once in the bar they were engulfed by people and a dozen introductions. Kapstein was perched unsteadily on a stool, with Escott, looking a shade worried, leaning against the bar. The Jewish actor smiled drunkenly at Jennifer.

'Mrs Silver, taking time out with our black brother already. Nice to see you here, my dear.' He closed his eyes slowly and reopened them, focusing on Joe Thomas. 'And what's Mr Thomas going to drink? You are allowed alcoholic refreshment aren't you, Joe? As well as the smokes I mean?' There was an undertow to his manner, as though he was spoiling for a fight.

'Give me a free day and an equal start and I'll drink you under the table any time,' said Joe with an easy grace. 'To be going on with I'll have a gin and tonic, but what about Jennifer?'

Jen ordered a tomato juice, adding that she was driving and had a lot of work to do that afternoon.

'So have I got work this afternoon,' challenged Kapstein, 'much work I got to do with your husband, but it doesn't stop me having a little drink at lunchtime.'

'He'll be the first alcoholic Shylock in the business,' muttered Ronald Escott. 'My daughter, my ducets and my gin.'

'Ah Mr Kapstein, you've had more experience than I,' Jennifer smiled.

'Sure, sure I've had more experience. I suppose in all fields, Mrs Jennifer Silver, or should I call you Frost? Morrie Kapstein could teach a young girl like you much in all fields.' He spluttered, rocking on his stool. 'In any field I could teach you much. Give me a summer's day, a field, and a young girl. . . .'

'Cheers, Morrie,' Joe Thomas cut in raising his glass.

'Cheers to you, you black bastard,' Kapstein gave him what was supposed to be a friendly grin.

There was a lull during which Ronald Escott asked Jennifer if she had settled in and liked Shireston; Joe Thomas stood glowering at Kapstein who now seemed wrapped in his own thoughts, lost for words.

'We've got a super apartment and I think –' Jennifer began, but Kapstein cut across her.

'What's this *Othello* going to be like then?' He sounded aggressive. 'You've been working with the great man all morning. How's it shaping?'

Joe looked at Jennifer, lifting his eyebrows as though asking permission to have a go at Kapstein. Jennifer shook her head.

'Secret signals, already,' boomed the fat actor intercepting the look between them. 'You don't need to have any secrets from Morrie. I am as a closed book.'

'The *Othello*'s going to be okay,' Joe said quietly.

'It ought to be okay,' Kapstein laughed loudly as though he had just thought of the joke of the century. 'It ought to be, it's got the right colour to it. I mean nobody has to black up or anything. That makes a change.'

Joe Thomas took a step forward and the atmosphere became charged with possible menace, which was only broken by the appearance of the head waitress from the restaurant who had come in to say their lunch was ready.

Joe nodded and Jennifer turned away, but before he followed her, Thomas pushed his head close to Kapstein. 'I'll see you again.' There was no warmth in the way he said it, holding his stance for five seconds or so before following Jennifer out of the bar.

Archie Swimmer, watching the whole thing over his pint in the corner of the bar, smiled to himself. Sparks, he thought, would fly in one direction or another before much longer, and, if Maurice Kapstein kept on knocking it back at this rate, the sparks would undoubtedly leap from him.

Thomas was magnificently cool about the whole business. 'Sorry about that,' he smiled pleasantly across the table when they were settled.

'I detest that sort of behaviour at the best of times, but within the profession it's unforgivable.'

'The profession makes no difference,' Joe laughed.

'How do you keep your nerve, your cool?'

'Sometimes I don't. That's my trouble, baby, I'm often too quick to pick up that kind of cheap crack. That's when I hit the headlines. Aw, forget it, the bum was drunk anyway.'

'He's drunk all right, and I can't see Douglas taking too kindly to that this afternoon.'

'Kapstein's experienced, I should imagine he knows well enough how to sober up quickly when he has to. Even I can do that.'

Jennifer took a long look at him. 'Do you have to face a lot of racist talk? A lot of things like Kapstein said? I would have thought a man like you would have been protected to a certain degree.'

He thought for a moment, a faint curve on his lips. 'You're right of course, I realized that when I arrived over here all by myself; that is without the characters I usually have around. Yes, I've been protected, but they can't do it all of the time, and I wouldn't want that anyhow, I'm not an Uncle Tom you know.'

'I know,' she smiled again.

'And I wasn't always protected; like everyone I live with my past and that's not always nice. It's a strange thing, even among the most liberal of whites, even among this company, you're never free from it.'

'What? The fact that you're. . . .'

'Black, Jennifer. I know it's become a cliché, so much so that people say we've got what we wanted now and we still aren't satisfied like your trade unions. The fact that I'm a black man. No person with a white skin can ever know what that means. Never. It's like some great gulf and it's never going to be bridged until both sides can learn to think differently. Sometimes I think maybe the great massacre's the only way it's ever going to happen.'

They were silent for a moment over their soup; the occasional guffaw came from Kapstein's party in the bar and there was the general hum of conversation around them, cocooning them in a kind of warmth.

'Hey, I didn't invite you out to bend your ear with race politics, Jennifer.'

'No? What did you invite me for?'

'I guess I wanted to get to know my Desdemona a little better.' He looked very much a man of the world, not unattractive, easy, a stylish character. They were both conscious of the interest that was being shown from other tables and from the bar; it was something that Jennifer had never completely mastered, the ability to remain naturally herself in public when she knew that most eyes were flicking in her direction simply because she was Jennifer Frost. She could admire Joe Thomas, now, for his outwardly casual approach, the way with which he dealt with situations as they arose. His command. No wonder, she reflected, he had a lot of girls, he was quite a different person here, alone with her in an English country pub, different from that which he had been last night for instance, with his little group of black actors and actresses at the party: the swinger, the loud and pushy kingpin making the girls, the leader of the group, the guy you saw on television.

'No, that's not really why I asked you out,' there was a flash of nervousness across Joe Thomas's face. 'I guess this'll sound stupid. . . .'

'What?'

'Well, Jennifer, I guess I asked you out for several reasons. Yes, to get to know my Desdemona, but also to get out with you because you're really somebody here, you're the director's wife, and I reckoned that with you I'd be safe.'

'That's flattering.'

'There's more. I wanted to talk with you because I'm scared out of my mind.'

Jennifer frowned. 'What about? Why?'

'*Othello*, that's what about. It's okay for you, baby, you've done the fancy acting scene, it's part of you. But how am I going to be? I'm an entertainer, not a stage actor. I thought I could do it in the start, but now I'm here . . . well I just don't know how I'm going to close my mind around Shakespeare and get through it all without everybody busting a gut and laughing their heads off.' He looked at her intently.

'You do it by being what you are; who you are.' Jennifer felt for the words, picking with care. 'By being the professional you are and by trusting Douglas.'

'And trusting you? Can I turn to you for help? Can you guide me through?'

'Not all of the time. . . .' She had to pause as the girl came to take their soup plates away and serve their steaks. When all was done, she continued. 'Joe, you have to trust yourself a lot. What I mean is you can't rely on Douglas, or myself, all of the time. But I'm sure everyone's going to contribute.'

'This is my problem. I've spent weeks learning the part, examining the man, trying to interpret. I did all that on my own, alone. Now I'm here and everybody seems so loose, so natural, taking it all in their stride, while I'm so tense. . . .'

'You didn't seem tense this morning.'

'Well at least I managed to hide that.' There was some genuine relief in his voice. 'I may not look it but I am tense about it, all knotted up. I mean we haven't begun yet and I'm

282

scared crazy that when I have to come out with my first lines the whole cast is going to jeer and tell me to forget it.'

'That isn't going to happen, Joe. You may be untried in this particular area, but you're a successful, seasoned performer.' She grinned at him, 'And don't come the non-actor bit with me. I've seen your movies.'

'The hell with the movies, this is different. I've never been so anxious.'

'It's a question of confidence, Joe, you know that. Douglas wouldn't have asked you, and you wouldn't have come if either of you had initially thought you were going to be that bad. I promise you that you won't have any trouble. I've never worked with Douglas before, but I've watched him work, he's careful and painstaking, and he never asks more than an actor can give, so stop sweating.'

He gave her an attractive lopsided smile. 'Yea, it's all a bit childish of me, I guess.'

'No, it's not childish. I'm glad you talked about it to me. Othello's the hell of a part for anybody to stake down, I can understand what you're going through.'

'Yea, Othello sure is a big, big man.'

'He's big and he's naïve, Joe. I think Douglas will want a lot of the naïvety spelled out to the audience.'

'You mean the bluff soldier statesman not used to the ways of women?' His voice took on a little screech note at the end, as though he was fooling around now.

'Just that.'

'Well how am I going to get that one? I know too much about women.'

'Lucky old you.'

'Now you're putting me on.'

'No, I just don't think any man really knows that much about women.'

'And Othello. . . .'

'Knows next to nothing, which does not mean he's not a good lover. You can be one hell of a lover and still know nothing about the woman you love; not the real, deep important things anyway.'

'You believe that?'

'Yes I do. A man can pour out his love, his affection, make you feel like an empress, say just the right things, be sexually satisfying and all that, without having the slightest knowledge about what goes on in his woman's brain. He can walk out of the house to his work in the morning and not have even a hint that the girl is in turmoil thinking she's going to lose him to the first woman that comes along, so she's in agony until he returns and starts the love ride again, lulling her into satisfaction. Or a man can go for years without knowing that the girl he loves and satisfies is desperate to talk to him about politics.'

'That's nuts, politics, that's the girl's fault if he doesn't know.'

'Not always. Think about it, Joe. Maybe you'll get some clues to Othello. Desdemona's a girl who wants to share everything and that's how I'm going to play her.' She almost savagely thrust a piece of steak in her mouth and chewed hard, looking at him with a fire that could have been interpreted as a challenge.

Douglas and Adrian Rolfe completed their meal and sat talking over coffee. They had covered all their separate problems, yet the nag in Douglas's mind left him edgy about the box office situation.

'I think I'll catch David here and now, fix a meeting for today,' he said rising and bringing their meal and discussion to a close.

'I'll be glad and relieved to know the outcome.' Adrian looked serious.

'Don't worry, you will; know the outcome I mean.'

They shook hands and Douglas walked over to the table where David sat engrossed in conversation with Rachel Cohen, their heads close.

Rachel looked up and smiled as he approached.

'You settling in?' Douglas asked.

'Fine, thanks, no complaints.'

'I should think not on the first day.' He turned to David. 'I wonder if you could look in and see me after rehearsal this afternoon.'

David asked what time and they agreed on five o'clock.

Outside, the rain had started up again, a thin, dismal drizzle soaking into everything. It was only two o'clock but Douglas, hunching his shoulders against the rain, started off at a trot towards the rehearsal hall.

He was glad to find the hall empty, smelling slightly of damp clothing and stale cigarette smoke. He prayed silently that nobody would arrive for fifteen minutes or so, throwing off his light coat and dropping into his chair behind the table, reaching for his notes on *The Merchant*. Once they began to really work, he told himself, things would settle into a more gentle routine; he could not expect everything to be right and easy on the first day. At the same time, Douglas was sharply aware that all this was a decidedly new experience for him. He had directed many plays, but always one at a time; now he was faced with doing two in tandem and, in a few weeks, the number would be doubled.

He took a deep breath and pressed all the anxieties away, including his most recent worry over the box office, that at least could be suitably shelved until late afternoon: now it was *The Merchant* which had to occupy his mind.

He flipped through his copy of the text and his notes, remembering all that he had planned: the idea of human corruption inherent in the brittle comedy. The whole style of his conception came back to mind. Raymond Leggat had provided five short pieces of music which they would use as a basic background score for the play and, while the composer was working on material for the rest of the season, Douglas still had to approve the pieces so that they could be properly orchestrated and put on tape for Art and Ronnie to splice in with whatever other effects were needed. Douglas had the music on a cassette tape, recorded on piano by Leggat himself, and he wanted the company's reaction before going any further. He checked the little cassette tape recorder before ticking off all they had to get through that afternoon: his opening remarks, again about how modern audiences should

285

see the play; the unpleasantness of those involved; the up-pointing of corruption; the music which, to his mind, was what he wanted, rapacious and debased: he had been tempted to go the whole hog and link the play rather as he was doing *Othello*, with the sounds of corruption, but instinct told him that you could not get away with the same tricks twice in one season. The costumes and settings would help to underlie what was already in the text and, now, in the music; the rest would have to come from within the actors and the style which Douglas Silver had to produce.

There was the sound of a car outside and a moment later Frank Ewes, looking flushed, came in with Liz Column.

'It droppeth like a bloody gentle dew,' Liz announced loudly, shaking the rain from her arms. 'God, this climate, take us to Venice, Douglas, as quickly as you can.'

Douglas rose. 'I'll do my best, but your magic has to be the power source for this little play.'

'Oh I know, I know.' Liz shook her head.

Frank had moved over to sit next to Douglas as Art, Ronnie and young Robin Alvin came in followed by a group of supers who would soon be rushing between the rustic pleasures of Belmont and the streets and the great halls of Venice in the play.

The hall began to fill and chatter drove the finer points from Douglas's mind. He saw Asher Grey come in with Peter Berger who would play Antonio, and his mind again slipped into the unresolved decision about Catellier's understudy; following Asher and Berger was the big Jamaican, Lonnie Barnes who had been cast in the small, but important, part of the Prince of Morocco, one of Portia's suitors who would have to go through the routine of choosing the correct casket business, thought Douglas; but, he supposed, there were some equally stupid rituals, and just as outmoded, connected with the choice of a bride or groom still active in the modern world: that was another point he must try to make in the production.

Mark Lynton, their Launcelot Gobbo, a small blond man, bouncy and full of energy, was sitting between Murray Fleet, the production's Bassanio, and Rachel Cohen who was now talking to Asher Grey: they would be the lovers, Lorenzo and Jessica, well cast, Douglas felt as he watched them.

It was nearly half past two now and he could see no sign of Kapstein or . . . the door opened and a breathless Carol Evans came into the hall brushing rain from a white trench coat with a hood which she had pulled up over her head. For a moment her appearance took him by surprise, then he realized that she was, of course, playing Nerissa, Portia's maid. Last night, Douglas had thought his feelings for the girl were dead, or at least anaesthetized, but now, in the afternoon light, the sight of her, rain glistening on her coat, the nervous smile as she looked around, brought back the unsubtle memories of their time together. He caught her eyes and smiled, hoping to convey at least something, he did not know quite what, maybe warmth, but she gave him only a brief smirk.

Asher Grey quickly excused himself from Rachel, leaping to Carol's aid, helping her off with her coat.

'We're two adrift,' said Ronnie quietly. 'Kapstein and Escott; and it's half past.'

'Give them a couple of minutes, then we'll have to start without them.' Douglas turned to Frank Ewes. 'If Mr Kapstein or Mr Escott aren't here when I begin, make some notes and fill them in after rehearsal, would you?'

Frank nodded, glum inside at the thought of having to brief Kapstein.

They waited for a couple of minutes. Nobody else arrived.

At last Douglas rose. 'We're not all here but I've got a lot to get through this afternoon so we'll have to start without our Shylock and our Old Gobbo,' he announced before launching quickly into his introductory remarks.

He had been talking for seven or eight minutes, and the company had settled, listening quietly to his views: about the stink of romantic decadence, greed and racial despisal, the caskets and orgies, the rigging of the trial and how they must work towards a unified production which, while not losing the comic aspects, must hit the audience with the evil of corruption.

He spoke briefly about Leggat's music for the play and was just going to switch on the cassette tape when the door burst open to reveal Ronald Escott and Maurice Kapstein. Douglas stopped speaking and stood in silence while the rest of the company shuffled and turned towards the commotion.

Escott looked all right, but it was obvious to even the most unpractised eye, that Maurice Kapstein was either unwell or more than a little drunk: his breathing was heavy and irregular and he stood, a swaying hulk, hanging on to the door as Escott, with a mumbled apology, slipped into the nearest available seat.

Kapstein straightened up, still holding on to the door, and took one shuffling, almost furtive, step forward; he raised his head to disclose features flushed a deep reddish blue and eyes wet and uncoordinated. 'My apologies, Mr Silver,' with a great sweep of his arm the grotesque figure lurched forward. 'And my apologies to all of you, a Shylock shouldn't be tardy. What news on the Rialto, eh?' Feet wide apart, Maurice Kapstein swayed again, began fumbling in his pockets and looked down to catch Liz Column's eye. He shook his head sadly, 'And special apologies to you, dear lady.'

There was a small explosion of laughter from the centre seats.

'Are you ready to join us, Mr Kapstein?' Douglas forced the civility in spite of himself; there was an intense anger building up within him and he knew that he could not restrain it for ever.

'I am ready and contrite. I apologize for keeping you good people waiting, I was engaged in matters spiritual. Now, you all wish to hear my Shylock, yes?'

'I have been talking about our approach to *The Merchant of Venice*,' said Douglas coldly, 'and I was about to play five short pieces of music which have been written for this production. I think the music underlines the approach we have to make. If you would sit down we can, perhaps, proceed.'

'Indeed. Music to soothe the savage . . . whatever it is. . . .' Kapstein tottered forward, lurching into an empty aisle

288

seat where he remained, slumped and still.

Douglas continued with the last of his remarks before switching on the cassette tape for the introductory piece.

The piano came out sharp and clear, three long discordant notes followed by an almost Rachmaninovian theme, not unlike the eighteenth variation on the Paganini theme, but off beat and key so that, while one was aware of the potential lyricism, the whole had an abrasive and hurtful quality. In spite of his irritation with Kapstein, and the rise of temper still throbbing in him, Douglas smiled at the skill with which Leggat had interpreted the director's needs. He caught Carol Evans looking at him and saw her return the smile; but it was simply that of two professionals appreciating the artistry of a third.

'Bloody awful row, Douglas Silver. Music? The food of love? Must be joking, 's not music; 's shunting of steam engines.' Maurice Kapstein had pulled himself into an upright position.

It was enough. Douglas snapped off the recording and Kapstein breathed aloud, 'Thank God for that.'

The remainder of the company were still. 'Do you require a doctor, Mr Kapstein?' Douglas asked in a precise, clear voice.

'Doctor? Why should I require a doctor? I have no need of doctors here. All doctors . . . charlatans.'

'You may well require one. Maurice, I warned you in private before you joined the company. As far as I'm concerned there can only be one warning. The board of trustees has put a lot of money into this season of plays. We have started the first rehearsal of *The Merchant of Venice* and you, our Shylock, are drunk and practically incapable. I told you before that I would not stand for any temperaments or difficult behaviour: and that applies to everyone, we haven't got time to play around at this.'

'Douglas. . . .' An unsteady conciliatory tone.

'You're drunk, Maurice, at the first rehearsal. It's irresponsible, unprofessional and I can't risk it happening again. You're fired.'

Douglas could hardly believe that he had said it; he heard a gasp from one of the girls and saw that someone behind Kapstein had half risen and then changed his mind, sitting down again. Ronnie muttered something about being careful.

Kapstein's mouth dropped open and he emitted a kind of shocked snarl. 'Fired, Douglas Silver? Who am I to be dismissed by a chit of a boy? I have a contract: can't fire me.'

'I just have, Maurice.' Douglas's mind reached back to the wording of the Standard Esher Contracts under which all members of the company were signed. 'Section L. Paragraph five, I think. Conduct on the part of an Artist inside or outside the theatre which is likely to bring the company into disrepute. It goes on to be most explicit about insobriety and stipulates that a person in your position has the right to call in a doctor to examine you at your own expense.'

'I'm a leading member of this company. . . . You're mad. . . . You can't do this . . . You . . . You . . .' Kapstein cast around him for the insult. His eye fell on Lonnie Barnes and then Carol. '. . . You. You nigger lover.'

Barnes rose, but Douglas motioned him back.

'I think that's enough, Morrie, get out.'

'Fuck you, Silver. I've never had such treatment; it should happen to a star actor? An actor of quality. . . . A household word. . . .' He lunged to his feet, now wild eyed in drunken fury.

Ronnie left Douglas's side and crossed the floor quickly.

'Don't come near me, you lackey. I am going to sue Silver and this whole shit-reeking festival.' Kapstein lurched towards the aisle, turning and staggering, reeling in his disbelief.

'Come on, Morrie.' Ronnie had reached him, but the actor refused to be helped.

'Away from me, you lynx . . . you jackal. . . . All of you, all lynxes and jackals. . . . Not one actor helps me. . . . Not even you, Escott. . . .' pointing an unsteady accusing finger. 'You sit there like sheep while this child . . . this boy . . . this apology for a director . . . abuses me in public. . . . Me. . . .

Maurice Kapstein. . . . He'll pay .. . My God he'll pay. . . .
You'll all. . . . Fired? Silver couldn't fire a cap pistol . . .
Silver . . . Yo-ho-ho and a bloody bottle of rum. . . .'

There was a little laughter starting to spread now at the
incredible whipped up drama as Kapstein bumped into the
edge of the door and made his unsteady theatrical exit still
chanting a flow of wrath and revenge.

Ronnie Gregor turned at the door, lifted his hands in the
age old stage Jewish act of supplication and followed the
burbling and furious man from the rehearsal hall.

Douglas, whose face had been white with rage, leaned
heavily on the table, arms straight. He looked around the
room as though seeking help, and, quite spontaneously,
someone began to applaud; the clapping grew and built until
the director had to quieten them with calming hand movements. When they had settled again he came round to the
front of the table, leaning against it, his buttocks firm on the
wooden edge, arms folded.

'I am quite within my rights to dismiss Mr Kapstein,' he
began, 'though, naturally, it is very much against the company's interests at this time. I must apologize for pushing an
impossible situation that far. In some ways it was inexcusable
of me.'

Cries of 'Nonsense.'

'However, Morrie's behaviour was also unforgivable, and
we can all perhaps learn from it. None of us can afford to be
undisciplined particularly during working hours. When we
have achieved something, then we can relax. In the meantime, working hours means morning, noon and night. I'll go
and do my best to salvage what I can; and I would be grateful
to you all if this incident was not spoken about outside the
immediate company.'

There was a general murmur of assent.

'Good,' Douglas nodded. 'We can probably still get some
work done this afternoon, so I suggest we listen to the rest of
Mr Leggat's music and then at least plot out and walk
through the first two scenes of act one: we don't need
Shylock until scene three.'

He half turned away and then thought better of it. 'For the benefit of those who were not at the *Othello* rehearsal this morning, I'd better make clear what I mean by plotting out the scenes. Some of you may think that it's an old-fashioned and rather rigid method: the director telling his actors exactly where they must move. Now be quite plain about this, I can move you around in the way which I think is most acceptable to the production, but the final result must rest with you. I don't expect you to always agree with me, and I don't want to be doing all the work. How you finally deal with a scene must come from you as actors and actresses. You know your own limits, so be quite free to speak out, and, most important of all, to develop the characters the way you feel best.'

Within half an hour they were well into plotting the first important scenes, getting under the skin of the *Merchant*'s world of argosies and gold in old Venice. The matter of Maurice Kapstein was, for the time being, forgotten.

Jennifer arrived back from lunching with Joe Thomas around three o'clock. She went straight to the apartment and worked alone on Desdemona until a little before five. The rain had stopped again and she felt in need of some fresh air. Coming out of the front door of Shireston House she met David Wills heading for his appointment with Douglas. The executive director smiled broadly and greeted her excitedly. 'Jennifer, I'm so glad I've bumped into you like this.'

Jennifer smiled her hello and let him continue.

'Has Douglas mentioned the poetry recitals yet?' David asked.

She knew Douglas had said something but could not quite bring the facts to mind. 'Yes, he has,' she said, not going into detail.

'I know we're not doing them until the summer, but I rather wanted to get started on the programmes as soon as possible.'

She remembered now that Douglas had said it would keep David happy if he had a hand in some form of creative project. 'Anything I can do to help?'

'I had thought of a small meeting to discuss things.'

'How small?'

'I wanted to ask you and Rachel, the boy who's playing Romeo. . . .'

'Asher . . .?'

'Yes, him and Carol Evans; and possibly Edward Crispin and Conrad.'

Jennifer nodded. 'Why don't I hold a little tea party for them, at the week-end, say Sunday.'

David was like a small boy in his enthusiasm. 'Could you? Could you really? That would be splendid.'

'Leave it to me then. I'll have them all at our place, about four.'

'You don't think Douglas'll mind?'

'I shouldn't think so for a minute. It'll probably be a good excuse for him to get out.'

David went on his way, happy with the chance meeting.

Douglas broke the rehearsal at four, going straight over to his office where Ronnie Gregor was waiting to give him the news that Kapstein had staggered across to the house, shouting abuse and calling a great deal of attention to himself, but had almost collapsed in the hall. Ronnie had got him upstairs to his flat, seen that the man was comfortably laid out, loosened his collar and tie, and left him in a snoring stupor. 'He must've drunk a gallon,' he commented.

'About a bottle and a half of gin,' said Art Drays who had come over with Douglas. 'I asked Ronald Escott. He went over for a quick beer and thought he'd better stay with him. Kapstein was there soon after the meeting finished this morning.'

'Where?' asked Douglas.

The Sheep, where else?'

Douglas sat down at his desk, picked up his telephone and put a call through to Kapstein's agent. The agent came on the line a couple of minutes later and there followed a protracted conversation: Douglas carefully breaking the news and then calmly explaining the whole situation, promising that he would not take any further steps if Kapstein apologized and agreed to at least a partial ban on drinking during working time. The agent in turn agreed to help by being unsympathetic with Morrie and pointing out the actor's best course of action but could not promise more.

'Douglas,' he said towards the end of their discussion, 'I'll do what I can, but you know what Morrie's like, mercurial sometimes. You can never tell, though, this might just shock him into behaving himself; it's enough I've got a big actor to deal with, I have to be his wet nurse as well; you've no idea what trouble he's caused with the television people in the past. . . .' And on, with Douglas sitting, the earpiece held away from him and his head nodding in agreement.

David Wills was kept waiting for fifteen minutes, and, just before Ronnie and Art left, Douglas told Art that he would speak with Asher Grey that evening about understudying Conrad Catellier. 'I'm still not sold on it, Art, but let me talk to him and see how he feels before we take it any further.'

David was eventually shown in and Douglas began a lengthy monologue on the advertising campaign, the block buster publicity they were mounting in the national press and on hoardings, the amount of personal publicity that would be given in features and articles, and the special links that had already been forged with tourist organizations, British Rail, hotels and schools. He went through all the figures he had already given to Adrian and told David about the need to sell the season and every seat in the place. 'You've seen our booking form?'

'The one Adrian's sent out, yes?'

'Have you any idea how many of those are going to come floating back at us after the campaign gets underway and the box office opens on the first of February?'

'I should imagine we'll be drenched with them,' David replied happily.

'Do you think the box office will be able to cope? After all, the box office is your pigeon.'

There was a moment's silence, the seeds of doubt slowly germinating in David's mind. 'Graham Harper isn't the most dashing character in the world, but he seems a decent enough fellow; capable enough.'

'Almost the same words I used to Adrian, David. But do you realize that for the last nine years or so this festival's been operating well below par. I can't give you the exact figures now, but I've seen them. I think the fullest house this theatre's seen in the past few years has been only half capacity, so I've got a sneaking suspicion that our gallant friends in the box office don't really know what's going to hit them.'

'I've talked to Harper, of course.'

'David, so have I. I wasn't fully conscious of the danger until lunchtime today. I want you to get in there and sort out the box office, sort Harper out if you have to; if you still think he's capable after you've had a session with him, let him stay. If not, get rid of him and bring in somebody else, fast. In any case they're going to need extra help; for the first few weeks they're going to be wading through those booking forms: with luck it'll be like a mail order firm the day they offer a ninety-nine per cent discount.'

David agreed to move in on the box office operation, but Douglas was left with the impression that his executive director's heart was not in the task. As he was leaving, David tried, a little abruptly, to turn the conversation on to the poetry recitals; Douglas understood the man's needs; basically he was a director and, while he was competent enough in an administrative job, the arrival of the company – the very physical presence of actors – had disturbed David; he wanted to be there on stage, working, not routing around the box office personnel. Douglas had consistently reminded himself, since David's appointment, that the man needed watching and pushing; just as consistently he had failed to watch or push him.

Feeling genuinely tired. Douglas signed the letters which Deborah had ready for him, dictated a dozen or so more on to tape, and left the office.

Jennifer, who knew how he planned to spend his evenings during the first couple of weeks, had a meal ready for him back at the apartment and their conversation turned naturally to the Kapstein drama. Jennifer was appalled, though not surprised, when her husband related the events during the afternoon rehearsal.

'He was terribly drunk by the time we got to The Sheep,' she told her husband. 'Very insulting to Joe.'

'For one of the chosen he's got a nasty streak of racial prejudice in him. How did lunch go?'

'Joe was sweet really, not as I expected him. You've got a frightened man on your hands, Doug.'

They talked for a while about the difficulties which Joe Thomas was undoubtedly going to meet.

'Don't be fooled by the sweet manner,' Douglas eventually told her. 'Thomas was quiet and malleable after the Heathrow business. He was nice and frightened today with you, but once he gets really confident, which he will, that guy can be seven different kinds of bastards.'

Before Douglas left, Jennifer mentioned her brief meeting with David Wills, and the tea party she was going to arrange for Sunday.

'Who does he want?' asked Douglas.

She reeled off the list and looked questioningly at the frowning face.

'I just hope to heaven he doesn't upset anybody.'

'Such as?'

'You're the director's wife, Jen. You're throwing a tea party for certain members of the company; those who are left out won't all get the message that it's a professional meeting. Temperaments, you know.'

'Christ, it's worse than living on a housing estate.'

'Much worse, love. We're both in the hot seat with our knickers down, exposed to the world. Jealousy, pride, the idea that there is a particular "in" crowd. It can be damaging.'

Jen shrugged. 'I shall use what tact I have left. Don't worry about it too much, love. Go and talk to your lovely Asher Grey while I try and muster the poetry readers.'

Later that night in bed, close to Douglas, Jennifer's mind turned, uninvited, to the physical presence of Joe Thomas: a picture of him leaning across the table towards her, jumbled with the vivid imaginings culled from newspaper stories; the women with whom he had been associated; his reputation; the natural energy which buzzed around him like some invisible force field.

The glow in her mind spread to her body, and, even though she tried to shake it, her sensuality was awakened like some burning irritation. The need was so great that she reached out for Douglas, deep in sleep, unresponsive and oblivious to her demanding hand and body thrust hard against him.

In the end she moved away from him and quietly went through the lonely ritual of self satisfaction. She was no stranger to it; the long separation from Douglas, when she was filming *Hidalgo*, had brought many lonely nights when the mind could take in nothing but the ache and need for that male pervasion to which she was now regularly accustomed: the movements, passions and experiments, the simple and straightforward joys which the pair of them shared. Removed and far away from Douglas her body had gone through regular patterns of withdrawal which could only be quelled by her own quick moving hand.

Tonight, though, it was different. When she had been parted from Douglas her mind had always been filled, at such moments, with thoughts of him, erotically poised or driving into her. Now, like a young virgin on heat in the first summer of full knowledge, it was Joe Thomas who was fabricated into her boiling thoughts: fantasies of him stripped and entering, a different way, new words and actions. The flush of guilt came at the moment of climax, after which she lay very still listening to Douglas's gentle breathing, ashamed at her own thoughts; yet, somehow, pleased with the new sensation.

Before they left the office for rehearsals on the following morning, Douglas took Art Drays to one side.

'I talked with Asher last night,' he told him. 'The boy's overjoyed, naturally, and swears to me that it's not overtaxing him to take on the *Richard* understudy.'

'Well, he's used to hard work in rep,' the productions manager replied.

'I went fairly deeply and he does seem to have got Lorenzo and Cassio under his belt. But we'll see how he works out during the next couple of weeks' rehearsals. He's spent a lot of time on Romeo as well, and I've told him that he needn't begin doing anything about understudying Catellier until we're well advanced with *Richard*.'

Art nodded. 'The same as all the other major understudies.'

'Yes, so you might as well put his name up and tell Conrad.'

'Fine. Then we're completely covered, except for poor old Morrie.'

'And it is poor old Morrie,' interjected Ronnie Gregor. 'I went up to make sure the old bugger was all right this morning and he's like the proverbial bear with a sore head. Told me to do the usual and stop bothering him. He was still breathing threats and fire against you, Douglas.'

Douglas chuckled. 'We'll hear from him when he's good and ready. In the meantime, if he doesn't submerge and come to suitable conclusions by this afternoon's rehearsals. . . .'

'Don't tell me. You're going to put in Joe Thomas so that we can have a black Shylock,' Art laughed loudly.

Douglas shook his head vigorously. 'Sammy Davis we'll need for that.' His face composed itself. 'No, I'm going to put more weight on Edward Crispin. If the worst really came to the worst he wouldn't have the drawing power of Kapstein but he'd do a good job. Let's see.'

Maurice Kapstein had spent a terrible night. After falling into his stupor during the afternoon, he half woke, with a parched throat, at around ten in the evening. He stumbled through to the kitchen and drained two glasses of water; befuddled, both from the heavy drinking of Sunday night and the memorable lunchtime at The Sheep, he fell into sleep again, not waking properly until just before five in the morning.

This time he felt really ill: his mouth sore and dry, a pain piercing behind the eyes and a stomach which seemed to be filled with vile poison. He vomited, gasping and sweating, in the bathroom, then stumbled, with aching limbs, into the kitchen to make coffee.

As he sat there, cold, wrapped in gloom and physical discomfort, Morrie dredged back into his mind which only seemed to be throwing up fragments of the past forty-eight hours. Then the big memory returned: the rehearsal and Douglas Silver telling him that he was fired. Agitation and fury began to take over from the feeling of self-pity: an anger which at first knew no logic, only the remorseless desire to hit back at the humiliation which he had undoubtedly suffered in the rehearsal hall.

With complete disregard for the time, Kapstein slammed about the small flat, adding physical dimensions to the manner in which he was rummaging around his mind for a solution. Instinct and past experience told him that it was useless to call his agent in the small hours. In the end he came to the only conclusion left: he would have to sit it out, sipping coffee, reviving body and mind, until the hands of the clock moved to a more advantageous hour. Time dragged, but as it ticked away, Maurice Kapstein's brain became more active, his anger more of a controlled fury laced with cunning. In the back of his thoughts there lurked the start of a plan to overthrow Douglas Silver. By eight he had convinced himself that his departure from the company would do irreparable harm to everybody but himself, and when Ronnie Gregor knocked at the door, around eight-fifteen, Kapstein exploded in a satisfying burst of invective.

Knowing that his agent usually reached his office about ten, Kapstein called him on the dot of the hour and was irritated to find him not yet there. He called his home number to discover that the man had left and was already on his way to the office.

Two frantic telephone calls, and half an hour later, a frustrated Kapstein got his agent on the line. Within fifteen minutes the actor's anger was as uncontrolled as before, his plans demolished and the future uncertain.

Morrie had started by recounting to his agent a quiet, and grossly inaccurate account of what had happened. He was amazed when the man spelled out the real facts to him: that Douglas Silver had every right to sack him; that the director had witnesses to prove, not only that Kapstein was drunk and incapable at the first rehearsal, but also that he had been abusive in the extreme; that the renewal of his television contract was in the balance anyway and if the news got out that Maurice Kapstein had been sacked from Shireston because of alcoholic instability it might well be the end; apart from this, the actor was made very aware that if he did not prove himself with a superlative Shylock at Shireston this season, the only person to suffer would be himself; his only reasonable course of action, therefore, was to throw himself on Douglas Silver's mercy and try for reinstatement, at the same time praying that the story did not find its way into the press.

The flare of resentment, following the conversation, finally resolved itself in another bout of self-pity. To start with, Kapstein wanted to go out and get drunk again, but there was enough of the old solid professional left in him to see that, however badly he felt, his agent was right. Once he had reached this point in thought, it was an easy step to centre his mind on the problem of how best to get off the hook without losing too much face.

At the age of forty-nine, Graham Harper knew deep within himself that he was a weak, ineffective failure. He knew it in little things like the fact that, while he tried to dress smartly the frayed cuffs and uneven shoes heels always showed; also the internal things, the knowledge that he had to take extra care because of natural smells and that too many cigarettes over the years had now not only robbed him of enjoying his food but also caused him to have bad breath. A Shireston man by birth, Harper had drifted for years before finally settling down in the job of box office manager at the festival, work which did not bring him much pleasure but at least provided a steady income, a small status and little in the way of really difficult mental or physical labour.

He tried not to think too deeply about his own private life: of the marriage which had pitifully been allowed to drift on for years, dead and hopeless, or the long affair which was now almost as dead as the marriage, shrivelled to one night a week at the pub with Elsie Williams and usually one night in her bed, puffing and sweating away at the oldest routine in history, the rite they had both gradually ceased to appreciate, neither of them being blessed with the agility, wit or imagination to make it stimulating or inventive.

Last night had been one of those evenings and, as always on the morning after, Harper allowed himself a little extra time, rarely arriving at the office much before eleven (a shade sooner during the season), never expecting Elsie to come in before time – that luxury had begun years ago as a pinch of mild pampering. Now it seemed to be the only mutual arrangement which worked for them.

As he drove up the hill from the town, Graham Harper thought about the previous evening, his stomach turning over in mild disgust: at himself, Elsie, the whole business. All the obligatory trimmings that were once part of the sweet icing that they had blindly thought of as love: silly small things like the black lace panties she always wore because eight years or so ago the sight of her in black underwear was a rousing assistance (now turning to fat Elsie always removed her girdle and pulled on tight nylon pants for one of their evenings so that, half stripped, her appearance had become almost bizarre); the fruitless, adolescent, and inept gropings and fumblings and kissings, wet and unarousing until the final undressing and, somehow, going through the necessary procedures of the act until one or the other of them reached some kind of mild satisfaction. Perhaps, thought Harper, it was his fault; plenty of his contemporaries seemed to thoroughly enjoy sex: unless they were lying, putting up a front; now it simply left him with a sense of embarrassment.

He turned in through the main gate, parked the car, locked

301

it and slowly walked in through the main door of the house, along the corridors, active and live with noise, to his office.

Harper sensed the presence of someone within as he turned the knob. David Wills, the executive director, sat at Harper's desk, idly thumbing through the files.

'Ah,' said David looking up and then, most pointedly, at his watch. 'I was beginning to think that you had been taken ill, Mr Harper.'

Despite his ineffectuality as a man, Harper had long since been able to cover most of his faults and ineptitudes. He smiled and spoke with some diffidence. 'There's not much on at the moment, Mr Wills. I usually allow myself one late morning a week.'

'Not much on?' queried David. 'Have you seen one of these yet?' He tossed the new booking form across the desk; it was a two-page colour leaflet, the cover embossed with the Shireston bell symbol and the names of the leading members of the company, together with the four plays; on its flip side there were details of the plays and how to book seats; the second leaf was detachable, with spaces for making any possible permutation of booking for any, or all, of the plays, leaving room for preferable and alternative dates.

Harper picked up the leaflet without really looking at it, then dropped it back on to the desk. 'Yes,' he said without noticeable enthusiasm. 'Yes, I've seen it. They tried something similar a couple of years ago. Didn't make much difference.'

'Really?' For the first time since Douglas had approached him about the box office, David Wills felt a violent reaction. 'Really, Mr Harper? How close to the ground do you keep your ear?'

The man shrugged. 'Well, you know. . . .'

'Have you read your newspapers, studied the memos that have been circulated here? Have you used your eyes? Do you know what we've got going here?'

'It's all been tried before, Mr Wills. All the gimmicks. People don't really go for gimmicks anymore. Some big names and a lick of paint here and there isn't going to

302

provoke a miracle. This place has been tottering on quietly for years and –'

'And it's going to stop tottering. On the first of February over one million of these booking leaflets will have been circulated. There will be a massive publicity campaign which I promise you is going to bring in orders for seats the like of which you have never seen. Our aim is a total sell-out for the entire season, and from what I can see here you're not even equipped to flog half a dozen of the cheaper seats in one day. Now, I'm answerable directly to Mr Silver, and I give you two days, two days to get off your arse and study exactly what we're trying to do and work out what the end result should be. I shall expect you to digest all that and come up with specifications of your requirements. You're going to need extra temporary staff to deal with the mail bookings and, I suspect, extra staff on the box office counter itself. You'd better go through those files and memos, Harper, and get yourself into the picture. I know exactly what you need, and if you don't come up with an approximation of what I have already worked out you'll be looking for a new job. Now get to it, and be in my office at nine o'clock on Thursday morning to face your moment of truth.' He rose and marched from the box office manager's office before the astonished Harper could utter a word of protest.

The morning's Othello rehearsal had gone well and Douglas was pleased with the progress; he was even more pleased when, just after noon, Frank took a call from Deborah in the office to say that Maurice Kapstein was anxious to see him. He sent a message back saying that he would see Kapstein at twelve-fifteen, knowing well enough that he would not get to his office until, at the earliest twelve-forty.

Kapstein had a half-hour wait, but Douglas was happy to note that the actor wore a distinctly shamefaced expression as he entered. The director knew that he had done the right thing: a show of strength at the start was worth a great deal.

'Well, Morrie?' he began.

'Douglas,' Kapstein spread his hands wide. 'What can I

say?'

'Sorry might be good for starters.' There was no doubt about Kapstein's dramatic ability, thought Douglas, it was all there: the look of contrition blended with dignity to hint that really he was a man who had been caught in one weak never-before-or-again moment. The voice was also modulated to just the right pitch, signifying that he was utterly penitent.

'Douglas, I'm sorry. Truly I am; an old man's fear at being among so much talent and faced with such a task. You must know that this sort of strain leads one to folly.'

'You crafty old devil,' chuckled Douglas. 'You don't deserve it but the matter won't be mentioned again if you make me three promises.'

'Anything, my boy, anything: you know me.'

'You apologize to *The Merchant* cast before this afternoon's rehearsal, and you stay off the heavy drinking for the rest of the season. You also make private apologies to Carol Evans and Lonnie Barnes for your unmitigated racial perversity; and, while you are at it, Joe Thomas and my wife.'

Kapstein looked stunned. The well-built characterization fell away for a second and his face flushed with anger.

'Well?' asked Douglas.

Slowly Kapstein nodded, speaking in a low husky voice. 'For you, Douglas Silver, for you I'll do it.'

Each morning at nine the whole company met in the rehearsal hall to exercise. The initial intention of these morning sessions was to relax the individual members of the company and therefore encourage concentration. Douglas had spent a good deal of time working with Frank and Robin, who always assisted at the morning periods, and together they had planned a course which would steadily progress through the season: beginning with simple yoga-based exercises, slow deep breathing, rhythmic movement, bending, stretching and pulling, the adoption of poses, such as the lotus; using these as a basis they would go on to the more dynamic exercises where actors and actresses would work in pairs and explore situations, sometimes in opposition to one another; there would also be physical examination exercises, again in pairs, one exploring the other's face with eyes closed, first with the hands, then nose, then ears; they might even move on to examination of the whole body.

The greater majority of the company took to the morning sessions with enthusiasm, dressed for work, in Levis and sweaters, they managed to accomplish in a few days a spirit which, under more conventional conditions, would have taken weeks.

Some of the more senior people, however, were naturally slower at becoming absorbed into one human team. Kapstein grumbled each morning, but Douglas could cope with him, turning the belligerence into a subject for humour; he was much more concerned by people like Felicity Durrant who, from talking to the younger actors, had built up horrendous anxieties in her mind about the later phases of the exercise class; or Conrad Catellier, who, like all actors, exercised regularly, yet had, over the years, built up his own scheme of training which he preferred to do alone; it was difficult to make him see that in order to develop the unified style, upon which Douglas had set his heart, they had to spend part of each day together as a company. To give him credit, Catellier turned up to most of the sessions and was obviously making an effort to overcome his natural suspicion of such things.

During the first week they accomplished much in rehearsals; Maurice Kapstein, now more malleable, began to throw himself into *The Merchant* rehearsals and, even after a few days it was easy to see that his Shylock could possibly become a major interpretation; Ronald Escott, as Old Gobbo, and Mark Lynton, as young Launcelot Gobbo, began to work out some very funny business, while Carol Evans, in the comparatively small role of Nerissa, started to give Liz Column's Portia a frame in which to shine during the early Belmont scenes.

As for *Othello*, that too began to lift, with Joe Thomas moving gently through his scenes. As yet there was no attempt at vocal attack, but Douglas impressed upon him that he had to start slowly, using Shakespeare's words to create the picture of a strong sane man, allowing the audience to glimpse the first fissures of breakdown as the scenes with Iago and Desdemona developed. It went without saying that Crispin's Iago was going to be a masterpiece of intrigue and neurosis, but Jennifer Frost seemed to be holding back her Desdemona, as if to keep in step with Joe Thomas.

By mid-week they had completed a full walk through and begun to work on some of the essential moves, such as the running *faena* between Iago and Roderigo and Iago and Othello. This had become such a popular idea that Douglas had to restrain Crispin, Laurence Pern (playing Roderigo) and Thomas from taking the actions too far.

Two of the big technical problems came right at the end of the play with Desdemona's murder and Othello's suicide, both of which Douglas wanted to be dramatically spectacular. While he had devised a brilliant and theatrical end for Othello, the director had shelved the actual moves for Desdemona's suffocation.

'I suppose it would be in keeping if you made a goring rush at her in the last moments, like a bull,' mused Douglas. 'But I don't know if that would be in tune with the text.'

'You ever see a movie about Othello?' asked Thomas. 'An old movie with Ronald Colman playing an actor obsessed with Desdemona's murder.'

'Yes, *A Double Life*; where he works out the business of smothering Desdemona with a kiss.'

'That's it: then he has to go and try it out on some babe to see if it works.' Joe grinned at Jennifer giving her the come on, 'Want to try it, kid?'

'I don't think we dare pinch that one,' Douglas maintained a serious demeanour. 'Let's just walk it through a couple of times; try the goring bull, Joe, it might work at that.'

Douglas had kept quiet about the final moves of the scene, working only with Tony Holt and, on the Sunday, with Joe Thomas, as the whole thing was devised to use Joe's acrobatic experience. Holt's setting for Desdemona's bedchamber had a great bed as the focal point; upstage from this an iron spiral staircase led to a short gallery, some twelve feet above the stage floor. The gallery had no protective railing, only a series of ornamental metal rails which curved up and outwards, then up again, secured under the gallery floor. Fitted to two of these rails were metal rings to which were attached strong small nylon rope nooses, the rails and gallery floor being specially strengthened.

The idea was that Joe would slowly mount the spiral staircase at the beginning of his penultimate speech, *Soft you; a word or two before you go*. He would move along the gallery and, towards the end of the speech, get his feet firmly into the rope nooses. At the last lines of the speech he would stab himself, releasing blood capsules sewn into his shirt.

At this point, Othello traditionally falls across Desdemona's body speaking the final lines: *I kiss'd thee ere I kill'd thee: no way but this*. Douglas's idea was that Joe should drop his dagger and, as he spoke the final line, stretch out his arms to Desdemona lying on the bed downstage, then pitch forward off the gallery. The nooses would take hold and the last seconds of the play would leave Othello hanging head downwards, blood dripping from his belly.

It was an ideal situation for Joe Thomas, and Douglas had purposely remained close about it so that they could gauge the shock effect in rehearsal. It called for accurate timing, nerve, and Thomas's confidence in the strength of the apparatus; the director had, therefore, insisted that Tony, with Archie Swimmer and his boys, should set up the staircase and gallery in the rehearsal hall on the Monday evening so that Joe could spend some time in private rehearsing the moves. He had, in fact, started working on Monday evening as soon as the prop was in position, going down late with Ronnie Gregor, first testing his weight on the ropes, dropping off the structure and holding the nooses in his hands, then fitting them to his feet and rolling gently from the gallery, building up to the complete routine.

Joe spent a great deal of his spare time down in the hall, and by Thursday, when they were starting to walk through the scene, he could just about manage the fall properly.

When the moment came, the shock effect on the *Othello* cast was indeed spectacular, at least two of the girls screamed, and a handful of the men came running across the room to his aid.

'Get away,' shouted Thomas, grinning, making himself look even more bizarre as he swung, head down, from the ropes. 'There's going to be a lot of blood dripping from here. I told you them mixed marriages wouldn't work, Douglas Silver.'

On the Friday of rehearsals, the *Shireston Gazette* carried both the story of the company's assembly at Shireston House, and the Joe Thomas drugs case, which had occurred too late for the previous week's issue.

TOP NAMES ARRIVE FOR NEW LOOK FESTIVAL screeched the front page banner headline; underneath was the cutting sub-heading: TV PERSONALITY PREDICTS ORGIES AT SHIRESTON HOUSE.

Between them, Janet Ridley and her editor, Hedley Moir, had performed a neat piece of journalistic butchery. The lead story was careful to stick to facts, yet it was written with a painful bias. Miss Ridley had taken numerous quotes out of context and made reference to things like *long haired actors mingled with short haired actresses, and towards the end of the evening there was wild dancing, led by famous coloured entertainer Joe Thomas, who recently appeared on a drugs charge before Uxbridge magistrates. (See story on this page.)*

As if this was not enough, Moir himself had written an editorial which seemed to be aimed directly at Douglas. He wrote of *Douglas Silver's first season at Shireston, which seems to be one of gross experiment if the, so far released, casting is anything to go by. The board of trustees has, it is rumoured, poured no less than two million pounds into this venture and the people of Shireston have a right to question what this investment will bring to their quiet town. So far, our residents have been able to remain aloof from the more unpleasant trends of contemporary life. The care with which our council watchdog committees have gone about their business has kept such things as the more undesir-*

able and sordid films from the two cinema screens in our midst.

The Shireston Festival, though admittedly never such a draw as places like Stratford, has usually maintained a standard of basically traditional Shakespearian productions. When they have been out of key, this newspaper, together with other local bodies, has always been quick to protest. Let us hope that the new leadership at the Shireston Festival is aware of local feeling and the power of local action.

Douglas was rightly furious. 'What do they think we are? Freaks?' he snarled at Adrian who, while taken aback at the attack, regarded it with a certain amount of humour.

'It's just small town, out-dated, scared-of-change newspaper talk, Douglas. Take no notice. You made your point when they had a go before.'

But Douglas could not sit back and do nothing about the newspaper. Before rehearsals that morning he made his views quite plain to the entire company. He wanted no idle chatter to reporters, either local or national, and restressed the question of private behaviour when newspapermen were around.

During the afternoon, BBC's *Nationwide* news programme called Adrian, asking if Douglas would appear, that evening, and perhaps comment on the views expressed in the *Gazette*. Adrian carefully probed and discovered that they planned to have Hedley Moir on the show as well, so, playing it safe, he advised them that Douglas Silver was too tied up with rehearsals to do any television for a week or so.

In the event, he breathed a sigh of relief that evening after the programme finished without a mention of the *Gazette*, Douglas, or the Shireston Festival.

The time would come for Douglas to hit back and it would be better if an interview could be taped when the director felt more cool about local opinion. Perhaps if one of the first two productions was a shattering success Adrian would move heaven and earth to put Douglas up with Moir on *Nationwide*, or any other television programme. Part of his job at this point was to protect his director and the company from press and television as well as to expose them.

309

On Sunday afternoon, Douglas announced that he would be having a lengthy meeting with Tony Holt about the *Richard* designs. It was the truth, though he had brought the whole thing forward to enable Jen to take full use of the apartment for David's tea party. He did not particularly want to be around and possibly cramp David's style; after all, it was the one chance his executive director would have to actually direct anything during this season.

By four-thirty, the main living-room was peopled with the small group which David had brought together. Rachel Cohen and David helped Jennifer with the chore of handing out tea, sandwiches and cakes to the seven actors and actresses who were present and in good spirits, having got through the first week of rehearsals with a sense of some small achievement; in the relaxed, friendly and easy atmosphere even Conrad Catellier seemed to unwind.

After tea, David talked informally about the four readings that had been proposed, displaying, Jennifer thought, a complete lack of preparation. Equally spaced through the summer, the readings were to be given in the theatre on Sunday evenings in late July and early August.

'I thought we should have three distinct themes, drawing material from all ages and sources,' David told them. 'And we might finish with some large and rather splendid performance.'

'Something like *The Hollow Crown*?' asked Conrad. The Royal Shakespeare's *The Hollow Crown*, a brilliant anthology on the *Fall and Foibles of the Kings and Queens of England*, had been a great international success in the sixties and would have well suited Conrad.

David said that he felt *The Hollow Crown* had probably run its course by now but certainly he was thinking of something along those lines.

'And what about the first three themes?' asked Jennifer during the pause which followed.

David hesitated. 'A bit obvious I'm afraid, and rather hackneyed, but they're the stuff of poetry.'

'Well?' Edward Crispin smiled.

'Life. Death. Love.'

'And we start off the Life programme with the Seven Ages of Man speech, I suppose,' said Conrad sounding weary.

'Read by you, Conrad, it can never miss,' David countered seriously.

Another pause, eventually filled by Rachel piping, 'Give me Love every time. If you want suggestions I know my favourite love poem.' Her voice dropped as if she suddenly felt foolish. 'Well it isn't a love poem really. It's about fear and bitterness really.'

David Wills nodded to her, indicating that they would like to hear it.

'It's a translation from Horace,' she began –

'The young men come less often – isn't it so? –
to rap at midnight on your fastened windows;
Much less often. How do you sleep these days?

There was a time when your door gave with proficiency
On easy hinges; now it seems apter at being shut.
I do not think you hear many lovers moaning

"Lydia, how can you sleep?"
"Lydia, the night is so long!"
"Oh, Lydia, I'm dying for you!"

No. The time is coming when you will moan
And cry to scornful men from an alley corner
In the dark of the moon when the wind's in a passion

With lust that would drive a mare wild
Raging in your ulcerous old viscera.
You'll be alone and burning then

To think how happy boys take their delight
In fresh and tender buds, the blush of myrtle,
Consigning dry leaves to the winter sea.'

311

Silence, because Rachel was no fool with the spoken word, before Edward Crispin said, 'That's certainly not a love poem, Rachel, but it's great erotica.'

'The bulk of all love poetry is basically erotica.' David pompously rose both to the bait and Rachel's defence.

Crispin grinned. 'Well, if we're having that, I insist on the Alex Comfort piece called *After Shakespeare*.'

'Can't say I know it.' From Conrad.

Crispin began:

'At the end of the third act, poetry gutters down –
at eleven, the best pentameters drag their feet;
Tragedy sinks to some old pother
and we find ourselves holding hands in the street,
suddenly tired of eloquence overdone
and wondering why we went, who have each other
in flesh and no pretence. We'll let the great dead stay dead.
That first act of our own
is still the best act left. Let's go to bed.'

Everyone laughed.

'A great put down for actors,' chuckled Asher Grey.

Catellier looked up grumpily. 'Should be retitled *After A Modern Movie*.'

More laughter, during which Jennifer caught Carol Evans sitting erect, eyes staring as though lost in thought. She did not know what prompted her, but even as she asked the question there was a jangle of premonition. 'Carol, have you got a favourite poem? A favourite love poem?'

Carol knew the Alex Comfort poem and, while it had no special significance for her, she found it took her mind leaping back to the weeks with Douglas, when life seemed to have taken up a new and warm spring. Funny, she could have sworn that all the feelings of then were dead. It is a strange unstable state, this emotion, she thought; Douglas in a thousand different poses slotting into her mind: you think it has all gone, and you know it has because the circumstances are against it, yet the memories are never destroyed completely and the fire is still there, just under the surface, a dormant volcano. Douglas, only a few short months ago, for one night in Malta; then the captured evenings and nights in London; and now sitting here, in his apartment, with his wife, a woman to be envied. She suddenly realized that Jennifer was speaking to her, asking her if she had a favourite poem; a favourite love poem.

'I'm not sure,' Carol stammered. 'I have a lot I like. I don't know if there's a favourite.' Douglas in her head, strong; in her bed; across the restaurant table; on the other side of the room; poetry listened together, learned at each other's knees and thighs. 'There is one, but I expect you'd all think it far too sentimental. I once heard someone describe it as untreated emotional sewage.'

'Go on love, there's nothing wrong with sentiment, as long as you know how to control it.' Asher Grey was talking to her from the far side of the room.

'Okay,' she heard herself say, and, as she spoke the first lines, the presence of Douglas Silver felt very close to her:

'There is no loving without losing.
You lose yourself to become part of somebody else,
That's just how it is.'

Jennifer Frost shivered; before the black girl spoke she had known, a fraction of a second before the first line jolted the whole tunnel that she called her life, just as it had been first knocked when Douglas told her there had been someone else. She knew that it was foolish, to be uncalm about something like this; the world had changed, people on the whole did not get confused about affairs that were done and finished; but neither Douglas nor she were people; for her life had begun with Douglas and she never doubted him until –

'I didn't expect to remain the same, but,
Oh I guess I didn't know what to expect.
It's different every time though.'

The black girl was speaking it the way Douglas had spoken it the one and only time Jennifer had heard it before. There was total recall of the moment, and what she had said – and what they had said:

('I didn't know you went for McKuen.'
'Neither did I.'
'You learned that with her, didn't you?'
'Yes, but that's all over now.'
'I'm glad.')
A new language invented,
A new system stumbled on,
Different from the old one.' Carol continued.

The bodies in Jennifer's brain; the imagined intertwinings, they had all been wrong, just as the faceless woman's face had been untinted; it had really been black; this girl, this woman, this black woman and Douglas.

'A new way of engaging,
And disengaging ourselves from each other.
God knows how often I've looked into your eyes,
But do you know, when I'm gone from you,
No matter how I try to remember,
Sometimes I forget the colour.'

Jennifer wondered if Douglas had forgotten the colour, and then saw the terrible irony; she was playing Desdemona while this black bitch played . . . she quelled the sense of melodrama rising within her.

'Yes, I've lost some things:
Friends you didn't approve of.
I get clobbered in the game of touch now,
Even with someone my own age.'

Douglas said it was all over. How could he say that and then allow her to come down to Shireston? Was Jennifer completely wrong? Was it a stupid, emotional jump to an overwrought conclusion? Yet it was all there in Carol's voice, as though the poem was some treacly love theme, played by a string-heavy orchestra, a backing to the romance which had been, or still was, must be –

'Sometimes I feel out of practice with people too;
'Well, what would I do,
If you went off,
Or something happened?'

Asher Grey looking intent because Carol was undoubtedly

314

speaking with a great deal of feeling; Edward Crispin, eyebrow tilted, his thoughts transparent; David Wills concentrated more on the way in which Carol was performing than on the words; Rachel Cohen visibly moved; the familiar things in the room: the armchairs, the leather buttoned settee, the Arnot collage; they were all familiar to Douglas, part of their world; Jennifer frowned at the knowledge that there was, or had been, another world, presumably filled with other objects, like this one bloody poem.

'I'm not equipped any more for relating to someone else;
I've lost,
Oh, only Jesus knows what I've lost,
As there is no loving without losing something.
What I have gained from being with you,
I guess I couldn't get anywhere else,
And I'll be damned if I'll ever try.'

A pause and then general gabble, argument, suggestion. Jennifer had the sensation of falling, dropping through a well of words, the rushing of wind in her ears coupled with fragments of poems quoted by those around her, out of context as if they were all vying for some prize. Above it that damned slush pounding in her head:

What I have gained from being with you,
I guess I couldn't get anywhere else,
And I'll be damned if I'll ever try.

How did that measure up against the words she could hear Edward Crispin speaking now:

'The big words from those ages when as yet
happening was visible are not for us,
Who talks of victory? To endure is all.'

The fragments and the sense of falling apart among the words.

Asher Grey was quoting:

'It seemed that out of battle I escaped
Down some profound dull tunnel long since scooped
Through granites which titanic wars had groined.
Yet also there encumbered sleepers groaned,'

Britten's music circling her consciousness; *The War*

Requiem, the words bringing back some performance, a performance listened to with Douglas: Wilfred Owen's words and Britten's music, a matched pair.

Now somebody else:

'Well, that Sunday Albert was home, they had a hot gammon,
And they asked me into dinner, to get the beauty of it hot —
HURRY UP PLEASE IT'S TIME
HURRY UP PLEASE IT'S TIME

Good night Bill, Good night Lou. Good night May. Good
night. Ta ta. Good night. Good night.

Good night, ladies, good night, sweet ladies, good night,
good night.'

It was Conrad.

'I've always wanted to do *The Waste Land.*'

'Couldn't we finish with an Eliot programme?'

'It's a possibility. What does everybody else think . . .?'

David, thought Jennifer, was like an uncertain school prefect, always wanting the advice of others in order to get a majority verdict. She was back in control of herself; back among her own things in her own room, looking across at the girl, black skin, jet hair, a sensual awareness with every movement; the long thighs rising under the mauve skirt; the rather terrible pain which came at the thought that Douglas had crept in between those thighs. It's the same the whole world over, and ever was, thought Jennifer. Two could play at coupling: if Juliet, then also Desdemona. She shackled the new private knowledge to her, leaving it to simmer in the mind. She had the whole summer to screw the hurt away.

316

CHAPTER TEN

The legend appeared towards the end of January: on railway stations, hoardings, in hotel foyers, among the clamour of a hundred other advertisements in the London Underground; in Birmingham, Manchester, Leeds and Liverpool. Black print against grey parchment, simulated by some astute paper manufacturer. The cracked bell symbol and the words SEE SHAKESPEARE AT SHIRESTON. Underneath, the names: Joe Thomas, Jennifer Frost, Conrad Catellier, Maurice Kapstein, and the others; then the names of the plays and their opening dates. It was a beautiful teaser poster, duplicated in the heavy Sunday newspapers and selected local weeklies.

In tourist agencies and on the smooth counters of luxury hotels the small brochures appeared, and in newspapers and magazines up and down the country the small references began to add up, the first printed reactions to Adrian's opening campaign:

Shireston has always struck one as being a most beautiful setting for an evening of Shakespeare. Unhappily in recent years the journey has been hardly worth the end product, for, on a summer evening, the cool lawns, the flower walks and trees, the great house and the theatre itself have not been enough to make up for mediocre direction, poor design and lackadaisical acting.

However, this year sees a change at Shireston with the advent of twenty-six-year-old Douglas Silver as overall director. Mr Silver is already possibly the brightest, shining star in the field of classical theatre direction, and they tell me that the changes he has already made at Shireston should be enough to have playgoers fighting for tickets.

Apart from a season which includes new productions of

Othello, The Merchant of Venice, Richard III *and* Romeo and Juliet, *Mr Silver has peopled his company with names we usually associate with our cinema screens. . . . There is also a new and luxurious restaurant, an exhibition and already you can book inclusive trips for an evening at Shireston through British Rail and four major coach tour operators. . . .*

David Wills's outburst at Graham Harper seemed to have had an effect. Before the beginning of February the box office manager had recruited, and put to work, four girls to deal exclusively with the mail order bookings, and another two to do duty at the box office counter itself.

However, the first week of February did not produce the tidal wave of expected bookings, and it was a wary and nervous David Wills who approached Douglas Silver at the end of the week.

'Before you read the figures, I'd better tell you that they aren't what we expected,' he said, handing the stapled folio copies across the director's desk.

Douglas's brow creased deeply; he had been gratefully aware of the changes which David had wrought in the box office, and Adrian's promotion campaign was there for all to see, therefore he had not allowed himself even to think of a drop in ticket sales. By rights at least the first three months should be a total sell-out, but a quick glance at the balance sheets showed that they were not even going to run in front of half-full houses on the present showing, and this included tickets already sold on a sale-or-return basis to agencies and tour operators (under their existing agreement, the agencies and tour organizations had to telephone the box office daily, between four and six, stating exactly what seats they wished to return, so that those tickets would be available for sale at the box office).

Douglas glanced through the sheets and dropped them on to his desk. 'What's Harper got to say? He's crowing, I suppose?'

'Not exactly crowing, because, according to him, we've done better than he expected.'

Douglas gave a sour grimace, lifting his eyebrows. 'Well,

it's only for the first three months, and it's all happened in one week which is not entirely bad. There's really nothing we can do except aim for the highest possible standard and spin our prayer wheels.'

'I'll go on pushing the box office people: keep on their tails if that'll help.'

'Everything helps.' Douglas felt uneasy, a blip in the back of his mind constantly telling him that, in the end, it was the public, and the public alone, who would decide the fate of Shireston. He could knock his guts out; come to that so could every member of the company, and Adrian, David, Tony Holt and all, yet it was still possible that the whole organization would collapse, melt slowly away like a gorgeous ice-cream cake in a warm room, if there was nobody there to appreciate it, eat it up and pay the piper.

The worry was not decreased by the sudden, and unexpected appearance, during the following week-end, of Sir Basil Daley making what he called, 'One of my quick trips of inspection'.

Sir Basil seemed pleased enough with what Douglas told him over lunch in the theatre restaurant; he asked no awkward questions and only mentioned the business of ticket sales just before he was due to take his leave.

Douglas said that they were certainly up on any previous year, at this point, but that it would take a few weeks more before any real breakthrough could be certain.

'You've got plenty of time,' smiled Sir Basil. 'I don't expect spectacular turnover until you've got a little way into the season itself, certainly not in the first week of bookings; and you don't have to make any up-to-date report, with the correct figures, until the twenty-first of May when we hold the trustees' meeting.'

Douglas had, naturally, known that there was a trustees' meeting somewhere near the start of the season, and another near the end, but he had not noted that the first one came as early as the twenty-first of May. The added knowledge served to compound his growing nag of worry.

It may well have been this state of mind which brought

about the director's change of mood regarding plans for *Richard III*. During the meeting he had held with Tony Holt, on the afternoon of the tea party to discuss David Wills's poetry readings, they had come to some definite decisions. *Richard* was the one production which seemed to be causing early worry. Right at the start, Douglas had thrown out Tony's original designs: the standing set of wooden scaffolding which Douglas referred to as 'Early Sean Kenny'. At that time he asked Tony to provide him with some very definite designs: up to Richard of Gloucester's coronation the setting had to reek of decadent opulence; after Richard was in power there had to be the overwhelming suggestion of fascism.

Tony carried out the brief brilliantly, both in the settings and costumes: the set still remained a basic standing structure, but was executed in different textures and with some ingenious moving and sliding panels which could be used to completely alter the depth and shape. This Douglas had accepted without any reservations, delighted at his designer's skill. But now, in the second week of February, he suddenly called a meeting with Tony, Art and Ronnie Gregor.

'Tony, you're going to be furious with me,' Douglas began, oozing his legendary charm.

Tony Holt's face was splashed with a wan smile. 'You're throwing out the *Richard* designs and set,' he said.

'Not the costume designs, they stay, but I want the setting changed.'

Art Drays gave out an almost silent 'Jesus'.

'I suppose they've started putting it together?' queried Douglas.

'Yes.' Tony nodded, tight lipped.

'I'm sorry but it's not right for what we have to do, mate.'

Ronnie looked up. 'Does this mean you've re-thought the whole thing?'

'No, I haven't re-thought it. I just want some changes in the working conditions. This is between the four of us at this point, but I feel that the weight of the production has got to fall on the actors, particularly on Conrad. If you've talked to him you must know that he's pretty lethargic about playing Richard, My guess is that if he could get out of the deal tomorrow he'd run a mile. He knows what I want of him, but he's not quite certain if he can do it. We have to make him, and we do it by giving him very little to lean upon, which means that the staging has got to be sparse.'

'You're going to let the company find their own way: feel their own way.' A bald statement from Art.

'To some extent.'

'You said we didn't have time for that.' Ronnie appeared quite agitated.

'I know what I said.' Douglas turned to Tony Holt. 'I want dirty white walls and one movable second level. I also want a central screen which we can drop in for projections.'

'You're going to find some old newsreel pictures of the battle of Bosworth and run them behind the action,' said Ronnie acidly.

Douglas grinned. 'No, the Grand National – "My kingdom for a horse". Yes, something like that. I want a screen there in case we can devise some projected stuff. Not pictures. Mobile abstracts probably. We've got the equipment, haven't we?'

'Oh yes, we've got everything,' said the stage director. 'You name it we've got it. The only problem is time. Douglas, if you let Conrad and that bunch off their leads they'll probably come up with some incredible stuff. It'll be *Richard III* à la Peter Brook *Dream*: plate spinning, acrobats, the lot. We've already got Joe Thomas swinging from his heels in a death sequence that'll give everyone heart attacks. Can you afford to –'

'I'd like to try,' Douglas cut in. 'Is it really too late, Tony?'

Tony Holt shrugged. 'You're the gaffer, if you want it all changed. . . .'

'I'd be grateful.'

'Then I'll have some rough drawings for you to see by tomorrow evening.'

Later, when Ronnie and Art were alone, the stage director expressed his feelings with a violence not natural to him.

'That production's going to be the biggest let-down of the season. It's going to bomb something horrible. Stupid bastard.'

'Why?'

'Why? You know Douglas, you've worked with him enough. Okay, so Conrad's heart may not be in it, but the real trouble is that Douglas has got the shakes. When he's full of enthusiasm there's never a dull moment; never a change of heart. When he's not quite with it, he niggles, finds fault, and he gets unsettled. I know the signs, Art. With this *Richard* he's going to give them an open space and a few props, the odd guide line and then he's going to let them get on with it. It'll be no more his production than fly. He's got *Othello* and *The Merchant* buttoned up and he'll use all his reserve energy for *Romeo*; *Richard*'s a bore for him: mark me.'

Since the Sunday afternoon in Jennifer Frost's apartment, Carol Evans had felt uneasy, listless: an anxious, butterfly lethargy. It was a sensation which she had not often experienced in her life; not just the uneasiness which is simple to analyse; the awareness that you are black or different, or because there is no work, or that you are worried about your family. This went deeper somehow, she could not quite put her finger on it, but she was aware that some of the sensation came from the fact of finding that her emotions for Douglas had not after all completely disappeared; also, part of it was purely sensual, she knew that bit only too well; the merely physical thing, the withdrawal symptoms, similar for men and women alike when a love affair ends abruptly. There had been no man since Douglas and, naturally, there were times when her body ached, not just for the easy pleasure of being ploughed by a male, but for the tenderness, the sense of adoration which had come with Douglas, and for which she now longed. She managed to sublimate much in working, but, with only her Nerissa in rehearsal, time hung a little heavy. She mixed well, yet found herself almost studiously avoiding the group of black actors and actresses who, while outwardly seeming to integrate themselves, still really remained a private breakaway clique. Carol had no wish to get drawn into the kind of black militancy which she felt was bound to emerge from their behaviour; she had been lucky, rarely feeling any of the hostility which friends found a constant burden that had to be made heavier by taking up bitter attitudes.

With the start of *Romeo and Juliet* rehearsals still three weeks away, Carol began to spend much of her spare time doing private work on Juliet, but the strange spring-like ache and lethargy still had to be fought.

One Wednesday in early February she spent the whole afternoon going through the text without a script, lying on the floor of her apartment. By five o'clock she was boggled with the poetry and blatantly randy with the emotions expressed: the walls seemed to press in on her like some medieval engine of torture and her nerves tingled.

Outside it was chilly but dry, so, throwing her heavy coat over the jeans and turtleneck she wore, Carol left her rooms for a brisk walk in the grounds, having learned long ago that the, now ridiculed, old maxims of English public schools, concerning brisk walks and cold showers, were at least a help when a woman was very much on her own.

There was still plenty of light, so she took the path behind the theatre restaurant, intending to cut through the orchard and paddock which lay behind the theatre, emerging in the drive, up by the main gates: in all a good three-quarters of a mile walk. The air felt clean and she had the sensation of being a shade intoxicated, floating through the evening shadows. As she entered the orchard, Carol was startled to see a dark, track-suited figure jogging through the trees towards her. As he drew near she recognized Joe Thomas who pulled up beside her with a broad grin on his face, though she could not help feeling that there was mockery around the eyes.

'Hi there. Forsooth 'tis Juliet,' brayed the singer.

'Hi.' Carol slowed to a halt. 'What're you doing? Ruining your health or out to frighten the local kids?'

'I'm learnin' to run so's I'll be in good shape after the first night of *Othello*. What's your excuse for being out alone in the woods? You lookin' for a man to leap on?'

'I don't need to look,' she laughed uneasily.

'No?' He raised his eyebrows and thickened his accent. 'I seen yo lookin' at that white boy.'

'Which white boy?' It came out with an unexpected rush, as though she had not realized that he was fooling around.

'Hey, that really caught you. Which white boy? Well I'll tell you, Carol Evans, there's a choice of two from where I sit looking at you. There's our esteemed director, Mr Douglas Silver, or there's your Romeo, Mr Asher Grey.'

For a moment she could not get her mind straight. Joe Thomas had to be either a lucky guesser or a very observant man and the first question was, did he simply watch her, or was it everybody? She wondered about that: he had detected something in Douglas Silver's manner, or her manner; that was clever, but the Asher Grey thing was even more astute because nobody but herself could know about it. Nowadays when she allowed her fantasies to roam uncontrolled, Douglas was usually the first to claim her attention; not unnaturally, for she knew his body and mind in detail, but Asher Grey was something else, occasionally the shadowy centre-piece to her sensual dreams. In rare moments she let herself admit to fancying him as a man, yet in reality she was far too aware, as indeed were the whole company, of Julia Philips's watchful omnipresence.

'Well?' Thomas was waiting for her answer.

She mentally pulled herself together, gave what might just pass for a coy smile and said, 'Don't tell me you never have little ding-a-dings with white woman.'

'All the time, baby, we're all brothers and sisters under the skin; but I also have room for my own kind. I'm not an Uncle Tom.'

'Implying that I am.' Unconsciously she had fallen into step beside him, walking back towards the theatre restaurant.

'You don't spend much time with your soul brothers and sisters.'

'They're all around me, Joe. They have been all my life.

I'm British, man, and my father and mother are British. They were born here and I was born here, we're not even immigrants.'

'Maybe, but you're black.'

'Tough. Doug Silver and Miss Frost are white: they've got colour too.'

'Don't give me any of that shit.'

She stopped walking, half-turning, looking up at him. 'Joe Thomas, you are just about the most irritating, self-opinionated, bumptious, stupid, overbearing, vain, crass, man I've ever met.'

'I'm kinda pretty too. Flattery don't rate any with me, kid.'

'You and your kind make me sick. Sure, the black people have got to fight. But, over here, what have they got to fight? A minority of bigots, and they *are* a minority, Joe. This country may be screwed up about a lot of things, but on the whole its racial problem stands more chance of getting sorted out than lots of other places.'

Joe held up his hand, the 'V' sign, palm outward. 'Right on. Peace, baby, peace. I don't have to argue with you: but may I give you just one small piece of advice? The situation may well be marginally better here, but we're getting it all together on a world-wide scale: it has to be settled that way so's we don't get the ultimate conflict; the one where it isn't West versus East, or Communism versus Capitalism, it's the one where black versus all other colours and that would be the clincher, the big one.'

'Joe. . . .'

'No, let's not argue. You're too pretty. Come on, I'll show you something that's really too much.'

'What?' She began to move with him again.

'Just a small thing I'm going to do in *Othello*. In the rehearsal hall. I got to finish my workout. Come on, I'm not all that bad.' Already Joe Thomas was feeling the challenge which, secretly, always took pride of place over politics, everything. At the reception for the company he had set his mind on making Carol Evans, if only for a one-time ball. This

325

might just be it.

The deserted rehearsal hall seemed oddly still, unused; Carol felt nervous and out of place, like a child trespassing on school property after hours.

'You often come here in the evening?' she whispered to Joe.

'Most every night,' he whispered back, grinning and picking up her mood. 'I got permission from the superintendent.'

Carol realized what she had been doing and laughed aloud. 'What've you brought me here for?'

'To have my evil way with you, kid. Just stand there and watch while I do my party trick.' He started towards the spiral staircase and gallery.

'That's part of the *Othello* set isn't it?'

'This is part of Desdemona's boudoir, would you believe?' He began to climb. 'After I knock off Desdemona I kinda climb up here, like they do in those stupid movies where the killer is cornered and makes for the roof.'

'Yes?'

Joe Thomas was on the narrow gallery floor now.

'Be careful, Joe,' Carol called up to him. 'There isn't much room up there. It could be dangerous.'

'That's why I come up here every night. Doug wants me to get used to the height. I jump around a little to get confidence.' He smiled to himself as he approached the nooses which he had personally reset on the previous evening!

'It's going to seem even higher on the stage. Do watch out for yourself, it reminds me of the old Astaire movie, where he gets smashed and has to do the dance on the high arch.'

'Yea,' Joe had his feet in the nooses now, 'and the idiot falls right off while they're singing and dancing.' He held his arms out wide and broke into *Heat Wave* –

'They're having a heat wave,
A tropical heat wave,
It isn't surprising,
The temperature's rising,
She certainly can,

Can-Can.
Then the dumb hoofer falls off.'
For a second he pretended to lose his balance.
'Look out, Joe.'
Partial recovery, then, with a gurgle of fear and a shout, Joe Thomas pitched forward and did his death drop.

Carol screamed, not able to move, hand to mouth, eyes wide as she watched the tall body fall forward. She hardly took in what was happening as the nooses caught hold and he jerked to a hanging stop. It was at that moment that she started towards him and became aware of his laugh echoing around the empty hall.

'What? What?'

'Don't fuss, baby, it's okay. Man, it works a treat. Douglas wants to frighten the ass off the audience.' He twisted his body, hands going for the short lengths of nylon rope straining above the nooses. He had worked out recovery from the hanging position and could now get himself back on the gallery ledge in less than ten seconds.

Carol was breathing heavily. 'Joe, my God you scared me. What is it? Why?'

'My death scene for *Othello*.' As he unfastened and reset the nooses he explained it to her.

'Well, Douglas Silver has no need to worry, it's very frightening,' Carol told him, a hand on her palpitating heart.

'Come on up to my place, you deserve a drink after having the pants frightened off you like that.'

'That's the only way they're coming off,' she warned with a smile.

After that she did not give it a second thought, listening contentedly as Joe Thomas talked about *Othello* and Douglas's production.

On entering his apartment, her first reaction was that he had not really put any personality stamp on it. There was an expensive stereo complex in the long bookcase which took up one wall of the main room, a stack of discs, but few books, and they, she could not help noticing, were mainly works on Shakespeare, voice control, acting. He slipped a disc on to

327

the turntable, inevitably one of his own, a soft, string and skins backed smoochy album which she also possessed: *Joe Thomas in the Quiet Hours*.

Carol slowly became conscious of the man's dedication. The short conversation on the way back from the rehearsal hall had been totally concerned with the problems of acting and staging Shakespeare; true, they were mainly his problems, but this was very professional talk, a long way from their small clash on racialism. Here, in this very ordinary room, she found herself warming to him. He was quiet, considerate, the things one did not associate with the person whom she had always admired as a performer yet hated in the image he projected off stage.

An hour passed without Carol realizing, relaxed as she was in the leather armchair with Joe Thomas sitting crosslegged in the middle of the room.

At a break in the conversation she stretched out her arms and looked at her watch. 'Is that the time? I must go.'

'Ah, not yet, baby. The night's young.'

Reality flooded back; the relaxation had gone too far, she even felt the first tweaks of sensual desire, and she knew her own body, the threshold of her resistance like the lines of her palms: too well, too graphically.

She gave Thomas a smile. 'You don't want me around. You'll be having company before long.'

'What's that supposed to mean?'

'Sylvia.' She pursed her lips.

'She drops in from time to time, sure. Not tonight, though, Sylvia's gone out with Lonnie.'

There was a long silence between them. Then she spoke. 'I don't lay it around, Joe.'

He looked puzzled. 'Who said you did? I only wanted to talk. . . . You think I asked you back for that? Oh no, lady. I like a good time, sure, I play the chicks. But I have respect.'

He seemed too open, too honest, that Carol was taken aback, so much that she even felt ashamed at having thought so basically.

Joe Thomas became moody, as though the insult that she

had inflicted on him had really hurt. Maybe it did, she reflected. She knew how you could so easily build a false picture of yourself deep within your own mind, and be badly injured when someone smashed it up with the truth. But her reaction was exactly that which Joe had prayed for, she began to over-compensate, going to sit on the floor, touching his arm, flattering.

Within half an hour she knew where it was going to end and she did not care anymore: to bother would have been laughably dramatic. Carol Evans wanted a man and this man was notorious. In a strange way they were both scalp hunting as they began the first stray movements towards sexual pleasure. The opening gambits progressed towards the kiss; delicate, gentle, but with a sharp sense of novelty; the new experience, the old game with a new body, the new words whispered with different intonations, the old moves with different expression. Both of them reacted slowly, though there soon came a point when the bodily urgency was more demanding: Joe's tongue fencing and her own probing as though mapping out his mouth, examining his response.

His cool had to be admired; at the moment of no return he disengaged from her, rolled away, and then rose to take off his clothes, a chore which he effected in a careful series of movements, as though it was some ritual always observed. Carol only wore ankle socks and pants under her jeans and turtleneck and she was out of them before Joe Thomas was completely undressed. She looked up at him with genuine admiration. 'Hey, you look great stripped.'

He grinned, slipping out of his pants and revealing himself. 'Spread it around, kid, spread it around.'

He was on the floor beside her and the dance began in earnest; the soft hand movements, skin and skin and hair and hair, the blood pumping, a shiver of pleasure as they touched one another, the increasing mount to the moment when Carol was breathing, 'Come in . . . Come into me, Joe. . . .' The pleasurable pain of assault, of being opened and filled in a different way, by a body unknown.

She came very quickly the first time, though later it was a

long and mutually enjoyable ride.

Dressed again and ready to leave with the throb of him still on her and his smell clinging to her own sweat, she put up her face to be kissed.

'Am I still an Uncle Tom?'

He put his head on one side. 'In some ways. You screw like a good black girl though, I will not deny. We must try it again some time.'

The remark, made so casually, stung, making her feel like a whore. It was several days before she could get the feeling out of her system. When she finally did, Carol was able to rationalize her emotions, seeing with clarity what had happened. She had behaved in the same way many times before, but always on her own terms. Because Joe Thomas had insinuated himself upon her, because she had enjoyed the experience and because, in the end, he had insulted her, she now felt guilt, and that was merely over-dramatized self-indulgence.

In the rehearsal she found herself watching Douglas Silver again with the same feelings of need, almost an anguish that had in no way been assuaged by Joe Thomas's body. It was like being on some roundabout and the uneasiness soon returned.

By this time Douglas Silver really only noticed Carol as an actress, just as he saw his wife in the same way, so tied up was he with the plays and their direction.

He was working with instinctive brilliance now, knowing exactly where the productions lagged or needed shoring up, resetting (like the arrival at Cyprus in *Othello*, which he changed twice before getting the grouping and movement exactly right).

Joe Thomas responded well to the encouragement which Douglas gave him, and nobody could deny that, what had been a rocky start, was now developing into a performance of outstanding promise. At the same time they were conscious, as all actors are, of the fact that, with the live arts, you cannot be certain of anything until the essential ingredient, an audience, was added: even then there was to be a spark, the leap and flash between actors and audience, to set the night alive. Douglas worked ceaselessly towards creating all the right conditions, his mind working with a dazzling speed and the energy pumping out as though he had some constant, unquenchable, source of vitality.

He was so involved, filled with the techniques of his company, crammed with clarified ideas, seeing the productions step by step and in sharp focus, that, on an evening at the end of February, he did not at first understand Jennifer's attitude when he returned to the apartment after a strenuous and rewarding *Merchant* rehearsal.

Jennifer had allowed her knowledge of Carol and Douglas to fester. On four occasions she went into *Merchant* rehearsals simply to observe Carol Evans and the girl's attitude towards Douglas. She saw what any woman in the same position would have seen: a girl constantly wrapped up in her director, hardly taking her eyes off him when he spoke, and, during the scenes when she was off, sitting, bunched up, usually on the stage floor, arms clasped round her knees, concentrating on Douglas as though he was the answer to all things in life.

Though she was deep inside Desdemona, and the *Othello* rehearsals were tiring, Jennifer had time to brood, her imagination snaking into swamps of mistrust, seeing new mental shapes and pictures, especially when Douglas was tied up, working, during the evenings. The jealous bud grew and flowered, seeped and wept until she could hold it no longer. In the moments of sanity and calm reason, she knew it would be wrong to bring the matter into the open again, not just wrong, but foolish and overemphatic.

They had moved *Othello* into the theatre, the refurbishing work having been completed, and Douglas was allowing members of the company, not in the *Othello* cast, so sit in at rehearsals (it had been one of the suggestions made during a company meeting). That morning, Joe and Jennifer had been through the difficult fourth scene in act three, with all the intricate business of the 'strawberry spotted' handkerchief, and Joe was, for some reason, not co-ordinating his moves as well as he should be. About eleven they broke for tea, Joe slinking away to sit alone in the Prompt Corner. Jennifer was concerned about him, and, after a couple of minutes with Douglas, she went over and sank down beside Thomas.

'You okay, Joe?'

'I'm not moving right.' Sullen.

'What's wrong?'

'Out there's what's wrong,' he inclined his head towards the auditorium. Jennifer followed his movement, there was a small group of company members sitting far back, almost out of sight, among them she picked out Carol Evans.

'What's wrong out there?' asked Jennifer, more interested now, knowing that the Evans girl was here to watch her husband at work.

'My little black sister.' He turned towards her speaking quietly. 'Jen, I'm a bastard, you know that, but I get bugged easily. Once with that Carol Evans, once only and she's following me around like Mary's lamb.'

'What are you talking about?'

'She's been sitting in at rehearsals for the last three days and it's starting to bug me. I don't like being followed around; girls like her give it one time and then expect a whole scene, the roses and organ music.'

'You had an affair with her?'

Joe Thomas laughed. 'No, Jen, baby, I had one night, not even a night. One evening we talked a lot and in the end she took her pants down. Now I find her sitting in at all my rehearsals; she's even around when I go to eat.'

It was nonsense of course, but Joe had been building up to one of his ego-inflated crises over the past few days.

'She's got a thing about you?' Jennifer asked.

'I don't know. I haven't talked with her since then. She's a nice kid, but I got other things to do. I work hard and play hard. Sure I had her, but that don't make her own me.'

In her mind, Jennifer seized the weapon and clung to it with joy. It did not matter that Joe Thomas's conclusions

332

were completely wrong, that Carol Evans was around at *Othello* rehearsals because that was where she could watch Douglas, not because of the big entertainer whom they were all licking into shape and who, beneath the easy exterior, was a complex mass of anxiety and worries.

So, that evening, after Douglas had guided Maurice Kapstein through three long sequences, she dragged it all into the open again.

It had become Douglas's custom to come in sometime between six and seven and pour drinks for them before they ate their evening meal. Tonight he went through the usual ritual, calling to Jennifer that he was home, tossing his notebooks and clip board on to his favourite chair, and crossing the room to slurp Bacardi into a pair of tumblers while Jennifer came in with the big coke bottle from the fridge.

It was not until they were both seated and Douglas had taken his first sip that Jennifer began.

'While I was away?' It was obviously the start of some interrogation, though Douglas, his mind on the problem of having put too much background business into the Trial scene, did not even catch the sentence as a question.

'Where?' he asked vaguely.

'While I was away making *Hidalgo*?'

'Jen, love, what's up? Are you asking or telling me something?'

'I'm doing both.'

'Well?' He put his drink on to the side table and gave up his concentration to her.

'While I was away doing *Hidalgo*, you had an affair.'

His brow crumpled, the familiar relief map of concern. 'Not again, Jen, please. It's all over. Things have settled back into place.'

'Have they? That's interesting, Douglas, because I'm not so certain. You had an affair with Carol Evans. And she's here. With the company.'

Douglas's initial reaction was of irritation: a large 'damn' in his head; no anxiety, that was reserved for the four productions, for his actors, for people like Joe Thomas, Kapstein, Catellier, Liz Column, Jen, Carol even.

'Forget it,' he said sharply.

'Forget it?' Almost a shout, bitterness bubbling up from the well of what had passed. 'You ask me to forget it. I come back and find that you've been having an involved, passionate, that's the word isn't it, passionate, attachment with somebody. You tell me that it's all over, and then I find out that the somebody's here, a member of the company, and you ask me to forget it: when she's still hanging round your neck?'

'She's not –'

'She's sitting in at the *Othello* rehearsals, and I've been in at the *Merchant*, she sits there like a moonstruck schoolgirl, Douglas: and you expect me to believe that it's over, it's over, it's over –?'

'Jennifer.' A bark, shutting her off like somebody pulling a switch. When he spoke again the usual calm had returned. 'Love, it *is* over. Yes, okay, it was Carol Evans and when we finished it I told her that she had to make a choice. She either had to come here and play Juliet, forgetting what had gone on between us, or not come at all. I was all set to have her replaced, but she came, and since she's been here there's been nothing but a correct professional relationship between us. That's the truth, Jen. Now can we drop it?'

'She's a whore.'

'Calling her names isn't going to help. I can understand you being upset, but there's too much at stake here. . . .'

'I'm not calling her names, I'm stating a fact. She's a whore. She's been at it with Joe Thomas.'

It rocked him: his deep pride, the vanity that is within all men; the indescribable and intolerable arrogance which makes a man jealous, even of that which is not now his.

'Does it really matter?' he said lamely. 'Does it make any difference? Another body, a need, a satisfaction, the quenching of fire. All good dramatic stuff. Ten years from now we could all laugh about it.'

'I've never been able to think that way, Douglas. Perhaps

it's my stolid middle-class upbringing. I love you and I'm married to you, and I know all the things that go on and that we're supposed to accept, but basically I've always believed in, and tried to live, for the two of us.'

'Well, believe it and live it now, Jen, because I've got my hands full of actors and designs and plotting, not to mention property, money and bookings and the general running of this place.'

'You expect me to be cool, nice and pleasant to your black whore.'

'Jennifer, let it lie. I start rehearsing *Richard* and *Romeo* next week. It's a miracle that we've kept to schedule so far. You've got enough to worry about with your work, have the sense to see that mine holds everything together, and put Carol out of your mind.'

It was an easy thing to say, and the juice of their quarrel worked in many ways. For Jennifer there was still anger and concern, she had no desire to lose Douglas in any sense, yet it was hard for her, resenting, as she did, the presence of the girl who had given so easily when she was not there.'

At the same time, Douglas was reawakened towards the fact of Carol: the lust creeping into the back of his mind when he least needed it; whether it was true about Carol and Joe Thomas was a side issue, its outward action was that his attitude towards Thomas now underwent a subtle change: he became more pushy, less sympathetic to the man's problems, his criticisms more astringent and his demands more pressing. In many ways it all assisted, for the more Douglas pushed, the greater the reaction from Thomas, adding finer points to his performance, exploiting Douglas's direction so that in performance the whole definition of character was being finely and dramatically revealed. Othello, the soldier statesman, lover; then the collapse into the true nature of the man, with jealousy gnawing at his entrails.

On their first full run through, all this, and more, was apparent, and, while Douglas had been initially thrown by Jennifer's assault and revelations, he now felt calmer about the production; happy also with Jennifer's own performance as Desdemona, a splendid mixture of joyous innocence and mistrusting fear, making a fitting contrast to this Othello's plunge into the emerald waters of unreason. Crispin's Iago was also a major contribution: sly, tricksy but with a stylish arrogance.

As for *The Merchant*, Douglas, not unnaturally, felt less tension when working on it, particularly as the production had begun to move with exciting precision: elegance off-set by the rat-race of business and the all-pervading atmosphere which the whole cast was bringing to bear, as though they were really planting the seeds of corruption. At the head of it all, Maurice Kapstein had started to produce a truly real tragi-comic character from Shakespeare's Shylock, even though he had taken to slipping in his old catch-phrase ('Don't trust anyone not even your own father, yet') on exits, or when he dried.

In the last week of February Douglas began to step up his schedule by bringing *Richard III* and *Romeo and Juliet* into rehearsal: the scheme of the week now running with *Richard* rehearsals on Monday, Wednesday and Friday mornings and *Othello* on those afternoons; *Romeo and Juliet* on Tuesday, Thursday and Saturday mornings and *The Merchant* in the afternoons. Conscious that this still did not give them enough rehearsal time, Douglas set Ronnie Gregor and Robin Alvin the task of bumping up a tighter timetable to come into use when they needed it most in a few weeks' time.

It was not until the Monday morning when they were about to start the *Richard* rehearsals that Douglas realized how much he had been dreading the play. True, he had given several hours to Conrad, during the past weeks, in order to carry on their discussion about the character of Richard, but now he had reached the starting gate, fear and depression dropped into the director's gut. To his surprise, Catellier was more enthusiastic than he had dared hope, making a great contribution from the first moment.

After the Monday morning company meeting, the *Richard* cast settled themselves and Douglas began talking, looking around himself to adjust to the particular group.

Conrad sat on the floor with Jennifer, who would make a brief appearance as Lady Anne; Crispin was there, not as his now familiar Iago, but as Richard's pawn, the Duke of Buckingham; Felicity Durrant, Liz Column and Rachel Cohen were grouped together (they would, respectively, be seen as the Duchess of York, Queen Margaret and Queen Elizabeth), while Douglas also took in the presence of men like Murray Fleet, now to play the Duke of Norfolk, Laurence Pern (Hastings) and Ronald Escott (The Bishop of Ely).

The director explained that he was not going to subject this particular cast to a rigorous block out of the scenes; with his production they would work as a group, the inspiration coming from all of them as they proceeded. He went on to describe the setting, with the help of Tony Holt and the small model which had been made. Lastly, he moved to the minor adjustments of text.

Apart from one or two small changes, like the addition of *Off with his head: so much for Buckingham*, the only major alteration was that which Olivier had made, both in the film version and in his *Richard* at the Old Vic in 1944: compounding the opening, *Now is the winter of our discontent*, with the passage from scene two in the third act of *Henry VI, Part III*, where, at the end, Richard of Gloucester proclaims:

I can . . . set the murderous Machiavel to school.
Can I do this, and cannot get a crown?
Tut! were it further off, I'll pluck it down.

Conrad, already perfect in word, had obviously spent his time at Shireston working hard and alone; now, in the opening moments of rehearsal, he held out to them almost the full dimensional character for which Douglas had asked: charm and bravura most apparent on the surface, a chilly ruthlessness in the heart. There was even the hint of homosexuality which Douglas, with some trepidation, had suggested at their first meeting.

As though spurred on by Catellier, the remainder of the cast followed his lead. What had, in the beginning been tense, now relaxed and they started to work together, bringing a corporate mind on to the production.

By lunchtime Douglas felt more at ease than he had done for several weeks.

Asher Grey had, literally, got Lorenzo and Cassio buttoned up. He had learned Romeo weeks ago, but only now did he have time to begin thinking about the flesh and blood with which to clothe the character. In many ways the solid block of work, which had consumed time since rehearsals began at Shireston, had been a domestic Godsend. Julia was also called upon to work hard, doing a serving maid to Portia (she even had a few lines, transposed from the serving man in act one, scene two), a series of changes in *Othello*: a lady-in-waiting to Desdemona and a citizen of Cyprus. She was also understudying Carol Evans's Nerissa and playing a lady-in-waiting in *Richard*; wisely, Douglas had seen to it that she was in no way concerned with *Romeo and Juliet*. So far, the tight timetable meant that, while they met in rehearsal, Asher and Julia only really came together in the evenings, often late, so some strain was taken off the young actor.

Asher thought deeply about Romeo, trying to see how he could bring some of his own experience to bear on the emotional dilemma of the young man. The key was, of course, the mad, hot, passion of love in its early stages, when everything is beautiful and all things rational are thrown away and life is lived wholly for the adored. That had nothing to do with his experience with Julia Philips: theirs was a relationship bound together solely by emotional blackmail and (he was the first to admit it) exceptional sexual pleasure: it was Julia's preoccupation with his body, and his with hers which made their state matter at all.

Julia's honest earthiness, and her knowledgeable approach to sex quickly stirred him, and while *Romeo and Juliet* certainly had to contain more than a little sexual stimulation, its quality had to be of a more pure and innocent nature, not quite puppy-like, but a blend of desire, need, romance: a bodily giving between both partners, all shrouded in floating joy which was turned easily to despair. There had, Asher considered, only once been a time like that for him and, even at his age, it seemed so long ago that he could not even grasp at the memory of feeling.

He must have been all of twenty-one years old, out of work, seeking a job during his looking round the agents' period (before Stanthorpe Repertory). She could not have been more than seventeen, in her first job, a secretary (which meant she was in the firm's typing pool) at some big city office, they sold furniture he suddenly recalled, and with that one fleck of knowledge a great deal more came rushing back to give him mental images: their meeting, passing the salt to her across the table of some tiny fried food restaurant; she being very impressed by the fact that he was an actor, even an out of work actor: her first question had been, 'Do you know Tom Courtenay?' The next evening he took her to a local movie. *A Clockwork Orange*, he seemed to remember, Kubrick was always a particular hero; there were afternoons, at week-ends, talk, talk, fun talking; laughter; holding hands and a lot of kisses; the sense of being oblivious to everything else but her, even being without work did not matter much. Then, in the middle of the joy, came the ecstatic agony of mind, the great decision which was no decision because they had both made up their minds, yet it had to be talked out; and the disaster of the first time. He had taken other girls before, but never a virgin, like Barbara, he now recalled her name and with it came the face, snub nosed, blonde hair which she had to wash a lot ('There's too much oil in my scalp.'), wide hazel eyes and striking white teeth: he could see the face screwed up in pain and hear her breathing the classic words, 'It hurts, God, it hurts. Go on. . . .'

He fumbled it, of course, but the next time was easier, and the next delirious. Then something happened; she had to leave London, something to do with her family in the Midlands. She wanted him to come and see her but he could not afford the fare; there were letters; waiting for the mail each day; passion in blue ink on pink paper and his semen caught in a tissue, the mind blown by thought of her absent body, the feel of her under her clothes, nipples like wild raspberries. Asher smiled to himself: the clash of phallic symbols.

Then what? Stanthorpe Rep? No, a change of pace and mood in her letters, that was the start of the decline; a trailing off into the wind; ragged trees at the end of autumn. Then nothing.

If he could only recapture those first days, their eloquence, madness, irresponsibility, the experience of being high on love. If he could do that, then his Romeo was made. Asher Grey tried to reach towards total recall.

At the first *Romeo and Juliet* rehearsal it was obvious in the minds of both Asher Grey and Carol Evans that, in spite of all their separate, previous or even present, emotional ties, their combination in this play put both of them at great personal risk. It was a thing apart, they knew that without saying anything. This was a thing removed from permanence and they felt the spider's web static flow between them, as it had at the company reception, and all nearby were aware of it. Douglas also saw and felt, and the professional in him warmed to it: he wanted this to be a dangerous production: as he explained to the company, he saw it mapped out in great dramatic colourful bursts, teetering on the brink of wide-screen romanticism, with youth in the foreground proclaiming the dangerous innocence of being young, together with that particular hot-headedness which clashed with the hard reality of the mature, already formed, world.

Within a couple of hours Douglas was fairly certain that he could get just what he wanted: the flash of steel contrasting with the rich colour of the moment, as age and tradition strove with wayward, thoughtless, beautiful and emotional young people.

'I knew you'd wear pink underwear.'

'David, you are a fool. You pervy old devil, thinking about my underwear. Well, I hope it brought you pleasure.'

'On. And off. Delicious. I love you, Rachel.'

Pause of five seconds as she props herself on one arm, moving a pillow with her other hand.

'Really love me? Or is it just . . . what does it say in the song? Just a passing fancy?' Depressed that he had brought it this far by saying it out aloud: she had played this scene before and knew that it ended badly. ('A little touch of Harry in the night.')

'I think it's real-type love. Is there any way of knowing?'

Another pause during which Rachel cannot look at him. 'No. No, I don't suppose there is. Have you had a lot of women? You're very good at it, David, very good.'

'You're pretty adroit yourself.'

'Well, I haven't done it in a long time. Have you?'

'Done it in a long time?'

'No, stupid, had a lot of women?'

'Not that many.'

'What's that supposed to mean? Twenty? Thirty?'

'More like a dozen.'

'Oh.'

'What about you as we're on the truth game?'

'Never had a woman in my life.'

'Idiot. Men?'

'Nine. But I know lots of girls who've had many more than that.'

'Who's the best ever?'

'Don't search for flattery. What're you . . . Oh David, again?'

'Come on, closer.'

'Oo. Oh. You're the best ever. Uhuh.'

'Open your legs. They're like the buds opening in May, your thighs.'

Noises.

'. . . *but, I do see you're mov'd;*
I am to pray you not to strain my speech
To grosser issues nor to larger reach
Than to suspicion.'

'*I will not.*'

'No, hold it. Joe, I thought we ironed that move out last week. You cross behind Edward, not in front.'

'Oh, sure, sorry, Douglas. Yea, you're right.'

341

'We changed it so that the cape movement –'

'The *pase de rodillas*.'

'Okay if you want to be technical, so that Edward's *pase de rodillas*, his move with the cape, would be more pronounced.'

'It's better than your pronunciation of *pase de rodillas*.'

'That's it. Okay, carry on.'

'Morning, Mr Swimmer. Usual?'

'Usual, Raquel, thanks.'

Four members of the company in the corner of the bar. Two strangers. Six regulars. Nodded towards and examined carefully at a distance. Laurence Pern and a boy called Mark (a walk-on), the girls looked identical, though he knew one by name, Eve Lester. Jeans, shirts, rubber soled shoes. They all looked dirty, but when you have to roll around on stages and floors all day you always look dirty. People expected actors to be all smart suits and carnations.

The pint on the counter, a tankard of sunshine; picked up and held to the light. The old joke, 'your horse is in perfect condition.'

'Thank you, Raquel.'

'Mr Swimmer.'

Cloud of white froth; your Raquel pulled a good pint; a smooth head, not too big but enough. Well-built girl; a year or two ago you'd have had that, Archie boy, like that big salesman from Shireston who came up most evenings in his Triumph to conquer and enjoy her plump thighs and swelling breasts which moved behind the glossy material of her blouse, all red swirling patterns. Ah, Archie, firm young breasts, a simple lascivious phrase that used to get the old saliva running; all fading away; you don't stand a chance now; time was, and it takes you back: the times you had with companies all anxious now to forget their ages (the ones that are still with us).

It was so simple then, flats and battens, a lighting plot operated by one man on the Prompt Side with his mind on other things: a couple of good scene painters, backdrops with no problems, a painted garden with a fountain up front and, maybe a bench on stage; no real problems; Shakespeare without the big modern techniques, not complex like today. Mind you, you could see how it could all go right back to that: the set they were building for *Richard III* for instance, a dirty white box with odd sections which came in and out of the rear wall. Very strange that looked, but it was the nearest thing he'd seen to an old-fashioned box set in years. Back to the simple way: cleat hooks and cleat lines.

The acting seemed easier then; you had to have a good strong voice and presence. 'The poetry is all that matters, my boy. Give them Shakespeare's poetry and you won't go wrong.' That's all that still matters to those stupid buggers down in Shireston. The bloody Shireston Festival Society; they'd never caught up with the change; Shakespeare at its simplest level with no underlining: that was what they wanted, unadulterated Shakespeare, meaningless Shakespeare, words that just sounded beautiful if spoken in a certain way with painted trees and walls, to show they had nothing to do with real life: declaimed bravely with a passion that had little to do with violence, politics or sex. Sex, that Eve Lester was a little mover. Archie, you should have been a bloody director not a stage carpenter. Another gulp from the jar, then back to supervising the building of Mr Holt's new set for *Richard III*.

'I trust we're not going to have any problems with this scene: either of the schoolboy variety, or the shocked, old-fashioned kind. There's no problem and it's perfectly straightforward. Romeo and Juliet have spent the night together, and it's love in a hot climate. They're both naked and I see no reason for either of them to be coy and start putting clothes on the moment dawn breaks. Asher and Carol have no reservations about playing it nude. If anyone else in the company has an objection, would they please make it now because we haven't got time to argue.'

'The press will have a beanfeast.'

'The press have not yet adjusted to the fact that nude scenes can be beautiful and, if used properly, they're perfectly natural. So let's forget about the press and get on with it. Asher and Carol in bed: I know you're fully clothed and lying on hard boards and that it's a chilly morning. But think bed, and hot. Right?'

'It's beautiful. You've done a first rate job.'

'It's a sixteen-page pamphlet on art paper with thin card covers and some difficult colour work, Mr Rolfe. Even for flattery I can't bring the price down.'

Adrian flicked through the programme under the tubular lighting of the printer's office. The cover insides and back carried advertising, the rest was a splendid layout job: colour, every device used for making space count, economy. A short article about the history of *Othello*. This production: two pages of black and white photographs of the company in rehearsal; a piece on Joe Thomas; a page of Tony Holt's designs; the centre spread of cast and credits littered with drawings; notes on members of the company.

'I'm not trying to flatter you. It's a bloody good programme. I doubt if any of the other festivals could match this quality.'

'Glad you like it, we're pretty pleased ourselves. Now, are you sure that first print is going to carry you for three weeks – the *Othello* and *Merchant* I mean?'

'That'll carry us, but what about the alterations?'

'Well, I've got to have them a good fortnight before we go for the second print, and we'll be coming up with the *Richard* and *Romeo* programmes by then.'

'You have my notes?'

'Yes. We slip page three for the second print. You're planning to give me a completely new page?'

'No, it's easy. The artwork stays, we simply lift the copy and insert extracts from the press reviews.'

'We have post-first-night comments instead of pre-first-night.'

'That's it. You'll have those within a week of opening on all plays.'

'Good.'

'Okay, that's the programmes. On to the second stage posters, stickers, advertising matter.'

'The individual play posters?'

'Yes, and the rest.'

'Well, we've had a slight problem with your Mr Holt's colour drawings for *The Merchant* poster.'

From: the Executive Director
To: The Director.
Date: 13th March, 1981

Please note that the attached current booking figures, for w/e 6th March, show a rise of 100 per cent on previous weeks.

'It's only the cuffs on this one. Far too tight. Fabulous blue. Feels super on.'

'It looks lovely, Miss Column. Make a note of the cuffs, Brenda.'

'Any more for me today?'

'Only the costume for the Trial scene, then that's you finished, Miss Column.'

'Liz. The wardrobe mistress always gets to call me Liz.'

'All right. Would you like to take that one off and change? Brenda, help Miss Column.'

'You very busy?'

'It's always a rush. We've got Miss Frost in at four o'clock and she has seven changes in *Othello*. All the odds and sods are done for the first two plays. It's only the principals now. Little fiddly alterations.'

'Like those cuffs.'

'Yes, like your cuffs.'

From: Director of Publicity
To: The Director.
Date: 14th March, 1981

For your attention I enclose the six new colour postcards of the house, gardens and theatre. These are best we could find and I have made arrangements for their sale in the foyer and at the exhibition. I am also pushing for a wider distribution through all available outlets.

Regarding our conversation two days ago. I have arranged for
Michael Lees to be present at all photo calls and would be
obliged if the principals would give him time for dress photo-
graphs to be used as extra postcards for sale in the theatre and
elsewhere.

Asher Grey and Rachel Cohen have just run through scene
one of act five in *The Merchant*: on stage using the set.

Douglas Silver looks annoyed.

'It's not sexy enough.'

'Doug, have you tried being sexy in a hammock?'

'God give me strength. That's the whole point of the
hammock, to get the laugh at the end. They always play this
scene for lyrical romanticism and it's so wrong. *In such a
night. . . . Did Thisbe fearfully o'ertrip the dew. . . . In such a
night Medea gather'd the enchanted herbs. . . .* Yuck, they pull
out all the stops and make it gooey. It comes out nine times
out of ten like the second movement of that piano concerto,
what is it, the second? By Saint-Saens. Loves, Lorenzo and
Jessica are finks. They've pinched the old man's bread; you,
Rachel, you're a randy, lusty little Jewess with no thought in
your head but clothes, playthings and screwing. . . .'

'The story of my life.'

'You even flogged your father's most cherished bit of
jewellery for a bloody monkey, remember? His prize ring for
a smelly little ape. Now the audience is supposed to see the
two of you as beautiful people full of lyrical romance together
in Portia's garden. Balls. There's a damn great hammock;
you've tried it most ways, so now you're going to try it in a
hammock. The words are romantic, but you've got to get
more lust, more purpose into it. Then you get disturbed by
Stephano and there's the usual discovered lovers' panic. In a
hammock it can be sexy and, at the end, very funny.'

'It's very interesting, I promise, especially with Asher.'

*It's hard to tell if Asher still really loves me like he used to. At least
like he used to say he did. He certainly humps enough, but he's
spending so much time rehearsing with randy birds. Doing his*

Romeo opposite that big black bit, Carol Evans, makes him come on terribly. I'm sure I'm only a substitute. What a pity we can't get into their minds and see who they're really fucking when they're at it.

However, life is far from dull here, if only I could be really certain of Asher it would be paradise. Work keeps all of us busy and it's going to be a marvellous summer, you can feel it all around. I'm heady with Shakespeare, desperately involved in the plays. You ask about Douglas Silver. He really is an inspiration to work with, and, between the two of us, I have designs on him. Think big, Julia, is what you used to say to me. . . .

'That's splendid, Conrad. I like the, *Is thy name Tyrell?*, and camping it up with the, *Art thou indeed?* It's a good contrast to the ruthless bitchiness with Buckingham.' Douglas turns to Ronnie Gregor. 'Look, while we've got Tyrell here, let's just reflect for a moment on scene three.'

'Tyrell's description of the princes' murder?'

'Yes.' Then looking up, loud to the company. 'We've been discussing how we might use some projected abstracts. You remember, as well as the gate and wall there's a screen we can drop into the back of the set. I think the description of the princes' murders might work with a projection.' Catellier catches his eye. 'Yes, Conrad?'

'Not film. I mean not acted out on film?'

'No. It would have to be something pretty horrible in abstract.'

'Two little hearts, in medical detail, working diagrams, pumping.' Frank flashes an unattractive smile, on and off. 'Then one struggles and stops. Then the other.'

'That's good. That's very good.'

'It's a bit naughty, isn't it?' Ronnie whispers.

A bleak look from Douglas. 'Very, but Tyrell isn't very good, is he?'

The images in Carol Evans's mind swarmed like hornets; velvet luxury; lust, the ripping apart. Which did her body need and crave for? Douglas with his firm approach and steady thrust into the mind as well as the body? No, the time with Joe Thomas, that remarkable energy which made her twist and roll like someone in a death agony. Faster yet. This one was different, unseen, tender, imagined, Asher Grey, her Romeo, lover, friend. Leaping the fence of passion, their bodies heaving to the same enormous swell. The long drawn agony, conscious of her swivelling buttocks against the sheet; then back to reality. It was going to be difficult, that scene, naked in bed with Asher Grey. She would be so aware, and he . . .? She had to be alone with him; she had to talk to Romeo.

In wardrobe they had all the costumes completed, but for minor detail, for the first two productions. The sets were finished, and operating, for *Othello*, *The Merchant* and *Romeo and Juliet*. Props were clear for *Othello* and *The Merchant*.

Each morning the company worked out together, their exercises becoming more complex, before rehearsals. Each day the productions advanced. March moved slowly towards its cold close and the air around Shireston stirred with the excitement of once more creating four new productions. New minds and bodies brought to bear on the Bard. It was all professional, all work and all concentration; the tensions would mount later. Spring was near and the opening of the season.

CHAPTER ELEVEN

Emilio Benneto was happy; in a little over a week his restaurant would be operating on a full and permanent basis. His chefs were up to it; he had spent much time with the five young waiters and the three girls he had been forced into accepting, against his better judgment, and they were all as ready as they ever would be. In the past weeks he had ironed out nearly all the catering problems in the entire organization; the buying of food had been reorganized, the kitchens put under more strict supervision; he even had an easy and friendly relationship going with the gaunt Mrs Doul. As he once observed to his young wife, Doris, 'I would like to know the whole history of Mrs Doul. In there somewhere is great personal tragedy. I sense it.'

On this Monday morning, Emilio was particularly happy, and, while he went through the accounts for the previous week, he reflected how lucky he had been; many men do not get second chances like him.

Back in their small house in Shireston, Doris Benneto finished off the week's washing, did a quick repair job on her face, put on her coat, the red one with big lapels and brass buttons which Emilio liked so much ('It makes you like a soldier. Wanton and desirable. The licentious soldiery.'), picked up her shopping basket and left to get half the week's groceries.

At eleven o'clock, just as Doris was shutting the front door of their home, Emilio began his weekly Monday morning inspection of the festival's catering facilities. It had become almost an occasion of military precision, but, by this time, most people had got used to it. Some still smiled: Benneto, a little Napoleon of the kitchens, but very professional. Accompanied by Mary Doul and the chief chef, Dominic, Emilio would make his way, first around his own kitchens at the theatre restaurant, then across to the permanent staff cafeteria, and finally to the company restaurant and the green room.

The driver of the lorry was a big Irishman called Dave Riley who had been piloting heavy vehicles for twenty years and should have known better. He took the hill too fast; there was no other traffic in sight; he slowed down, but not enough; he realized that he was taking the turn too wide and fast, but could do nothing about it; he did not even see the women in the red coat until it was hopeless. Riley swore, pushed both feet on to the brake pedal, pumping furiously; wrenching at the wheel so that the lorry bumped and ground, swinging violently. Then the crunch and bang.

Doris Benneto did not feel a thing. If anything she only experienced momentary horror, suddenly confronted by the inescapable, the rear end of the lorry mounting the pavement, striking her full on into blackness. Her body was thrown against the wall where the side of the truck, rebounding, struck it again, crushing.

They laughed a little in the permanent staff cafeteria because the fish had been under-ordered last week. It was unusual, normally they were in excess by Saturday. Last week there had been an unaccustomed demand for fish.

'I think we get Mr Silver to give us a research assistant to find out when things will be in greatest demand,' Emilio Benneto said.

The police and ambulance were at the scene within minutes. Riley was treated on the spot for cuts, bruises and shock. What remained of Doris Benneto was identified, wrapped in a blanket and taken to the mortuary at Shireston Hospital about a mile away. It was half an hour before the police discovered the next of kin was the dead woman's husband,

Emilio Benneto, restaurateur to the Shireston Festival Theatre.

By the time Emilio was back in his office the police were sitting with David Wills.

'Someone's got to break it to him, sir,' the uniformed inspector told the executive director. 'You're his immediate superior.'

David's horror was the most complete emotion he had yet experienced, and on top of it came the terror of having to break the news. He needed help desperately, but this time there was nobody for him to turn to: Douglas was in a *Richard* rehearsal and could not be disturbed; he thought of Rachel but she was also in rehearsal.

'Isn't there some friend?' He looked at the police officer for help, but his eye met the look of cold immobility. The inspector shook his head. 'Apparently they had few friends.'

'How do I. . . ?'

'Tell him, sir?'

'Yes.'

'You make sure he's sitting down and you're as careful and sympathetic as possible. It's never easy. I'll have to be with you if that's any help.'

'Have to be with me?'

'I have the harder job, sir. I have to ask him to come and identify. . . .'

'He has to?'

'I'm afraid so, and it's not at all pleasant. We really should be getting on with it.'

It was appalling. For David a private nightmare. At first Emilio could not grasp what David was telling him, and when he did it was tinged with the utter disbelief which is usually present, until the inspector added a word or two and reality set in. The restaurateur's face took on the grey parchment pallor of death, and, for a minute, they thought he was going to collapse altogether.

'It can't be. No. I was with her this morning, last night we. . . .' And he lapsed into a flow of Italian, laced with anger. The real grief would come later.

Douglas was told as soon as the rehearsal broke, and he exploded with rage at David, for having let Emilio go off with the police by himself. He took Jennifer to one side and broke the news to her and together they got the car and Mrs Doul. Douglas quickly instructed Ronnie, Frank and Robin to carry on with the normal *Othello* run-through in the afternoon if he did not get back in time; then they drove to the hospital in silence; once there it took fifteen minutes to discover that Emilio had been sedated and taken home by the police.

The restaurateur opened his own door to them, a wreck, as though the flesh and blood had disappeared from his body and the skin had sunk on to his bones, red eyed, his hands clutching at a dress. Down the hall a young policeman and policewoman shuffled in embarrassment.

'Is there anyone you can go to, Emilio?' Douglas's hand on the man's arm.

'There are only her parents. I wasa never close to them. The police hava told them. They haven't come 'ere and I don' want them to come 'ere.'

'Why not come back to the house, to the festival?' Jennifer stepped towards him. 'We've got a spare apartment, I'm sure.'

'Someone could look after you there,' Mary Doul, her thin face bleached with the shock felt on Emilio's behalf. 'Even I could look after you there,' she looked up at Douglas, an inquiring face.

Douglas nodded in reply and turned back to Benneto. 'Emilio have you got a solicitor? A lawyer?'

'No.'

'Well, don't worry about a thing, Emilio. Come back with us, please.'

'All her things . . . here. . . .' His arm went out in a limp gesture.

'That's exactly why you shouldn't be here.'

When they got back, Jennifer took Mrs Doul and Benneto to their apartment while Douglas routed out David Wills.

'You get hold of Robert Hughes and tell him I said he

would deal with everything, get in touch with the girl's parents, make the funeral arrangements, everything. Right? Now I want some spare accommodation. At least a room for Mrs Doul who seems to be the obvious person to look after Benneto at the moment. And we'll need a whole flat for him. We can't let the man stay completely alone at a time like this.'

'I'll fix it.' David most anxious to make up for his earlier bungling.

Asher Grey had been through a hard day. He had started to sit in at some of the *Richard* rehearsals in order to observe Conrad at work, even though Douglas had told him that it was not necessary at this point. So he spent the morning watching Conrad. The run-through of *Othello* in the afternoon was tiring, particularly as Douglas did not get in until around four o'clock. Then, the full news of the tragedy depressed the young actor.

The news, in fact, spread quickly and was felt by all. Nobody, apart from Dominic and a few of the catering staff, had known Doris Benneto well, but they all liked the little Italian restaurateur, and the very nature of the tragedy made it almost a personal shock to company and permanent staff alike.

When they finally broke at five Julia went over to tell Asher that she was getting a lift down to Shireston with Liz Column and asked if he would like to come; the shops were mostly open until six and there were one or two things she had to buy.

'I think I'll just go back to the flat and take a shower, love.'

'You sure? I hate leaving you alone, Ash.'

'I'm sure. You won't be long, will you?'

'About an hour.'

Asher waved good-bye and set out for the house. On the stairs he met Carol Evans and for a second felt that she had been loitering there in the hope of seeing him.

'Hi, you okay?' she asked.

'You heard about Benneto's wife?'

'Yes, it's terrible, I can't get it out of my head.' Then, as

353

though she had just realized that he was alone, 'Where's Julia?'

'Gone into Shireston with Liz Column and Frank Ewes.'

As he said it the butterflies began low in his stomach and his hair tingled at the nape of his neck. There was a long pause.

'I think we've got things to talk about.' She leaned back against the bannister rail; he could see the small curve of her stomach hard against the denim skirt.

'We have to talk about your Juliet.'

'And your Romeo.'

'Yes.'

'We can talk in my place.'

Asher nodded.

Inside her rooms there was air and light. Even though Julia professed to love the country so much she was no fresh air fiend when indoors; rarely was a window left open. Now alone, the particular, almost electronic, communication between Asher Grey and Carol Evans seemed to rise.

'When's it going to happen?' she asked.

'There's little chance.'

'It has to be before we do the love scene properly. I couldn't meet you in public, if you see what I mean.'

'It's been worrying me. It could be embarrassing for both of us.'

'What is it, Ash? I feel like a whore.'

'Don't. Don't talk like that. I don't know what it is. Perhaps it's. . . .'

'Don't say, love, it isn't that.'

'No, I was going to say that perhaps it's simply the two of us playing Romeo and Juliet. It's more than just a physical thing.'

'I don't know. My feeling is definitely physical.'

'Come here, then.'

'No, in bed, under the sheet, Asher, like it will be.'

They reached the bedroom before the frenzy broke over them, washing away Douglas, Julia, Joe Thomas, everyone who might get in the way, clog their memories. Clawing at each other's clothing, mouths wide, bodies not in complete control. In a pinpoint corner of his consciousness, Asher wondered if this was what Shakespeare had in mind. The scene not played. Grab the experience, hold it tight, so that you can recall it when you awoke with her on stage in a contrived dawn with the audience watching. Naked now, they rolled on to the bed, her fingers around him and his hand reaching for her, wet and running with desire.

Carol's own body filled her mind, then beyond it the sensation of flying through colour. Asher was bigger than she had expected and so a small pain at first, but not now in the heaving wild gasping storm.

Emilio Benneto on the bed staring out of the window; his face vacant, though the mind's eye crammed full of pain: unbelievable; Doris, his other self, the only person, active and alive; young, moving, now all gone, finished, disappeared. That could not be; yet it was; the awful sick joke of life, the tunnel to nothing, and there was not a thing one could do about it. Where are you? Where? The images so brilliant, close and clear, bringing only agony and warm tears.

'Cry. Cry now and as much as you can.' A thin hand on his shoulder. Mary Doul standing beside the bed. 'If I had cried it would have made life easier for me.'

'She was. . . .'

'I know. I promise, Emilio, I know exactly what you're going through.'

'Why Doris?'

'Why anyone? Why you, eventually? That's why I wanted to look after you, because I know about it. I've been through it.'

Asher got back to his apartment only five minutes before Julia returned from Shireston. He and Carol had lain together when it was over, bathing in each other's warmth and afterglow.

'Is that how it always is for you?'

'With Julia you mean?'

'With anybody.'

'It's very good with Julia, but not like that. And you?'

'It was something different, something for the memory.'

'Really it's what we have to describe through the text.'

'I know it. That was everything that Shakespeare wrote about them, even if they never existed.'

Asher chuckled and the laugh built between them.

'Our secret?' she asked.

He placed a finger on her lips. 'Our secret.'

Julia came into the bathroom as he was showering, and he had to turn away, put his back to her so that she would not glimpse the redness, praying that Carol had not clawed too deeply around his shoulders.

'Is he modest, then?' Julia coming too close for comfort. 'You've taken a long time to shower.'

'I lazed about some. How was the big city?'

Happily she headed for the door. 'Brash, as always.' She stopped at the door. 'Ash, what happens when you die? What's happened to Mrs Benneto?'

He slung a towel around his waist. 'That's the big one. The end product of life. For my money the end product is nothing.'

'But that's illogical.'

'Life?'

'Everything. It makes nonsense out of it all.'

'Perhaps. Maybe that's the trick, living for every moment. With no end product, the fact is here and now. Nothing more.'

They buried Doris Benneto on April the first, Wednesday afternoon, a chilly day with rain in the offing. Douglas, Jennifer, David, Mrs Doul and most of the catering staff, a dozen or so members of the company. A depressing ceremony after which they were thrust into the final days before the first night of the season which was to open on the Tuesday with *Othello*.

The technical dress rehearsal was a shambles: the changes all taking too long and the tape not matching in with the lighting plot, or the actors, on four separate occasions.

The stopping dress rehearsal was no better. Douglas, leaping around the auditorium, discovered for the first time that Joe Thomas had developed the bad habit of dropping his voice whenever he had to turn away from the audience, therefore becoming inaudible. It meant a lot of extra work. They began the stopping dress at nine o'clock on the Saturday evening and it was still in progress at three on the Sunday morning. When they finally broke, Douglas told the company that they were free until the photo call at seven-thirty on Sunday evening. The full dress rehearsal would go up at three on Monday afternoon. Final notes afterwards, and a technical run-through, without actors, on Tuesday morning at ten.

At the same time they were working on *The Merchant* which was due to go in on the Friday night; the technical dress, stopping dress and full dress being scheduled for Wednesday night, after *Othello* had come down, Thursday afternoon and Friday morning. It was going to be a non-stop and very tightly run week.

On Sunday evening, just after eight, Douglas went over to the theatre to make sure all was well with the photo call. It would be a long evening as they were doing shots from both opening productions. The press were given one hour with three different set-ups, and time for individual work with the principals as they were available; after that the leads had to be ready for Michael Lees who was coming in to do the portraits for the postcards. There would follow a good two hours for Adrian's other photographer commissioned to do the stills for programmes and blow-ups for the exhibition.

Adrian was somewhere on stage with the herd of press photographers pushing, standing, kneeling around Joe, Jennifer and Edward Crispin in costume. Art Drays was also up there helping things to move as smoothly and quickly as possible (they had half the stage staff in for photo calls). At the back of the auditorium David Wills stood with Ronnie Gregor. Douglas went quietly up to them.

'I trust my assistants are around.'

Ronnie looked up. 'Frank and Robin?'

The director nodded.

'They're here, clucking about like little mother hens back there somewhere.' Ronnie inclined his head towards the stage.

'Everything else under control?'

'As far as it can be. David and I've been over at the exhibition all afternoon. Tony's still there with as many spare hands as he can muster, and Adrian's joining him as soon as we've finished with this lot.'

'Christ,' Douglas looked weary. 'I haven't been near yet. How goes it, David?'

'I think it's going to be fine. You want to look over it now or do you want to wait until we're fully operational?'

'Let's have a look see.'

The marquee was larger than Douglas imagined. He had, of course, been aware of its erection and had read the regular reports from all concerned with the progress of the exhibition. Yet, now, he was suddenly most impressed by the whole project as they passed through the relatively narrow entrance into the first section, the one dealing with the history of Shireston itself. In the centre of the area stood a full size replica of the cracked bell from Shireston Parish Church. At the far end, flanking the small corridor which led on to the next section, where two tall cut-out trees, faded and wilting slightly, the remains of some pre-World War Two production. The other exhibits were set, with some elegance, around the walls which had been built, in front of the canvas, to resemble the red brickwork of Shireston House, with ledges and panels, slanting desk tops and glass cases inserted for each item. There was a painting of the house made soon after it was built; family portraits of the Longwells and, below a fading print of Richard Longwell, fifth earl of Shireston, the famous will, which had set the festival in motion; the original designs of the theatre; photographs, maps, programmes, costumes, prompt books and drawings galore.

'It'll be really impressive when we have the tapes going.' David looked anxious.

'I think it's impressive enough already. I saw the draft for all tapes, but I only had time for a quick look.'

'They've come out well.'

They moved on into the small second area which dealt with historic performances and productions of the four plays of the current season. Again, many photographs, programmes and a lot of memorabilia: Douglas noted a big photograph of Johnston Forbes-Robertson as Othello and another of Paul Robeson which almost evoked the power of that big man's beautiful voice; there was the famous Dali painting of Sir Laurence Olivier as Richard III, showing the great actor in character, full face and three-quarter profile (originally commissioned by Sir Alexander Korda, the painting had been loaned by Sir Laurence). There were also two huge blow-ups of famous *Romeo and Juliet* productions: John Gielgud and Peggy Ashcroft at the New Theatre in 1935, and the mind-clasping Zeffirelli at the Old Vic in 1960, John Stride and Judi Dench looking out with a devoted fervour. Above a false archway leading into the third section was a large reproduction of Emlyn Williams as Shylock at Stratford in 1956, a portrait by Angus McBean, shot from low down on the right profile on to a wispy-bearded, slit-eyed, hook-nosed make-up, the face betraying the craft and cunning of ages.

The third section was chaos, Tony Holt working like a maniac to create a picture of the current season's productions; spaces everywhere waiting to be filled by items either not yet available or completed.

'Please move on, Douglas,' pleaded Tony pointing on to the last, and largest, part of the exhibition. 'We've finished in there and quite proud of it. But give the credit to David, all the ideas are his, I only got the stuff together.'

On coming through the opening into the fourth section, one was immediately confronted by a massive imitation wrought iron frame archway which bade the visitor welcome to THE LIFE AND TIMES OF WILLIAM SHAKESPEARE. Douglas's eye took in what seemed to be millions of exhibits, including a full size centre-piece reproduction of the Stratford-upon-Avon Gower Memorial: Shakespeare himself seated above

Puck, Falstaff, Lady Macbeth and Prince Hal. The upper sections of the long walls to left and right were covered by giant copies of the Norden maps of London and Westminster of Shakespeare's day, while the far wall was dominated by a seven-foot-high copy of the Droeshot engraving (Douglas remembered Tony saying, 'Even if it is a fake it'll look bloody good.'). Below the maps and engraving, the exhibits were set into an authentic looking wooden panelling.

Moving on to the exhibits, Douglas found that David and Tony had pursued the life of Shakespeare using the simple, masterly technique of taking the many extant documents concerning the Bard, reproducing them and using each as the key to some setting, model or visual symbol.

So, the extract from the Stratford Parish Register, 26th April, 1564, *Guliemus filius Johannes Shakspere* was illustrated by a wooden cot in the foreground and a long perspective view reaching towards a golden sunburst, with objects suspended, floating, as the view receded: a quill, a knife, parchment, the masks of comedy and tragedy.

The bond exempting the Bishop of Worcester from liability if the marriage of *William Shagspere on thone partie, and Anne Hathwey of Stratford in the Dioces of Worcester maiden* should be unlawful, was simply surmounted by a deep velvet cushion upon which lay a pair of broken gold rings. The christening of Susanna; the christening of Hamnet and Judith; on 26th and 27th December, 1594, the fact that *Willm Kempe, Willm Shakespeare, & Richard Burbage seruantes to the Lord Chamberleyne* received payment for Court performances (a model of arches surrounding a simple platform, in the background a cyclorama, beautifully decorated, giving the impression of a rich court with the queen in their midst).

The death of Hamnet (a child's coat, roughly thrown across a stool). Then, slotted in between the documents, there were simple illustrations of the plays, some three-dimensional, others done with line drawings, the *Histories*, *Titus* and *The Tempest* done in large abstract oils; for *Othello* a photograph of two swans, one black and one white; *Hamlet*, a sprig of rosemary and a rapier; *Coriolanus*, a laurel wreath sprayed gold and torn apart at one side; *The Dream*, a purple pansy entwined by a snake.

In 1602 *Williemus Shakespeare generosus* secures a warranty for New Place (a colour photograph of the New Place Gardens as they are today). The marriage of *Susanna Shaxpere* to John Hall; the Globe burned down during a performance of *Henry VIII* in June 1613; and on until, finally, the death, burial and will (Yorick's skull against unremitting black).

Yet still the exhibits continued, a glorious montage of present-day Shakespeare festivals ranging from Stratford-upon-Avon to Shireston, to the Canadian Stratford, Ontario and Stratford, Connecticut, the American Shakespeare Festival in Balboa Park with its recreated Globe Theatre (roofed in, not for protection from rain, but to provide air conditioning within); the annual Shakespearian performances in Regent's Park and Central Park.

Douglas emerged with a sense of wonder. 'That's magic, David. What it'll be like with the tapes running I daren't think.'

'It's not bad, is it?' David preened himself.

'I'll come back on Tuesday when you're open properly.'

CHAPTER TWELVE

It was raining on Tuesday. Jennifer knew it as soon as she opened her eyes, and in the same second remembered what the day was and wanted no part of it. Then, as consciousness wakened fully, the sense of fear turned to an excited tingle coupled with a healthy respect for the unknown which the night would bring.

She could smell coffee, and, as she lifted her head, saw the small parcel, silver gift-wrapped, on the bedside table. She gingerly put out her hand (noises from the kitchen) and picked up the package. It was impossible to open the wrapping without rending or tearing: inside, a small box, and, on soft cotton wool within, a gold medallion, about one inch in diameter, hung on a gold chain, around the edge the repeated words *Desdemona Othello Desdemona*, and at the bottom *Shireston 1981*, in the centre two hands engraved, clasped together, one heavily shaded, the other clear.

Douglas opened the door fully and appeared carrying a breakfast tray.

'It's super, Doug. Oh, thank you, thank you.'

'A present for a good Desdemona.'

'Don't say that, not until it's all over.'

'When it's all over it's just beginning, girl.'

She fumbled in the bedside table drawer. 'Desdemona didn't forget her director either.' She held out the little box. 'It isn't wrapped because I was really saving it until tonight, but, as you've jumped the gun and given me mine. . . .'

It was a gold signet ring, square, chunky, modern, engraved with the cracked bell of Shireston. Douglas had given her the tray before taking the box, now it got in their way.

The technical run-through ironed out some of the hitches: now there was no more Douglas could do, except be on hand, wish each actor and actress well, and pray within.

He came out of the theatre just before one o'clock (still a thin drizzle, he remembered that it had rained on the dramatic first day of rehearsals); he started to cross the lawn at a lope, when a shout from the theatre made him turn; David Wills was coming towards him, almost running.

'I just missed you at the theatre, Douglas, we've got a problem.' Breathless, his face lined with worry.

Douglas quickly reflected that David's jobs that morning were concerned with the exhibition, the box office and checking the company.

'What kind of problem?'

'Joe Thomas is missing.'

'Missing?'

'Nobody's set eyes on him since last night. His bed hasn't been slept in, and there's no trace of him anywhere on the festival property.'

For a second, Douglas knew what it felt like to have your blood freeze. 'You questioned everybody?' he heard himself asking.

'Most people. Lonniè Barnes saw him going up to his room at around ten last night; Edward Crispin wanted a word with him and tried to call him at quarter to eleven but got no reply.'

'He was okay when we finished the dress.' The dress rehearsal on the previous evening had not been brilliant, but they had got through within the timing: Douglas had not expected it to be anyway near perfect and had been pleased enough to feel the underlying potential of a performance in front of an audience. Now, he searched his mind in an attempt to pinpoint any moment, word, action which might have thrown the hair-trigger mechanism within Thomas. He did not want to bother Jennifer, who was spending the day resting at the flat, so they walked over to the office in silence.

Frank Ewes, already alerted, was there, looking anxious. He had been with David earlier when they discovered that Thomas was missing. Now the three of them gathered in Douglas's office like a group of edgy conspirators.

'I suppose we call in the police.' David sounded glum.

'There doesn't seem to be any alternative,' Douglas pacing the floor, a caged leopard, 'but I don't like it. There must be some rational explanation.'

Deborah buzzed through to ask if Douglas would see Edward Crispin.

'I came over to see if there was anything I could help with. At least it would give me something to do. Getting through the day of a first night is bad enough, but this. . . .' The actor lifted his hands in a gesture of concern.

'What about our switchboard?' asked Frank.

'What about it?' Douglas aggressive in his anxiety.

'Do we keep any note of local calls?' Frank clutching at straws.

'There's a note of course.' David quick with the answer. 'Antiquated bloody system, but you know how it works. If you're calling from your room you have to go through the operator. That's a good idea, Frank, nip off and check on any outside calls made from Joe's room last night.' Looking up at Douglas, 'Okay?'

Douglas nodded.

Frank left the room bustling, shrouded in an air of self-importance.

While they were waiting, Douglas put a call through to Robert Hughes, the solicitor. 'I'm speaking on an unofficial and friendly basis, because I think you might be able to help: in the last resort. Joe Thomas has gone missing.'

'Christ, on his first night.'

'Quite. We've only really just discovered it, and I don't want to call the police until we've done a thorough check out here.'

'Of course you don't. That man's caused you a lot of concern one way and another.'

'It'll be worth it if tonight goes well. Actors can be strange at this time in a production; I don't want a lot of noise and publicity if there's no need. How are you with the local coppers?'

'I have an ear with the chief superintendent.'

'Enough to start something on a quiet basis?'

'I think so.'

'Can I call you back if it's necessary?'

'Of course. If it looks really difficult I'll do all I can.'

Douglas thanked him and cradled the telephone. Frank returned some twenty minutes later; Douglas, David and Edward Crispin having sat almost in silence, knowing that as the minutes ticked past, their inactivity brought them closer to the edge of panic.

Douglas's mind was sprawled full of disaster. If something had happened to Thomas, or if he had chickened out at the last minute, then . . . No, he just would not do such a thing and the director could not contemplate it.

Frank brought back the start of an answer.

'Joe made two outside calls between ten and ten-fifteen last night.'

'Do we know who he called?'

'They're checking the numbers now, they'll come on to you, Douglas.'

Five more minutes before the telephone rang. Douglas listened quietly as the impersonal voice of the girl on the switchboard gave him the details. When he replaced the receiver some of the strain had gone out of his face.

'Joe called the Blue Boar Hotel in Shireston just after ten last night. He then got on to a local taxi firm.'

'Getting away from it all?' suggested Crispin.

'More than likely. David, you'd better come down to the Boar with me. Edward, thanks for you help, but please go and rest now, you've got a bitch of a night ahead.'

At first, the manager of the Blue Boar was reluctant to say anything. A small grey man, who knew as well as anybody that his hotel was fourth rate, a man who fought a losing battle against staff shortages, rising prices, inefficiency, slovenly work, he had no wish to antagonize the Shireston

Festival in general and neither Joe Thomas nor Douglas Silver in person.

'Look,' Douglas eventually rounded on him. 'I'm running a professional theatre company. I have reason to believe that you've got one of my leading actors here, holed up. He's probably told you that he must not be disturbed under any circumstances. Well, I'm not going to disturb him. All I have to know is whether he intends coming back to the festival and appearing on stage tonight.'

The manager looked distraught, then finally capitulated. 'Mr Thomas rang us last night,' he said quietly. 'He asked if we had a single room and booked in at about ten-thirty. He's left instructions that nobody is to be told he's here; a meal is ordered for half past four this afternoon and he is checking out around half past five.' He relaxed like a man who has got a great load off his mind.

'You did right to tell me.' Douglas said. 'Who else knows?'

'Only the night porter. Mr Thomas booked in under the name of Smith.'

'Not too imaginative these actors. Will the night porter . . .?'

'Keep quiet? No doubt at all, sir. Mr Thomas is, what they call in the trade, a heavy tipper.'

Douglas nodded. 'All I ask is that he gets back to the festival and into the theatre in good time.' An added worry struck him. 'He's checking out at five-thirty. Do you know what arrangements he's made?'

'Oh yes, sir, it's perfectly all right. The taxi that brought him down last night has been booked to take him back. I gathered that he simply wanted to be away from everybody up at the house.'

'That figures.'

Back at the house, Douglas telephoned Edward Crispin and then Robert Hughes, to put their minds at rest. It was four-thirty before he got back to the flat where Jennifer was using all her control to keep mind and body in check.

Douglas told her about Thomas.

'I don't blame him at all. If I could, I would get a million miles away. How do you really think it's going to go, Doug?'

'I told you last night. If you all keep the pace steady and don't start getting ragged, and, between ourselves, if Joe Thomas doesn't lose his nerve, I think it might just be a knock-out.' He had made an enthusiastic speech after the dress, designed to bolster any signs of sagging moral, only too conscious that his own stomach was in a nervous twist.

Just after five, Douglas got into the bath and began to prepare for the long evening ahead.

They started to arrive shortly after five-thirty. The restaurant was solidly booked from six onwards and the exhibition had officially opened at three that afternoon. They came in cars and taxis, while the first special coaches rumbled in through the main gates a little before five-forty-five. The British Rail special from Waterloo got into Shireston station at a quarter to six, met by coaches; Adrian and two of his staff waiting with cars to add a small slice of luxury, and flattery, for the reviewers who had chosen this method of transport.

The rain seemed to have gone, though it was still a chilly evening; yet, in spite of the weather, the grounds seemed to be full of people, a holiday mood taking over the whole area.

Among the company and theatre staff, however, there was the natural strain and concern. No panic, simply sustained anxiety.

The technicians did their last checks on equipment. For the hundredth time, Archie Swimmer, who had been in the theatre all day, went through his list of changes. Just after six o'clock, members of the company began to drift in through the stage door.

Douglas, now dressed in a dark blue double breasted velvet suit, passed through the crowds, noticed at this time of day by only a few, and headed for his rendezvous with Art, Ronnie, Frank and Robin, on stage at six-fifteen. None of them would dine until it was over.

The others were already there by the time Douglas arrived, and they prepared to begin what amounted to an almost ritual leave taking, the final words with the company. Tonight they would be out front, their job now was to be back stage until the ASM called 'the half' (with curtain up at seven-thirty, it is usual for the assistant stage manager to keep actors informed of the time by calling 'the half' over the backstage inter-communications system at five minutes to seven; 'the quarter' at seven-ten; 'five minutes' at seven-twenty; and 'beginners on stage' at twenty-five past. In this way, actors have a vocal time system to which they can refer).

After a last word with personal staff, Douglas sent them off on their trek around the dressing-rooms. He was far from being a religious man, but there was an old superstition of his, an undying habit to which he had adhered through the years. Now, alone on Tony Holt's opening set for *Othello*, Douglas Silver knelt down and made the sign of the cross.

Joe Thomas sat in front of the mirror in his dressing-room and saw that he looked exactly how he felt, frightened out of his life. Wilson, his dresser, a little rabbit man who, like Archie Swimmer, had tended actors in the theatre at Shires-ton for over forty years, had come in at six-thirty to find Thomas sitting just as he was sitting now.

'Come back at the quarter,' Joe had said quietly. 'I'll dress then. Just don't bother me until the quarter.'

Wilson knew better than to argue with him on a night like this.

A tap on the door and Douglas's head peeping round. 'Just looking in to make sure you're okay, Joe?'

'Come in, Doug, baby.'

The director could feel the strain and terrible tension which had built up. 'You had a quiet day?' He tried to sound casual.

'I skipped out last night. Holed up in Shireston so nobody could get at me. I probably did the wrong thing.'

'I knew where you were. It's sometimes good to be alone.'

'I don't know. Douglas, I'm frightened out of my life.'

'Now he tells me.' Douglas grinned. 'Joe, what the hell's the matter? You've been before larger audiences than you'll see tonight.'

'Yeah, but I ain't done *this* in front of audiences. Everybody expects so much. . . .' He waved his hand limply at the framework of telegrams and cablegrams which surrounded the mirror.

'I only expect you to do what you've been doing in rehearsal. Just go on and do it, Joe; there are no problems, I promise.' Before he could take it any further, there was another tap on the door and Jennifer was in the room, a long towelling robe over her underwear, her face calm, not showing the swirling apprehension within.

'Good luck, Joe.' She bent to kiss him.

'And to you, honey. I'll do my best.' The very act of seeing his Desdemona seemed to reassure him.

'You're going to be great,' Jennifer smiled, then looked up at Douglas. 'Good luck, Doug, darling.'

'Just do it all. Good luck, it'll be fine.'

Jennifer took her husband's hand and gave it a long squeeze, then turned and left the room.

For the next fifteen minutes it was a constant chorus of good lucks as Douglas toured the dressing-rooms, and, for him alone, that terrible sense that it had all fallen away; that the work they had done together was about to be thrown into the open to become almost a sexual act in the centre of the marketplace, rending all trust and mutual respect between actors and director.

The dressing-rooms all had the smell, known only to Theatre people: stale sweat, perfume, make-up. Everywhere the sense of communications breaking down.

Asher Grey pacing the room, dressed and ready, even before the half; Laurence Pern adjusting a buckle; Ronald Escott putting on his beard for Brabantio, looking up, then quickly away as Douglas came in; Liz Column, cool and talking about clothes to Rachel Cohen, both of them trying to blind themselves to the fact that, in barely twenty minutes, they would be on. He popped in to see Jennifer once more and she was twisting the Christmas ring on to her finger. She had not worn it at any of the rehearsals, but now, as she had promised, it had become her Desdemona ring. He grinned at her and held up crossed fingers and she blew him a kiss.

They called the quarter.

Douglas headed towards the stage door where Frank Ewes and Ronnie Gregor caught up with him. There was some commotion at the end of the corridor and Douglas looked up to see Tommy Carr, Joe Thomas's manager, and Smiley come hurrying from the direction of the stage door. Douglas breathed an obscenity before Tommy Carr called out loudly.

'Hey, there's that Douglas Silver now. Hi, Douglas Silver, how've you been, man?'

He was obviously a little drunk.

'Hi, Tommy,' Douglas lifted his hand in greeting.

'We're just goin' to wish our boy well before he goes on.' Carr's face grotesque in smiles.

'He know you're here?' asked Douglas.

'No, thought we'd give him a surprise.'

'Yeah, a surprise,' echoed Smiley.

'As his director, I'd be glad if you didn't.' Douglas pulled himself up to his full height.

'Hey, man, we want to give him a lift, like surprise him.'

'You already told me that. I'm telling you that it would be better to surprise him after the performance.'

The smile faded from Carr's face. 'Look, Silver, I'm his personal manager. When I want to see him I see him.'

'And I'm his director for this production; this is my theatre, my company, my *Othello*. In fifteen minutes they'll be starting. They're all twitchy back there, particularly Joe. It's a big night for him, Tommy. If you want the truth he's already spent twenty-four hours running away from it. It is just possible that he could be very great tonight. It is also possible that he could die a thousand deaths out there; he's certainly going to do just that if you bust in on him now. He'll blow it for sure, Tommy, so get out and into your seats and stay there until it's all over.'

The speech came out so forcefully that Carr and Smiley only had a second's thought before making some disgruntled noises, turning on their heels and heading back the way they had come.

By this time, Ronnie had joined Douglas and Frank. Robin and Art were following. On the way out, Douglas left the stage doorkeeper in no doubt that nobody, except theatre staff, was to be allowed through until they had come down at the end of the production.

With the help of his staff, Adrian was looking after the press, making sure they were all there and catered for; that they had transport home, or a hotel room into which they could retire when the night was over; or facilities for writing and telephoning in their copy. All the senior men were there from the nationals and Sundays, while the bigger provincial daily papers were well represented. Locally, Adrian saw that Hedley Moir himself was covering for the *Gazette*. With thought only for the festival, the PR man went across to invite the editor to the press bar in the interval; but he was met by a sharp rebuff.

'I am not in the habit of taking any kind of bribe.' The editor's lips pursed neatly.

'It's not a bribe, merely a social courtesy. I know previous directors have not allowed the custom to develop, but this year we've got all the important critics here. So I do hope you'll come and join your colleagues.'

'I think not.' Rudely, Moir turned away.

By this time the foyer was packed full, and Adrian could see that there were press men covering the audience as well as the play, the surroundings being lit spasmodically by the flare of photo-flashes.

All members of the company who were not in the *Othello* cast had been asked to attend, and they had turned out in force and style. Catellier was talking hard to a London producer; Kapstein had a mob of television people around him, there were pop stars and actors, big names from the whole entertainment industry, from all walks and all strata.

Douglas arrived with his small retinue and the flashes exploded again, newsmen hustling for shots. The director found that even getting to his seat was tricky, a business of being accosted by someone every couple of steps.

Adrian finally got to him. 'They've really turned out for

you tonight, Doug. Good luck.'

Douglas muttered a perfunctory thanks, saying that it was Joe they had turned out for, then immediately asked, 'Did anyone find out how Emilio was coping in the restaurant?'

'Yes,' Adrian had to almost shout above the prattle and noise. 'I went over there myself. He was fine, packed out but cool. Everything like clockwork.'

Eventually Douglas got to his seat and discovered that, momentarily, his apprehension had been drowned by the general excitement.

People waving to one another across the auditorium, the rustling of programmes, confused chatter. Carol Evans looking outrageously beautiful in a long white lace gown. Despair: Douglas felt the anxious loneliness and a sense of being totally deserted by everybody: even Ronnie sat silent by his side. Then the moment, as though someone was pulling a dimmer on the noise.

The houselights went down and Raymond Leggat's raucous fanfare split the ears, followed by the loud medley of night noises coming from the stage, a black cavern. Though he had heard them all many times before, Douglas felt the audience react to the noises and he with them: the tingle low in the spine and at the back of the neck, the shudder he had asked for passed through the auditorium as the night street noises built, echoing and grating with increasing volume – something which could have been a cat yet sounded shocking in its confused echo; the mutilated cry of a baby which made the very bowels tremble with fear; a muffled shout and cry which could only have come from the most terror-struck darkest recess of a mentally warped mind, then, through it all, Laurence Pern's voice, as Roderigo, on the tape and as though from down a long street –

Tush; never tell me; I take it much unkindly
That thou, Iago, who has had my purse
As if the strings were thine, shouldst know of this, –

The stage lights came up to reveal Tony Holt's lowering setting and Edward Crispin, Iago, dancing attendance on Roderigo. It worked, through the first scene, worked marvellously, the noises, the hint of the grand *corrida* to come, the action and the poetry.

Then, to the end of the scene, the noises of intrigue stabbing through the darkness as Archie Swimmer's boys got Brabantio's house off; then the quick *pasodoble* and Crispin on stage with Joe Thomas and the others, the lighting plot working with the flickering torches, throwing great moving shadows.

Douglas hunched down in his seat as though trying to disappear. For a couple of minutes he thought he had made a terrible mistake with Joe Thomas: within the darkness and light from the torches the man appeared to have diminished, not looking as lordly or beautifully dominating as he should. His first lines came out without the real force, but suddenly, on the arrival of Brabantio's search party, and at the words '*Keep up your bright swords, for the dew will rust them* Thomas seemed to have got it together: the dignity, unruffled calm, the strength; in a blink he became Shakespeare's creation. It was the first spark of many. Both Joe Thomas and Crispin seemed inspired, like men throwing down lightning bolts, while between them, Jennifer flashed a brilliant theatrical conception of Desdemona. Crispin's Iago sparkling with subtlety, the matador motif always a fraction below the surface, and Thomas's Othello uncompromisingly great, both to see and hear. Douglas could not entirely trust his emotions but did not remember ever hearing the major speeches done so well by anybody, let alone Crispin and Thomas.

It seemed also that Douglas's directorial underlining and counter pointing did its job: the *faena* sequences, the soundtrack noises, the crowds at the arrival in Cyprus, the drinking scene, Tony's great hot Cyprus settings. By the interval it was as though the audience was watching the play as if they had never seen it before.

In the interval, Douglas hurried through to Joe's dressing-room to find the man lying on his couch, Wilson bathing the sweat from him. The director scarcely knew what he said, but the words of encouragement seemed to help before he left for Crispin's room, and lastly to Jennifer, who was now at a quivering pitch of ultimate control.

Slowly, as Iago dismantled the greatness of the Moor, Douglas thought the audience were viewing the action with a rising sense of horror, Joe Thomas connecting hard with the soul of the play; it was what he had intended, but now the moment was here, Douglas was once more assailed by doubts and concern: most conscious of Ronnie Gregor, calm and writing notes as he sat beside him.

The wretched handkerchief did its work, plot weaved with sub-plot, the grandeur of the language echoed in the mind and, before they knew it, they were engulfed by the final moments of the play: Othello dissolved into the raging mad wounded jealous bull, ravaging and smothering Desdemona. Then the quiet anguish of what follows. The truth slowly impinging on his mind. The climb up the staircase and the walk along the unprotected gallery –

'. . . *Set you down this;*
And say besides, that in Aleppo once,
Where a malignant and a turban'd Turk
Beat a Venetian and traduc'd the state,'

The voice held to one note, rising imperceptibly, almost sung. The bodies of Desdemona and Emilia; Asher Grey, as Cassio, wounded and held up by two soldiers; Murray Fleet's Gratiano, Paul Berger and Mark Lynton stock still as Montano and Lodovica; Edward Crispin being restrained by another pair of soldiers. Tension complete and all eyes on Thomas, no, net Thomas, the complete Othello standing high on the gallery –

'*I took by th' throat the circumcized dog,*
And smote him – thus.'

The arm up and the flash of light on the blade, the thump they had devised on the tape, again and again the thump as he stabs himself, the thin wail from the tape (they had done it with an electronic organ), so slight at first, and so much part of the whole, that nobody could really hear it, but rising to its crescendo by the last lines of the play.

'*O bloody period!'* Just enough projection from a heavy-hearted Lodovico.

And from Gratiano –

'*All that's spoke is marr'd.*'

Thomas, gore soaked now, having burst the blood pellets and still with one in his mouth ready to bite, sways and drops the long dagger, puts out his arms, the audience perched to a man on their seats, tension cutable. Arms out to Desdemona's corpse –

'*I kiss'd thee ere I kill'd thee; no way but this,*
Killing myself to die upon a kiss.'

The hand just makes his mouth, then flaps forward as he bites the blood pellet and pitches off the gallery.

Genuine screams from three points in the house, and noise towards the back of the stalls which spoke of someone fainting. Thomas, Othello, swinging and dripping blood; the high whine getting louder over Lodovico's closing speech, then the whole noise erupting in one brassy bray, a fragmentary shout of *aficionados*, then darkness and silence for the count of five before the audience also erupted.

It was like standing in a great white light and suddenly the rain came. At first a small patter, rising, though he could not feel its force or wetness. The raindrops got bigger and louder until it teemed around him and Joe Thomas stood there alone among the ferocious applause and the shouts and cheers. He had known adulation and the sense of achievement before, but never anything like this. He looked to the wings and saw Jennifer coming towards him, a look of other worlds on her face as she clasped him to her in front of the whole company. Then Edward, holding his hand, patting him on the back.

Douglas Silver sat in silence surrounded by the gleaming noise and remembering something a great director, he thought it was Guthrie, had once said to him. 'Never trust first night applause; the bulk of the house is friendly anyway. Wait, if there is hysteria, and see if it happens a second, third, or fourth time.'

The trick was in keeping the mood buoyant, and the emotions

in check, holding the crest until the second and third performances. At first it was pandemonium back stage, the corridors and dressing-rooms crowded and the sharp sense of success heady in the air. Over the loudspeaker system, Ronnie's voice persistent. 'Notes for the *Othello* company at ten-thirty sharp, on stage tomorrow morning. The next performance will be at two-thirty tomorrow afternoon.'

In the dressing-rooms it was smiles and constant cackle.

You were marvellous, darling.

Beautiful, that finale. I thought I'd die.

Ash, that was splendid.

What a night.

Marvellous, darling.

The best Othello since I saw Robeson in fifty-nine.

Douglas, conscious of the praise heaped on him as well as the actors, threaded his way from dressing-room to dressing-room, tempering his own congratulations to his company with a low-key reservation.

Tommy Carr and Smiley were among the crowd that had gathered in and around Joe Thomas's room, even so, Douglas was glad that Thomas gave a yelp the moment his director pushed through.

'Doug, baby, thank you. How about that? Just how about that?'

'Great. Fine, there are only one or two things I need to talk about in the morning, Joe baby.'

For the first time that day, Thomas threw him an aggressive look.

'See you later.' Douglas pushed his way out again, heading for Edward Crispin's room, and, after that, to Jennifer.

Near Jennifer's dressing-room he met Carol Evans in the crush. 'Fantastic, Douglas,' her face gleamed. 'I'm dumb with awe.'

'Thanks. It's too small a word, but thanks. I guess I'm a little awe-struck too. See you later, maybe.'

'That would be nice. I look forward to it.'

Jennifer had got rid of the visitors and was struggling into a slinky white creation.

'Yes, Cinderella, you may go to that ball.' Douglas put his arms around her.

'And at midnight?'

'Who knows, personally I like tattered Levis, and stuffed pumpkin is something else.' He looked at her solemnly. 'That was about the most perfect Desdemona I ever wish to see.'

'Douglas.' Warm, the gratitude in her eyes. 'But what about Joe? Wasn't he fantastic? That voice, we didn't hear that quality at rehearsals.'

'I don't believe it. So good. I'm afraid I've been a bit naughty, I cooled him in his dressing-room just now: gave the impression I wasn't altogether happy.'

Jennifer's excited smile turned to a look of concern. 'You're the boss; if you think that's how it should be handled.'

'His bloody manager's turned up from the States. I'm just anxious that Joe doesn't get thrown. It would be so easy for him to walk it now, Jen, and if he begins doing that the whole show'll come crashing down. That man has got to be kept under pressure for the whole season.'

'I still think a little praise. . . .'

'Okay, I'll give him one of my famous pep talks at the party.'

She kissed him lightly. 'And so will I. He'll be a better person for that.'

They both laughed.

Knowing that the first night of the season could mean the letting down of hair and a complete abandonment of discipline, Douglas had organized things so that there could be some kind of control. The last thing he wanted was a series of spontaneous, or organized parties going on all over the house and theatre. So, to make certain, there was to be an official Opening Of The Season Party in the theatre restaurant, to which the whole company and their friends were invited: the party beginning one hour after *Othello* came down.

It was essentially Joe Thomas's night, Douglas caught the general feeling as soon as they reached the restaurant, the thing bubbled with the singer's success and, while Tommy Carr was keeping close to his client, he could in no way monopolize him; Joe was in constant demand. Even Conrad Catellier went out of his way to discuss the performance and tell him how good it was. There was music, unlimited talk, a lot of laughter and many important guests. On their way in, Douglas and Jennifer met Asher Grey with Julia Philips clinging on tightly.

'Wasn't he super, Douglas? Absolutely super,' gushed Julia.

'I've been trying to get to you, Ash. Splendid, congratulations and thanks.' Douglas clasped the actor's hand firmly.

It set the mood for Douglas, and the next hour became a continuation of the conversations in which he had been engulfed back stage. Eventually he even got to Joe Thomas and poured a little honey on his leading man. Thomas was obviously being puffed full of praise, but there was a change in him: Douglas felt that he was talking to a much stronger character than the one with whom he had spoken in Vegas, it seemed a million years ago now.

'You mind if I dance with your wife?' Thomas asked after a few minutes conversation against the babble and music.

'If you can find her.' They had been split up on arrival. 'Alas, she's your Desdemona, as well as my wife.' Douglas laughed, turning away straight into David Wills and Rachel Cohen who seemed to have little time for anybody but each other. Again mutual compliments. (Rachel's Bianca was, in Douglas's mind, the most neatly conceived piece of characterization among the smaller roles, and his praise was sincere: she played Bianca, the whore, without recourse to any of the stagey tricks which so many actresses use when giving an impression of what they believe to be carefully observed whorish traits.)

'I bet you haven't been over to the exhibition now that it's all happening,' said David.

They had decided to leave the exhibition open until after the party so that members of the company could all see it in a certain amount of privacy. 'No, but I'm going over in a minute. It's on my schedule, David. How've they done over there?'

The executive director grinned broadly. 'A sell-out. We reckon that just about everybody who was in the theatre tonight went round the exhibition as well. If that keeps up right through the season we're made men.'

A few minutes later, Douglas caught sight of Jennifer dancing with Joe Thomas; it was impossible to catch her eye, she was laughing a lot, moving well to Thomas's rhythm. It had become increasingly hot in the restaurant and Douglas felt that he needed a break from the smoke; obligatory back-scratching and noise. Almost stealthily he made for the exit, the exhibition uppermost in his mind.

Jennifer knew she should not have drunk four glasses of champagne so quickly as she now bounced to the strong beat with Joe Thomas; she was aware of the light-headedness. Then there was something else, something she had felt during the later rehearsals of *Othello*, and again, on stage, that night: during the more tender scenes her nipples had hardened and she had been conscious of the reek of sensuality wandering through her mind and body. It was all part of playing Desdemona, part of the character, she told herself: she had to have some earthy feelings for Joe as Othello, otherwise she could not project the emotions. Now, with the alcohol relaxing her, she felt the sensuous strain again and knew it for what it really was: one part of her fancied Joe Thomas in the most basic of ways, another fancied him for what he had proved to be that night, and a third was obsessed with screwing the world, simply to show Douglas and that black bitch. There was, of course, particular irony here with Joe Thomas.

'You look hot, baby.' Joe shouted above the din.

'I am hot. It's stifling in here.'

'You want some air?'

The nip inside her and the rising sense of her sex: the throbbing, tingling pulse low down.

'Yes, come on.'

With the tapes running and the lighting properly set, the exhibition seemed to assume new dimensions. Douglas had viewed it with a kind of reverence on his previous visit, but now the magic increased and his mind had nothing but gratitude, tinged with wonder, for what David and Tony had managed to invent.

The sounds within the first section, The History of the Shireston Festival, were neatly interwoven: music, combined with the noises of the countryside (birds and animals, cries, the sounds of the seasons), and, behind them, extracts from Shakespeare, spoken by members of the company, and well chosen for their allusions to the fields, woods and country life: Conrad spoke the Duke's lines from *As You Like It* –

And this our life exempt from public haunt,
Finds tongues in trees, books in the running brooks,
Sermons in stones, and good in everything:
I would not change it.

On top of this a girl's voice, he thought it was Rachel singing –

And merry larks are ploughmen's clocks,
When turtles tread, and rooks, and daws,
And maidens bleach their summer smocks,
The cuckoo then, on every tree,
Mocks married men; for thus sings he,
                    Cuckoo;
Cuckoo, cuckoo: O word of fear,
Unpleasing to a married ear!

Jennifer and Joe walked across the lawn in the direction of the theatre, now in darkness.

'You enjoyed tonight?' Jennifer forcing herself to be serious, the champagne had brought on an attack of frivolity combined with the raging randiness.

'I wouldn't say I enjoyed it, honey. I like it now it's over and I know I can do it. Hey, that's a gas, isn't it? This feeling?'

'Yes, it's the whole experience. But you've had it before, Joe.'

'Not quite this way. You know, Jen, I wasn't so happy when Tommy and Smiley turned up tonight after the show. They're from another part of my life that has nothing to do with this. I really believed I've found something out about myself here: here with you people.'

'A change of mood and pace?'

'No, a change of style, language, thought, the way you learn to use your mind in this medium, the way you learn to use your voice, move your body.'

Jennifer giggled in spite of herself. 'You move your body all right, Joe. I bet you use it really well.' She could hardly believe that it was herself talking, the entire night exploding in her head; legs unsteady, stomach trembling. The adolescent volcano.

Joe Thomas caught hold of her hand, stopped and moved closer. He could feel the grass under the soles of his shoes, his body rising to meet Jennifer's.

'You really want to prove that old Othello-Desdemona legend, baby?'

'I think so, don't rush me though, Joe. I feel something. I don't know.' The automatic, self-imposed cut-outs of her whole moral background already working behind the natural desires.

'We can go to my dressing-room and talk, anyhow. I got a spare bottle of that French fizz water in there.'

Douglas had moved on through two more sections of the exhibition: famous productions of the four plays was backed by some wonderful voices from the past, recordings culled from the BBC Sound Archives. In the section on the Four Current Productions at Shireston the voices were more familiar, those of the present company, cross-cut with Leggat's music, the whole giving an electrifying effect.

Now Douglas stood at the entrance to THE LIFE AND TIMES OF WILLIAM SHAKESPEARE and again marvelled at the way in which the project had been put together. Here, the sounds were diffused, as though a hundred voices were whispering from all corners of the long room, interspersed with fragments and snatches of music. He quickly discovered that what they had done was to work one particular segment of poetry, prose or music for each individual exhibit, using a phased loudspeaker system.

The exhibition was beginning to fill with couples who had drifted over from the party; Douglas turned back, pausing for a second beside the exhibit showing the bond exempting the Bishop from liability should William's marriage to Anne be proved unlawful, with its illustration of the pair of broken rings. Edward Crispin's voice came softly from the loudspeakers –

I knew a boy went wandering in a wood,
Drunken with common dew and beauty-mad
And moonstruck.
Then there came a nightshade witch,
Locked hands with him, small hands, hot hands, down drew him,
Sighing – 'Love me, love me!' as a ring-dove sighs,
(How white a woman is under the moon!)
She was scarce human.

Douglas began to move away with a puzzled frown.

'You look worried, Doug.' It was Carol Evans who had come up quietly behind him.

'Hello. I couldn't place that passage.'

The loudspeaker cycle went on and finally the voice of Edward Crispin again repeated the piece. Carol smiled. 'I know where it comes from.'

'Where?'

'Oh, I only know because I was in on this recording session and they had a laugh about "*How white a woman is under the moon.*" It's from a 1920s play called *Will Shakespeare*, by Clemence Dane.'

'Before my time.' Douglas gave a wry smile. 'You come here with somebody?'

'No, I came looking for you.'

'Yes?'

'Yes. To give you some information from tonight's play.'

'Go on.' He felt a small stream of apprehension in his

blood.

She came close to him and whispered. '*Even now, an old black ram is tupping your white ewe.*'

At first, Douglas did not grasp the significance. Then, 'Jennifer?' he queried, voice small against the whispers and music of the exhibition. 'Jen and Joe Thomas?'

'Yes, at least I think so. They left the party together. I saw them and it had that look.'

'No, Jen wouldn't. . . .'

'We did,' soft, her hand on his velvet sleeve.

The fury crossed his face and he saw that his fist was tightly balled. 'I'll bloody well. . . .'

'No, Doug. Please. All I know is that they're together and it looked, well, you know how people look. It wouldn't be a serious thing. It's to do with *Othello* if it's anything.'

'Sod *Othello*. It's to do with my wife.'

'And you're the last person to interfere. Don't do anything you'd regret.'

He relaxed slightly, shrugging his shoulders. 'I suppose you're right. I'd better go and find her though. I still can't believe. . . .'

'I don't suppose she could believe it about you either. We were very close, Doug; and people are pretty much the same, I guess; having our cake and eating it; not wanting to get involved with things that are unpleasant. I don't want to get caught up in this race thing, but I'm black and you're white; none of us want violence until there's some guy stealing your paper money, or your property and so you fight back; we all share; we all breathe the same air, drink the same water, share the same pollution.'

Douglas bobbed his head up and down slowly, gave her hand a small squeeze and walked away, unhurried.

The silence in the theatre had a depth and vastness to it, Jennifer almost hearing her heart-beat, crossed with their footsteps, echoing down the whitewashed corridors. Joe's dressing-room had been cleaned and aired, the *Othello* costumes hung neatly, ready for the next afternoon. Inside, he

383

leaned against the door and she saw his hand move down to the key. He turned the key and they collided with mutual consent, her fingers digging into his shoulders as he kissed her, the first time, on the lips, then she knew she was biting him as he pressed harder, sliding his stiff tongue into her mouth, the miniature of the act itself. They must have stayed locked together, mouths and lips sucking and playing, for a good minute (he kissed her with tiny jabs all over her face and neck; she felt the tingling within and the oncoming rigidity of her nipples). Then she drew away and Joe began to unbutton his shirt.

Jennifer put her hands behind her neck, slipped the hooks and eyes, then drew down on the zip. The dress was of a heavy material and she wore only a brief pair of white pants underneath. She caught a glimpse of herself in the long wall mirror as she stepped out of the dress, her breasts hanging full; she let the dress drop and looked up at the mirror again. Between her breasts the shining medallion, which Douglas had given her that morning, hung like a small golden sun between the two smooth mounds. It seemed as though in a second a whole jagged montage of moments and actions came alive in her brain: the arrival back from the States; the Christmas angel, and the knowledge of Douglas having needed someone else, outdated maybe, but the pain still soared; the moment in the apartment when she really knew and Carol Evans was reading *Loving and Losing*. The truth that this thing now had nothing to do with Joe or Othello or Desdemona, that it was really only the bitch in her spitting at Douglas.

Joe was undoing his belt as she picked up the dress. 'Joe?'

He stood still, comprehension of his face. 'You're going to put that on again, aren't you?'

'Yes.'

A small explosion of air from his mouth, perhaps a smothered oath.

'Don't get mad, Joe. I know it's wrong of me. A girl who says no at the last minute deserves –'

'All she gets, which in different circumstances would be

384

six cracked teeth.' He did not smile. 'It'll be okay, Jen, just get that goddamn dress on and move yourself out of here fast.'

Her stomach was an open pit wherein a large coarse hand opened, closed, opened, flexed its fingers and closed again; she felt sick, the saliva running like a fountain and her eyes burned with the first threat of tears.

Jennifer did not, later, remember putting on the dress, shoes, unlocking the door. There was a picture of the dim corridors and the darkness once outside, the grass and the people as she ran back over the lawns to the house.

She was unlocking the door to the apartment when Douglas appeared at the far end of the passage, from the direction of Joe Thomas's apartment: that registered. Douglas's face bleak with rage. It was the first time she had seen him truly encompassed by such fury, reaching for her shoulder and propelling her into the apartment like a small, offending, child.

'Joe Thomas,' he clipped out as though speaking an obscenity.

She could not put together the thought processes which had brought him to this point of hate, or jealousy, or whatever the emotion was. Jennifer could only stammer half-formed sentences.

'You and Joe Thomas, tonight.' Douglas spoke loudly, not questioning, simply a demand.

'Douglas. . . .' Pleading.

'You left the party with Joe Thomas nearly three-quarters of an hour ago. You weren't at the exhibition, or in his apartment. Where were you?'

'Doug, please, why so uptight?'

'And what were you doing? Why? Because a member of the company quoted *Othello* at me tonight. *An old black ram is tupping your white ewe.*'

A sudden anger, injustice, burned in her.

'A few months ago they could have misquoted that and been accurate: an old white ram is tupping your black ewe.' She shot hard.

'It's not the colour.'

'Of course it isn't. It wouldn't matter if she had been a puce martian.'

'Right, Jen, or he candy striped and green. It's us.'

In spite of herself, Jennifer began to giggle.

'I don't see. . . .' Douglas began.

'It's all right, darling, I promise. Nothing happened with Joe Thomas. Oh God, you're so funny when you get pompous. Just like a bloody man; I'm away and you have a great lovelorn thing and screw Carol Evans from here to whenever, and you expect me to understand and be sympathetic. Then I go missing for half an hour with Joe Thomas and that's the deadly sin. I come back and you're standing there, metaphorical whip in hand, almost telling me to bend over your desk. Really, Doug, you're the bloody end.'

For ten seconds the silence was strained, then the atmosphere leaped on to another plane.

'Oh Jesus,' Douglas started to laugh. 'Jen, I'm sorry.'

'You will be, love. Nothing happened tonight, but it nearly did, so you'll have to sweat out Othello and Desdemona for the rest of the season.'

Douglas stopped laughing, the corners of his mouth still upturned in a smile. 'We'll see about that. You ever had a dress torn off your back?'

'Try me.'

Joe Thomas, still whirling from the first high, a combination of promised success and alcohol, now dropped to the gloom of despair. For a couple of hours he had ridden a cloud of happiness, the culmination was the pledge of a new, and desired, body in which to cool his mounting lust. Then, without warning, that opportunity had been removed. Jennifer left and he was alone in the dressing-room.

His loins sang, the fire in his head burned with a raging brilliance, locking out everything but the need for satisfaction, some part of a woman, preferably her basic self, around him soothing the ache. Christ he wanted Jennifer Frost, almost to the point of madness:

'I do confess the vices of my blood,
So justly to your grave ears I'll present
How I did thrive in this fair lady's love . . .'

He quoted aloud, cutting the words, conscious that he was concerned more with lust than love, as he unlocked the private cupboard above the dressing-room mirrors. Joe always kept the cupboard locked, for it contained his private stock of liquor. He took down a tumbler and jug together with an unopened bottle of Teacher's. He ran water into the sink until it was really cold: there was no ice, but that did not matter.

The party spun towards its climax; in another hour or so it would all be over, the drunks comatose, lovers paired, the rest to their double or single beds, to sleep or ache, dream or hope. Emilio Benneto relaxed for the first time that day. In the short period which had passed since Doris had been snuffed from his side, Mary Doul had been an almost constant companion, a prop, shoring up the imminent collapse of his being. To take his mind from the intense personal grief, she talked to him much about her own problems: born into an Army family, Mary's father had been a regular officer with an iron hand and total reliance on the power of hard discipline, so when, at the age of eighteen, she fell deeply and unreasonably in love with a pacifist artist whose talent was outweighed by the fervour of his political and social convictions, there was the inevitable family clash. The result led to Mary romantically eloping with young Richard Doul, her father playing the heavy parent and cutting her off without the proverbial penny. Doul himself enjoyed a brief success: no doubt spurred on by his young wife's ardour, he produced a series of abstracts which excited the imagination of several critics, giving him a certain standing; so, for around three years, the young couple were able to live in a position from which they could cock a calm snook at Mary's outraged parents. Then, for no apparent reason, Richard Doul collapsed one morning and was dead by evening of a brain haemorrhage.

There followed the long hell of Mary Doul. Her parents were intractable and her grief long sustained. Thrown back upon herself with the shadow of a rigid upbringing stamped deep into her personality, her thin body stacked with bitterness and resentment she lived, at first a nomadic life among temporary jobs, trekking from one bedsitter to another: a displaced person in her own land.

In the end the catering trade claimed her, a petty martinet of the kitchens of a dozen hotels until she arrived on the Shireston scene. It was an outdated, romantic story, but the fragments of it that she was able to impart to Emilio Benneto were a solace to the Italian. He, being a romantic, by race as well as condition, was able to appreciate her personal agonies which helped to put his own shattered work into perspective.

The grief and shock were still, unmercifully, with him, but the presence of Mary Doul, her softening towards him, were already, in this short time, starting to compensate.

During this difficult first day of the season she had, many times, left her own work to slip over to the theatre restaurant for a quick word and reassuring look. During the party that night, she had been there, helping him. Now, they stood together, apart from the main throng.

'They have enjoyed themselves, these actors, eh?'

'I've never seen a party like it at Shireston, Emilio. You should be proud.'

There was a long silence, augmented by the blast from the loudspeakers piping music for the dancing, and the happy babble of the crowd. Emilio's voice broke as he said, 'Doris would have enjoyed tonight. At the reception for the company she was so happy; and at Christmas.'

'I know, Emilio, it's so hard, but you've entered into a new phase now. You have to accept it, my dear man. It is all part of life whichever way you look at it.'

Laurence Pern was deliriously drunk, happily drunk in a bewildered, hopeless, falling down state. Ronald Escott and Mark Lynton carried him, screeching and helpless with inebriated mirth, over to the house and bedded him down, unceremonially, and still fully dressed, in his room.

David Wills spent the evening trying to persuade Rachel Cohen to marry him. Before the first performance he sent her a dozen red roses, which he could ill afford, and since then he had taken every available step: at the party and the exhibition, which he showed off to her with the pride of a schoolboy revealing his art exhibits on an open day, in order to press an answer from her.

A week before, Rachel had asked him for a little more time, to think; they were happy enough, she said, after all their mutual enjoyment, both physical and mental, could not be greater ('Darling we never stop talking and we're like a couple of riggish rabbits. We couldn't get more if we tried.'), so why the hurry?

Secretly, even though David knew all about the affair with Harry, the thought of marrying worried Rachel: she had tied herself so completely, without legal binding, to Harry, that part of her would, she felt, inevitably always belong to him. Even tonight, with the whole festival celebrating, and glory flavouring the moment, she could not give David any immediate or convincing answer.

'But I love you, Rachel. I know the problems.'

She frowned, leaning in his arms. 'Can't we just go on as we are for the time being, love? I really don't know if I believe in marriage, not the kind of marriage our parents believed in anyway.'

'The provider and the little woman? You know I don't altogether believe in that either, but I do believe that you can build up a unit with someone, something more flexible than the old idea, but a marriage nevertheless.'

'Just a little longer, David, please.'

Edward Crispin quietly enjoyed himself, wholly self-reliant in his own way. His few friends were of his own choice and his life lay within the boundaries of his work. Tonight he felt satisfied, at ease and fulfilled. His Iago, if not brilliant, had the stamp of depth and complete characterization to it, he

389

knew that. To have created and interpreted as he had done gave Crispin more contentment than most men got from the usual sidekicks in life, the things after which they seemed to hustle so urgently, like sex or power, or drink even. Edward Crispin relaxed with a gin and tonic, did not push or obtrude, he merely sat back, a shade pretentiously perhaps, knowing that if there was some bonanza to come, some added pleasure, it would arrive in his path without him having to sweat around looking for it.

Maurice Kapstein was behaving himself and it paid off in large dividends. Slowly, during rehearsals, he had wrapped Shylock around himself, and the knowledge that his night was near seemed to give him new accuracy of balance and judgment. At the party he took little to drink and was affable to everybody. It was around midnight that he sought out the pretty Eve Lester, with whom he had clashed at the reception for the company and who, that night, had walked on in *Othello* and, on Friday, we would be walking on in *The Merchant*.

'I have reason to believe that you have been avoiding me.'

'Oh, Mr Kapstein.' The girl felt the disturbing flush of embarrassment. 'Avoiding you? No.' Inexpertly lied.

'My dear girl, you have been avoiding me since the day of my arrival here, and it is no wonder. I made a lewd, salacious pass at you during the party for the company. I was rather drunk and now I apologize.'

'There's really no need. . . .'

'There is a great deal of need. Can I talk to you now?'

She was naturally hesitant. 'Of course, but aren't there people here who you need to . . . I mean there are important people.'

'Important? Who's important?'

She mentioned the names of two powerful television men with whom Kapstein had been for most of the evening.

'Those predators?' There was the right amount of loathing in his tone. 'Do you know what important people, like those people, will do to you? They'll take you and fill you with pride, they'll feed you on it until you are fat and juicy; then they'll ravage you with their fangs, chew you into small pieces, suck every ounce of sweet talent from you and spit out the remains, like husks from a combine harvester.'

'That's a very cynical attitude.'

'Cynical? What else can a man be at my time of life? There is nothing else to be at my age, in this shallow and fearful time, but cynical. Even you, the youth of the moment, have a great strain of cynicism and disbelief running through your ways.'

She warmed to him, sober, Maurice Kapstein was a much more interesting possibility. 'Ah, but we're only cynical because of the results we can see; the results of the generations that have gone before us. We see the inaccurate standards, the false motives, the faked picture, the political confidence trick that's led to guilt, war, misery, famine, poverty, pollution, agony.'

Kapstein, smiling, held up a hand. 'Child, don't talk to me about poverty, pollution or agony. I promise you that your generation will not make much difference to that: no more than mine did. Maybe you are all more aware: and that's because your fathers have almost perfected the communications industry. But I doubt, in the end, if you'll use your early wisdom with any more ability than we did.'

They talked for over an hour, Morrie at his best, making remarks calculated to bait the girl into friendly attack. Slowly they drifted from politics to individual achievement, and he talked to her about his own life, the fascinating stories of the theatre as it had been, glittering illustrations of the great names he had known; when he was on form like this, Kapstein could paint three-dimensional pictures with words, turning the mind into a living galaxy of time past. Without realizing it, Eve Lester was trapped by the actor's personality. A few months ago she had lain on her bed, sick with loathing at the thought of being alone, or close, to Kapstein. That night, she returned with him to his room as docile as a hand-reared lamb, and then behaved with an abandon she had never approached with the handful of boys who were, until now, her only intimate experience.

It restored Kapstein's faith in himself also. After a long naked churning and wrestling, during which he brought her to a climax twice (the second time with himself), he did as he always claimed: turned her over, slapped her three hearty times on her backside, and boomed –

'Now you see what it's like to be with a man.'

All she could do was marvel at both the man and her own tingling, new and exciting experience.

Carol Evans waited for five minutes after Douglas left the exhibition, before wandering off again towards the theatre restaurant and the party. She had a roving eye tonight, though it was Douglas whom she really felt need for. Asher Grey was firmly locked within the clattering jaws of Julia Philips, so there was no joy to be had there. Carol took a couple of drinks and joined in the general chatter, dancing with a couple of the unattached company members, always at the edge of turning on but never quite making it.

At around twelve-thirty, she decided to call it a night and made for the main door. It was crisply cold by this time, the night clear but more wintery than early spring. She stood for a moment allowing her eyes to adjust to the darkness, then set off towards the house, taking a dozen paces before seeing the dark shape lumbering unsteadily to her right from the edge of the lawn.

She quickened her step, then, with a quiver of fear in the back of her throat, called out, 'Who's there? Who is it?'

'That's the black and beauteous Carol Evans. C'm'ere Carol Evans.' Joe Thomas, slurred and throaty.

'Joe?'

'Yeah. Come to me, you livin' symbol of desire; you roisterin', bucking piece of magnificence.'

She laughed, beginning to move towards him. 'You're pretty drunk, Joe.'

'Pissed out of my ragin' skull, babe. C'mon, help your poor strugglin' soul brother.'

'Mind how you go.' She put an arm around him for support; he reeked of whisky and obviously found walking impractical, his progress charted in a tacking motion.

By holding on to his upper arms, Carol was able to steer him safely into the house. Getting upstairs proved to be a long and unsteady business, each stair being a new and delicate obstacle, but, by the time they got to Joe's landing he seemed more in control of himself.

'Thanks, baby,' he breathed when they arrived at his door. He took a deep breath and started to sort through his keys, finally getting the right one and opening the Yale lock. She switched on the lights for him and stood back so that he could enter.

'After you, lady.' The smile lopsided, though his eyes seemed in better focus.

'No, I'll leave you now, Joe. Time you were in bed.'

'Agreed, agreed. After you.'

More to humour him, Carol moved inside the apartment, she felt tired now, wanting only the comfort of her own bed and the soft sensation of sheets around her naked body.

Joe came in slowly, more steady now, the grin as stupid though. Quietly he closed the door.

'You're what I've needed all night, honey.' Low.

'Open the door, Joe, I'm going home to bed. You're too drunk anyway.'

His face became alive with anger; it was like triggering an explosion. 'You git your clothes off and your frame on to that bed through there and I'll show you if I'm too drunk.'

'Joe.' Not even pleading, he was becoming a bore.

'I said git in there.' Sharp, with a pace forward, and for the first time Carol experienced real fear. She tried to sound calm.

'Joe, it's late. You've got a heavy day tomorrow.'

'Do as you are told.'

She did not see his arm come up, only the flash of pain as the palm caught her cheek, sending her sprawling sideways. She hit the floor heavily, more pain sharp on the right side of her body, one hand leaping to her burning cheek.

'Git up and into that bedroom.'

Slowly she began to rise, but he grabbed her, pulling her

up into a standing position and pushing her backwards. With a burst of energy, Carol tore herself clear, but his hand came up again, paddling hard across her face, the pain sudden and fierce. He must have struck her eight or nine times.

She backed away, opening her mouth, screaming in panic.

The scream stopped Thomas for a second, and Carol sprang clear as he lunged at her again with a spluttered oath. But the alcohol took its toll and Joe's balance was off once more. He slipped and fell forward, leaving Carol with enough time to make the door and run down the passage, distraught, her whole body sharp with the hurt on her cheeks and side, the stink of stale liquor in her nose and the horror of the sudden, unprovoked violence swirling around her throbbing head.

By the time she reached the stairs Carol was too bewildered for instant decision, she paused breathing heavily, her weight against the balustrade, not even knowing if Thomas was following. Clear within her disturbed and fractured mind there came one thought, one person to whom she could turn, one woman. A couple of minutes later she was knocking on Felicity Durrant's door.

Conrad Catellier left the party relatively early; apart from his natural mistrust of such occasions, he needed to be alone now that he was so deeply entrenched in his *Richard III*; at the same time he was most conscious of the experience of Thomas's *Othello*, not that he was completely in tune with all that Douglas Silver had pulled out of the air, but, as an actor, he felt nothing but respect for the ballad singer who had proved himself so masterful with Shakespeare's language.

'Your understanding of the role is quite profound and you have that rare gift of complete interpretation; your audience knows and understands you immediately,' he told Joe Thomas.

Thomas had thanked him, and said that if it was so, then, he supposed the many years of singing modern songs with meaningful lyrics must be partly responsible.

Conrad undressed and got into bed, glad that he had

entered into no particular liaison with any other member of the Company; his text for *Richard III* was on the side table, and he worked on it for an hour before finally putting off the light, taking his sleeping capsules and closing his eyes.

Liz Column hardly stopped talking after *Othello* came down. Throughout the party she made a constant verbal assault on Frank, repeatedly asking him what he really felt about her Emilia. Now, with Frank beside her, dropping with sleep, tucked into her bed like some cuddly teddy bear, there as a prop to comfort her, she cajoled him with queries about her Portia: had Douglas said anything to him about her performance? Did he (Frank) think she was playing this or that scene in keeping with the general conception of the production? That move in the Trial scene, in the 'mercy' speech, was it too dramatic?

'Liz, can't we go to sleep?' Frank at last pleaded.

A silence almost painful in its stunned atmosphere.

'Darling, have you gone mad?' she shrieked in a stagy upper register. 'I can't sleep on a first night without being laid. Go to, boy, go to.'

Douglas and Jennifer were at peace, warm clasped as lovers in each other's arms, their abrasive friction eased away in more tender attrition; their minds at rest and swords put up.

Felicity Durrant was always a light sleeper, so she heard Carol's knock almost as the girl's knuckles touched the wooden panel of the door.

Her face registered shock as she opened to the sight of Carol leaning against the jamb.

'My dear girl, what's happened? Have you been in an accident? Come in; Oh come along in, child, my goodness me. . . .'

She fussed around constructively, wanting to send for a doctor, but Carol persuaded her against it assuring her that no bones were broken. Felicity bathed the bruises, and the little blood on Carol's right cheek, where Thomas's nail had scratched her; there was a warm drink, sympathy and a ready ear as Carol sobbed out part of what had happened.

'You go straight down to Douglas in the morning and tell him the whole thing.'

'No, Joe didn't mean it. He wasn't himself. He was so drunk, I'm sure something terrible had upset him.'

'You're a very foolish girl if you don't tell Douglas. Now, off with your clothes, I'm getting you into bed.'

It was as though their roles in *Romeo and Juliet* had broken through the fabric of the play to become reality. Carol, suffering slight shock, needed nothing better than the tender care as the older woman helped her to undress, tutted when she refused to borrow a nightdress, gave up her own bed, tucked Carol between the sheets and kissed her affectionately on both cheeks before retiring to the couch in the living-room.

And as they approach the first fence at the now refurbished Shireston Festival, it is Othello in the lead. Othello, a stayer, by El Cordobes out of Noises Off. That is Douglas Silver's production anyway: loud, with strange sounds as scene smoothly dissolves into scene, a technique almost cinematic. No doubt some things will jar, for we have Iago, played at athletic pitch by Edward Crispin, as a heavyweight matador goading Othello with his cape in a flurry of veronicas, naturales and derechasoz . . . the award must go to Joe Thomas for his Othello whom he presents as a complete and believable human being, rendering the verse in a voice which almost sings Shakespeare's words and certainly passes their full weight and comprehension to the audience. His acting ability is enormous, and . . . (Daily Mail)

I have seen Joe Thomas live in Las Vegas, listened to him charm audiences at Plaza Nine in New York, and heard his particular kind of magic soothe and inspire at the Talk of the Town here in London. I did not, in the wildest flights of imagination, think I would ever see his Othello. I did not think I would see it here in England at the Shireston Festival, and I certainly did not think that it would be as it is – brilliant and complete. . . . Joe Thomas speaks a moody blue Othello, so profound that you cannot fail to be moved. . . . Jennifer Frost's Desdemona, looking like a souped-up Joan of Arc, with cropped hair, gives the role tender dimensions by making the woman have a blind spot to Othello's true needs. . . . (Daily Express)

In spite of staging and production technique more suitable to Carmen, Douglas Silver gets a double first for his Othello, which opened at the Shireston Festival last night. Much of the credit goes to Joe Thomas whose Othello begins as a whole man, the very presence of a soldier-diplomat, and really progresses, seemingly in voice, manner and body, down the flinty road to outraged, unreasoned, brain-cracked jealous violence. I doubt if I have ever heard the great verse of this play rendered with such power, attack, understanding or emotional control. . . . (Daily Telegraph)

Shakespeare's Othello is a complete labyrinth; a vast landscape of mental peaks, valleys, crevasses . . . the theatricality of Douglas Silver's production: he sets Iago and Othello in juxtaposition, as matador and bull, with background noises redolent of the corrida as well as the central themes of the play. The problem with Othello has always. . . . Thomas's Othello is a rare dramatic experience. . . . Jennifer Frost's touching, bewildered, unaware Desdemona . . . Edward Crispin's Iago is a professional con man, fully conscious of what harvest he will reap. . . . Elizabeth Column's gentle Emelia; a nicely scored Bianca by Rachel Cohen and a powerful Cassio from Asher Grey (A young man worth watching, for he is to play Romeo later in the season). . . . (The Times)

A dazzling Othello opens the Shireston Festival this week in a production packed with brilliant spectacle, sex and violence, Othello himself, played by the unlikely Joe Thomas, a performance of explosive skill which you should sell your bed to see. . . . (Sun)

Douglas called in at Adrian Rolfe's office before going over to give notes to the *Othello* company on the following morning. They both had the same sense of elation over the reviews.

'Nearest thing to raves that you're going to get this season,' announced Adrian.

Douglas pulled a face. 'Wait for the Sundays; you ought to know that rule. We're healthy now, but those Sunday boys are something else.'

'Ah, don't worry, I've got enough good selling quotes here to have them fighting for tickets. I'll tell you what we've really got to look out for though.'

'That quality weekly the *Shireston Gazette*. That joy comes on Friday.'

'So does *The Merchant*, mate, things really get heavy now.'

Carol ached and felt stiff down the right side of her body and, worst of all, there was a large ugly purple bruise down the right side of her face, the cheekbone painful to the touch; there was little she could do about it.

Felicity Durrant continued her tirade against Joe Thomas over breakfast, saying that Carol was an idiot if she did not report the matter to Douglas.

'Douglas has enough on his place at the moment without me bothering him with this.'

She got back to her own apartment just after nine-thirty to hear the telephone ringing madly.

'Hello.'

'Carol?' His voice was a throaty wreck.

'Yes.'

'Baby, you okay? I'm sorry, honey, I feel terrible; don't know what happened to me. . . .'

'Oh.'

'I've been calling you since eight-thirty. When you didn't answer. . . .'

'I'm okay, Joe. Just a few bruises that show. The best thing you can do is stay out of my way.'

'I didn't mean. . . . Gee, I don't. . . . Isn't there anything I can do?'

'You've got notes at ten-thirty. I think you'd better be

there and go on turning in the performance you gave on stage last night without trying to louse up my body as well as my life.'

'I just want you to know I'm sorry.'

'Being sorry isn't enough, Joe.'

It was the Wednesday evening performance, and Douglas crept into the producer's box to sit beside Ronnie Gregor.

'Strong so far,' whispered Ronnie.

Douglas nodded, three-quarters of his mind wanting the performance to leap ahead so that he could begin the technical dress rehearsal of *The Merchant*. The day had been arduous and tonight would also be long and hard. After the initial exuberation of reading the reviews, Douglas suddenly hit a down-draught of concern when he first walked into the theatre that morning. Joe Thomas looked terrible, as though a bomb had exploded inside his skull, so much that Douglas had to do an aside to Frank Ewes, ordering his assistant to get a doctor to check Joe over and, maybe, bolster him up before the afternoon performance.

There were two hours of notes for the *Othello* company, and Douglas was pleased to see that, before they went up at two-thirty, Joe looked, and sounded, considerably better. He spent much of the afternoon catching up on paper work in the office, slipping over to the theatre to do spot checks on how the afternoon performance was going. The company had been kept right up to scratch and there was no lagging or sag during the afternoon; now, at the evening performance, it looked as though the pitch would be maintained.

Douglas, in an understandably restless mood, hovered between the producer's box and the dressing-rooms all evening, ending up in the prompt corner for the closing moments of the play, his stomach thrilling to the tumult of applause which seemed to hit a higher, everestine, note than on the opening night.

He waited until the auditorium had cleared and the stage crew had begun to clear and prepare for *The Merchant* technical dress. It would be a good half an hour before anybody could possibly be in even a near state of readiness: a large number of the *Othello* cast had to change into their *Merchant* costumes and grab quick cups of coffee; the strictly *Merchant* people had to get in and be assimilated into already comfortably full dressing-rooms; a certain amount of confusion was inevitable.

Jennifer came up in her towelling robe and stood beside Douglas as he gave instructions to Frank.

'You want me to stay so we can go home together after?' she asked when the assistant had moved away.

'That's sweet of you.' He looked and sounded fatigued. 'Did I tell you how great you were tonight?'

'No.'

'Well, you were.'

'It did seem to go well. Did I lie still tonight?' During the post-first-performance notes, that morning Douglas had made reference to his wife's twitchiness as the dead corpse of Desdemona.

'Not a flicker.'

'Good, I tried hard. You want me to stay?'

'If you sit down in front and remain silent.' He flashed her a grin, called to Frank, telling him it was about time they started to call *The Merchant* company on stage. 'Prod 'em a bit.'

'I'll go and slip into some jeans.' Jennifer left him to his work.

Members of *The Merchant* company began to drift on to the stage in costume. They were not required to wear character make-up, for tonight's rehearsal would be concerned only with those parts of the production which required technical assistance from the stage crew: cues and changes of scene.

Maurice Kapstein came up in enormous good humour; Douglas also noticed Rachel Cohen and Asher (their Jessica and Lorenzo) and, at the far side of the stage, Carol Evans, her back towards him. She was walking away but her poise did not seem natural, a stiffness about the manner in which she moved. An unnatural concern flowered in Douglas's mind and he went over to her.

400

'Happy in your work, Carol?'

She turned and he saw her face, even the heavier evening make-up she was wearing could not completely disguise the extent of bruising.

'I'm fine.'

'You are hell. What happened? You get the number of the truck?'

She gave an apologetic little smile. 'No looking where I was going; that's the trouble with us drunks: I fell down the stairs last night.'

It did not ring true, but he wasn't going to stop and argue with her at this point. He had so wanted the impossible, an ideal theatre society, an integrated company, working together without clash or friction: that was impossible, but violence was something else; he smelled violence here.

'How much of you's hurt?'

'Just my face.'

'You're a liar, you're walking badly.'

'I bruised my side as well. Only a little.'

'Seen a doctor?'

'No.'

Douglas called over to Frank Ewes who came up at a trot.

'You arrange for a doctor to see Miss Evans in her apartment tomorrow morning. As early as possible. Right?'

'Right.'

'And check the time with Miss Evans.'

'Check.'

'Okay, Carol, love, there you go; no heavy lifting tonight, you'll get looked at in the morning.'

He was still uncertain about her story; no definite clues on to which he could lock, but her manner was almost furtive. He mentioned the business to Ronnie when they finally completed the technical dress rehearsal around three in the morning. (They had to cope with several difficult moments: the hydraulic lift mechanism, used to bring the corner of Shylock's house up to stage level became temperamental and stuck: as this device was used several times during the play this caused heavy delays; then an archway, used for one of the

401

Belmont exteriors, got fouled up in the fly tower, and two bulbs burned out on number three batten necessitating dropping the batten from the grid to stage level, replacing the bulbs and flying the batten again, an operation which cost them more than twenty minutes.)

Ronnie agreed to nose around and see what he could find out about Carol Evans's 'accident'.

On the following afternoon they got through the stopping dress rehearsal in almost record time. Friday was quickly on them bringing with it fury and chaos.

The same old first night anxiety flowered and buzzed in the pits of two score stomachs as the company and staff woke on Friday morning, the whole organization seeming to flex itself in preparation for a day which would include both a full dress rehearsal and a first performance.

Douglas was up early, glancing through the *Daily Mail* and the *Express* during breakfast. He would get a resumé of *The Times* later from Frank Ewes, and he was on to his second cup of coffee before picking up the weekly *Shireston Gazette*. Straight away he turned to Harvey Moir's review, immediately annoyed by the heading – MINSTREL SHOW AT FESTIVAL.

Moir began with a lengthy, pseudo-scholastic, examination of *Othello* as a play before going on to recall great *Othellos* he had seen at Shireston: there had been very few but this did not deter the journalist who used up at least half his space before getting down to the point. Douglas hardly credited what he read –

. . . Not only is Douglas Silver's production of Othello a piece of irreverent iconoclasm, it is probably the noisiest that audiences will ever have to suffer: blurring the poetry and action with a collection of strange, out-of-place sounds including shrieks, moans, clanking, music from Spanish bullfights and other horrors which have little or nothing to do with the Bard's great tragedy.

It could be called an exercise of mind over matter: Mr Silver does not seem to mind and, to him, the audience does not matter.

This terrible murder of Shakespeare is heightened by the fact that it also either drowns or stifles the, so called, actors. Joe

402

Thomas (Othello) is a nightclub singer and performs like one . . .
the only characteristic he shares with Othello is that they are both
black . . . Jennifer Frost's Desdemona reminds me of the kind of
acting we get on bad television, but this must be expected as she is
essentially a lady of the cinema . . . Edward Crispin plays Iago
as a third rate matador, more concerned with his cape than his
capability of speaking well. . . .

Douglas flung down the newspaper and made for the
telephone; but there was no reply from the *Shireston Gazette*.
By the time he put down the receiver, he realized that Jennifer had read the piece.

'Doug,' she called quietly, 'it's only a little puffed up local
bigot trying to be clever. Much safer to ignore him.'

'Ignore him, hell. I'm going to knock his teeth out.'

He had calmed only slightly by the time he reached
Adrian's office. The paper was on the PR man's desk and the
director pointed at it, stabbing with his finger. 'Have you
seen that?'

'Cool it, Doug. I've seen, read, marked and inwardly
digested, and. . . .'

'I've tried to get hold of the creep . . .'

'You've what?'

'Tried to get hold of him.'

'I trust he wasn't available.'

'Couldn't get through. No reply.'

'Douglas, calm down,' Adrian had to shout. 'You sounding off at Moir isn't going to do any good.'

'But that isn't a review, it's a string of calculated insults.
Personal insults.'

'Quite. Calculated to make you blow your top and say, or
do, something provocative.'

'They're not even good insults.'

'No, but they've done their job. You *are* outraged.'

Silence, edged with Douglas's fragmented fury. At last the
director dropped into a chair. 'Adrian, we can't leave this
unanswered.'

'Nor will we, Doug. It's a weighted, inaccurate piece of
journalistic folly, but we mustn't show that we're in any way

rattled. We take no notice of it, and if he does the same thing with *The Merchant* we take direct action.'

'What kind of action?'

'We withdraw reviewing facilities.'

'That won't stop him.'

'Wait and see. We'll scatter him to the four winds, chum. So take no notice. Leave it with me.'

'What about the company? Joe, Edward . . .?'

'Leave them to me as well. You've got a dress rehearsal and you're already late for your staff meeting.'

It was a nervous dress rehearsal, with people playing considerably under par, a natural enough reaction considering that they had a first public performance within a very few hours. However, there were no major hitches; Douglas sitting hunched in the stalls, still smarting under the *Gazette* review, making copious, niggling notes, most of which he, intuitively, did not give to the company.

Douglas found that, in spite of both Jennifer and Edward Crispin lightheartedly joking about the *Gazette* review, his fury with Moir had thrown part of his mind into turmoil. During the afternoon, when he had to attend to a myriad administration matters, the fact that the local newspaper man had gone to such pains to knock him, and succeeded, was always near to the surface of his mind.

As with the first night of *Othello*, the theatre was crowded for the initial performance of *The Merchant*, the air electric with promise. Douglas did his tour of the dressing-rooms before joining Jennifer to go into the foyer. The last person he visited was Carol Evans. Late in the afternoon, Ronnie had come over to the office and told him the result of the inquiries he had been making within the company. Felicity Durrant had told him, in confidence, what she knew of the truth and the facts now related to Douglas disturbed the director almost as much as Moir's review. His first reaction was to get hold of Joe Thomas and give him a serious warning, but, after quick and careful thought, he shelved the whole thing, especially not mentioning it to Carol when he saw her in the dressing-room. Her stage make-up covered the bruising and the doctor's report confirmed that no bones were broken, but she had to admit that she found fast movement a painful business: this, in turn, added to the director's concern; his Nerissa had a lot of fast, almost balletic movements in the production.

He sat, close to Jennifer, in the stalls, the usual first night crackle going on around him (Joe Thomas with Tommy Carr and Smiley making an impressive entrance; a very famous American film actor waving delightedly across the auditorium to Jennifer; a top TV comedy double act pushing through to their seats making comments which sparked the whole row of people into frantic laughter), a trail of anxiety, like a line of disintegrated stars running through his head. A week ago he had not been in the least worried about *The Merchant*, the company had risen to all his ideas with a precise and professional zest; but now, sitting there within an act of the production beginning, Douglas had horrendous second thoughts, as though he was suddenly seeing that nothing in his production had sound roots.

In the event he was quite wrong. The scent of success seeped from the stage almost as soon as the houselights went down and Tony's wide chequered piazza was revealed with the melancholic Antonio and his friends setting the scene of dominant business, trade and cut-throat merchant gambling, etching out Douglas's interpretation of Shakespeare's basic theme of human corruption. Quickly the various threads of plot began to weave into the harsh fabric of the play: Bassanio besotted with love for Portia; Antonio and the pernicious bone made with Shylock in order to lend Bassanio money and so push forward his suit with Portia; the Lorenzo-Jessica and Gratiano-Nerissa sub-plots; they all caught meaning and an almost Chekhovian truth in Douglas's hands.

From his first entrance (*Three thousand ducats – well*) Maurice Kapstein made a powerful, and totally believable, Shylock completely locked within the confines of his race, religion and profession, the hatred of Christians streaming almost visibly from him. In fact, Douglas had tried, throughout the production, to make all the cast work on a

405

basis of realism and belief in the characters which they portrayed.

'They're such a load of self-indulgent people and they become alive only when you do what Shakespeare is telling you to do in the text.'

Vocally, everybody rose to the night, making a clear and comprehensible sound picture, while visually the set pieces, which Tony and Douglas had devised, worked in the best interests of Theatre: the most notable instances came early in the play, the first scene at Belmont being set in an open garden at night with Portia and Nerissa dining together in extreme luxury; later came the first casket sequence. Douglas had found the whole business of the caskets one of the major stumbling blocks in the production; the idea of suitors having to choose the right casket from three – gold, silver and lead – in order to marry Portia, and the audience already knowing that Bassanio had to be the one to choose correctly, seemed to negate the earlier scenes where the Princes of Morocco and Aragon went through their wordy rituals. You either had to skip through the scenes or embroider them; Douglas had set out to make them interesting outside their intention within the play.

The first scene in which the Prince of Morocco, played by Lonnie Barnes, greets Portia had been reset to include the later sequence in which he makes his wrong choice, and Douglas had hit on what seemed to be a splendid device. The scene was played in an enclosed courtyard, Morocco making his entrance dressed rightly in scarlet flecked with gold thread, jewels flashing, deep greens and purple, his fingers ringed with gold, encrusted with sapphires and rubies, he was accompanied by an equally accoutred entourage and Douglas had purposely built the scene into a beautiful, if old-fashioned, theatrical picture.

Morocco made his first speech and Liz Column, as Portia, replied, ending with the words –

Youself, renowned Prince, then stood as fair
As any comer I have look'd on yet
For my affection.'

Lonnie Barnes, using his deep bass voice to great effect, replied, slowly taking the centre of the stage –

'Even for that I thank you:
Therefore, I pray you, lead me to the caskets,
To try my fortune. By this scimitar,
That slew the Sophy and a Persian prince . . .'

Here he drew the great curved scimitar, holding it in an aggressive pose for the rest of the short speech. The scimitar was, in fact, a stage illusionist's sword, the blade hollowed out to take a series of neatly folded large silk squares each of which could be released and delivered to the point of the scimitar in turn by a spring-loaded mechanism operated through the hand grip.

At the end of the speech, Lonnie cleaved the air with the blade, reached out dramatically and appeared to catch a dark red silk at its point, out of nowhere. Once more, a cut through the air, a lunge forward followed by a sideways movement and a second silk, dark blue, rippling at the scimitar's point; another, orange; and another, green, until the stage around Lonnie was piled, colourful, with silk; Portia, Nerissa and the servants registering happy wonder.

The moves which followed had required a long, painstaking amount of research and work. One of Morocco's assistants brought forward a burnished copper jar which the prince showed to be empty, while another assistant stood to one side with a large glass, globe-shaped, bowl. With a flourish, the prince began to pour water from the empty copper jar into the bowl, again showing the jar empty, and again pouring water, until the bowl was full. He then plunged his hand into the water, swirling it around to demonstrate its reality. Once more the hand into the water and this time it clouded and became ink black. An assistant hurried to him with a towel on which he dried his hands, while the other assistant brought a tray upon which stood three smaller copper basins.

Lonnie picked up the first basin, allowing its contents, green coloured dry sand, to run into his hand, then back into the basin. This he did several times before holding the basin high over the bowl of black water, letting the green sand stream out in a falling ribbon into the water, which he stirred, again drying his hands and going through a similar procedure with the second basin, which held red dry sand, and the third, yellow dry sand.

He turned to Portia with a bow, and then, showing his hand empty, reached once more into the bowl, bringing the hand out clenched and dripping, holding it over one of the basins on the tray, slowly letting a thin stream of dry green sand trickle down into the basin (delighted gasps from Portia and her retinue). Lonnie repeated the colourful effect with the red and yellow sand, then plunged his hand into the bowl again, swirling the water for the final time, and, as he did so, the blackness disappeared, leaving the water clear, showing no trace of sand, or anything else, within the bowl.

Portia and her attendants politely applauded (accompanied this time by the audience who rose to the theatrical wonder), while the prince's assistants ranged themselves on either side of the stage, each holding an elaborate candelabrum.

Another flourish and Lonnie appeared to pluck a ball of flickering fire from the air, crossing the stage to light the four candles on the first candelabrum on the prompt side. Another ball of fire, held, it seemed, between finger and thumb, to light the candles on the opposite side, and so on until all the candles were lighted and the prince turned to Portia with an extravagant gesture, the Lady applauding him before starting her speech –

'You must take your chance;
And either not attempt to choose at all
Or swear before you choose, – if you choose wrong,
Never to speak to lady afterward
In way of marriage: therefore be advised.'

Douglas breathed relief, the magic performed by Morocco took no more than four minutes of the production, but had to be dispatched with beauty and art to gild the scene. The audience appeared to have accepted it for what it was, an essential aspect of theatre.

Douglas was not so certain about the sequence, later, when the Prince of Aragon came to make his choice. Ronnie Gregor had been a trifle dubious about the magic for Morocco and even more discouraging when it came to Douglas's ideas concerning Aragon's casket choice. Again the scene was played out in the same courtyard, this time lit by the leaping flames of torches bracketed on to the walls, and Douglas had directed the embellishment so that it came immediately upon the prince's entrance. Like Morocco, Aragon entered with a large train of followers, notably including a guitarist and two gipsy girls, Aragon himself swathed in a long cloak reaching to the ground. Portia, with her attendants, took up positions by the caskets, ranged on a table down-stage; but before the action could begin, Aragon (played by Laurence Pern, swarthy in an olive-skinned make-up) bowed to the ladies, swept off his cloak to reveal flamenco costume; the compelling guitar rhythm started, and, joined by the two girls, Pern performed five minutes of twirling, hot, highly exciting and professional flamenco dance.

'It's too much, Doug,' Ronnie had said.

'I'm still going to use it,' Douglas was arrogantly stubborn. 'Those two scenes have to be lifted, otherwise they just go for nothing. I might as well be hung for a sheep as a lamb.'

Now, as Laurence spun and clattered through the dance, the director knew he had been right and that the extra hours spent by Pern with the Spanish dance director they had engaged for four weeks to do the choreography, had all been worth while. Doubtless it would be knocked hard by the critics, but it provided excellent theatrical spectacle as well as up-pointing the extremes of decadence which Douglas wanted the whole production to convey.

Between the two casket scenes there was a mass of action: the comedy with Launcelot Gobbo and his old father; the Jessica-Lorenzo elopement; the company carried the play forward in an upsweep of splendidly accurate work: Kapstein not overplaying the stage Jew, keeping him wholly credible (the later scene with the Jew's friend, Tubal, brought both the dimensions of grief and dignity to the character as well as the mercenary undertow –

> '*One of them show'd me a ring that he had of your daughter for a monkey.*'
>
> '*Out upon her! Thou torturest me, Tubal: it was my turquoise; I had it of Leah when I was a bachelor: I would not have given it for a wilderness of monkeys.*')

Plot crossed with sub-plot: Antonio's fortunes changed, he was forced either to pay the three thousand ducats or forfeit his bond, the pound of flesh. So to the rigged trial with the disguised Portia and the 'mercy' speech (Liz Column using her voice to woo the court with long sweeps of sound); thence to Belmont and the final moments of moonlight: a captivated, amused, entertained and enraptured audience.

Jennifer squeezed Douglas's hand as the welcome applause broke, but, in spite of the smoothness of the performance, production and the audience's undoubted pleasure, the director still felt the edge of his earlier depression: his mind holding pictures of a grinning oily Hedley Moir and the bruised face of Carol Evans.

On the following morning the reviews were oddly mixed. They all praised Maurice Kapstein's Shylock, Liz's Portia, and singled out Mark Lynton's Launcelot Gobbo. The *Daily Mail* and the *Express*, surprisingly, agreed and were in favour, but *The Times* and the *Guardian* chose to be cuttingly snide about some of the production detail, *The Times* writing about . . . *the overweight directorial scoring of the casket scenes, combined with almost camp situations, such as the beautiful poetic love scene between Lorenzo and Jessica at the end of the piece being played all-out for laughs, with the lovers plunging about in a hammock, making one think that Mr Silver was directing 'Carry On Merchant' instead of Shakespeare's play*.

It worried Douglas, who genuinely wondered if he had overdirected; yet the proof was in the audience's reaction and enjoyment (deep in his mind, Douglas knew he should not take much notice of the critics). He went into *The Merchant* matinée on Saturday afternoon, and again in the evening, delighted to see that the audience were reacting exactly as he had hoped, Shakespeare's music being clear and unblurred, coming out strongly and with meaning from behind the direction.

The Sunday newspapers, guardians of public taste and critical seal, devoted a great deal of space to the *Shireston Festival*, particularly the heavy papers, though the big selling, more popular press, like the *People, Mirror, News of the World*, all gave at least some mention (the *Mirror* even used a photograph from *Othello*). *The Sunday Times, Telegraph* and *Observer*, not only reviewed both opening productions, but also carried articles on Shireston, the *Observer* reprinting the directorial map which Tony Holt had designed for the programmes. They all drew attention to the exhibition, lavishing praise on it and calling the festival *a new 'must' for tourists, from home or abroad,* and *a threat to the kingly positions of the Royal Shakespeare, The National Theatre and Chichester.* The *Observer* even referred to it as . . . *the future Glyndebourne of English classic theatre.*

On the whole, the major reviewers seemed to go out of their way to pick up the good points: all giving outstanding approbation to the performances of Joe Thomas, Maurice Kapstein, Jennifer Frost, Edward Crispin and Liz Column. The *Observer* commented . . . *whatever Mr Douglas Silver does, or does not do, directorially within the productions, he certainly proves that William Shakespeare is able to reach forward through the centuries and tap us hard on our shoulders as easily as he did to his own contemporaries . . .*

While *The Sunday Times* reviewer wrote, *The two opening productions at Shireston leave us with no doubt that Shakespeare's genius is truly concerned with the human condition in all ages. This Othello makes us aware of the thin line upon which each one of us treads, and the ghastly tragedy of mankind's emotional instability; while the rat-race fanaticism of Shylock's Venice, coupled with the absurd, almost corrupt, waywardness of the characters in The Merchant of Venice, gives us cause to reflect on how little the world changes, echoing with the Book of Ecclesiastes, 'there is no new thing under the sun'.*

The bruising on Carol's face still looked painful, even though

411

she was smiling across Douglas's desk. He had called her in on the Monday morning, after rehearsal, not allowing himself to defer a confrontation about the true cause of her injuries.

'You look happy enough. How do you really feel?'

'I'm fine, Douglas. Truly.'

'No problems?'

'We've all got problems.'

He paused on the edge of the plunge. Then –

'I think I should tell you that I know you didn't get those bruises from an accidental fall.'

'Oh.'

'I know who gave them to you, Carol. I don't know all the details, and before you start telling me that it's none of my business, I'd like to point out that it's very much my business. If one leading actress in this company can get herself beaten up by a leading actor, then it can happen again. I can't have that; I can't take the risk.'

She was glum again, looking at the floor. Eventually she asked, 'How much *do* you know?'

'Enough. I know that Joe Thomas got very high, and I know he sorted you out.'

'It was my own fault.' Her voice flat and steady.

'You want to tell me?'

'I've behaved . . . Oh hell, let's say indiscriminately, since I've been here. . . .'

'My fault?' He did not look at her, his attention focused on his hands clasped in front of him.

'I don't know. Who can say? A bit of reaction, maybe; trying to show you – you know what I mean?'

Douglas turned down the corners of his mouth. 'Christ, every single action we take goes full circle, doesn't it? We never really know what we're doing to other people. We can leave hurricane trails without every being conscious of them.'

'It was only once with Joe.' She laughed. 'A lengthy quickie some people would call it. Then I found him drunk out of his mind after the party. I helped him, Douglas, I helped him back to his place. Then he sobered up a bit and demanded. I

412

suppose that's the worst thing a woman can do, give and then refuse when the guy asks again.'

'I don't think it's the worst thing, but it's obviously the most dangerous when the man happens to be Joe Thomas and he's stoned. But I feel so badly about this.' He was thinking, knowing that he held the other key to the situation and so had a very good idea why Joe Thomas was so drunk; and in part that also was his responsibility.

'You have no need to feel badly, Doug. Joe's still in one hell of a state about it; keeps calling me, asking me what he can do to make up.'

'I'll keep quiet and just watch from the wings.'

'It would be best. How do you feel about *Romeo*?' It was not simply an attempt to change the subject.

'I think his Juliet's superb.'

'No, seriously, how do you think we're coming?'

During the past week they had all been so concerned with the first nights of *Othello* and *The Merchant* that the other two productions had become eclipsed. Carol's question brought Douglas down to earth hard. They had just under a month to go before *Richard* and *Romeo* had to be in the Season; he was also conscious of the fact that soon after *Romeo* was in he would have to present his director's report to the board of trustees. It was a moment when Douglas felt himself poised on the edge of a great chasm; then, suddenly, events took hold of him, forcing him to action.

The telephone rang and Deborah was telling him that a David Seltzhiem was on the line. It was obvious to Douglas that Deborah did not have the faintest idea who Seltzhiem was, apart from someone undoubtedly in the theatrical stratosphere. Douglas knew well what the name meant: Seltzhiem was perhaps the biggest American theatrical impresario, in recent years even overshadowing the legendary David Merrick in his skill for picking winning London productions and shuttling them to New York, or vice versa. Without a second thought he told his secretary to put Seltzhiem through.

'Douglas Silver?' The voice gruff, gravel stained with the

hint of one who expected obedience.

'What can I do for you, Mr Seltzhiem?'

'I want to know the availability of your *Othello*. The Joe Thomas *Othello*.'

'I didn't know you'd seen it; when were you down?'

'I slipped in on Wednesday last week. Quietly, I knew you'd be having a tough time so I came incognito as it were.'

The thought of Seltzhiem going anywhere incognito baffled Douglas, the man was over six feet tall and very well built into the bargain: you could pick him out of a crowd at five hundred yards. It struck the director that his staff had slipped badly in not spotting the man, or reporting his presence.

'You've got something with that *Othello*,' continued the impressario.

'Well, thank you, but I can't help much about its availability,' Douglas tried to sound diffident. 'You see we have our actors only under seasonal contract. What were you thinking about?'

'I can give it two weeks in Boston and a minimum of six in New York. With Thomas it could run for ever, but we can't expect that.'

'I'd have to take it up with the board of trustees, after that it would be a case of negotiation with the individuals. I should imagine Joe Thomas would be tough.'

'He can have a percentage of the take. So can you. It should be a sizeable sell-out.'

'Can I talk to the chairman of our board and then come back to you?'

'Sure. Make it quick though.'

'I can't promise anything very fast.'

Another problem, but the kind which Douglas enjoyed; the thought of taking a Shireston production to the States was a matter of prestige; for him, money was not at stake here, though it would be with Joe Thomas.

He talked on the telephone with Sir Basil that evening, and the chairman told him this was a matter for the director's discretion alone. It would mean talking first with the leading

414

members of the *Othello* cast, and then with the company as a whole.

He called Seltzhiem on the following day, saying that he could not take the matter much further until his other two productions were in, but would try to get it on to some firm basis before May twenty-first: in this way he might just have another weapon when he made the director's report.

On the next Friday, the *Shireston Gazette* came out with an even more cutting, vituperative and biased review of *The Merchant of Venice*, together with a selection of reader's letters wholly in agreement with the *Othello* review. All the letters were from members of the Shireston Festival Society, undoubtedly doing their best to prove themselves the most active bigots in the business.

Adrian Rolfe once more had to quieten Douglas.

'Don't worry,' he told his director. 'I'll sort them out once and for all. Moir will have no review tickets for the first nights of *Richard* and *Romeo*; and I'll see that he is refused admission to the theatre, he's bound to get tickets from somewhere.'

'Can we do that?'

'Douglas, look on the back of your own theatre tickets, man. *The management reserves the right of admission*. From now on we reserve the right of admission to Mr Hedley Moir.'

'And we test it on the first night of *Richard*?'

'On the first night of *Richard*.'

CHAPTER THIRTEEN

The month sped past, and before anyone could realize the schedule became bowstring tight, the pre-production tension descending once more, and they were at the week-end immediately before the two first nights.

The stopping dress rehearsal for *Richard*, on the Sunday, over-ran, not because of terrible complications, but caused by the fact that the company was determined to pull off another explosive success; the sense in everyone that each tiny fragment of the production had to be right. Douglas got back to the apartment, with Jen, in the early hours and catnapped, leaving his wife in bed: Lady Anne was a comparatively small role, but Jennifer now tired quickly, feeling the first strains of the season, later her body and mind would adjust to the routine pattern and life would once more be easier.

Douglas was up, showered and shaved, early, going over to the theatre to collect some of his notes inadvertently left in the auditorium.

The stress of constant work, the fact of two productions already in the repertoire, and two near to their peak of preparation, combined with the constant flow of administration business, which ranged from trivia like signing check lists for people such as Wilfred Brownhill who, apparently, could not order a dozen electric light bulbs without Douglas's signature on the invoice, to the giant problems of the deal with Seltzhiem: all these things gave the director a warped picture, a sense that he alone carried the full weight (which, in the final score, he did) and that it was he alone who did any work. It came as something of a surprise when he entered the auditorium at around seven-thirty in the morning, to find Asher Grey with Laurence Pern, hard at it, Ronnie Gregor leaping around them, the distinctive clash of rapiers and daggers, blades meeting and circling (like a fly washing its legs, Douglas thought) working on the Tybalt-Romeo duel. Ronnie was directing all the fights.

At ten o'clock they started the *Richard* dress, smooth as honey, an illustration of how a company should operate at full stretch with the stage staff, the individuals blending to the action, Conrad never better, pushing out the charm disguising the villainy then giving it full power, a creation of immense talent supported splendidly by the company.

They came down at twelve-forty-five and Douglas completed his notes by one o'clock, following Conrad to his dressing-room and sitting with the actor while he removed his make-up.

'I've no need to tell you how much I thank heaven you invited me to play Richard.' The actor concentrating on his mirror, removing the dark wig and setting it neatly on its stand.

'You're giving exactly what I envisaged, and more. I feel I've contributed little.'

Conrad laughed vigorously. 'Contributed little? The fact you asked me, got me involved with these people,' he turned, the line of make-up showing where he had removed the wig. 'In some ways you've made a new man of me. Douglas, I know I'm a difficult devil, introspective, with my own problems – close mew'd up, as Richard himself would say. This is just what I needed at this particular point in my career. I want you to know that.'

Though he recognized that *Richard III* was not really his production, but a corporate effort, dominated by Conrad Catellier, Douglas felt more tranquil than he had at either of the Season's earlier first nights. Backstage there was more than a feeling of confidence: it radiated, a tangible thing, the first night excitement doused by something more solid, a positive trust between the separate members of the company.

Conrad seemed a little distracted when the director saw

him in his dressing-room before the performance; not nervous, but a small tension which had not been there before. Douglas did not dwell on it, you could not be certain about actors' behaviour before first performances. He wished Catellier good luck and reached the foyer, in company with Art Drays, just in time to witness the extrusion of Hedley Moir.

As they pushed through the bubble and tightly packed foyer heading for the most convenient stalls entrance, Art suddenly caught hold of Douglas's sleeve. The director looked towards his productions' manager who inclined his head forwards. Directly in front of them, Hedley Moir was making for the same entrance, and, out of the corner of his eye, Douglas could see Adrian Rolfe trying to head him off, at the same time making signs to the usher who stood at the entrance.

Douglas and Art were only a few feet behind Moir as he reached the usher who took the ticket politely.

'If you would wait just one moment, Mr Moir.'

Adrian, who had briefed all the ushers, arrived, taking the ticket and asking Moir if he would be good enough to come to one of the offices.

Moir spoke out loudly, anger inflaming the simple words. 'No, I will not come to any office. I bought this ticket in good faith because your people failed to send me my usual complimentary seats and you were never available when I telephoned. The performance starts in a little over five minutes; I am a journalist, a critic, I have to be in my seat.'

'I'm sorry, Mr Moir,' Adrian was quiet, well under control. 'It isn't your seat, it's one of the theatre's seats. Your money will be refunded, but, as far as tonight's, or any other performance is concerned, we cannot allow you to enter this theatre.'

Moir spluttered: what right had they? Why? What reason could they give? And so on. People began to crowd, stop and listen.

'We have every right, Mr Moir.' Adrian tried to edge the man away, still speaking quietly. 'If you look on the back of your ticket you'll see that we reserve the right to admit you. We're doing just that. You've made yourself a nuisance locally and we can't allow it to go on. We're banning you from this theatre as a biased critic.'

Moir seemed stunned, coloured scarlet; Art took the lull as an opportunity and pushed Douglas hurriedly on, behind the journalist, and through the entrance.

Once in his seat, Douglas attempted to expunge the wretched man from his mind by savouring, in advance, what he was about to experience with the audience.

In his mind's eye he saw Conrad, the tall, lean figure in costume as Richard, lank black hair, only a trace of the deformity, one shoulder held slightly higher than the other; he could hear the way in which the actor hit upon the core of evil, played the charmer, wooed, plotted with Buckingham and took each chance as it presented itself, until he carved a path to the throne, and then, once there, made a desperate, and treacherous, despotic bid against his unseating. Douglas saw the smile, the cunning in the eyes and Conrad's mouth half open in disbelief as the old Queen Margaret, Queen Elizabeth and his aged mother, the Duchess of York, shot out their litany of disgust against him (a scene usually played with great ritualistic formality, here done with naturalism); and on to the final horrors with the dreams before Bosworth. Again, they had tried to blend realism here, with the symbolism of the haunting, by the troop of dead whom Richard had used like stepping stones to power, presented not as ghosts in the accepted sense, but as figments of the king's conscience. The tents elaborate, Richard's on the Prompt Side (Douglas had got a word in here about it being the only side to use, stage left, the sinister side from which in the medieval Morality Plays, the Devil made his entrance); Richmond's opposite prompt; both tents made of scrim so that they could be lit from behind to reveal the interiors; Conrad entering his tent and slipping out of the back, being substituted by another actor so that he could be seen sleeping within and yet take a definite part in the dream of hauntings – a Freudian conception which had a chilling effect in rehearsal.

The houselights went down and Douglas felt the hairs rise on the back of his neck as Raymond Leggat's loud, vociferous, drum roll caught the audience's attention. The screen at the back of the set became a white hanging oblong in the darkness, then alive, fulminating with colour, not psychedelic patterns, but a mixture of smoke, fire, lightning, blood, combined with noises, diffused sounds of battle gradually dimming until a fanfare and the image of a crown, held for a brief moment on the screen before it finally dimmed and the stage became fully lit, the screen now replaced by an archway, the dirty white box of walls, empty, with the sounds of revelry coming from a long way off, swelling from time to time as though a door was suddenly opened and closed.

Conrad Catellier, as Richard, lay, half sprawled against one of the walls, almost in the angle on Prompt Side. Douglas waited for the movement and the first, almost whispered, words, so effective in rehearsal. They came –

'Now is the winter of our discontent . . .'

But something was lacking; Conrad was three-quarters of the way through the brooding opening soliloquy before Douglas realized that the man was not pushing the character with his usual power; it was as though a beautifully precisioned machine had suddenly began to run unevenly. They played the scene with Clarence on his way to the Tower, and then the wooing of Lady Anne (Jennifer well into the role) and there was still no fire, no glimmer, Conrad reaching for the words like some schoolboy giving a reasonable reading of the part. The others were all working flat out, excelling themselves, as if to drive Conrad into the pitch he had so ably created among them, but nothing worked, the realism went for little and Richard became a vocally weak puppet who appeared to be manoeuvred by those around him.

Douglas could hardly believe it, watching moment after moment, so strong in rehearsal, go for absolutely nothing. The naturalism of the political confidence trick at Baynard's Castle, just before the interval break, dwindled to a matter of words spoken within a well-set picture –

'Long live King Richard, England's worthy king!'
'Amen.'
'To-morrow, may it please you to be crown'd?'
'Even when you please, since you will have it so.'
'To-morrow, then, we will attend your Grace:
And so, most joyfully, we take our leave.'
'Come let us to our holy work again –'
'Farewell, good cousin; farewell, gentle friends.'

What had been a peak was a trough. The house-lights came up and the buzz of conversation in the auditorium had about it a disappointed note. Douglas rushed backstage; Jennifer was standing by the pass-door waiting for him, Ronnie Gregor hovered in the background.

'He's ill, Doug, I'm sure he's ill.' Her face a map of anxiety.

'Ronnie?' Douglas's voice squeaky.

'He won't let anyone near him. Touchy as a bear.'

'He'll let me near.' And Douglas was off down the passage.

Wilson, who also acted as dresser for Conrad, was outside the dressing-room door.

'I think we should get a doctor, Mr Silver.'

'Let me in.'

The elderly man nodded and opened the door for the director.

Conrad was slumped in his chair and spoke before Douglas had a chance to open his mouth.

'I'm sorry, Douglas. My pace has gone to pot and I don't seem to be able to push it. The second half will be all right, I'm getting my wind now.'

Douglas had no option but to go along with the actor. 'Are you sure you'll be all right? You don't feel ill or anything?'

'I feel fine, a bit tired, perhaps. It'll go. We'll get shocking reviews but I'll put it together. Just bear with me.'

Outside again, Douglas was confronted by Ronnie and Art. 'Tell everybody to help him, use any tricks they know, upstage him, cut in on him, just get him through it.'

He returned to his seat, mind in confusion, stomach boiling.

421

In retrospect, Douglas only had a jumbled memory of that second half: Conrad visibly slowly down, missing lines and bits of business, the other performances so exact they could not help but throw his shoddy work into relief.

Felicity Durrant's Duchess of York, strident age shrieking her assault upon the tyrant.

Liz Column doing Queen Margaret as a burning husk of a woman, making her long speeches of defilement linger home like slow exquisite torture.

These were the only moments in an otherwise theatrically grim evening. Bosworth Field and the tents of Richard and Richmond: Conrad having difficulty in finding his way out of the back of the tent so that the substitute Richard had trouble getting in and Conrad missed his cue. The final battle between the unhorsed, broken Richard and young Richmond, played knee-deep in swirling mist, but so slowly that it had all the feeling of an action replay on television.

To Conrad it was unbelievable hell. In the interval he had been dishonest with Douglas, having felt unwell all day and worse only ten minutes into the play. Now it was like a terrible nightmare where all his reflexes seemed to slow up; he knew it and could do nothing to stop it, and there were moments when he felt like a man standing outside himself, watching disaster.

At the end, he lay, slain by Richmond, but panting, clawing for breath (steel bands around his chest) until the stage lights went down and he heaved himself up, lumbering unsteadily off, stumbling over invisible furniture, not waiting for any calls, desperate for the safety of his dressing-room.

Edward Crispin and Jennifer Frost at his elbow speaking yet no words reaching his ears, only a rushing and the thump of something within him. It was hot and even the air around him seemed to constrict, like an odious gas.

Wilson took his arm and between them they carried him into the dressing-room, putting him gently on the couch.

'For God's sake, get a doctor.' Jennifer distraught after the manner of people who feel utterly useless, without the know-

422

ledge or qualifications to help someone in acute distress.

'Ronnie's already gone to find one.'

Douglas was in the doorway, above the murmurs Conrad's breathing was loud and laboured, his face the colour of thin parchment. The director reached the edge of the couch as the actor suddenly seemed to lift his head, as though straining upwards for more air. Then a long outsweep of breath and he fell backwards, a small white foam around the lips, no movement.

Jennifer grabbed at a handkerchief, wiped the lips and tried to push her fingers into Catellier's mouth to get at his tongue and start administering the kiss of life (she had seen it done on television) but could not get past the clenched teeth. Then Ronnie arrived with the doctor. Everyone was swept from the room, leaving Douglas, Jennifer and Ronnie watching as the doctor, a small, benevolent man Ronnie had found among the crowd leaving the theatre.

The macabre scene remained frozen until the doctor turned from kneeling by the couch.

'I'm sorry.' He had a west country burr to his accent. 'I'm very sorry, but Mr Catellier is dead. There's nothing more anyone can do for him.'

They had known it, but this official confirmation seemed to leave them in immobile shock; the moment suspended for Douglas whose mind became a bowl of empty questions, his arm around Jennifer's shaking shoulders; Ronnie white, staring at the thing, still in Richard's armour, which had been Conrad Catellier. The door opened and David Wills appeared with Art.

'How?' Douglas heard himself addressing the doctor.

'A coronary I should imagine. There'll have to be an inquest and a post mortem of course. I'm not a local man, there's not much. . . . I'll wait for your own doctor to get here, it would be best. . . .'

'Of course, of course.' The thousand queries floating, jumbled, in the director's head.

Then Ronnie asking, 'What do we do?' A real cry for help.

What indeed? Douglas began to fumble, then took hold, as

though he quite suddenly comprehended the true crisis.

'David.' It was a command and David Wills took a step forward. 'I want you to deal with things here. Get hold of our doctor. Have the body removed. Notify the authorities. If you don't know what to do I suggest you grab Archie Swimmer. I should imagine he's had experience.' Douglas knew that he was subjecting David to the most dismal job, but the executive director had already been through his baptism at Doris Benneto's death. Douglas turned to Art and Ronnie. 'Art, get hold of Asher Grey and take him to his dressing-room. By the time you're there I should have arrived, but don't leave him alone, and don't tell him anything. Ronnie, I don't care where they are, or what they're doing, I want the company, all of them, and the stage staff, on stage in fifteen minutes. Everyone.'

He thanked the doctor, leaving him with David, and helped Jennifer into the corridor; by the time they got out of the room the assistant stage manager's voice was coming through, clear on the loudspeaker system. 'All members of the company and stage staff on stage in fifteen minutes.' Repeated like some order within a crippled warship.

'You all right?' Douglas asked Jennifer.

'I'll be okay. It's just. . . .' She dissolved into the mist of natural tears once more.

Douglas took her down, found Liz Column and Rachel Cohen and left her in their care. He then went straight to Asher Grey's dressing-room.

The young actor looked nervous, sitting on the edge of his chair talking to Art. Douglas nodded, giving Art the signal to leave them alone, then he went over to the couch, sat down and lit a cigarette.

'Is it true?' asked Asher with the natural hint of anxiety, his face solemn.

'About Conrad?' equally grave.

The young actor nodded.

'Yes, Ash. I'm sorry but Conrad is dead. They think it was a coronary.' He took a long pull at the cigarette. 'I'll be perfectly honest with you; I don't know what to do. The only

424

thing I could think of was to get you down here and talk before we consult the company.'

'I know what Conrad would have wanted.'

Douglas took a deep breath. 'Oh yes, Ash, we know what Conrad would want. The show must go on and all that stuff. It's emotional thinking, mate, but we have to be realistic, practical. Is it feasible for the show to go on? Do you realize what you'd be letting yourself in for?'

'I think so.'

'Asher, you're already playing Cassio and Lorenzo. During the next three days you've got to get through a technical dress rehearsal, a stopping dress and a full dress of *Romeo*, not to mention a first night, and it's a bloody long play. Now this terrible thing, tragedy, has happened and you're also faced with a performance of *Richard*, which you've never played, never rehearsed, tomorrow afternoon. . . .'

'I know Conrad's Richard inside out, backwards, forwards, standing on my head.' He said it with all the arrogance of his art.

'But can you do it all? Physically it'll. . . .'

Asher was on his feet. 'I'm a repertory actor, Douglas. Yes, I'll cope, more than cope. I'll be bloody tired by Sunday, but. . . .'

'And what about after Sunday? What about all the nights until the end of the season?'

'What about all the nights before you invited me here, Douglas? It's what I've been doing, for Christ's sake; a bit more complex perhaps, but I'm a repertory actor. Conrad was a very great actor. The public have the right to see his *Richard*; I can't give them mine, but I'm probably the only person who can reveal Conrad's *Richard* to them. Come on, Douglas; I can do it, and Romeo, and Lorenzo, and Cassio. What's your alternative? Close the festival for a week's mourning?'

Douglas thought for a moment, pondering the actor's ambition and confidence in terms of endurance, the whole shape and scope of the season, even his own personal situation. 'All right,' he finally said. 'We'll reschedule the rehearsals so that you can get one run-through tomorrow morning for *Richard*. Okay?'

'It's more than I need.'

'Let's hope you can stay that positive.'

They went up on stage where the company sat in a large semi-circle, silent, a strangely subdued, almost reverent awe gripping them with fact that one of their number, an important actor in any context, had been removed so swiftly from them.

Douglas spoke for the best part of twenty minutes: first of the shock and pain that had come so quickly and finally; then of Catellier, the man as he had come to know him; the professionalism and attack; the painstaking painting of character; his final immersion in Richard; their last real conversation when Conrad had told him that playing Richard was just what he had needed at this point in his career. He then went on to talk of things practical, rearranging a run-through of *Richard* for the following morning at nine, with Asher Grey playing the lead; a technical dress rehearsal of *Romeo* after *Richard* came down on Wednesday night; the stopping dress on Thursday morning, starting at ten-thirty, and the dress on Friday morning at ten, with the first performance on Friday night. He did not need to suggest that they all got to bed as soon as possible.

Adrian was waiting on stage when he finished, and Jennifer came up still looking shaky and white.

'I'll have to ask you to come into the office now,' said Adrian. 'There are at least three national newspapers waiting to speak with you, and I have to arrange for you to tape a couple of television tributes.'

Douglas nodded, beckoning to Ronnie and Frank who had just appeared. 'Jen,' he turned to his wife. 'I'm going to ask Ronnie to take you home. I'll be up as soon as possible, but I want you to get to bed. Frank, I want you with me now.'

The group broke up, Jennifer clinging to her husband for a second before they parted, as though willing a small part of courage into him. He alone had to face the reporters, the cameras and the obituary writers.

'What's happening about the press? The critics I mean.' Douglas asked Adrian as they left the theatre and headed through the darkness for the house.

'Once they know Asher's doing it they'll be knocking on the doors to get in. I'll have to get at Graham Harper and see what he's got left available for tomorrow night. I'll give the Sundays priority, but that's going to be my headache, you mustn't worry about it. You think Asher can do Richard?'

'Convinced, so don't throw any doubts my way. How did you end up with friend Moir?'

'There's going to be bad sweat there, but leave that to me as well. Jesus, he got hysterical in the office, calling down William and all his ancestors on you and the company, not to mention the wrath of the Shireston Festival Society and the late earl. Out to get you, I should imagine.'

'That's all I need, Moir and a posse of militant Shakespeare-only-done-as-art-and-beauty people littering up the lawn and throwing stones.'

'You want me to get a riot squad?'

'Only to control Joe Thomas.'

Douglas eventually got to bed at two-thirty, Jennifer still awake, looking frightened and ill.

'Come on, Jen, love, we've got a great deal on our plates, I can't have you cracking up. I need you, baby, not just as an actress either.'

She gave him a small smile. Conrad's death had obliterated any of the other realities which surrounded them. 'I know. He must have been a very lonely man, Doug.'

'There's loneliness and loneliness. He had a great talent which, maybe, called for that odd aloofness he seemed to wrap around him.' He sensed her emotion rising again. 'Let's stop talking about it, Jen. I've been doing nothing else with the press since I left you. Sorry, but I need sleep to tackle tomorrow.'

She reached up to kiss him and they entwined for some two minutes.

'I love you, Doug.'

Together, close in bed, they clung to each other, not

speaking, but understanding in the last moments before sleep. Jennifer told herself that they had now ridden out the storm which had once threatened to swamp them. The future was safe within reason and, more to the point, in some strange way the respect she held for Douglas had been restored to its old high proportion. Her mind slipped on to the immense task which Asher Grey had undertaken and, in the darkness, she crossed her fingers.

Asher, with good sense, had purposely underplayed during the morning run-through, but, at the matinée and, now, the evening performance of *Richard* it was clear to all the company what he was doing: a sustained and brilliantly dignified imitation of Conrad Catellier's Richard III; every line, word, action, facial movement copied in meticulous detail as the actor had noted it in rehearsal. Much later in the season, Asher admitted to Douglas that the early performances were basically instinctive, relying completely upon what his memory had retained, including the vocal trick habits which were entirely Conrad's. The play and production appeared perfectly married to the actor; Asher took it so far that, when he went forward for his call after the evening performance, he did not even smile at the warmth of the reception, his whole being so taken up with the idea of ultimate evil swathed in elegant charm. Nor was it simply the audience who were doing the applauding, the company rose to Asher's performance and their praise rang out long after the audience had started to leave.

It was a different matter with *Romeo and Juliet*; here, Asher was concerned with his own creation of character, just as Douglas was anxious with the complexity of his production, made technically difficult by Tony's settings, the streets worked out in up to four different levels, houses and balconies overhanging cobbles, the interiors wide with huge archways and supporting columns: they were a nightmare for Archie Swimmer who had to completely clear the grid for *Romeo*.

With *Romeo and Juliet* Douglas had been concerned with

classicism, poetry of colour and movement as well as the tragic poetry of the play, and was excited from the start by working within the somewhat operatic sets, not allowing them to dominate him, but using them to their full stretch, filling them with people, yet letting attention be focused only on the two or three people playing the scene. It had been a challenge and all these things had caused initial problems, now dealt with and resolved so that the production had become tightly worked, full of movement and action. He told the company, 'I want to prove that you can play this piece classically and still come up with something as box office as *Love Story* which says twice as much about where it's at; to show people you don't necessarily have to do *West Side Story* to make this play sing, dance, snap its fingers and shout its message.'

At another time he said, 'The human condition doesn't change all that much. What was true of the youth of fourteenth-century Italy is still true today. They experience the same basic emotions, they hold in and then explode with the same frustrated violence.'

True, the director had argued that he was not in any way going to up-point the racial theme, but he had not been in rehearsal long before discovering that by the very action of giving the play a black Juliet (with black relations, and only the odd white retainer, Felicity Durrant's Nurse, for instance) he had automatically thrown the play into the passionate, violent arena of racist politics, the whole theme taking on a different tone: not just a romantic tragedy of great beauty which spoke of the ageless ferment of youth, but the added dimensions of love and hate between the races; the finale becoming a damning condemnation against all who thrive on racial discord.

Asher and Carol were both most conscious of this last point; on stage in performance, they both related to the one experience they had lovingly shared together, their warmth towards one another being clear for all to see. In the back of his mind Douglas half wondered what the outcome would be once Julia Philips saw the production on the first night.

429

Together they worked, through the *Richard* performances, the technical dress and the stopping dress of *Romeo*. On Friday morning the press gave its glowing verdict on *Richard*: all except the *Shireston Gazette* from which blurted the disgruntled headline – OUR CRITIC IS BARRED FROM FESTIVAL, followed by a long and wordy diatribe against the festival as a whole, under its current management, and Douglas Silver's directorship in particular.

Adrian pointed to the short obituary they had printed for Conrad at the bottom of the front page. 'You can see how well they've got their priorities sorted.'

Douglas shrugged, he had neither the time nor energy to worry about the trivial protest of a biased editor. They had to get through the dress rehearsal of *Romeo* and at three o'clock he was to be present at Conrad's inquest, while the first performance of *Romeo* was scheduled, as usual, for seven-thirty; there might, he reflected, be a moment for breath when it was all over.

Asher was in the midst of battle, the clash, clamour and screams aching on his head.

'*Fight, gentlemen of England! fight bold yeoman!*
Draw, archers, draw your arrows to the head!
Spur your proud horses hard, and ride in blood;
Amaze the welkin with your broken staves!'

But why were they fighting in front of Shylock's house? It was the wrong play and now Edward Crispin was giving him a cue –

'*Will you hear 't again?*'

What was the line? They were in the drinking scene and now it was Cassio's line –

'*No; for I hold him to be unworthy of his place that does those things –*'

No, wrong again, for he was in bed –

'*It was the lark, the herald of the morn,*
No nightingale; look, love, what envious streaks . . .'

But this was not Carol's supple body beside him. Slowly Asher came to consciousness, dragging his senses into the

430

day. Friday; he had been correct the last time: today he had to be, stay being, Romeo. He eased his body, stretching and rubbing his back into the mattress, testing his muscles, aching from the unaccustomed Richard. He was erect, that consciousness he could not avoid, and for a second he turned, his arm beginning to stretch out towards the still sleeping Julia; but he sank back again, fondling himself, it was not Julia he wanted; as Asher Grey and Romeo his need was for the dark Carol Evans, his Juliet; the urge so deep, the desire so specific that he even had a mild attack of guilt for being so close to the naked Julia. Asher did not try to analyse his emotions. On waking he desired Juliet, Carol Evans; it was plain and simple, the manner in which his mind and body reached out for her, shrinking from Julia Philips, who, throughout the frenzied activity which followed Conrad's death, had never for a moment, when they were alone, stopped demanding, like a child who is not getting attention.

Asher slipped quietly out of bed; it was eight-thirty and he had to be in the theatre by nine-fifteen at the latest if they were going up at ten. He showered, shaved, dressed and swallowed a cup of coffee, pleased that Julia had not awakened, so that he could steal from the flat without being engaged in some barrage of words.

The tensions had returned, the company concentrating on the vast production, but they got through the dress rehearsal with a minimum number of problems (Archie's stage crew taking half a minute too long over a crucial change, throwing the lighting plot a fraction; Felicity Durrant missing one cue, and Joe Thomas, as Capulet, drying during the last moments of the play). It was enough to fray some tempers and set moods on edge. Douglas gave his notes on stage afterwards, conscious that he had to imbue all of them with a sense of calm.

They broke at one-forty-five, Asher finding himself walking off with Carol; they had been together during Douglas's notes, Carol's hand lying gently on his. Now she stopped, turning to him.

'I suppose this is where I wish you all the luck in the world for tonight. I'll give you all I can, love, you know that.'

'You've got nothing to worry about; you're going to be great.' He paused to allow Liz Column, who played Lady Montague, and Murray Fleet (Paris) to pass. 'I think we should be together before tonight.'

She looked at him eagerly, a slight inclination of the head.

'My dressing-room at six?' he raised his eyebrows.

Her brow furrowed. 'Is that safe for you? There'll be people around.'

'I'm only concerned for us, and for tonight.'

'Please, Ash,' a hand on his arm. 'I want to, you don't know how much; I'm not trying to find excuses, but, well, physically won't it bush you?'

'It'll be the same for you. Under normal circumstances the answer would be yes. But I don't know, won't the performance benefit from the performance, so to speak?'

She gave him a smile, lighting up the whole of her face. 'Six o'clock.'

The Coroner's Court returned a verdict of death from natural causes on Conrad Catellier, the post mortem proving, without doubt, that the actor had suffered a massive coronary thrombosis. Douglas got back to the house around four, depressed at having to listen to the evidence, and give his own small contribution. The funeral was to take place on Monday in London, and there would be a memorial service next month.

Jennifer was in high spirits, she had no part in *Romeo* so would be with her husband all evening. By five o'clock she had started to prepare for the evening, lying in a hot bath before the statutory hour in front of the mirror at the dressing-table, her long white evening gown laid out on the bed.

Douglas, stripped and in his bath robe, waiting to use the bathroom, watched her as she came through wearing only her pretty white underclothes.

'I suppose it'll be all go in the bedroom after tonight?' She laughed, catching his eyes on her.

'You know me,' he grinned. 'Once I've stopped creating in

theatre the urge has to come out in other ways.'

She pursed her lips, blowing him a kiss. 'About bloody time.' She held up a hand as he moved towards her. 'And don't start now or we'll be late for your opera.'

Asher sat quietly in his dressing-room at six o'clock. It was early and there were not many members of the company in yet, but he had taken the precaution of seeing his dresser, telling him that his services would not be required until seven o'clock, and hanging a DO NOT DISTURB sign on the door. All day he had managed to avoid Julia, knowing that, for him, it was essential to get the first night over before being plunged into her harassment again. He felt perfectly at ease, with only the normally light mixture of excitement and nervousness about the night.

A quiet tapping on the door and Carol slipped into the room, wearing a turquoise silky robe which clung to her body as she moved.

Asher rose, extending his arms to her. 'We're going to slay them stupid tonight.'

She kissed him quickly on the mouth. 'There won't be a dry eye in the house.' Then, as he pulled her closer she whispered, 'Get the tension out of me, Ash. Take me like before.'

She wore nothing under the robe, and the couch, though a narrow bed, was big enough to take both of them. There was nothing quick about it, in spite of Carol's urgency: a steady and slow, tender, loving experience, sliding into each other, and then up among those indescribable shapes and colours which gloss the mental images, the landscape of minds mounting the sexual plane together.

Half an hour later they wished each other well for the night, kissing at parting, knowing that when they met again it would be as Shakespeare's star-cross'd lovers, and, by their intimate knowledge, they might convey to the audience the same passions which they had just engendered.

Douglas and Jennifer were about to leave the apartment, at almost twenty minutes to seven, when the telephone rang. It was Adrian for Douglas, unexcited but with a cold fire in his voice. Douglas took the telephone and greeted him cheerfully.

'Our friend Moir's out for revenge,' said Adrian.

'He's here? On the premises?'

'I don't know if he's here, but all his pals from the bloody Shireston Festival Society are. We have a demonstration on our hands, Doug.'

'What sort of a demonstration?'

'Peaceful, I think, but there are a dozen or so protesting in front of the theatre.'

'How protesting?'

'Marching up and down with banners.'

'Are they out for trouble?'

'Difficult to say. Looks untidy though. The press have been taking pictures.'

'Put someone on to it: Frank or Robin. If it gets out of hand send for the police to clear them out, but don't let any of our people go near.'

As it turned out, the protest did little immediate harm. Douglas and Jennifer saw them as they made their way over the crowded lawns to the theatre: a group of mainly middle-aged, shabby-looking men and women parading up and down carrying banners which read – WE DEMAND SHAKESPEARE AS RICHARD LONGWELL INTENDED – THE GOLD OF POETRY NOT THE TARNISHED WORK OF SILVER – OUT WITH SILVER'S PAPERBACK CHEAP PRODUCTION – HANDS OFF SHAKESPEARE: GIVE US THE TRUTH.

'They look just what they are,' Douglas muttered. 'People locked inside tiny, unimaginative minds. Out-dated pseudo-intellectuals, fallen behind.'

Of any of the protesting Shireston Festival Society had bothered to go into the theatre that night they would have been able to hear the pure gold of Shakespeare. True they would also have been appalled by the racist theme which resulted from a black Juliet, the opening moments lit strongly, so that the heat of an Italian summer glanced from the walls of Tony Holt's streets, and from the thinly dressed, sultry bodies of the company, the girls lingering on balconies to watch the black Capulets tangle with white Montagues in tumbling, strenuous, frightening violence.

The ball: with Raymond Leggat's updated beat music heavy, yet blending with the colour and glitter of the renaissance costumes, making the scene instantly classic, yet as modern as tomorrow's pop song.

The outstanding moments, as expected, came from Asher and Carol, the distinctive beauty of Shakespeare's love scenes given a full naturalistic glow so that the poetry shone through against the urgent impetuosity which is the final undoing of the lovers.

To Douglas it was as though he had not seen the production before; together, Asher and Carol gave everything a new lift making moments authentically moving. At the balcony scene (Tony had created a single, large and solid white stone balcony which seemed to hang in darkness supported only by a slim pillar, rising some eight feet from the stage floor) Asher leaped down for his exit speech, radiant, not bearing to leave Juliet, yet with all the sexy puppy love which is essential to both roles –

'Sleep dwell upon thine eyes, peace in thy breast!'

Seeing Carol, as Juliet, still on the balcony, he did not turn away for the last three lines, as they had consistently rehearsed, but climbed swiftly back up the pillar for another fast embrace, getting down to the stage floor again just in time to shout the words about going to Friar Lawrence's cell as the lighting plot slowly dimmed.

Later, the audience watched, attentive, charged with emotional static as dawn came up on Juliet's bedroom and the discordant dawn chorus screeched out before the lovers slipped stark naked from their bed to stand, clasped in each other's arms at the great window.

So, while there was beauty, splendour and richness about the night, there was also the edge of danger as black clashed with white. By turns one could sense the audience being outraged and deeply moved as the events of the tale took their inevitable toll: the romantic Mercutio (Edward Crispin giving a memorable Queen Mab speech) killed; the Nurse fussing over her charge, alternately tender and ribald; the death of Tybalt; the baulked plot which sends Romeo to the Tomb not knowing that his Juliet is only feigning death; the slaying of Paris; Romeo's final speech over the sleeping Juliet (for a second, Douglas's mind went back to his first meeting with Asher Grey and the audition in the shabby rehearsal room; he little thought then that Asher would be the saviour of the festival); Juliet's waking to the terrible truth, her suicide and the forging of new bonds between the rival families, black hands clasping white in a sustained moment of high emotion.

Everything that followed was an anti-climax. Not only Asher, but also the whole company, felt drained, as though they had been through some highly strung period of unbearable pressure, when minds and bodies were subjected to the ultimate strain. The aftermath of gloom, from Catellier's death, still hung, like a pocket of foul air, over them, and in that climate nobody had taken any steps to arrange celebrations after the first night of the season's final production. For the leading members of the company there was relief in this, as most of them wanted a brief respite.

Asher was not destined to get immediate mental peace. When the dressing-room cleared, he showered, changed, looked in on Carol, who was only just beginning to unwind, and told her that he would see her at the nine o'clock work out, which was to be followed by Douglas's notes from tonight's performance; he then, unwillingly, made his way back to the house, his head full of the things he felt had not been quite right about tonight's work, the dissatisfaction of any professional.

Julia sat on the bed, her face flushed and mouth in a sulky pout; it was only then that Asher realized she had not even come back to his dressing-room after the performance.

'Where did you get to?' he asked, trying to be easy and natural in spite of the nervous anxieties which had begun to crowd in as soon as he saw her.

'Did you expect me to get anywhere?'

'What do you mean?'

'You know what I mean.'

'Sorry, love, I'm really not with you. It's been a tough day as they say in the trade. Is something wrong?'

'You have the gall to ask that? Something wrong?' Voice hitting the high, uncontrollable pitch.

'For Christ's sake, Julia.' More tired than angry.

'You and your black whore, that's what I'm talking about, that's what's wrong. Anyone who knows you, has half an eye, could tell.'

'I don't know –'

'What I'm talking about? No, I bet you don't. Well, I'll be generous, I'll spell it out. I'm talking about you and your precious Juliet, your beloved Carol bloody Evans, that nig-nog tart.'

'What about me and Carol?' Suddenly, in the eye of fatigue, he went cold with decision.

'I know you too well.' She sat, very still, like some danger-ous reptile about to strike, Asher thought. 'Such warmth and passion, they'll all say. You can't do all that on Stanislavsky or RADA training. You've been laying her, you bastard, making me look a stupid fool. No wonder Douglas took bloody good care to make sure I didn't get into any *Romeo* rehearsals. Well, Mr Asher Grey, nigger lover of nineteen eighty-one, you're going to have to make up your mind, because I'm not hanging around here as your bit of spare, to be made a laughing stock. You can go with Carol Evans or –'

'Julia,' he roared, eyes closed, blazing. 'Will you be a professional for one minute and shut that stupid clack. I've had just about enough, not only tonight, but the whole damn. . . .' He reached for the words. 'You're a bore, a bitch and a bore; selfish, unfeeling, emotionally unstable, and a misery to live with; I've had it, all that I can take; you're only good for one thing, Julia, and frankly I'm getting bored with the way you do that. Make your own arrangements, stay or go, it doesn't matter. I'm fucking tired and I want some rest and sleep.' He turned and marched out of the room, through the living-room, slamming the door behind him, padding down the stairs, out and across the lawn to the theatre.

They had employed a nightwatchman since the start of the season and he recognized Asher at once, letting the actor in, even making him a cup of tea, before he retired to the couch in his dressing-room (there was still the light scent of Carol's body on the leather) to drop into a sleep disturbed by patterns of unpleasant dreams. In the dim rear of his consciousness he knew what he wanted and what he would do next.

Inevitably, the newspapers on Saturday, and especially on Sunday, took Douglas to task for altering the natural context of Shakespeare's *Romeo and Juliet* by introducing the racist theme. They all grudgingly admitted that the added excitement did explode a contemporary topic into magnificent theatre, but argued that it had nothing to do with the Bard's original intention.

However much the press was at odds with Douglas's productions, there was lavish praise for the company; the Sunday nationals reviewed both *Richard III* and *Romeo*, singling out Asher Grey for the main attention (though Carol stole some of the *Romeo* notices), *The Sunday Times* saying that *the two performances bestride the very poles of character, so much that it is, at times, difficult to comprehend the fact that the same actor is playing the fiend Richard and the love-sick young Romeo. He is the brightest thing to have reached the theatre in the last five years.*

The *Observer* quoted Asher as *a genuine, unique talent which all lovers of Theatre will watch with increasing interest.*

Edward was praised, both for his Buckingham and Mercutio; Carol Evans had ravishing compliments for her Juliet (*a bodily grace which defies description added to a voice which conjures a golden quality out of the air*, said the *Sunday Telegraph*); Felicity Durrant, Liz Column and Rachel all came in for their share. Yet the reviews were really stolen by Asher.

One of the people who read, marked and took note was Ivor Armstrong.

At the age of thirty-one, the tall, distinguished Ivor Armstrong already had six solid profit-making films to his credit as a producer-director; a man of excessive energy and talent he had recently acquired a property titled *The Lord Deputy*, a brilliant screenplay based upon the exploits of the second earl of Essex, his ill-fated mission to Ireland and the resultant, so-called, Essex Rebellion in the City of London. The treatment was ingeniously up to date, using visual technique more than language to create mood, situations and tensions, yet written with authentic style and excitement.

A man of Armstrong's ability had little trouble in promoting *The Lord Deputy*, which he planned to shoot, in England and Ireland, next spring. He was currently on the verge of casting, looking for new faces and new talents. Asher Grey's name, coupled with the high references and descriptive praise of the reviewers, came out of the blue to him as a possible godsend.

He made an immediate note for his secretary to book him into an hotel at Shireston and reserve tickets for both *Richard III* and *Romeo and Juliet*.

If Douglas Silver hoped for a period of relaxation once his last production was in, the expectation was in vain. His presence was much in demand as director of the Shireston Festival, in both his administrative and artistic capacities. The discipline of company life had to be maintained, so the morning work periods continued; there were the personal problems of individual company members; and also his own work on the director's report, soon to be presented to the board of trustees. For Douglas this was now the most important matter: the immediate future, for himself and many members of the company and staff, rested on his reappointment as director, a decision which would allow him to prepare for the next season, give him an opening to plan, approach actors concerning their availability, and generally get things under way at an early stage.

Seltzhiem had almost completed his negotiations, and it was practically certain that the *Othello* company would be off to America for eight weeks as soon as the season ended in September.

It was from Ronnie Gregor that Douglas got the first

intimations of Asher Grey's domestic problem.

'I gather he's moved most of his stuff into Carol's apartment, and Julia's freaking out on every possible occasion.'

'I suppose I'd better talk to him,' said Douglas. 'Though I'd prefer to leave it until after the twenty-first when I've seen the board.'

'Well, it doesn't seem to have affected his work,' commented Ronnie. 'Certainly not his Romeo; with Carol he's incredibly good.'

'Let's hold it a little longer then. Give me a little air.'

But Asher got to Douglas first. On the Tuesday before the meeting of the board, they played *Romeo and Juliet*. There had been a *Richard* performance on the Monday, and Asher felt naturally fatigued when he came off, irritated when his dresser said that someone was asking for him at the stage door. The vexation left as soon as he discovered that it was Ivor Armstrong who wanted him, Armstrong's name was immediately identifiable to anyone in the profession.

Working so tightly, and within such a closed framework, combined with the stress of walking out on Julia had left Asher with little time to ponder on the difference his success within the season could make to his future. He was, therefore, amazed when the producer shook him warmly by the hand and told him he had a proposition to make. When the details were revealed Asher was even more taken aback.

'I know I have to talk with your agent, but what I'm offering is a flat fee of twenty thousand pounds for a maximum fourteen weeks' shooting, starting in April of next year. That gives you plenty of time, but I have to have a fast answer,' Armstrong had said.

'How fast? I mean I've got to read the screenplay and . . .'

The producer laughed. 'I don't mean tomorrow, Asher, but I have to be a man of quick, sometimes instinctive, decisions myself. I'm basing the offer of this part on what I've seen you do here; for all I know you might come out like Dracula's mother on film, but I don't think so. No, you've got a couple of weeks to make up your mind.'

Asher read the screenplay that night and it lit up areas of

his mind which had been dormant since he left RADA as an enthusiastic actor, thinking he held the world by the throat. The dilemma was further increased by his own knowledge of his needs and capacity as an actor: what he really needed was one more season in a situation like Shireston. The next morning he asked to see Douglas urgently. Douglas, imagining that the domestic situation had taken a drastic turn for the worse, gave him an interview straight away.

Asher went through Armstrong's proposition in detail. 'The screenplay's a smash, it can't fail,' he told the director. 'I know I'd make it.'

'Then where's your problem?'

'Deep down I don't feel ready yet. Oh, the acting's all right, but I don't want to face the other things without some more experience; you know, all the things you hear about when people make it big. The pressures.'

Douglas nodded. 'But you've been through them, you're going through them, here. What you're really asking me, Ash, is do I need you here, at Shireston, next season, right?'

'I suppose so.'

'Well, I can't help you. Not yet anyway. I won't know if I'm going to be in charge until Friday when the board meets and I deliver my report. Even then there's just a slight chance that they'll delay their decision, they don't have to tell me until September by the terms of my contract. If you're going to be free, then of course I'll want you here, but, at the same time I wouldn't wish to stand in the way of something like this.'

'Can I come and see you after the board meeting then?'

'Yes,' he hesitated, uncertain whether he should bring up the domestic issue at this point. 'Ash, how are things? I gather you and Julia. . . .'

Asher Grey sighed. 'I don't know how things are, Doug. I couldn't take Julia and give of my best at this particular moment, so I've had to pull out.'

'But you're living with Carol?'

'I'm living in Carol's apartment. Oh sure, yes, we have a thing, but there's nothing permanent. I wish I could get into

441

a situation as clear cut as that. I've been with Julia for a long time, there's a sort of natural love-hate relationship upon which we both used to thrive. It sounds like a paradox, but I seem to need friction to spark me.'

'I guess the friction would come in time with Carol.' Douglas felt a trace of sadness, he also knew what it was like with the black girl, the enthusiasm she had to bolster a tired confidence, making you into a kind of marvellous human being. Did he mean making you feel like a God?

Asher chuckled. 'I expect it happens with every relationship given time. Leave me to sort that one out, Douglas. I'll find my own level, no doubt.'

For a good fifteen minutes after the young actor left his office, Douglas sat and thought about the strange patterns made by life: the way in which one relationship led to another, the chance meeting or sudden idea blooming into a completely new way of life . . . or something else.

After a while, he shook himself free of the wandering thoughts, returning his attentions to the facts and figures of his report.

Friday, twenty-first of May was a warm day and Douglas found that time had a trick of turning full circle on him; there he was, back in the trustees' board room, the pretentiously panelled chamber with the oil painting of Richard Longwell hanging behind the chairman's place at the end of the long oak table; and there was still the scent which reminded Douglas of that 1964 Exhibition in Stratford-upon-Avon.

Only four of the trustees were present: Sir Basil, smiling encouragement to Douglas, Rupert Crown and William Dempsey, both looking sour, and George Tupnall, the local solicitor, as sad and precise as ever. Promptly at two o'clock Sir Basil called the meeting to order; they went through the minutes and preliminaries, after which the chairman asked Douglas if he would make his formal report.

Douglas got to his feet where he remained for the next three-quarters of an hour, first giving a detailed account of what had been done to the property, the refurbishing, the

442

work on the new theatre restaurant, within the theatre itself; he then went on to comment on the company and the productions, pausing to pay tribute to Conrad Catellier; he talked about the achievements in artistic terms, and the exhibition, giving due praise to Tony Holt and David Wills; then the forthcoming American tour, stressing that this was the first time a Shireston company had played outside the festival, let alone the country, and coming, at last, to their financial statement. Things were in a good and healthy state, they were playing to houses with a ninety-eight per cent capacity and the bookings were well up to this standard for the remainder of the first three-quarters of the season; there was no reason to think that there would be any drop in houses once the last quarter's bookings were open to the public. On top of this the exhibition was already showing a profit and the restaurant would undoubtedly give them at least a fifteen per cent margin by the end of the season; at this stage it was difficult to give an exact figure regarding total profits from extras like programmes for the theatre or exhibition, sales of postcards and the like, but they were certain to at least break even, and possibly might come out with a five per cent profit. In all, Douglas was confident that he would be able to show at least three-quarters of the board's original investment returned to them.

He had hardly sat down when Dempsey began to quiz him over the figures, pompous as ever, some of his questions even verged on being impertinent, but Douglas had made sure that his figures were accurate and nobody could change the fact that, provided the bookings continued to come in at the same level, Douglas would be well inside the board's margin, maybe even higher.

At last, Dempsey seemed to have exhausted his queries, and Sir Basil began to speak.

'I take the greatest pleasure in congratulating Mr Silver on the success of his first season at Shireston. I can think of no area in which improvement has not been made –'

'I can,' from the hangdog George Tupnall. Douglas knew what was to come, Tupnall was a local man and had undoubtedly been approached.

'I am most concerned,' continued the solicitor, 'about the situation which has developed with regard to the relationship between the festival and the town.'

'By the town I presume you mean the local newspaper,' Douglas replied acidly. 'The *Shireston Gazette*.'

'No, I mean important local people.'

'The Shireston Festival Society.'

'Some are members of that body. But we should remember that there are people concerned here who were once personal friends of the late earl. Mr Silver and his staff have seen fit to ban the local newspaper from access to the theatre. There have even been protests – physical protests; and there are rumours of gross immorality and wild orgies at Shireston House. I must admit that some of the actors here look as though they needed a good wash and a change of clothing.'

'I can assure the board that there have been no orgies, nor, to my knowledge, has anyone been corrupted. The way in which individuals dress is, to my way of thinking, a personal matter. I am not running a school for young people here, I'm running a festival company.' Douglas met the accusation calmly. 'As for protests, there has been one, very lame protest. Half a dozen local people, very much a minority group, paraded in front of the theatre with banners which seemed to imply that they were the guardians of all Shakespearian theatre.'

'They have a right to be heard.'

'They have been heard; they've aired their bigoted views in the local press. I understand from my director of publicity that some have written letters to *The Times* and the editor of that august newspaper has not seen fit to publish them. I can bring evidence of their bigotry if the board wishes to waste its time, but –'

'What about the banning of the local newspaper?' Sir Basil sounded concerned.

'Most serious consideration was given to that. Again the evidence is in the press reports. Mr Hedley Moir, the editor of the *Gazette*, with whom I presume you are all acquainted, is also the dramatic critic. From the day of my appointment he has made disparaging remarks about the company and the season. When it came to reviewing the plays it is quite obvious, if you read him in context of all the other reviews, that the man is biased out of all proportion. We came to the conclusion that his reviews could only aggravate the local situation, so we barred him from admission to the theatre.'

'Thank you, Mr Silver,' Sir Basil appeared to have accepted Douglas's version. 'The board will let you know if an individual report on this matter is needed. We would like you to leave us now so that we can deliberate on the matter of whether your contract is to be extended and if so for what period. You must be aware, of course, that we are doing this today at your request; that we are in no way obliged to come to a decision at this stage.'

Douglas pursed his lips. 'I understand, Sir Basil, but may I briefly explain to the board that, if I'm to accompany *Othello* to the United States, a later decision will hold next season in jeopardy. If I am to follow through with a second season, I do need to start planning and signing people in the immediate future. I'm also thinking about the availability of actors and actresses, many members of the company are already coming to me for advice about their futures.'

'I shouldn't have thought actors were scarce,' unfeelingly from William Dempsey. 'I hear there are twenty-two thousand of them out of work in this country.'

'That is precisely why some of the company are concerned,' retorted the director.

Sir Basil gave Douglas a knowing look as he left the room for his long, somewhat agonizing, wait. He was not summoned to return until almost five o'clock, and it was obvious, from the atmosphere, that things had not gone easily. Basil Daley looked furious and spoke with some embarrassment.

'Mr Silver, the board has had some difficulty in coming to an agreement. All of us are not over anxious about the situation between festival and town, but we would appreciate it if you would do all in your power to heal the breach. Now, with regard to your continued status as director here, the board is again divided. The larger majority feels that, while it looks certain that you can financially justify the festival, it would be importunate to make the final decision until the last booking phase has shown concrete stability. We, therefore, reluctantly, ask you to await our final decision which will be made on Monday the second of August.'

Douglas tried not to show his fury; the immediate reaction was to hand in his resignation, but common sense and judgment held him back.

'They're a hard-headed lot,' Sir Basil explained later. 'They now see you as a future goldmine. But they're cautious men. I'm sorry, all I can hope is that you'll wait until August.'

Douglas talked to Adrian about the local situation, and the publicity man promised to make at least an approach to Moir.

'It'll be a start anyway,' said Douglas. 'I can't stand the man myself, but I must do as the board asks.'

He then had a long session with David Wills to make perfectly certain that the booking figures could be maintained.

'Old Harper's a strange bird,' David told him. 'He doesn't really believe what's happening; you can't get him to admit that we're topping anything that's been done here before; but I'll push him. I would suggest that you replace him before next season, his diffidence does not inspire confidence.'

'Let's see if any of us are here,' Douglas sighed.

'Yes.' David seemed to be miles away, he was still pushing Rachel Cohen for an answer to his proposal of marriage, but she remained reluctant to commit herself.

Asher Grey was in a state of despair now that Douglas would not have a definite answer for him until August. He could not wait that long before giving his answer to Ivor Armstrong, and his uncertainty began to overflow into his performances; Ronnie also noticed that his drink bill in the green room was rising sharply, and pointed this out to Douglas who sent for the actor.

'Is it just your answer to Armstrong about *The Lord Deputy*, or the other decision as well?' the director asked.

'Only the film. I really don't know what to do, Douglas; I'm torn in half.'

'I'm sorry, Ash. My answer is the same as it was before. Yes, if I'm still the director, I will be asking you to join the company for next season, but I wouldn't want that to influence your decision about doing the film. When have you got to give your answer?'

'Armstrong's coming in to *The Merchant* on Tuesday. I'm having dinner with him afterwards.'

'We need you cool, Ash, I wish I could help.'

The business was resolved in a strange, coincidental way. On the next Tuesday morning, Carol Evans woke with a severe attack of vomiting. Asher called Ronnie, who sent for the doctor. He pronounced a mild stomach infection and ordered her to stay in bed for the rest of the day, suggesting that it would be better if she did not work that night. Douglas was informed and called a *Merchant* rehearsal for that afternoon in order to check out the understudy (Frank Ewes and Robin Alvin had, since the first night of *Romeo and Juliet*, been studiously going through understudy rehearsals). Carol's understudy for Nerissa was Julia Philips.

Personal differences were forgotten in the moment of crisis and even Asher tightened into the atmosphere as they took the nervous Julia through her scenes. In performance that night she gave a confident interpretation of the small part, different from Carol, adding an extra edge of bitchiness which pleased Douglas and prompted praise from most of the company.

Ivor Armstrong was late getting to Asher's dressing-room afterwards.

'Guess I must smell lucky at the moment,' said the producer, rubbing his hands. 'I think I'm going to sign up somebody else for *The Lord Deputy*, only a small part, but important: the Whore, the girl who plays that scene with Essex in Ireland, you know, the long sexy scene before he returns to England.'

Asher remembered the scene, difficult and lengthy with some clever camera work. 'Who've you offered it to?' he asked, genuinely interested.

'The girl who played Nerissa tonight, the understudy, what's her name? Julia, Julia Philips. The understudy thing'll make good publicity and she's right for the part. I think she's going to accept, I have to call her agent in the morning.'

On their way to the theatre restaurant, Asher made up his mind, taking the first real decision he had made about his life for a long time. Over dinner he told Armstrong that he could not accept the Essex role. The producer did not even try to argue with him, long ago he had learned the art of taking actors at their word. He would wait for a month before approaching anyone else, if Asher did not get back to him by then, it would be offered elsewhere.

Spring turned into summer and Shireston blossomed; play succeeded play as audience followed audience: Joe Thomas's Othello, Jennifer's Desdemona, Morrie Kapstein's Shylock, Asher's Richard and Romeo, Carol's Juliet. Early in July, just after the final booking period had opened, and looked, in its early stages, to be holding up well, Emilio Benneto came to see Douglas.

'It's your advice I need, Mr Silver.'

'Don't say you're going to resign. There's nothing but praise for the restaurant.'

'No, it's not that. I'm a lucky man to have such a good job. No, Mr Silver, this is a personal problem.'

'You're certainly looking better.' Douglas had the evidence of his eyes that the restaurateur was making a complete recovery from his wife's sudden and tragic death.

'Thank you, I sometimes think I should not feel as good as I do.'

'Come on, Emilio, we can't go on grieving. It's not easy, but we have to put life into perspective.'

'This is what I wish to talk about, Mr Silver. You see, Mrs Doul and I. . . .'

'Yes?'

'It is so soon after my poor Doris. Back home they would

think it terrible. . . .' He stopped, all the words blocked and stuck in his throat.

'Are you trying to tell me that you want to marry Mrs Doul?' You did not have to be either a genius or a fortune teller, the pair were inseparable around the festival.

'This is so. Yes, we wish to marry. I am concerned because I think maybe it is too quick after Doris.'

'My dear fellow,' Douglas rose, offering his hand. 'I couldn't be more pleased. Truly, I think it would be the best thing in the world, both for you and Mrs Doul.'

'I am thinking of her also. She has been alone for so many years. We have much in common.' The man smiled. 'It is not exactly an affair of passion you understand. We have common interests, a mutual ground.'

'I really am delighted.'

'You don't think people will say I am a bad, thoughtless man?'

'I think they'll say you're a very sensible man.'

Also in July David Wills's Recitals took place, before a depleted audience, on three consecutive Sunday evenings. It was a pity about the audiences, because the programmes deserved a better hearing. Douglas knew that Adrian had been spending a lot of time in Shireston, but he restrained himself from asking how he had worked the oracle: Hedley Moir was readmitted for the three recitals and the *Gazette* gave pleasant tributes both to the choice of verse and the manner in which it was delivered. It was not for many months that Douglas found out the possible reason for the change of heart when he noticed that Sir Basil Daley's name was on the board of the newspaper group which owned the *Gazette*.

It was in the last week of the month, with Douglas beginning to feel the bite of agitation and nervousness about the outcome of the board's decision, that Maurice Kapstein decided to make a nuisance of himself once more.

Kapstein had been on one of his stints at the television studios for a couple of days, returning to the house early on a

Thursday afternoon. He had lunched well, but was not overtly drunk (Morrie was not likely to make that mistake again). Eve Lester went up to his room at about four. She was used to his animal appetite (something she shared in common with him) and, seeing him in bed, stripped and climbed in beside him. Kapstein woke from his short slumber and grinned.

'So you have come to me, huh?'

'You've been away. I know you, Morrie. You'll not settle until you're satisfied.'

The actor gave a long contented groan and reached out for her, but in the kissing, fumbling, smoothing and frenzied groping which took place during the next hour, Maurice Kapstein was incapable of even entering the girl.

Eve was sensible and tried to soothe. 'Morrie, darling, you've been working very hard. You're tired.'

'But it is not normal, not for me, not for Morrie Kapstein. I know. I haven't ever been like this before. Age is ruining me, this is the first sign, emasculation. . . .'

It was the full farcical scene, with Kapstein overdramatizing and Eve getting anxious. (It was a *Romeo* night and she had to be in the theatre, one of the sultry girls of Verona.)

Just after the quarter had been called, Maurice Kapstein came into the theatre, through the stage door, at last wandering into Felicity Durrant's dressing-room, unzipping his fly and exposing himself directly to her.

'Wouldn't you say that wasn't bad for a man of my age?' he asked in all seriousness.

Miss Durrant had experienced many things in life and was not easily distressed, but the sight of Morrie shaking his great mane of hair and asking her opinion of his sexual organ was too much. She laid about him with her clenched fists, finally pushing him into a corner, where he lay, dejected, as she swept out of the room in search of Ronnie Gregor, demanding that Kapstein be removed from the theatre before she would go on.

Maurice was gently prodded back to his apartment where Douglas saw him later that evening.

'You're a bloody old fool, Morrie. Who the hell do you think you are, a mixture of Bacchus and eternal youth? I've never known a man like you, openly screwing one of the youngest girls in the company, working like a horse and expecting to go on doing it. I'd see a doctor if I were you, otherwise, one of these days you're going to go out like a light.'

It was the kind of storm that Douglas could well do without. He managed to get Maurice to apologize to Felicity Durrant the next morning, and for her to accept the apology; by the next evening, when they were playing *The Merchant*, Morrie seemed to be his old self again, at least Douglas spied him going across the lawn to the theatre, Eve Lester by his side, arms entwined around each other, and a burst of laughter floating over the air. The incident became a roaring joke for the rest of the company, but, not unnaturally, remained an embarrassment for Felicity Durrant.

On the evening of the second of August, Douglas received a short telephone call from Sir Basil Daley.

'I thought you'd like to know that the board met in London this afternoon. Their decision is to ask you to stay on as director for a further three years. I hope you accept.'

There was no hesitation on Douglas's part, it was like unlocking a section of his mind, he knew the broad outline of what he wanted to achieve at Shireston and began to take immediate steps.

On the next morning he talked to Adrian and David, who both agreed to stay for at least another year. Frank Ewes had already accepted a job at Chichester, where Liz Column was playing as a member of the company in the following season, but Robin Alvin would stay; there was no problem about Ronnie and Art, from their manner and style they might easily become permanent fixtures.

Edward Crispin was booked for two films, so Douglas did not even approach him. Laurence Pern would come back, as would Ronald Escott. Late in the afternoon Douglas spoke with Rachel Cohen, who seemed overjoyed at the thought;

then he talked to Asher Grey.

'I can't promise to find anything for Carol, though,' he told the young actor.

'I want to stay for another year, of course, Doug. As for Carol, I don't think she'll settle or find permanence for a long time. I don't know what it is, Doug, apparently there was this big love in her life and she hasn't really got unbugged from him yet. Would you mind if she was around for some of the time? If she's not working?'

'Of course not.' But Douglas had already left the actor, his mind far back in time.

David came in to see him towards the end of the day, particularly to ask if he could have a double apartment. 'I've persuaded Rachel to at least share with me,' he said, looking considerably brighter than he had done during the past weeks. 'Douglas, I really think she might just marry me when we get back from the States.'

That night, as they were preparing for bed, Jennifer, in the midst of removing her day make-up, asked Douglas if he wanted to know her availability for next season.

'Why?'

'The place is buzzing: who's been invited to stay, who hasn't and why not? You haven't even mentioned it to me, apart from telling me that you're going to be director of Shireston for the next three years.'

Douglas smiled and sat down beside her. She was half lying on the bed, a stand mirror propped against her pillow, her jars of cream and box of cotton wool littering the counterpane.

'I was going to ask your availability as the director's wife,' he said quietly.

She went on sweeping her face with the cotton wool. 'For three years?'

'For ever, but at least for a year without doing anything else.'

'I'm available. For ever if you really want it.'

Joe Thomas was still under pressure. Tommy Carr had fixed

452

three long recording sessions and he was to do a concert, with the London Philharmonic Orchestra, at the Albert Hall on one of the non-*Othello* nights in early September.

'If Tony Bennett can do it so can you,' the manager had told him.

The *Othello* still stood up well, but Douglas knew the strain must be great for Thomas and that he would have to take the whole company through some stiff, disciplined rehearsals before they left for Boston and New York.

For Joe the strain became a little too much on a hot night towards the end of August. He had been in London for two days, a day recording and another rehearsing for the concert. That night his performance was good, steady with no hint of what was to come.

They got to the final scene, Joe mounting the spiral staircase and padding along the gallery –

'. . . *Set you down this:*
And say, besides, that in Aleppo once,
Where a malignant and a turban'd Turk. . . .'

He seemed to falter, his feet in the nooses. Then, slowly, one hand came up as though holding a microphone, his body changing position.

'Aw, let's call it a night, folks. What say I sing you a song?'

Shuffling and murmurs from the audience. Ronnie, who happened to be in the prompt corner, reacted, his hand moving to the telephone link with the control box.

'No?' Thomas swayed. 'Okay. But I want you to know you've been a great audience, the best since I've been here, so come back real soon. God bless you and let's live in peace.'

He plunged the dagger in and broke the blood pellets, toppling forward to the usual intake of breath from the audience.

Mark Lynton had the presence of mind to go straight into Lodovico's closing speech. Ronnie was already whispering into the house phone, calling Douglas over to the theatre.

'I don't know what happened, Doug, I'm sorry, baby, suddenly I didn't want to go on.'

'It was bloody unprofessional.' Douglas stood in Thomas's dressing-room looking down at the singer who sat, slumped in a huddle in his chair.

'What did you want to prove, Joe?' The question cracked down.

'I didn't want to prove anything. Doug, I'll do the run of *Othello* in the States and then get back to my own line. I'm no actor.'

'You're Othello's a knock-out, except when you do stupid things like tonight.'

'Cut it out, Doug. Yeah, sure, I'm great. But do you know what it's like going out there every night?'

'I've got a fair idea.'

'No, I mean for me? I'm used to doing my own thing being Joe Thomas. It doesn't matter if I decide to light a cigarette, or chat up the folks in the audience. Going out there and doing *Othello* again and again is like something else.'

'What do you think it's like for someone like Asher, playing four big, important roles, a different one each night?'

Joe looked up slyly and grinned. 'It's like a bullfight, man. Every night's a sodding bullfight, when the moves have to be so accurate or you're a dead duck; either the bull gets you or the audience does. Every night's a bullfight, Douglas, baby.'

Douglas grinned back in comprehension.

Imperceptibly the days passed and summer began to turn to autumn. Suddenly they were in the last week.

The closing night was an *Othello* performance. All day the atmosphere built; a party was planned in the restaurant to begin once the play had come down. After the *Othello* calls the whole company were to appear on stage, and Douglas had agreed to make a short speech.

There was the natural sense of change, of the company breaking up, of productions ceasing to be living things, only memories.

Douglas could not bring himself to go in for any of the performance, bathing, changing and walking over to the

454

theatre just before *Othello* was due to finish.

It was a mild, clear night, and he stood on the lawn in front of the theatre's white façade, looking, looking back at the bulk of Shireston House, like the hulk of some great old ship, a dark ungainly splodge against the night sky. His mind raced towards next season, following that huge, endless wheel of work which always turns for festivals like Shireston. He wanted to do *The Shrew*, there were some things about feminist concepts there; and, most of all, there was this conception he had for *The Tempest*: Antonio, Alonso and Ferdinand as space travellers wrecked on Prospero's planet, the magic island. There were so many ideas there.

From the theatre he heard the applause rising and signaling the end of *Othello*.

With a smile, Douglas Silver turned and began to walk slowly towards the theatre. Behind the applause he could hear, deep in his mind, an actor's voice, not Conrad's, but quite like it, speaking Prospero's lines –

Our revels now are ended. These our actors,
As I foretold you, were all spirits, and
Are melted into air, into thin air:
And, like the baseless fabric of this vision,
The cloud capp'd towers, the gorgeous palaces,
The solemn temples, the great globe itself,
Yea, all which it inherit, shall dissolve,
And, like this insubstantial pageant faded,
Leave not a rack behind. We are such stuff
As dreams are made on; and our little life
Is rounded with a sleep –

STAR BESTSELLERS

0352 309350	**WHISPERS** Dean R Koontz (GF)	1.95*
0352 310804	**ROGUE OF GOR** John Norman (Sci. Fantasy)	1.95*
0352 310413	**AFTERMATH** Roger Williams (GF)	1.60
0352 310170	**A MAN WITH A MAID** Anonymous (GF)	1.60*
0352 310928	**A MAN WITH A MAID VOL. II** Anonymous (GF)	1.60*
0352 395621	**THE STUD** Jackie Collins (GF)	1.60
0352 300701	**LOVEHEAD** Jackie Collins (GF)	1.50
0352 398663	**THE WORLD IS FULL OF DIVORCED WOMEN** Jackie Collins (GF)	1.60
0352 398752	**THE WORLD IS FULL OF MARRIED MEN** Jackie Collins (GF)	1.50
0352 311339	**THE GARMENT** Catherine Cookson (GF)	1.25
0426 163524	**HANNAH MASSEY** Catherine Cookson (GF)	1.25
0426 163605	**SLINKY JANE** Catherine Cookson (GF)	1.25
0352 310634	**THE OFFICERS' WIVES** Thomas Fleming (GF)	2.50*
0352 302720	**DELTA OF VENUS** Anais Nin (GF)	1.50*
0352 306157	**LITTLE BIRDS** Anais Nin (GF)	1.25*
0352 310359	**BITE OF THE APPLE** Molly Parkin (GF)	1.35

* Not for sale in Canada   Prices are subject to alteration

STAR BESTSELLERS

0352 300965	**LONELINESS OF THE LONG-DISTANCE RUNNER** Alan Sillitoe (GF)	1.50
0352 300981	**SATURDAY NIGHT AND SUNDAY MORNING** Alan Sillitoe (GF)	1.35
0352 310863	**BEST FRIENDS** Kelly Stearn (GF)	1.75
0352 310456	**GHOSTS OF AFRICA** William Stevenson (GF)	1.95*
0352 306351	**GOLGOTHA** John Gardner (Thriller)	1.50
0352 300078	**THE FIRST DEADLY SIN** Lawrence Sanders (Thriller)	1.95*
0352 30099X	**DIRTY HARRY** Philip Rock (Thriller)	1.25*
0352 307390	**THE GOOD THE BAD AND THE UGLY** Joe Millard (Western)	85p*
0352 305231	**CROSSFIRE TRAIL** Louis L'Amour (Western)	1.25*
0352 306750	**THE SUNSET WARRIOR** Eric Van Lustbader (Sci. Fic.)	1.75*
0352 306769	**SHALLOWS OF NIGHT** Eric Van Lustbader (Sci. Fic.)	1.75*
0352 306777	**DAI-SAN** Eric Van Lustbader (Sci. Fic.)	1.75*
0352 309237	**101 REASONS NOT TO HAVE SEX TONIGHT** I M Potent, M.D. (Humour)	1.25*
0352 396121	**BODYGUARD OF LIES** Antony Cave Brown (Gen. Non. Fic.)	2.50*
0352 310146	**THE COMPLETE CB RADIO** Richard Nichols (Gen. Non. Fic.)	2.50
0352 310731	**PERSONAL COMPUTERS** Peter Rodwell (Gen. Non. Fic.)	1.50

* Not for sale in Canada   Prices are subject to alteration

STAR Books are obtainable from many booksellers
and newsagents. If you have any difficulty please send
purchase price plus postage on the scale below to:-

Star Cash Sales
P.O. Box 11
Falmouth
Cornwall

OR

Star Book Service,
G.P.O. Box 29,
Douglas,
Isle of Man,
British Isles.

While every effort is made to keep prices low, it is
sometimes necessary to increase prices at short
notice. Star Books reserve the right to show new retail
prices on covers which may differ from those adver-
tised in the text or elsewhere.

Postage and Packing Rate
UK: 45p for the first book, 20p for the second book and
14p for each additional book ordered to a maximum
charge of £1.63. BFPO and EIRE: 45p for the first book,
20p for the second book, 14p per copy for the next
7 books thereafter 8p per book. Overseas: 75p for the
first book and 21p per copy for each additional book.